Other Books by Michael W. Burns

Fiction

The Worlds of Harry Logan
Sunset House

Non-fiction

Into the Blue Far Distance

THE
TRANSFORMATION
OF
HARRY LOGAN

MICHAEL W. BURNS

authorHOUSE®

AuthorHouse™ LLC
1663 Liberty Drive
Bloomington, IN 47403
www.authorhouse.com
Phone: 1-800-839-8640

Published by AuthorHouse 12/04/2013

ISBN: 978-1-4918-3182-3 (sc)
ISBN: 978-1-4918-3181-6 (e)

Library of Congress Control Number: 2013920275

For Joanne, always

PREFACE

This second journey into the world of Harry Logan is longer and more perilous than the first. From his introduction to readers in *The Worlds of Harry Logan* until the end of this book, Harry is by turns, outrageous, obsessive, opinionated, selfish, annoying, humorous, and compassionate. He is a man ever changing and trying to understanding what to expect of his life and what expectations he should have of others.

Fictional characters such as Harry that spring from the landscape of one's imagination are just that and they are expected to recede back into that fog shrouded place. Yet Harry begged to be better explained and clarified. I hope that, with the words set down here, I have let him.

My thanks go to those friends and family who have put up with my obsession with the life of Harry Logan. I want to thank also the people at AuthorHouse who were kind enough to help with both journeys.

Michael W. Burns
Carlsbad, California
December 2013

CHAPTER ONE

Haunted by the memory of another fall day, Harry Logan looked down at the tree-lined streets of Hamilton. Anita said goodbye to him on this platform then and although they would see each other again briefly in the years since, it was really the only goodbye that mattered. There was a book for Harry to sell and, as she predicted, their life together was over when he boarded the train. He couldn't turn away from the bright lights of the world that waited for him beyond here and she refused to live in their reflection.

No Free Country became a success, an important book far beyond his expectations. He was proud of that, of his talent to do it but unsure the accolades were worth the price of a life forfeited with the good and kind Anita DeFoe.

He once believed he would live the rest of his life with her in this pleasant verdant place yet he was back now only to see friends and to sell his beloved Craftsman style house. He would surely miss Hamilton, but he would miss Anita most of all.

Bill Powers pulled into the car park five minutes later and greeted him with a handshake, a hug, and a smile and spoke in that odd locution he reserved only for Harry, "Hey pal, early, huh? Must be a new guy runnin' the trains."

"I am William, how are you and where is the lovely Martha?" Harry said addressing him by his full Christian name as he always did when they were engaged in the parry and thrust of their good-humored conversations.

"She's home slavin' over a hot stove makin' a dinner she'd only take time to make for you. I'm jealous and a bit offended to tell ya the truth."

"Are you? Well perhaps it's good I finally came. Now you'll get to enjoy it. It must have been awful waiting for it all these years."

"Well, I gotta' say havin' you in town is a treat, but how much I enjoy the meal depends on how much ya spout your pompous nonsense while you stuff your face."

"Ah William, I see your rapier wit is still as sharp as ever," Harry said with a chuckle as he tossed his bags in the open trunk.

They drove to what passed for suburbs in this small city. Harry's house was in town while Bill and Martha's house was on an acre farther out. It was famous for its freestanding basketball court where Bill taught his boys to play. In the years Harry lived here Bill regularly beat him here at every opportunity using his three inch height advantage and superior shooting skill. Harry remembered the games more for their camaraderie and exercise than one-sidedness. He and Bill settled many things on that court. They talked as much as they played.

As they passed through the city Harry's memory was stirred by familiar places. The Playhouse, the Pub, and down that street the Library where Anita worked and they met while he served on the Library Board. As they drove by the Coffee Time Café, Bill said nothing more than, "Still there." Yet they both knew it was more than just a coffee shop. It was where Harry's ritual early morning walk ended, Bill drank his first coffee there most mornings and Harry's whining and lectures began. It was also where he first met and began his faux romance with the lovely Amanda Quince. It was a place of laughter among friends. Debates of great consequence, or deemed great at the time, were held there. It was in its way their kitchen table.

When they reached the house, Bill jumped out and yelled from the already open trunk,

"Come on Harry, if ya want all this inside, I ain't carryin' it. That just ain't gonna happen."

Harry shook himself from his reverie and climbed out to an effusive greeting from Bill's wife Martha who looked as joyful as ever. She was a wonderful conversationalist, doer of good works and, Harry once remarked, always looked as if she were about to burst out laughing. While he hugged her warmly, Bill asked him about the luggage again.

"Oh stop it Bill," Martha said, "Be glad he's finally here. That can wait."

"No, no, he feels compelled to have it all inside, Martha, so I'll oblige him. Now William do you think you can manage that small one?"

"Course I can, ya dope, what the hell you got all this stuff with you for, anyway?"

"I've lived out of these suitcases these past few years, William. I could have left them in a locker at the airport, I suppose, but I didn't get a chance to sort things so I brought them all with me. Being homeless is a bit of a chore. You should know that should Martha ask you to leave."

"Yeah, yeah, let's get inside."

Dinner was both lively and delicious. Bill pestered him as always about the women in his life while he and Martha caught up on the locals and the playhouse in which she was still quite active. While their boys were in prep school in the east, she became more and more involved in the community, its arts, and its more humanitarian endeavors. Harry congratulated her as always on her avocation of keeping Hamilton a good place to live. She laughed uproariously when Harry suggested she run for mayor. Bill said he thought she already had enough influence, but wryly remarked if the bribes were good, it might help pay the bills.

After dinner they walked to the basketball court and idly tossed a ball back and forth. Bill asked about Elspeth Henson, Harry's agent whom he'd met when he came to New York for the awards dinner. Harry learned the details of Bill's new responsibilities as the area supervisor while he remained an agent for commercial insurance. Life was good for the Powers family. The boys liked the east coast so much it was hard to get them home, but everyone was healthy and happy and Bill said the money still worked the same way, He made it, and Martha spent it so he had to make more. These two friends who married in college were still very much in love and they were happy here. Hamilton was good to them.

"So ya didn't fall in love this trip Harry? Why not?"

"I didn't want to. I met some interesting people, who were very nice to me. Campus life has changed since we were there as you can imagine. I found the woman of the junior faculty interesting. It was fun."

"So you dallied with them, huh?"

"They were very nice to me."

"Bet they were."

"I did rather enjoy the lecture tour."

"Sounds like you did. Back in the bad old days your sense of women was so badly impaired you found a bunch of goofy ones, didn't ya? You couldn't live with' em, couldn't write when they were around and never stopped talkin' about any of it. God you were annoying."

Harry had his first good laugh of the trip. "Why William, you sound as if you've miss it."

As they crossed the patio on the way back in, Bill replied, "I do, the games and the laughs were good."

"Yes they were."

"You understand any better what happened with you and Anita now?"

Harry shook his head, "Sadly, I may never fully understand it, although I try. It surely didn't work out as I hoped and I'm still not sure I know why."

It would not have been a night at the Powers house without a sporting event of one sort or another on the oversized television in the den and Martha pestering Bill to turn it off while they talked. He muted it. Tonight there was a hockey game on and he would occasionally leap to his feet and issue rude admonitions to a player or the referee despite appearing to be paying no attention at all. Bill loved all sports, played basketball with Harry in Prep School, and went to Stanford on scholarship where he met and married Martha who was a scholarship swimmer.

By the time the reminiscing slowed down, Harry was suffering from one of the frequent severe headaches that plagued him for the past six months.

"I need to go up now, my head hurts. What have you two planned tomorrow?"

"Nothing unless you and Bill need to go out for coffee, just come down when you like." Martha said.

"What of that William? Is there a reason to go to the Café? It is the weekend."

"Nah," Bill replied, "Still the same there on Saturdays from what I've heard. Bunch of the newly married running around there doin' a lot of bad parenting is all. Might find Amanda in there on Monday."

"Is my Amanda still as beautiful as ever?"

"She is. Maybe you can two can finally agree to sleep together."

"Please William, don't be crude. There was sadness for us both that our love remained unrequited. You make it sound so tawdry."

"Yeah, well the way you said it sounded that way too."

Harry laughed, said he would see them both in the morning, and went upstairs hoping a mild dose of medication would get him through the night.

He showered in the guest suite and lay down. He was still very much awake for some reason. He knew being here wasn't going to resolve any of his lingering doubts about his relationship with Anita yet the proximity made him think about it. Harry was not a believer in things like closure. He thought it an artifice. He never forgot how he felt when his mother was killed so many years ago. He lived with that open wound even now when he thought about her. So it was with this. He returned here to sell the house, not to make amends yet he still searched for an understanding of what happened.

He was happy here with her until that trip to New York. Once he went, he became caught up in the world of literature, the tour, his new book, and New York's literary society. Writing was his passion and he knew in the act staying longer than the initial book promotion, he'd made the choice between her and that passion.

She was living a quiet, nearly cloistered life when he met her perhaps out of fear of being abused again. She was timid with him at first but grew to trust him and despite a nearly intrinsic dislike of men admitted affection for him she could never adequately explain. Improbably enough they became inseparable. In the last months while he went back and forth to the city doing the nearly interminable editing and publicity planning they spent most waking moments together here. She took the pompous, bombastic, obsessive and very public Harry and the private, gentle, humorous, and generous one who lived behind that façade and helped him in her quiet way become the best of both. He believed that. He believed she in part responsible for whom he was now, was still becoming. She helped him understand there were two Harry Logans who needed to learn to get along with each other were he ever to truly grow up. She was a wonderful friend to him and in him she found a man she could trust, one that gave her the confidence to see the world as a happier place. They were content with that platonic closeness. It was what he needed in the frenzy to finish his book and prepare to leave and sell it. It was what she needed to get beyond the disastrous and abusive relationships with the men before him. He wanted the book done and the tour over before it became more complicated. She wanted him here. He wanted her to come with him. He was leaving, she was not, and they both stubborn enough to want whatever it became on their terms.

She clearly wanted him back here and while he said he wanted to be, she was equally sure he couldn't break away from the world of the *literati* if the book was as successful as he so desperately wanted it to be. She made it clear she wanted no part of that life. When *Country* became a huge success, far greater than he ever anticipated, the world of authors that wrote books as successful as that overtook him. In the months that followed he begged her to come with him. Yet she stubbornly believed if they were to be happy it would be here. This woman who fought off the demons in her life to reach this measure of personal peace and success did not want to go to the party and stand in his reflection and wait for it to be over. She was emphatic about it before he went and when he returned weeks later even more so. Anita Defoe's life was here. She wasn't leaving it for him.

Her point was simple really. If he wanted to be with her he could come back here to write. If he didn't, he could live in the literary circles he enjoyed so much without her. She was unyielding in that, as unyielding as he was in wanting her to come. When he received a National Book Award he asked her to come with Bill and Martha hoping she would see that it wasn't a world to hate but a comfortable place for them together. When Harry asked her to stay on she said it was a nice way to spend a weekend but not a life and came home. He went on his lecture tour and while he still called occasionally the humor and light touch that was uniquely theirs was gone. Walls were built in the subconscious need to protect themselves from the inevitable.

Harry was helpless in the face of his own success, being pulled in many directions, and having his ego stroked by so many people and—he admitted—was enjoying it. Yet he wanted desperately to try to save their relationship so he returned once more nearly a year later.

She agreed to lunch and thanked him again for his help in bringing her back to a normalcy in her life she thought she would never find yet remained adamant about remaining in Hamilton. He remembered the last conversation they had with searing clarity.

"I'm seeing someone else Harry. He's fun and is very good to me. I don't love him. Perhaps I will someday. He wants to be here with me. I can't go with you, you know that, and you aren't coming back here, I know that too. So I'm trying to get on with my life now and you need to as well. You're still the best friend I ever had. I'll never forget you."

Harry tried hard to say all the right things and be happy for her and surely failed miserably. He left Hamilton two weeks later for the last time until tonight. He didn't see Bill and Martha again until they came to New York last year.

He was downstairs staring out the den window still in his robe and slippers when Bill found him about five in the morning. He'd slept but a few hours. Bill made coffee and said nothing. Harry's head ached badly. He went back upstairs, put on clothes, took some pills, and returned to the den. There was coffee next to the chair he'd been in and Bill occupied another across from him.

"You sleep at all?" Bull asked quietly.

"Some. I was thinking."

"Wanna tell me?"

Harry looked him directly,

"I spent much of the night thinking about my years here, specifically about the last one with Anita."

Bill said nothing, just returned his gaze, sipped coffee and waited.

"How we met, what we did, where we went, how she changed, how much she helped change me, the last thing she said to me, everything."

"Sounds hard."

"I don't know. It was sad. I do know that. It was very, very sad."

"You still miss her that much?"

Harry sipped his coffee, "At times I do. I mean, I've moved on, as I did when my mother died, but I find no solace in it."

"So is that how you see her? Like your mother? Gone?"

"I have to Bill. If I saw it any other way I'd be paralyzed by 'what ifs' or standing at her door asking for another chance. I was the one who made the choice. I told you once she said I brought her back to a normal life and if I helped with that then I did some good. She's back to a normal life, or so she told me, and I'm glad of that. Yet that normalcy doesn't include me does it, and I know it's my fault."

"It goes around in a circle doesn't it?" Bill said gently.

Harry shrugged, "I suppose it does." He folded his hands, and looked at Bill. "I left to promote a book and I worked very hard to do it well. Perhaps too hard, perhaps it meant too much, but that's what I chose and I did it. I never hurt her. We called each other best friends and we were. There were emotional problems she still needed to resolve and I needed to sell my book, and a platonic relationship suited us both. Yet we felt more than that in the end and while we never acted on it, we both knew it. When I came back the first time we faced a conundrum. I was leaving again, she was staying, and no matter what I said she wasn't coming with me. The book sold beyond my wildest dreams. The publisher wanted me in New York. I became their commodity then. It was the biggest seller they ever had. I succeeded at my passion and I admit I loved it. They published me and I owed them."

"I suppose you did. After all, without you or them it wouldn't have happened."

"Exactly. I was a hostage to my good fortune. One doesn't say, thank you, this was all quite wonderful but I need to go now, there's a woman back in the northwest waiting. I mean could I have done that?"

"You? No, you couldn't. Someone else might, but you were succeeding at what you cared about most. You wanted it a long time. It's more than a passion for you, Harry, it defines you."

Harry looked at Bill, "So you agree that the Harry Logan you've known all these years on and off as it were had to do what he did?"

"Yeah I do. Doesn't mean I think it was good or right, but I do."

"What could I have done differently?"

"If you weren't Harry Logan you could have come back and married her. Marriage was what you both said you wanted. But you were Harry

Logan and you needed to control it and her so you wanted her to come to you, give up what she had here for you. I'm not sure it would've worked in the end, not even sure you really loved her or she loved you and I think you know that."

"So my selfish need to control my world is what caused the relationship to fail? That's hard for me to accept, Bill, I mean, at the time I had no choice. Whatever else could I have done?"

"Nothing. You don't have another gear, Harry. You know that. You believe your world is writing and selling books. Anita knew it, still knows it. She stayed here for a lot of reasons. They're not all good. Fear of being hurt out there in a world that hurt her badly before is the one that we know the most about. That fear's still there I'd guess. There's more. She likes her work, Hamilton, and she was smart enough to understand that your passion was more important." He looked up from his cup, "Tell me honestly Harry, would you stop writing for her?"

Harry sat back now and drank the fresh coffee Martha had brought in to them. His head was pounding again. He thought of what Bill just said,

"I've asked myself that question often the last few years, Bill. She was special, but no, not so special that I would stop for her if I'm honest about it. I've not met a woman yet that I need as much as I need to write. I should be able to treat the two things equally—love of work and a woman—yet I couldn't with her. I wish it were different but it isn't. I hope I did the right thing," he finished softly.

"You'll never answer that, pal, so get past it. You did her some good, never hurt her, or took advantage of her fragility. Then you left and did what you had to do to make you happy. She's over it I'd guess. You should be too. Keep writing because you're very good at it and you deserve to succeed. Anita's got a life. You have too. You aren't part of hers. She's not part of yours. That's sad, maybe, but it's a fact. You can love her if you want, but she's out of your life because you put her out by giving her no choice, so get on with it."

"I'd like to believe that someday I could love someone and write as well. I mean, Anita helped me understand that there was more for Harry Logan than books and tours and lectures and the pursuit of awards. Yet for reasons that will forever remain beyond my comprehension, that someone wasn't her."

"No, it wasn't, but like I said, you want control over all that and may still believe it could've worked if she'd only come with you. I just don't see it that way."

Bill was always so practical when they talked of these things. *Get past it* . . . is what he said. Harry knew he was right. He stood now, "Should I do anything now?"

Bill shook his head, "What? Is there somethin' you can do to change it all now? It'll only make you hurt a little more. Time to let it go. Maybe you'll become the Harry who can do both, but it sure as hell ain't gonna' be with her."

Harry sighed, "You're right. Now, I need to lie down. I'm tired and I still have a headache. Do we have plans?"

"Martha is gonna be in and out. I'll be working here. No hurry until we eat."

"Thanks, and thanks for listening too. It helped. It always does."

"No worries Harry, you know I'll always try."

Harry woke around one. The day was overcast and gloomy. It matched his mood. He understood it better now and needed to move on. He hated it nonetheless. Bill Powers was a good man, perhaps the brother he never had. He and Martha were his only close friends and, in their way, his family now. He always brought his problems here. His mother's death in his childhood and his father's, shortly before he came here five years ago, left Harry very much alone. Bill was his conscience in his way now. As he dressed he thought of how lucky he was to have him, to have someone to share his hopes, and he thought grimly, his failures too.

When he went downstairs, Martha met him. Bill told her everything. She knew what happened. She took his hand,

"Are you all right Harry?"

"I will be Martha. Bill's right, it's time to get past it. I'm glad I came. You're husband is a great help to me."

"You're a brother to him Harry, you know that. He brags about you all the time."

Harry was both pleased and startled. He chuckled, "Not something he'll share with me, I'd suppose."

She laughed her vast laugh and squeezed his hand, "You know him better than that."

When they came back from a late dinner he excused himself early. He wanted to get a good night's sleep. He agreed to Bill's entreaty to go for coffee on Monday before he went to the house for the closing paperwork. He would be back in the city by evening.

After taking a heavy dose of medication for his headache he went almost immediately to sleep. He woke after seven to a brighter sky and the smell of bacon. As he dressed he knew he was done here now. There was no one to confront or a reason to raise his voice in frustration when he spoke of her any longer. It was over and nothing would change that. It was the only answer that made sense.

It was busy at seven o'clock Monday morning at the Coffee Time Café. Most were just running to grab their needed caffeine and leaving for work. It felt strange having to tell the woman what he wanted. In the old days it was on the counter when he got there. They were out on the deck when he turned to see the gorgeous and statuesque Amanda Quince, Attorney at Law smiling widely as she came quickly up the steps,

"Harry? My God, have you really come back?" She said loudly and without a care as to who heard it, "I missed you so and was certain you'd abandoned me. Wait here, please! Just let me get some coffee."

Harry and Bill both threw back their heads and laughed.

"Guess she remembers ya, huh?"

"Oh stop it William, you called her, I'm sure. She never gets in here this early."

Bill shrugged, "could be she changed her schedule."

"I know better than that."

"I knew you'd want to see Amanda. Maybe she'll propose and make the trip worth it."

Harry rose as Amanda returned and she hugged him so hard she nearly knocked him down. In her incredibly high heels she was probably taller than he was. Her expensive designer suit and matching coat looked wonderful on her. Her long blonde hair was swept up in a twist at the back of her neck, and she smelled delicious. She kissed him warmly on the lips, and then held him tight as she exclaimed, "Harry, you have no idea how much I missed you. I've lain awake at night and ached for you. Why did I ever let you leave me?"

Bill laughed so hard he spit out some of his coffee and Harry was having trouble composing a proper riposte because he so enjoyed seeing his beautiful, wacky, brilliant, and melodramatic friend. She was the first woman in Hamilton who ever spoke to him and their faux love affair played out here in the morning for years.

"Amanda you dear sweet woman, I have missed your timeless beauty and so longed to hear your voice and laugh that tears have come to my eyes. It's wonderful to see you again."

Amanda pecked Bill on the head wished him a good morning and sat.

"Where in the world have you been, Harry? I do miss having you here." She said putting on that false frown she used whenever complaining of Harry's insensitivity toward her.

Harry chuckled, "There aren't enough hours left in the day to cover that one my dear. You look smashing as always. You have such wonderful taste and you're more beautiful than ever."

"You are a love, this is just something I threw on because the Judge has summoned me."

"Well it's lovely, and you in it makes it even better. I'm sure the Judge will be pleased."

"Why thank you, Harry dear. Do remind me, why did I never run off with you and become the mother of your children?"

"You wouldn't have me despite my desperate entreaties, Amanda. Sadly, our love was destined to be unrequited," he sighed deeply, "I so regret that."

She laughed that wonderful big laugh he heard so many mornings here, "Jesus, Harry, back in the days when I was drinking, you could have asked me in the Pub any Friday night and I probably would have requited you right there."

He laughed, knowing it was her way of letting him know she was still sober, "Your evenings at the Pub were, shall we say, memorable? I don't recall them being amorous so far as I was concerned. You always had other interests."

"If you say so, I don't remember much about the bad old days. By the time I became a designated driver, you and the lovely Anita were inseparable." She sat up straight now and crossed her legs, her chin in a cupped hand,

"Now, why you are here?"

"I came to see Bill and Martha and sign the papers that will make the house sale final. I'm going back to the city today after I do."

"Are you writing?"

"I have an outline done. Characters, plot, minor things, but I haven't begun in earnest. Perhaps in a month, maybe two. I need to finish the contract with the publisher and see my editor."

"Do we have time for an opera in the city? You always promised me one."

"I did, Amanda, but you've forgotten that you hate opera because they sing in German and other foreign tongues."

"Oh god yes, there is that. Could I go and just sit in the reflection of your fame?"

"Fame is a fleeting thing, my dear. I won a prize and if I write a bit of trash now, they will bury me."

"Oh don't get mawkish. You're a wonderful writer. You were a love to send me my very own copy. I found it riveting and look forward to the next."

"You deserved it. God knows you suffered through it with me."

"I didn't suffer at all my dear. We drank coffee and laughed a lot and then you would disappear into that perfectly horrid dank and smelly garage and write until nearly the next morning. You lived on raw meat or ate fish from a can or something for months."

Harry laughed. "Perhaps I should put that on the cover when the next paperback reprint is done. You know, 'authored by a man in a cave being fed raw squid,' it might make someone buy it."

"Well you know how I feel about all that, Harry. I think what you do and particularly how you do it is very, very strange. Perhaps that's why I've subconsciously withheld my favors."

"My desire for you has always been too great to simply accept that Amanda, but then you know my view on the law as a profession as well."

"Ah Harry, had we only been more *simpatico,* who knows how happy we might have been?"

After they stopped laughing, Bill urged Amanda to tell Harry news of his many infatuations that passed in and out of the Café. Of the two best known to her, one left town for a foreign country and the other married and now was with child for the second time in three years and of the rest Amanda knew only amusing anecdotes that may or may not have been the whole truth. Most in her opinion joined the legions of not so very young married women that walked briskly up and down the residential streets now pushing jogging strollers talking to either each other or their husbands on their cell phones.

"It's a most curious practice, Harry, don't you agree? I mean there's no visible benefit to the child, is there? It seems so pointless to me. Perhaps I've missed some hidden benefit."

It was a wonderful reunion. Amanda jumped to her feet thirty minutes later and made profuse apologies for having to rush off and asked Harry to promise to come back soon. She hugged him and kissed him again and told him how much she would miss him, grabbed her second coffee and was gone.

"Ya gotta admit that was worth comin' for. She's still something special." Bill said.

"She's as beautiful and funny as she was three years ago."

"She's always like that. Glad you got to see her. She's really doin' well. Quince Pedersen and Blaine is too."

"I'm glad to hear it. I can't fathom why she isn't married by now. Are the men around here blind?"

"Nah, she likes tradin' in her toys pretty regular. Don't see much of her in here but she always shows up at the fundraisers for Martha's causes. Always has a handsome dude on her arm. She's more tied to her work now than she lets on. She's the managing partner again and still the best litigator in the state from what I hear, so maybe she's more like you than you think."

As they rose to leave, Harry said, "What an awful shame if that's true. I just hope she's happy that's all."

"Seems to be," he shrugged, "bout all we can know, huh?"

"Well thanks for getting her here. It was a treat to see her."

"Knew it would be. You're gonna be late for the paperwork exchange if we don't get movin'."

They settled in the car and went to the house. They didn't speak again until they pulled into the drive.

"I'll wait." Bill said simply.

"I can get a ride with the agent. I'm sure you've enough work to do."

Bill looked at him squarely over the roof of the car. "I'll be here."

Harry waved in response and took his briefcase with him as he went up the familiar front steps and across the porch. Madeline Grenville, the agent who handled the sale for him, met him at the door. She was very beautiful and very young. Harry was meeting her for the first time. They had done all the listing information and the contracting for the estate sale by telephone and fax. She was from Barton's Realty in town, ironically one that Harry knew well from his liaison with another particularly beautiful woman who was an associate there what now seemed a long time ago.

"Mr. Logan! What a pleasure to meet you at last." She smiled a most radiant smile and held the door for him. The others were gathered in the dining room. Harry conveyed some of the furniture on the first floor in the sale at the new owner's request and they sat waiting at his aunt's antique dining table. He smiled broadly and took her proffered hand in both of his,

"Madeline Glenville, the pleasure is all mine I assure you. You're one of those wonderful people whose looks are as pleasing to the eye as the voice is to the ear. I hope you have a few moments for me when we finish. There are a few loose ends to tie up. Oh, and do call me Harry, Mr. Logan makes me sound even stuffier than I really am."

She laughed, "Of course Harry, I have all the time you need. I was hoping we might have lunch."

Harry thought how appealing that might be, but replied,

"That would be lovely, but I'm taking the train to the city so I'm terribly short of time and I have someone waiting for me."

"Then let me introduce you to the others and we can get this part done."

For the next half hour the drone of the Escrow Officer's voice, the rustling of paper, and the scratching of pens were the predominate sounds in the room. The new owners seemed a nice young couple and Madeline was quite good at clarifying the stupefying pieces of business that came out of the mouth of the small, wizened man, who spoke atonally and as if from a script. When it was done, there were handshakes and assurances from the new owners that they would love and care for the old Craftsman as much as Harry and his aunt before him. Madeline and Harry watched them leave from the porch. He wanted to check his office and be sure everything was removed from there. While the house was rented in his absence it had been locked with only the garage portion available to the tenants. They went across the yard and Harry looked in wondering now how a novel as important as the world found his was written in here. They sat at the desk and talked of the disposal of the rest of the things in the house as well as the things here. Madeline took notes and when they were done, thanked Harry again for the listing and all the extra work. He said he always thought highly of her agency and was glad her competency matched their reputation. She smiled,

"I'm told there was a time that your view of Barton's may have been quite different, but I suppose that was on a more personal level, wasn't it?"

Harry looked at her, "You mean my friendship with Jamie Wells?"

"Yes. From the lore of the agency I understand that might not have ended in, shall I say the most pleasant circumstances?"

"It didn't. But that wasn't the agency's fault."

"Oh, I understand. It's just that some found it odd that you choose us to represent you."

"I would never hold what happened with Jamie against the agency. They handled matters quite efficiently when my aunt died and I acquired this place."

"Well, I only met her once but she does still hold a place in Barton's history. Jamie Wells' stories still flourish, but I suppose you knew her better than they did."

"I don't know that. We were intimate for quite some time if that's your point. I'm not at all certain I held exclusive rights."

She blushed a bit at that. "I don't know," she shrugged her shoulders then smiled, "and it doesn't matter now."

Harry nodded, "No, it doesn't."

She pointed at Bill leaning on the car as they reached the drive, "Is he a friend of yours or just a driver waiting for you?"

"A friend. Why?"

"I would have been glad to take you back." She said coyly, "I hoped to change your mind about lunch."

Harry nodded in Bill's direction, "he and I go back as far as Prep School, and I haven't seen much of him since I left here to sell my book.

We're catching up on a good deal of old business this weekend. I'll be in touch, perhaps we'll lunch another time. You have my number if anything goes awry?"

"Of course. Thank you again and I look forward to hearing from you." She shook his hand, squeezed it, and walked to her car. Harry smiled glad someone that young and beautiful would want to flirt with him.

He and Bill ate at a lunch counter they both liked in town. They both wished there was more time, particularly for their basketball rivalry. As they sat on a bench waiting for the train now, Bill asked,

"Where ya headed after the meetings in the city?"

"My last lecture series is for the English Department at Pepperdine University. I'm staying with Wedgie. I've told you of Carlton Wedge before, I'm sure. He worked in commercials and cartoons with me in LA when I was teaching and hoping for a career as an actor."

"Yeah, I remember. Goofy guy, New Yorker like you? Hollywood or bust type, wasn't he?"

Harry laughed, "In those days we both were."

"He's still down there, huh?"

"He is and quite successful now. He sold an idea to some studio a few years ago. It made lots of money so now he's independent and producing all these new digital animations that I'm sure your kids know all about. He moved to Malibu a few weeks ago. He and his lady with the unlikely name of Chloe—unlikely perhaps for anywhere but Hollywood—are excited about living on the beach. The University is in Malibu, so I'll stay with him and that will end the tour. I have as usual, great expectations for the new book and I want to get on with it. I just wish these awful headaches would go away."

"You ever try to find out what's causin' them?"

"No. I just got some pain medication from a GP in New York, but haven't seen anyone. That was months ago. I have the name of a doctor who practiced in New York who's now at the University of Arizona. Neurosurgeon. He got some big research grant or something so he moved there. Supposed to be one of the best."

"Think you oughta' see him. You had one every day you were here and it was about the only thing you complained about."

"Why William, you sound concerned, I'm touched. I've delayed in the hope it was just the travel. I guess I should look into it."

"Not should Harry, must, hear me? Could be somethin' awful for chrissake. Take care of yourself will ya? You're out there all alone tryin' to become the new Willie Faulkner or somebody. That ain't gonna happen if ya drop dead. Go see the guy—soon."

Harry was startled at Bill's agitation. He was denying it. He knew that. He didn't have time to be sick so was refusing to accept that it was more than a sinus problem, stress, or eye strain.

"All right, after I get things done in the city, I'll go over and see him before LA. It is beginning to worry me. I'll call him when I get to the city."

He stood. Bill needed to get to the office he knew and would be there half the night now because of the time he spent with Harry.

"Thanks for everything. You and Martha have been wonderful." His gaze went past him as he looked at the city, "I feel a lot better about leaving here now, thank you for that too."

"No worries Harry, we're always glad to have you. Wanna come back and marry Amanda that would be good too. If not, then stay in touch and plan a weekend or two here when you get back to the city."

Harry laughed, "You'll have to work on Amanda for me, but I promise I'll be back. I enjoyed it."

"Next time we'll get serious on the court and I promise I will leave you whimpering like a new born baby child."

They laughed, shook hands, and hugged briefly as the train rolled in and Bill went back down the steps with a wave and yelled, "Tell me what the doctors says."

Harry nodded, gave him thumbs up, and went to be sure his bags got on the train.

CHAPTER TWO

He booked at The Regent, the hotel he always used in the city. The concierge was quick to tell him she read his book, loved it, and congratulated him on his award. His head hurt and hearing that made him feel better and less annoyed at the construction going on in the lobby and the public rooms on the ground floor. He went into the bar for a small scotch before he met Elspeth for dinner. He didn't see anyone he knew so sat on a banquette facing the door toying with his glass and letting both the good and bad memories of the place wash over him. This was the scene—surely an apt word for what happened that evening—of his last prolonged and stupefying conversation with beautiful and insane Jamie Wells. Yet there were good times here too. In all, he liked the place. He left when he saw the time. He wanted to change before he met Elspeth at mid-town. They were having one of their planning dinners and, given the location, he was sure she was going to the opera afterwards so she was relying on his punctuality.

He met her as she exited a cab looking no older and fashionably dressed as always.

"My dear Elspeth," he said, genuinely pleased to see her. He gave her a quick hug, "you look absolutely stunning."

"That's very nice of you, Harry. I've missed our dinners. Did you enjoy seeing your friends?"

"It was very nice. I was blessed with good weather until I got off the train here." He said as he held her chair for her.

"Well, we do specialize in moisture this time of year. I'm sure you don't miss it."

"I don't mind it, actually. The green is quite lovely. After all, I have been to some awfully drab places since I started slogging back and forth across the country first selling the book and then selling me as I sopped up the lucre given an author as lucky as I was on the lecture circuit."

"It was genius Harry, not luck."

"Perhaps the book was, but the awards were pure politics, we both know that. I needed to drag you all the way to New York to be sure I was charming to the right people so they would be possible."

Elspeth laughed, "Oh Harry, don't be humble, it isn't like you. You worked hard for both and I'm proud of you. Yes, its politics, but my dear, what isn't these days?"

"Well," he said raising his glass, "I thank you very much for your help in all of it. I did enjoy it. As for humility, I continue my quest for that. This lecture tour was fun, perhaps because I had no expectations of it. I hope my impossibility quotient is down a bit as we begin this new adventure."

"Good lord, I certainly wouldn't mind that," She said with a laugh.

"There's still much work to be done there, unfortunately, but I try. Now, are we going to see the grand Pooh Bah in the morning to settle contracts and other distasteful matters?"

"Yes, we'll see Drew who has tentatively agreed on a timeline and an advance. I have those numbers here," she said as she gave him a piece of paper, "I didn't want them in e-mail."

"I appreciate that." Harry scanned it. "Well the money is fine and the time seems enough. I presume this is fair for like-grossing authors?"

"It's in line with it, yes."

"Good. We ought to be able to settle that quickly then. I'll try to make this as easy as I can, El, I do mean that. I've thanked you for your patience the last time around, but never apologized, so please accept it now."

"Oh never mind that. We did well in the end and you learned a great deal about process, I must say. I am pleased that you've done some preparation this time. I know writing plot outlines isn't your style but it helped me in my meeting with Drew."

As they ate, she went over the rest of the schedule. He was beginning to feel that sense of being held captive again, but tried not to dwell on it. His head was beginning to pound by the time coffee came. They would have a meeting with Christine Morgan the new supervising editor if the rest could be settled by afternoon and then he could have a full day with his editor, Charles Winchester, on Friday if he liked. That seemed a bit intense to him, given how badly he was feeling and how little he'd done so far but he needed to work out logistics and give Charlie some sense of what he was going to write this time. He asked again why he was meeting Ms. Morgan and Elspeth said she thought it was because Christine was new and the meeting was just a courtesy.

"Where are you going to write this one Harry, back in Hamilton?" She asked innocently. Elspeth never knew about Anita or that he'd now sold the house. Once he stopped seeing Jamie and began writing well he'd stopped telling El all about his personal life. She was a good agent and once he understood that was the only expectation he should have of her, he gave up talking of his private life and they only discussed business, opera, and symphonies. After all, she wasn't a spiritual advisor she just sold his books. She glanced at her watch and he knew she would want to be in her seat for the first act so he stayed vague for now.

"No. Not in Hamilton. I'm not at all certain where yet."

"We'll discuss it later, then." She said distractedly.

"Yes, yes we will," Harry replied. "Now I know you didn't dress just to dazzle me so you must be going to the opera."

She stood and they headed for the door, "It's very good of you to remember, Harry. I'll see you in the lobby in the morning at nine. Perhaps Drew will have some decent coffee."

Harry laughed, pecked her cheek, and put her in a cab. The rain was over for now so he walked the eight blocks back to the hotel. By the time he reached it he was more tired than he should be, so he went straight to his room rather than to the bar as he usually did. It depressed him that he needed something to rid him of the pain in his head more than a stimulating conversation. The old Harry would never have missed a chance at that and tonight he wanted to be him again.

He called the office of Paul Zuckerman, M.D. in Tucson when he got up. They were able schedule the preliminary tests if he came in a few days. The senior Fellow called him back. He was one of the five physicians that worked with Zuckerman. He took some of his history and turned him over to a most pleasant woman named Marion to schedule him.

Harry and Elspeth met Drew, the Senior Vice President in the executive conference room. During coffee in real china and a scone, he made effusive noises about Harry's past success and hope for this book. Two of the firm's lawyers slipped into the room and they talked about the new contract. Harry disliked lawyers. Amanda Quince and his father's old friend in New York who handled his Will and Trust Fund the only exceptions. He reserved a lower opinion for those who practiced in a corporate setting. Elspeth's lawyer was over these papers a week ago and Harry accepted Elspeth's judgment that he knew what he was doing. There were some questions about the advance without the promise of an option for another book after this. Harry wasn't interested in committing to more. They were a small boutique publishing house trying to protect their interests in the ever changing world of publishing and he understood that yet for that reason did not want to commit to more than one book. One of the lawyers, Frank Burns, annoyingly clucked his tongue like someone's grandmother scolding a four year old while Harry defended his position. He was about to lose his temper and tell them he'd find someone else who might be interested when Drew interrupted and gave him what he wanted. The lawyers scurried off to finalize the paperwork. By twelve he signed and they shook hands all 'round. They went off to have a quick lunch before he met Miss Morgan and Elspeth declared the morning a success. His head was killing him. He wasn't happy about having to be nice to the supervising editor even if she just wanted to meet their most successful author. He hoped it would be a short session with no questions of substance.

Christine Morgan was a gracious woman about Harry's age. She was dressed quite fashionably in a blue silk suit, and had long auburn hair. She was of average height and attractive in her way. She possessed a most direct and self-confident manner and quick wit. The "getting to know you" was comfortable and lasted a half hour as they traded stories as to who knew whom and about the last tour.

She cleared her throat, and to Harry's surprise, produced her reading glasses and a copy of his outline and began to idly page through it. She looked up and said,

"Why do you want to write about this, Harry?"

"Why?"

"Yes, why this subject, why these people?"

He looked quickly at El. Why did she care? Why did she even have the outline? Her job was to make sure Harry and Charlie got along, not delve into his subconscious.

"I was researching non-fiction subjects," he replied evenly, "I was persuaded, however, that the regard for my fiction suggested that I stay in that genre. Thus, the story of a man who tries to quell his demons and salvage his life by giving back to his community came to be the vehicle I chose. It sprung from a real incident I read about. I'm adapting it from that."

She smiled. "Have you any doubts it will flesh out to a full novel?"

"No, I think it will be fine once I begin to write."

She shook her head, "There isn't much here."

"I'm afraid I don't understand."

"If this is to be worthy of your last work, I don't see it here."

"You don't."

"No. It doesn't seem very developed, more something you might have written anytime."

"I see, and this, this revelation of thinness and age came to you, when? Just now?"

"No, I saw this after Drew approved your book concept. I like to talk to authors to get a sense of what they want to write and why. You're new to me and I thought there might be additional thoughts you'd share."

"With you? Isn't Charlie Winchester still my editor?"

"Of course."

Harry was annoyed now and his head was pounding worse than ever. He turned to Elspeth. He wondered what she was thinking. Her head was down but she quickly raised it and spoke into the silence,

"Miss Morgan, this is a merely a bare plot outline, a roughing out of the major characters that was useful to me and Drew. I'm as perplexed as Harry is as to why you find it unacceptable."

"Oh it's not unacceptable. I simply find it sparse."

Harry's head was screaming for a dose of pills now and he nearly tore the papers from her hand. He took a deep breath, asked if he could be excused, went to the men's room, took his pills, and splashed water on his face. He knew screaming wasn't going to help. Harry never wrote an expansive plot and character outline and thought them useless. She apparently thought otherwise. When he returned she and El looked at him expectantly. He sat down trying to relax and began in a conversational tone,

"Do you mind being called Christine, or do you prefer Miss Morgan? I don't think we've settled that yet."

"Christine or Chris is fine. I like my given name much better," She said with a big smile that Harry, given her most recent remarks, found disconcerting.

"Thank you." He favored her with a small smile of his own. He was speaking very softly given he was now wearing his full public persona,

"I'd like to be sure I understand the issues you raised. First, I sense you think this is an old idea from some time in the past that I am bringing forth to ride the coattails of my previous success."

"I—

"May I finish?"

"Of course."

Harry cleared his throat, sipped some water and continued,

"Now, you said a few moments ago that you thought it best to discuss an outline in person. I'm confused by that since this was intended for Elspeth and, to some extent, the VP should he seek an understanding of what I was going to write about this time. Do I have that right?"

She looked unhappy but said nothing so he continued,

"In addition, you've made judgments based on this vague and admittedly sparse outline and not a finished manuscript, as is usually the case with a work of fiction. I haven't shaped the first chapters, yet you see this as a project not worth doing without more thought on my part. Most curiously, you have some existential need to know why I want to write about this subject, which, in my view, is no one's business but mine. Do I have that about right as well?"

"I think you've misunderstood."

"Have I? How did I misunderstand exactly?"

Christine stood frowning and walked to the conference room windows. Finally after some minutes of what he hoped was thought, she turned,

"I believe you've misunderstood because I was less than precise in my comments. I'm relatively new here. I like meeting all the authors whoever their primary editors are. I'm not imposing my view, I simply prefer more before a book proceeds. That was my point, not whether it would be a good book in the end, it was about what it is now," she said, waving her hand at the outline. "My personal opinion is that you might benefit from describing it more fully before you start."

"You think that an outline of an idea should make all that clear before writing the book?"

She replied testily, "As an editor, I find it useful."

"So re-writing a plot summary will help me do—what? Write a better book? Understand my own thoughts? Assist Charlie in some way? Please, I am trying to grasp your point and I don't."

"I know *No Free Country* was written without an outline at all. Yet you wrote this one and gave us a look into how you want to write this book. I don't feel any sense after reading it of where this is going except to an ending and I'm uncertain as to what the characters will do to reach it."

"What you are saying is you want to know how the book will read before it is written, that it must meet that expectation now?"

"I think it would benefit from further thought, that's all. I know some authors, you among them, don't like these summaries. I think they're useful."

Harry was standing now and felt his anger rise, "That's quite lovely, Christine. However I'm not here to do useful things for you. I have written two best sellers without any outline. Charlie and I did *Country* almost chapter by chapter. He'll see having this, which you find tragically inept, as a plus. I won't re-write it. Not because I wish to be contrarian but because I won't write a better one or a better book if I do. This isn't an outline for a thesis. I don't need to defend it. It's a bare outline for a work of fiction so my agent and the VP would know what it was about. You're applying your opinion to my process, not my substance. I object to that. That," he waved his hand again at the stack of papers, "was written only to make El more comfortable in presenting the idea.

My contract says nothing about getting a gold star for an outline. Aside from the subject, the plot outline has little to do with what will finally be published. It isn't important."

"Are you finished?" There was no warmth in her voice.

"Quite. Thank you for your time." Harry said as strode quickly across the room.

"Are you leaving?" She seemed astonished.

"Yes. Goodnight," Harry said as he closed the door.

He was in the elevator before he realized that Elspeth wasn't with him. He shrugged. Perhaps she could smooth the woman's feathers. He was sure she would call. His headache was nearly unbearable now so he took a cab to the hotel. Lying down in the dark after another dose of medication for an hour or so was most appealing. He was angry. After all, he would stand or fall by what he produced. No awards were given for the best summary. He grudgingly admitted that editing is a hard job that makes a book better and each editor has their own style and could accept that, but asking existential questions about *why* he wanted to write about this subject seemed ludicrous. Charlie didn't give a whit of thought as to why he wrote about a subject. He only cared that it made sense and he did it well. Harry's characters would take up residence in his mind throughout the writing and it would end as it should not necessarily as planned. Harry believed that was how it worked for him and he found it curious that she didn't see that given his previous works. He sighed and closed his eyes to the remaining light.

He woke to the ringing of his cell phone. It was Elspeth. She spent a few minutes with Christine after he left. She agreed with him that she didn't understand the tenor of the meeting. Christine apologized to her for making him angry and causing such misunderstanding. She said she was curious about his motivation and was only trying to express her own view about process.

"Well, I rely on you in these matters, El, what should I do? I don't want to fight with her. I don't want her looking over Charlie's shoulder either."

"I'll have a talk with her boss, George Crampton, and tell him we met with her and what happened."

"I don't want to make life difficult for either of us, El, or her necessarily."

"Don't worry about that now."

"If you think it will help then yes, talk to him."

"I'll see if I can call him before he leaves today."

"She must be very good to be where she is, mustn't she, El? I mean one has to be to become the supervising editor, doesn't one?"

"Yes. Perhaps there are reasons the meeting was so odd. This is my first encounter with her too, and I have three other clients ready to publish there and I can't imagine any of them handling her as well as you did today."

"I'm not sure I did much except revert to my natural pomposity."

"However you did it she was properly devastated and it was no act. I know theater when I see it. You're leaving upset her a great deal and I think she was genuine in her apologies."

"Well, call George then. Call me back and tell me what I should do."

"I will."

He lay down again. His head felt better but not great. It concerned him that he felt so frequently debilitated.

George was distressed to learn that their highest grossing author was displeased. He said Christine spoke to him about Harry. Since she was new, she wanted to meet him and ask a few questions. He saw no harm in it so agreed. He thought well of her and was sure there was some misunderstanding. He spoke to Christine, who after apologizing to him for today, asked if she could meet with Harry again to explain. Seeing no reason to leave any animus between them Harry agreed to see her in the morning.

They met in the same conference room at ten the next morning. Her smile was warm as she stood and held out her hand,

"Good morning, Harry. Thank you for seeing me again."

"I'm glad it could be arranged, Christine."

She offered him coffee and they sat sipping for a few moments. He waited for her. It was her meeting.

"This is awkward. I don't know where to begin."

Harry nodded, "I'm sure you'll find your place."

She smiled, "Yes, I'm sure I will. The first thing to say is I'm sorry. I meant no offense to you. That certainly wasn't my intention. I wanted to meet you and secondarily, to know why you write about what you do because you do it so well. I was surprised when I saw your plot outline was written in such a different style than either of your books. I was a bit nervous and I phrased things badly at the start and no doubt sounded like a writing teacher. I asked about your motivation because I was genuinely interested in it. You took that wrong and it went downhill from there as we got tangled up in process. I mean, I do have strong views about that, but I'm not your editor and you are hardly a neophyte. I was wrong to say as much as I did about it. I want it to be clear as well, since George seems to think otherwise, and you may as well, that I am well aware that your only editor is Charlie Winchester."

Harry was silent, waiting to see if there was more.

"I'm being inadequate in explaining myself now, but on reflection, I suppose I never should have asked about your outline, but I did and I accept the consequences of that."

What she said seemed honest. He heard no trace of guile in her throaty voice,

"Thank you Christine, I appreciate your honesty. I didn't mean to be rude, but what you said and perhaps the way you said it, struck a most discordant note and likely brought out the worst in me."

She smiled, "You do know how to make your point. Frankly, I haven't been lectured quite that way in a very long time. However, since I deserved it, I'll remember it with fondness."

Harry looked up quickly to see if she was mocking him. Her eyes were warm and her smile seemed sincere. He wasn't sure how much he could warm up to her but she seemed a very nice woman really, perhaps yesterday was just a bad day.

"Well," Harry said as he exhaled slowly, "I'm not sure I will. I mean remember it fondly. I don't enjoy the tension it creates. Verbal jousting should be a sport not part of the work day."

She shifted in her chair now, crossing her legs and relaxing,

"You enjoy word play as amusement?"

"Words are how we, you and I, make our living. I think bringing them out and having fun with them, particularly those not used often is amusing," he said. "Of course, you'd want to avoid combining them in quite the way you did yesterday."

She laughed with genuine amusement, "I'm sure you'll find it strange Harry," she said looking at him directly again, "But I might look forward to a game of words with you."

"Would you?"

"Do you think we could have one or am I forever tarnished?"

Harry stood and she did as well. As they walked to the door he replied, "Forever is a very long time Christine."

She stopped as they reached the closed door and turned to face him with her arms folded. "It is."

Harry smiled, "Do you have a card? Perhaps I could drop by and see you when I'm here again and we can have another conversation as civil as this one. I can even let you know how the book is going."

She stared at him a minute. "Charlie will be the only one who'll need to know that if that was your meaning. Here," she said as she handed him a card from the credenza near the door. "I'd be happy to have you stop by however, and appreciate you're seeing me this morning."

"I was making conversation just now, not conveying any meaning."

"Then I must be too sensitive, I'm sorry. Are you leaving the city soon?"

Harry nodded, "I need to see Charlie and go over the plan of how we'll work this time and perhaps give him a few rough chapters so he can get an idea of how I plan to do this. I have one more lecture series to prepare for as well."

"You live near here don't you?"

"I did. I've sold my house in Hamilton. I've travelled for two years and won't be going back."

"Where are you lecturing?"

"Pepperdine University."

"Well Malibu should have nicer weather than here."

"Yes I'm sure it will. Then I'll need to find a place to write."

"Really? Do you need suggestions? I have some, but am not anxious to share them unless you're receptive to that sort of thing."

"I don't fly into bombastic outrage at suggestions, Christine. If you have anything, I'd be glad to know about it."

"I'd be happy to do it then. Further atonement for my bad behavior," she said with a laugh, "perhaps we can talk again before you go and you can be more specific as to what you want. Where are you staying?"

"I'm at The Regent."

"Why do you stay all the way uptown? There are lots of hotels down here. I'm sorry, that was a personal question."

"It was, but I don't mind them in context. I've used The Regent since I moved up this way, even before Hamilton. Alas, I'm looking for another hotel now at least for this trip. The renovations they have going on are annoying."

"What about The Universal? It's just down the side street here. It's more modern but many of our people stay there now when they come in for editorial conferences."

"I don't know it."

"It's new and probably wasn't there when you were here last. You may like its location if you plan to see Charlie. Do you want me to have someone call?"

"No, no thanks, I'll do that."

"I'll ask some of my authors for some suggestions for places to write as well."

Harry smiled. "Will you call this week if you have anything?"

"Of course, and thanks again for coming in today. It was a pleasure. I hadn't expected that."

"I doubt either of us did," he said with a smile and walked out to the elevator.

He was trading stories of the bad old days with a smiling Charlie Winchester by noon. He never seemed to change. He was still taciturn, saying more with his expression than with words. He was stoic in the face of Harry's bluster, perhaps why they worked well together. He had glanced at the outline and remarked acerbically that at least there was one this time. They went over the logistics. Charlie agreed that fewer meetings would be fine with him.

As he left, Harry thanked him again for his work on *Country* and Charlie expressed the hope that this time things would go easier. Harry laughed and said that he shouldn't expect too much. He rolled his eyes and smiled.

Christine had not exaggerated the lushness of The Universal. It was a lovely hotel. Perhaps too sleek and modern for his tastes but the service was excellent and the rooms large and airy. After checking in, he sent an e-mail expressing as many thanks as he could to Bill and Martha, promised he would call soon, and worked on his lecture.

Harry ate at the hotel the next morning because it was simplest and the weather was turning and he didn't feel like walking. His headache was continuous since last night. He sat in the lobby and tried to read a newspaper while he had a nice chat about the city with an older man who seemed in no more of a hurry to get on with his day than Harry was. He eventually went upstairs, took medication, and drafted two early chapters. He got lost in it as the pain eased and was startled to find it was after five when the phone rang. He didn't recognize the number.

"Hello?"

"Hi, Harry, It's Chris."

"Hello Chris."

"Are you at The Universal?"

"Yes, yes, I am."

"Are you busy?"

"I'm drafting some chapters for Charlie to review."

"I have some listings for you and two suggestions an author gave me. Do you want to walk over here and I'll tell you about them or I could meet you in the lobby over there if you like on my way out."

"The lobby would be better."

"When are you leaving?"

"Excellent question, I haven't checked flights yet. I need to go to Tucson for a few days first and should go tomorrow. Thanks for reminding me. Did you say you were about to leave?"

"Well, close. Give me thirty minutes to clear up what I'm doing. See you in a bit."

He stood and stretched. His headache was only a dull ache now. He'd see if a scotch helped.

He found a table in the lobby bar and saw Christine come in and look around. He stood. She smiled when she saw him.

"Hello, Christine, it's nice to see you. I have a place over here."

She smiled brightly, "Why thank you, Harry. I wasn't sure it would be nice."

He chuckled as they sat, "We'll give it a try."

"Good. What is that?" she pointed at his drink as a waitress came into view.

"Just single malt scotch and some water."

"I'd like one," Harry must have shown some surprise since she said, "I don't drink often Harry, but I like scotch very much. Not one for white wine."

He chuckled, "You're full of surprises aren't you?"

"Yes."

"Yes?"

She shrugged as her scotch arrived and she took a sip. "That seemed sufficient. God this is wonderful."

He sat back and appraised her as she sipped at her glass again and looked around the huge glass lobby area. Was she strange or have a sense of humor? He supposed he'd know soon enough. She looked at him squarely,

"Now, its five-thirty and my office closed. I know writers don't understand such concepts because you tinker with things day and night, but I stop editing at five, so can you call me Chris now?"

"If that's what you like."

"Well, when you see me around the building, feel free to use the more pompous Christine or Miss Morgan if you feel the need."

She managed to say it with humor and wasn't the least offending. He looked at her and wondered what he should make of this woman. Her humor was refreshing and unexpected given their history.

"Do you need another?" He said pointing at her now near empty glass.

"Need? No. Want? Yes. I don't want to get roaring drunk and be poured into a cab, however."

"And that would be the result if you had another two ounces of scotch diluted in water?"

"Well, no, but you know how that leads to two more and then two more."

"I see. Well, I think you should have another and share the results of you're no doubt exhaustive research into where Harry Logan should write his next book."

"Are you having one with me?" Harry's glass was only half-empty.

"Presently perhaps, I'll have more of this first." He waved down the waitress and asked for hers and a glass of water for him.

"Okay. Here are the listings I have and the addresses of the places my author gave me. Be easy to refine the list if I knew more."

"More what?"

She looked around, as if perhaps he was asking the question of another standing behind her,

"Are you mocking me now? Do you want to talk about this or just have a drink and see if I can make you laugh?"

"I prefer both."

"Good, we agree on something. A first, perhaps in our case. Now, can we go on?"

"Do you need your glasses?" He said mockingly.

She sat back, "You're impossible."

"I am actually. Charlie gets that. It's why we thrive."

"You're making that up. Charlie hates that sort of thing."

"No, he finds me quite charming, lovable even. Can't wait for the book."

"He finds you . . . ? That's the most preposterous thing you've said tonight."

"Really?" Harry was sitting back quite relaxed and finding this fun. She seemed a woman with a nice sense of humor.

"Yes."

"Okay."

"Please, can we be serious for a few minutes?"

"You started it."

"I realize that."

He narrowed his eyes, "You refuse to stop, don't you?"

She stared back. She had merry, impish eyes Harry thought. Finally she said,

"I have no reason to, it's fun."

"It is," he said, "but ask your questions now."

"Okay, do you want to be warm, cold or do you like seasons?"

"I like the seasons, but if I'm wrapped up in the writing, I won't notice unless it's extreme."

"I'll put you down as 'temperate' then. Since you need to get here for meetings, do you want to be near here or just have an easy fly-in?"

"Either one. Perhaps I should give a better idea of what's important."

"Anything is going to be better than an hour quiz which is where this is going if you don't help me here."

"Sorry, I thought I gave you my preferences when we talked the other day."

"There you go again."

"Go? Whatever do you mean?"

"You did it earlier. You seemed to think you'd told me something you hadn't. Are you okay?" She said lightly.

"I did that?"

"Yes, I thought you were being funny, but yes, it was as if you forgot."

"I really did?"

She nodded, "You do remember what we're talking about now, don't you?"

"Of course I do," Harry answered with more irritation in his voice than he meant and looked up quickly, "I'm sorry, I didn't mean to use that tone. It's just a bit frightening to forget like that."

"It happens to everyone," she said with a wave of her hand in dismissal, "just tell me what you like, and we'll go from there."

He summarized it for her, including the preference for a town, the need for people around him at least some of the time, and no cities or apartments. When he was done he looked at her, she was concentrating on what he said.

"So that's about it. Anything spring immediately to mind?"

"Yes and no."

"Gee, not undecided are we?"

She smiled, "How do you feel about cabins?"

"Cabins. You mean in the woods?"

"Near a town and on a lake but yes, in the woods."

"Ambivalent. Can I walk to town?"

"It's a long walk, but doable on a nice day."

"More ambivalence."

"Okay. What about the desert?"

"Deserts are brown, hot. I'm not certain I would thrive there."

"Not all of them are bad and winter is coming. I'll give you that they are mostly brown, but there are some with charm."

"It doesn't sound plausible. I hate air conditioning. I don't sleep well in it and prefer none at all if possible."

"Have you ever heard of the Sabino Pass? The Santa Catalina Mountains?"

"No."

"Near Tucson. Desert, but cooler because of the altitude. Even rains in July, snows every year or two. Has green things growing around there too."

"Would I survive the summer?"

"In that adobe house on the list there, yes. It's a real adobe with walls nearly four feet thick. Not those faux thing contractors build these days."

"Interesting. And how do you know about it?"

She smiled, "We can get to that if you don't rule it out."

"It would be different. Anything else?"

"Take a look at what I gave you and let me know."

They talked of the city, which she liked a great deal, especially living near work. He learned she was from Seattle and lived in a number of places including Chicago, New York, and Arizona and had always been involved in publishing in some way.

"Thanks for the help Chris, It was much more than I expected."

She looked up at him, "Have you had dinner?"

"Not yet, why?"

"We could."

"There are rules about that aren't there?"

"From the publisher? There's a general admonishment to editors regarding sleeping with their authors. I have my own rules about fraternizing with you people as well."

"And what would they be?"

"This," she said waving her hand, "having a drink is okay. Although being in your hotel is a close call under rule five which deals with drinking. Dinner is rule six."

"How many are there?"

"I'm not sure. Eleven. Let's say eleven."

"So it could be more, then?"

"Well, something may come up I've never experienced before so why not just say I have eleven? If I need another one, it will be twelve."

"They don't sound very rigid if they are meant to be rules."

"Not rigid, perhaps just complicated."

Harry just shook his head and laughed.

"I've never applied them to authors I wasn't editing, however. I mean, you're a first. I never drank with an author that I wasn't working with or dined with one either. So," she gave a huge grin now, "do the rules apply at all?"

Harry groaned audibly while she laughed and finished her scotch.

"You needn't answer. It was rhetorical but perhaps worthy of discussion sometime."

"Yes, let's save that," he replied as he looked at the check he was going to sign,

"As amusing as I'm sure I would find dining with you, Chris, I'm sorry I haven't time tonight. I need to finish preparing my lecture notes if I'm leaving here tomorrow."

"This was fun," she said as they walked to the main lobby door, "You're a surprisingly funny man. I'll keep your secret from the publishers. They see you much differently over there."

"Ah yes, as the pompous, bombastic, and imperious Harry Logan."

She laughed, "Close enough."

Harry walked her to the cabstand in front. On the way she reminded him to book his tickets to Tucson.

"I will in the morning. I hate doing it, especially with connections. I find it annoying and confusing."

She got in, gave the driver her address, and waved as they pulled away.

He thought briefly of his lapses in memory. The doctor asked about them and he'd denied it. He wasn't happy about it. He'd write a note about the flight so he'd see it in the morning.

When he woke, there were two messages on his phone from Chris. After he showered, he called her,

"What is it Chris?"

"What time's your flight?"

"I don't know. I was about to try to figure it out."

"You've missed the last decent connection today."

"I have?"

"You have, and it would be sad but I sent over your boarding passes an hour ago. You have three hours to get to the airport."

"You made my reservations?"

"Don't be offended, I'm still atoning. I remembered that you said Tucson and you hate doing it. Since you wanted to get out of here today, I thought the earlier it was booked the better. The connections can be horrible. I lived over there remember? It was easy enough to do when I came in, and I find it a challenge. The last good connection was through San Francisco. I knew you flew First Class when we send you so assumed you always do, did I get that right?"

"Why yes, yes, you did," Harry said with a laugh, "Did you book it all the way through?"

"No, it's easier to drive from Phoenix, trust me I've done it, although there is still time to change that."

"I'm speechless."

"Sure you are. Anyway, there's a car reserved at Phoenix and that information is at the desk as well so pack and get over there. You can reimburse the publisher. I'm sure you're e-mail is all over the building, do you mind if I use it? I have some more suggestions from another author."

"Of course not, or just call. You're very good to have gone to this trouble."

"Am I? Well, that's nice to know. I hope you have a good trip and the lectures go well."

"Thank you, I'll look forward to hearing from you."

"Good."

Harry was as surprised by the call as he was by her behavior the first time he met her. He shook his head and went to find breakfast.

Paul Zuckerman was there to meet him the next morning in his office adjacent to the University of Arizona Hospital. He was highly recommended by friends in New York who knew only that Harry was being bothered by what he described as tension headaches. They claimed Dr. Zuckerman was the finest neurological diagnostician in the country. He was forty-five, ten years older than Harry. He was six feet tall, well tanned and fit, and his sandy hair made him look younger. Harry liked him as soon as they met.

After two days of routine medical tests and a host of x-rays and scans to which Harry submitted with a minimum of questions and a meekness not seen by many in his life, they were meeting to discuss the preliminary results. Harry was just getting off the telephone with Madeline in Hamilton who assured him the estate sale was done and escrow account closed when Zuckerman entered and began questioning Harry without preamble.

"How long ago did you first notice anything unusual, Mr. Logan? Your history says you've had headaches all your life. What makes these different?"

"The last year or so they've become quite intense, at times debilitating in the sense that I can't concentrate. Of late, they've become nearly continuous."

"Anything else?"

"A colleague up north suggested that I may have a short term memory problem. I'm not certain about that."

"Okay, let me show you what we see in the images."

Zuckerman was moving to another desk that had a large computer screen and two chairs. The dye-enhanced image of what looked to Harry like the inside of a pomegranate was glowing on the screen. The lights were lowered by one of the Neurological Fellows and Zuckerman continued,

"In this area here," he said, "you can see a white spot. That's not a mass, probably an aneurism. It's small and looks as if it's been there for some time, perhaps most of your life."

Harry asked, "What does it mean?"

"It could be the trouble . . . See it?" He put the stylus the on the bulge in the vessel, "but if it's been there as long as I suspect, and you report no singular and crushing, totally off the scale headache, it isn't a worry. We don't have another earlier one to compare it with so I can't say whether it's getting larger."

"Is that what's causing the headaches?"

"It could, but it's unlikely. You have this other area near the right ear. Here," He moved the pointer forward now, "this is a concern because I don't know what it is. It could be a clot or you may have a tumor. I'm not sure. This is the only shot we have of it. It wasn't apparent in any of the other views. Is your vision any different now than say a year ago? Have you been nauseous for no reason? Had dizzy spells when you stood quickly?"

"No, nothing like that on any regular basis. I have, as you know, been in a perpetual travel status for at least two years now. I change places and time zones quite frequently so the fatigue I feel is greater than normal, as is the eyestrain and that sort of thing."

"Humm . . . . when were you off the road last, relaxed and didn't work for any period of time?"

"I haven't lived at home in the conventional sense for three years. I lived in New York for several months. I was in hotels, however, and I was working throughout. That is, not writing but doing what one does when a novel is published. There's been no time away from that since the initial publishing tour although I was home for a few days at a time back in the early days of that."

Zuckerman grinned. "I had no idea authors put in those kinds of hours. Sounds like a surgical residency."

"Hardly that, I stand around gripping hands, grinning and spouting clichés at people who have come to have a drink or dinner, and praise or purchase a book. Lately I've done a great deal of public speaking. That's hardly the pressure of a young surgeon, is it?"

"I understand, but moving from place to place as often as you do isn't without stress is it?"

Harry nodded, "It may be the worst kind. I mean, you know, the kind of stress that's irrational. The worry of being late, not getting to an interview, missing a connection, bad weather and the rest when there isn't much you can do about it. You can feel pretty awful when you arrive in a new time zone every day with a different climate and in the wrong clothes. Do you think that thing may have something to do with my headaches?" Harry said, pointing at the screen.

"Not sure. We don't know as much as you think. What causes these things is one of them. Maybe you've had this a long time and now as you get older," he shrugged, "I can't say how it got there, or when because I have no early history."

"I see." Harry said thoughtfully as he studied the image trying to understand.

Harry and Dr. Zuckerman talked for another hour about what it meant. Harry, who wanted to know nothing more than how to get his head to stop hurting wasn't much interested in the words surgery and radiation which popped up now and then as possibilities. He wanted to relieve his pain, to get on with it. He was clear with Paul—they were Paul and Harry by now—that his wish was for the quickest solution. Paul prescribed a different pain medication and a relaxant for sleep. He wanted Harry to come back for more extensive test as soon as he could. Harry wanted two weeks and Paul finally agreed.

On the drive back to Phoenix and the short flight to Los Angeles he tried to absorb all he'd heard. He found it most annoying since his life was busy, and he couldn't take time out now for some wretched physical problem. He was riding a big wave and he was in no mood for debilitating headaches to make him get off. He was frightened too, and didn't want to share that fear or his problem. He needed to tell Bill what he learned and there was no choice but to come back here for more tests after his trip to Los Angeles.

Harry taught at a small college in Los Angeles for a time while he tried acting. His mellifluous voice found him steady work in commercials and then even more lucrative work as cartoon characters, although very little as an actor. Carlton Wedge, a fellow expatriate from New York City worked with him then and they'd stayed in touch over the years. Carlton's new studio was doing very well and, by Hollywood standards, he was nearly an "A list" personality. Harry looked forward to a few days with him and Chloe if he could avoid the parties with the pseudo-glitterati that Carlton called friends, many of whom he'd met when he passed through on his book tour.

The next four days were relaxing. The English Chair at Pepperdine was a vivacious woman named Caroline Grayson whom he enjoyed having at his lecture the first day and having lunch with the following day. He attended the obligatory Dean's dinner with her and her dry sarcastic humor and charm made it more entertaining than many that he'd attended over the past two years. Carlton still had a strange group of friends who seemed to be more interested in drinking and partying than doing much work. He had some friendly neighbors in Malibu and Harry enjoyed playing beach volleyball with them and the freedom from any other obligations while he was there.

He reached Bill before he went to the dinner with Caroline by tracking him down through his secretary. He was beginning to understand that Bill was a lot busier now than he was three years ago.

"Hey Harry, what's up? You never call here."

"Your cell is either dead or off and Martha isn't home, William, or I wouldn't now. I wanted to tell you that I went to see the specialist in Tucson. I'll be going back for more tests this week."

"They find something?"

"Yes, but what is still an open question. They'll run more extensive tests and I hope for something more definitive then. He doesn't like whatever it is."

"Doesn't sound promising."

"Hard to tell. There was mumbling about a need for some sort of intervention."

"You in Malibu?"

"I am. I have to go to an obligatory Dean's dinner tonight, but the rest has been fun, even my head feels better. Carlton, despite his new wealth, drop dead gorgeous woman, and fantastic beachfront house has changed very little. He still sounds like a man on Seventh Avenue about to order a salted bagel. He left this morning to do a shoot up the coast so I have the place to myself for a day or two."

Bill chuckled, "Sounds like tough duty. You got any Hollywood lovelies with ya there?"

"No, actually. The University is about four miles from here so I haven't been downtown since I got off the plane. Malibu has its pleasures however."

"Yeah, I bet it does. I think I heard all I need about it for now. Not much good news so far."

"No, and who knows what will happen to my writing schedule. Beyond that, well, it scares me."

"Would anybody Harry. Take it easy for now and then get back over there and see what they find. Ya gotta do that."

"I know I do but part of me doesn't want to know. I'm busy and too young for this Bill. I shouldn't have to deal with this now."

"Don't worry so much, could be somethin' easy."

"Perhaps. I felt worse in the city and my short term memory seems to be affected, so it's more worrisome. I'll need to go back up there and will try to see you and Martha before anything gets done. It's not clear there is any great rush unless my symptoms worsen."

"Just be careful Harry, don't push it."

"I'll try to be reasonable, although anger is all I associate with it right now."

"Just don't assume anything. Call me when you know more, or when you're comin' back. We should be here the rest of this month."

"My love to Martha then," he glanced at his watch, "and go home for dinner."

"Yeah, sure."

By the time Harry saw it, the next day was warm and bright with only a hint of coastal fog off the beach and a gentle breeze. He slept well and his head was remarkably clear. Even the dull ache that was always there was nearly gone. Since Chloe and Carlton were cooking-impaired there were menus from every place that delivered in Malibu. After coffee, he called out to the local breakfast place and he sat out on the deck afterward. It was quiet on a weekday. Only gulls screeching and the waves breaking broke the silence.

Success and wealth had come young, quickly, and in some ways by accident, tragic and otherwise to Harry Logan. For someone in his mid-thirties he'd done a great deal he knew, but he wanted to do a great deal more. Yet now he needed to deal with the fact that he could be seriously ill. It both annoyed and scared him. He needed to know more from Paul Zuckerman before he started anything new now. He hated the thought of losing the time to doing something to get his health right before he could write again.

Moreover, he was essentially homeless. He knew selling was the right thing, that going back to Hamilton wasn't possible for him, but it did leave him at sixes and sevens as to where next to hang his hat. He needed to find a place to live, yet he needed to know how ill he really was first and make room for that as well. It meant changing the contract he'd just signed too since he had to allow for a recuperative period if Paul couldn't find a way to control it until after the book was done. Having to do all that made Harry tired just thinking about it. He wanted to write his book and sell it. He was good at that. This illness business was beginning to overwhelm him and he wasn't even sure what was wrong yet. He loved writing and in a different way loved selling books. He didn't want to contemplate having to do anything else and it made him angry that he might. Worse perhaps, he would do it alone. He had no one really. He had friends surely and people who cared about him but he was without the conventional family most would have for support through something like this. He'd made such a habit of being solitary that his friends expected it of him. Yet now he may need help and he wasn't sure how to ask. He never had before. Except with Bill, he held his feeling close. While the loud and annoying and obsessive part of him was largely out of his private life now, it was just outside the door. Balancing any sort of private life relationship and his public life seemed beyond his meager social skills. The past two years were as happy as they were because he hadn't tried to be more than the public man, except for the pitifully fruitless attempts to convince Anita to love him on his terms. He was enjoying his work. His relationships were facile or flirtatious. None lasted long, meant much nor did he have any expectations of them. He was uncomfortable believing that was all he was capable of but it was what seemed to work. Perhaps there could be more as Bill said, he didn't know. He'd have to work at it and after Anita he was disinterested or perhaps just afraid to try.

He shook himself from his thoughts and looked at the time. It was nearly two now. The long evening—night really—with Caroline and his attempt to sort out his thoughts left him tired. He wasn't going to solve any of this today he knew, but it needed more thought. There were grown up decisions to be made and only he could make them.

Paul Zuckerman called and asked questions that Harry failed to appreciate but knew must be relevant since Paul wasn't one to waste time. He asked about his activities, exertion level, and was very specific about how he felt in various situations. Harry tried to remember everything. When they were done, Paul spoke quietly but sternly,

"I'd like you to come back here sooner. You need to have the tests we discussed."

"I can arrange it any time now."

"Good, call Marion then and schedule it. The Fellows will do the work up. We'll talk when you're done."

"Fine."

"You'll need to stay in the hospital this time. It will take about two days to get it all done."

"Is that necessary?"

"It'll be easier on you actually since there's some sedation involved. See you soon."

He rang off abruptly. Harry wondered what he was facing but had to know all he could now.

Tucson was as brown and arid as Malibu was blue and green. After the short ride to the hospital he was filling out paperwork for Marion by four.

He was in Paul Zuckerman's office for their conference two days later. It was late. He wanted no more hospital food or care. Paul was leaving for New York tonight, so he wanted to go over the results now. One of the physicians in training under Paul, those he knew as Fellows regardless of gender, asked some additional questions while they waited. Paul came in and got straight to the tests with a brusqueness Harry had not seen before.

"We have decent pictures of all of your head this time Harry so we know a little more about it. I believe it's a tumor and relatively new. I don't like the looks of it and it's going to continue to cause pressure unless we do something about it. You need to take care of it sooner rather than later."

"Take care of it?" Harry was feeling numb.

"Yes, you're going to have to tell me what you want to do. Surgery is the best option. It's small and appears encapsulated. I should be able to get it all and your headaches will go away as well your other symptoms. I can't say exactly what the postoperative effects will be, but I can tell you leaving it alone won't make you better. If I were to find no more than coagulation we can use blood-thinning drugs and make it go away. In my opinion it's not a bleed though, it's too well defined."

Harry sat and stared at his hands. A tumor. How?

"Did it come from elsewhere?" Harry knew that brain tumors were often secondary to others.

Paul shook his head, "If it did, we can't find it. It's why we did the spinal tap and the rest of the tests. I think we can say it is new and it's solitary and isn't from another place. That's the good news. The bad news is it's there. Tumors of this type are benign in nearly all cases, but a biopsy is the only way to know for certain."

"Are you going to do it?"

"In conjunction with surgery. We could do a needle biopsy but I'd need to bore a hole in the side of your head for that anyway so I might as well do the rest of the job while I'm in there."

"So doing the biopsy without surgery is pointless?"

Paul nodded, "In my opinion," Paul looked at him a moment longer and then said, "There are a range of treatments here Harry and you need to know the risks and benefits of all of them. I believe this is best but I'd like to have some others look at the films and the test results and make sure I didn't miss something before we decide. Is that all right with you?"

"Of course. Is it what's causing the headaches?"

"Yes, or rather it's raising you ICPs, sorry, Intracranial Pressures. Sure of that now. This spot here that we talked about when you first came, here, back in this area in what's known as the Circle of Willis where all the blood vessels are—he pointed at the base of the skull on the film—is that small aneurysm. That may be as old as you are. You don't report a family history of such problems but you also don't relate any history on your mother's side because you don't know it. I'm assuming it's congenital. We need to keep an eye on it, but I have no plans for it. We have a good baseline now and the lumbar puncture showed no blood in the spinal fluid, so I'm sanguine. Many people have aneurysms and never know it—maybe ten, twenty per cent of the population—so I wouldn't worry. They usually get discovered this way, when we look for something else. Now, what are your plans for the next month?"

"I need to go up north and see my publishers. I would like to be there at least ten days."

"Hmm . . . well it's up to you."

"Yes it is."

"Just don't get dug in Harry. Keep an open mind about this. I may be able to make you good as new with no fatigue or headaches. I can't believe your still tolerating those actually."

"Then again, you may not, correct?"

Paul looked at him steadily. "I may not. Tell you what. I'll stay in touch and let you know if I want you to see anyone else. Why don't we say two weeks? I would feel better if we got it out of there now, but you apparently don't so we'll deal with it as you wish. I'll call if there is any urgency based on what the others say and you call here if you have worsening symptoms."

"What about medications?"

"Take what you think you need of what I prescribed the last time in the same way while you're working."

Harry asked about activity levels and Paul assured him he could do whatever he could tolerate. Finally, he looked at him hard,

"Do the reading about this. The staff will give you all the references and journal articles you could possibly want. Call us for more if you're not satisfied. Just stay the hell away from the general internet stuff because all that'll do is scare you or give you the false hope that some witch doctor will make it go away. Don't be afraid to learn about it. It will make it less of a worry. I know this shocked you."

"It does everyone, doesn't it?"

"Yes it does. There are worse things however even if you don't believe that now."

CHAPTER THREE

Harry's trip back to the northwest was a series of interminable hours in airports broken up by several hours of flight. When he checked in at The Universal he thought he would go blind from the pain. He went to bed and remained there until noon. He found no rejuvenation in a shower. He ordered room service, ate, and then slept for another two hours before he was even able to dress. The debilitation scared him. He couldn't remember in all time he spent traveling ever being that tired.

Throughout the layovers the previous day he read everything they'd given him twice and while it made him more familiar, he felt no more comfortable. He had an intimate knowledge of aneurysms and ventricular meningioma, yet it gave him no comfort. One of the Fellows called him in the afternoon and asked how he was feeling and whether he had any questions. The physician said Paul would reach him tomorrow. When done, he called Bill, who was on the road with three associates. He said he'd talk to him in a day or so, but that he thought he'd see him this weekend and they left it at that.

By then, Harry was beginning to recover. It was near four so he walked out into the light mist and crossed the street to see if he could find Charlie. He was, as always when not with a client, reading at his desk. They talked over the chapters he'd left with him. Charlie said he understood the book's direction but had no suggestions based on the early drafts. Harry said he only wanted to see if he understood them and say hello. Charlie seemed pleased by that and Harry left realizing the visit was more a need to talk to someone who understood his world. He was depressed about how ill he felt more and more. He needed to decide how much to tell Elspeth and while he looked forward to seeing Bill and Martha he knew the look in their eyes would be one of sympathy and he didn't want that. He got off the elevator in the lobby and heard his name.

Christine Morgan got off the other bank across the hall and was coming towards him smiling. He still hadn't read Elspeth's e-mail about her.

"Hello Chris."

"How are you Harry? What brings you in? You have chapters with Charlie already?"

"So many questions, Chris. I sent Charlie some early drafts to show him the direction I want to go but I haven't done any real writing yet, it was more to say hello than anything. I still have things to settle."

"Here?"

"Yes, I have to have a contract meeting this week, and I hope to get to Hamilton for a couple of days."

"When did you get in?"

"Late last night and I came all the way from Tucson and without your booking skills I ended up in three airports with very long layovers."

"Driving from Phoenix is more rational. When I lived there I did it all the time."

They reached the street door now and the mist was still falling. She pulled her coat tight,

"Have you eaten?"

"No."

"I know a place you might like. Would you consider dinner?"

Harry smiled for the first time. "What about the rules?"

"You remember?"

"Of course. They seemed as complicated as the Kyoto Protocols. How could I forget?"

She laughed, "I'm glad you worry about my rules."

"I don't worry about them. I just try to follow them as I do my own. Since you were good enough to get me to Tucson on time, I owe you dinner, however."

"Good, I'd rather walk unless you mind the rain."

"No, I could use a walk."

They crossed the busy street and went three blocks uptown. She abruptly turned into a small Bistro in the next block. They shed their coats, she went off to the ladies room, and he was shown a table in the back. It was a quiet neighborhood place, which made him think of comfortable food. He needed that and talking to Chris would surely be better than the solitary meal he faced twenty minutes ago. He ordered a single malt scotch for each of them and water as well. His head was reminding him it was there again, although it was a mild compared to last night. She came back smiling and slid into a chair,

"Gail must be working. She always gives me this table. Is that scotch?"

"It is."

She gave him a broad smile, sipped at it, rolled her eyes upward, and gave off a sensual sound of satisfaction. He laughed,

"Is that the first scotch you've had since I left?"

She settled back, "It is. Thank you for that."

Harry nodded his head.

"I'm glad I ran into you. Eating with boring Bernice was not something I was looking forward to with great pleasure."

"You had plans? You should have said."

"God no, I'm just glad I didn't go down the hall to find her before I left."

He chuckled, "a bit strange that rule six was broken so easily. Are you sure there is such a rule?"

"You may recall, Mr. Logan, the last time we wandered into that rhetorical thicket it was a question of whether it would apply to all people I meet as a result of my employment or only if I am their editor. The rules were made for those whose books on which I am working."

"I do remember."

"Rule six doesn't apply to you then since we have no professional relationship."

"Interesting. The lawyers would argue that we do, however. You work for my publisher and you're the immediate supervisor of my editor, so there is a relationship, albeit tenuous."

"Is there?"

"Yes, were someone to question our eating together, it would not be unreasonable for them argue that."

"That's absurd."

"Of course it is. Yet lawyers are absurd, aren't they? They could further argue that I was guilty of unprofessionalism and we won't even discuss the personal harassment issues. That is a thicket not worth entering."

"Hmm. So what are we to do? Never eat together?"

Harry raised his chin, "Well, you may have your rules and decide how to apply them, but there are other consequences that spring from our actions that might damage the reputation or employment of one or the other of us. We may do as we wish, but there are consequences, intended and unintended."

Chris sat up straight, "Jesus that was stunning. Even I, who was once the object of your scorn, didn't think you could summon a complicated argument like that from your ordinarily amusing mind on a whim."

Harry smiled, "Apparently I'm still able to do it. Now what have you been up to since you whisked me out of town nearly against my will?"

She laughed and sat back again. "You know, I have a hard time getting my head around your act. Do your friends find you difficult?"

"Yes, but I'm rarely with them. I only have two."

Harry looked up at the approaching waitress who smiled and greeted Chris by name. Chris said she'd wave when they were ready.

"Is this the place you hang out?"

"No. I like the food here and Bernice lives two blocks from here which is how I found this place."

"Where then?"

"I'm not sure I want you to know that. You could be a stalker."

"I could. I'm not, by the way,"

"Good to know," She said laughing and grabbed a menu and told Harry at some length what she liked best.

They ate and laughed at his anecdotes about the lectures at Pepperdine and Carlton's party and his friends. She told him about some film festival involving only old black and white movies, some with subtitles which he didn't fully comprehend.

Neither were interested in desert or more liquor. She leaned back and looked serious now. He wondered why and as the silence stretched longer than he thought she was capable so he spoke into it,

"What is it?"

"I was thinking."

"Given your acumen, I don't find that unusual. About what?"

"I want to ask you a question, but it really is none of my business."

"How bad could it be? We've insulting each other all evening."

"Yeah, but that was all in fun."

"What do you want to ask that isn't fun?"

"You may get angry."

"I have free will. I may not answer. You're exasperating me now, so ask if you are."

She looked up quickly, frowning. "Why were you in Tucson?"

He was startled by the question. He didn't want to answer it,

"It was a personal matter."

"Will you tell me more?"

He looked at her a long minute, thinking. Did he trust her? There was no reason he should. After all he met her under difficult circumstances and now had one apologetic meeting, drinks, and dinner. She was a very funny woman and on the surface he enjoyed her company, But she worked for the publisher. They couldn't know the truth now and she might tell them. Harry never lied so what was he to say to her? Her shoulders were sagging and the smile was gone. Finally he said,

"There isn't much to it, Chris. I have headaches. I went to Tucson to get an opinion about them."

She looked at him a long time as she slumped down in her chair. Finally Harry spoke,

"What led to your question?"

"You led me to my question. You were headed for Pepperdine. I sent you to Tucson from here, so you were there twice since you told me you came in from there last night." She shrugged, "It seemed strange."

Harry said nothing. If she could put all that together, did he slip up somewhere else? Did others know? It was important that no one did. He wasn't sure why, but that was his problem, not hers.

"You're not angry?"

"Not at you."

"I'm sorry, that was my lack of elegance again. Are you all right?"

"I've said all I want to say."

"I wasn't spying Harry. I was . . . well, maybe worried about you."

"Worried."

"See, now you've taken that the wrong way. I just meant it was odd and I was . . . let's try concerned this time."

"Okay."

"I hope I can at least be concerned."

Harry drew a breath and let it out slowly, he drank the second cup of coffee and said seriously and quietly,

"If you like."

"Okay, look. I know you have a problem of some kind because I figured it out and you told me the truth. I don't need to know more.

That's fine," She shrugged, "I just want to be of some help if you need it, however that works out, okay?"

"Okay, Chris I appreciate it."

They managed a normal and trivial conversation after that. She had a father in Arizona, a Masters in English, a love for music and a middling talent for playing the piano and her badly thought out marriage lasted only through graduate school in Chicago.

They agreed to share a cab as the rain fell harder now. He dropped her at her building, said he'd call before he left and went back to the hotel.

By the time he got through his e-mail and the coffee he ordered it was nearly eleven. Elspeth returned his earlier call from across the street. He had read her e-mail about Chris now and thankfully it was positive.

"El, do you have time to talk? Perhaps we could grab a bite. I'm at The Universal again and they have a lovely little bistro."

She laughed. "Yes, Harry, I've been there a few times. Is The Regent still renovating?"

"Actually, I have no idea. I flew in and stayed here because it was fine the last time and more central. Perhaps I'm capable of change."

She chuckled, "To answer your question, yes, I just finished up. I have to be somewhere else by one, is that enough time?"

"More than enough. I'll find a table."

The pleasant Bistro was busy when she made her entrance shortly. Elspeth never just slipped into a room, she entered one and drew attention when she did. Nearing fifty she was surely still that attractive and always that well dressed.

"First, thanks for the mail on Christine. You didn't seem to see any evil intent in her."

"No, I didn't and I must say she is editing one of my clients now and she loves her. She thinks she's a very smart and insightful editor with excellent language skills. She is one who loves long and involved outlines so perhaps they're kindred spirits. I still don't know what was going on the day you met her."

"I don't know either and suppose we never will so we can let that dog sleep where it lies now I should think."

"How quaint Harry. A nicely turned phrase however."

He chuckled, "Now, here's why I called. We need to set something up with the VP and the lawyers. I will tell you why, but I would hope we don't have to say much to them."

"What is it now?" She said with some irritation.

"Nothing tawdry or stupid. It may amount to nothing but I'd like to get some time added to the manuscript submission date. I'll do it for the same advance. Perhaps your lawyer can figure out how to word it and we can try to amend the current contract. It's quite serious, Elspeth, or I wouldn't ask."

"How long is 'some time' Harry?"

"A good question, but I should think six months. I would agree to a simple ratable reduction of the original amount to the longer time. I don't know how to write that. Can your man write an amendment do you think?"

"Well, of course he can but why do you feel you'll need it?"

"For now can I just say it's personal and serious and leave it at that? I'll tell you when I learn more. It needs to be done so that neither you nor I have a problem because of a promise made contractually that I can't keep."

"All right. Let me do this. My lawyer has the original contract so would know where the change would need to be made Let me have him call you. If he explains it are you comfortable arguing for it?"

"Yes, yes, I would be. I know what I need. It's quite simple really. I merely need to understand the place we need put it in the contract, that's all."

El dabbed at her lips, "Is it that serious Harry?"

"It is. It involves something I may need to do before I can start writing. I would rather tell you the rest when I have all the facts."

"All right then, I know you wouldn't ask unless you needed it. If there's anything I can do to help, tell me."

"Thank you El, but for now I only need your help getting this concession. By the way, how are sales? I haven't had time to look in a week or so."

"Surprisingly good and it won't hurt your case. The paperback and electronic versions are doing very well considering how long it's been out."

"Good. Now, how are you?"

"I'm fine, I have the symphony tonight. A new guest conductor will be here the rest of the week. You should go. They're doing some Bach and a good bit of Elgar. The paper has the details."

"Hmm, interesting. I do like Elgar."

"I'll try to get this done in a day or two but I can't promise they'll agree to meet that soon. What's your schedule?"

"I need to take care of this, go see Bill and Martha while I'm here, and get on with things."

"So a day or two here isn't a problem?"

"No, not at all. If they can't do it in the next two days, I'll overnight in Hamilton and return. I don't want to make this more difficult than having to ask for it."

"For you Harry that is most kind."

He laughed and walked out with her to the street and waved for a cab,

"I told you I was capable of change El, you need to believe me."

She laughed, waved, and disappeared into the back seat.

He missed a call from Paul while he was at lunch. He got Marion, who promised to track him down and have him call back in a few minutes.

Ten minutes later he was talking to Paul who was in New York.

"Harry, how are you?"

"No worse at the moment. The trip was horrible and it was never a problem on the road before. The layovers were awful, but I usually get through them better than that."

"Where are you?"

"At my publishers. If what I read in the references is going to apply to me, I have to try to re-negotiate the length of my contract."

"Sounds stressful."

"It will be."

"Here's why I called and I'm sorry this will have to be short. I brought your films to a conference here. Three other people for whom I have great respect looked at them. One has a contrary view, Stan Morris from the Mayo Clinic. He's an older thoughtful sort and has seen many of these. He'll get the whole file from Marion this week. He's going to look at it and send a report. He doesn't need to see you so that will save you a trip unless you want a formal second opinion from him or someone else."

"No, this sounds fine."

"I have the other reports and will be back in the desert the end of the week. I want you to plan to come back as soon as you can."

"I have at least three days here, perhaps less. I'm going north for two days so I would think given the horrible logistics that it would be next week before I would be there. I can stay in touch with Marion if it will help."

"It would. She can always find me. Meanwhile try to keep the stress down, although this week sounds hard if I know anything about lawyers. I apologize for cutting this short, but we'll have time next week. Call the emergency number if anything seems worse."

"Fine, Paul. See you soon."

Harry grabbed a bottle of water from the complimentary stack. The maids were knocking so he let them in and went down to the lobby and called Bill.

"William, are you terribly busy?"

"Nah, workin' at home actually. What's your story?"

"I'm in the city. I thought I would see what your schedule was and try to get to see you."

"When?"

"I'm not sure yet. Two or three days from now is my best guess. I have to get the publisher to revise the contract in case I have to delay the book and that may take a day or so. Alternately, they may drag their feet about meeting and I could come before I see them."

"Either one is all right this week."

"Good."

"Doin' the contract again so soon doesn't sound like fun."

"It won't be. I can think of many, many things more pleasant than discussing a contract amendment with corporate lawyers. It will be like being neutered."

Bill laughed, "Yeah, it'll hurt. I can't imagine what it'll feel like in your condition."

He quickly explained to Bill what he proposed to offer.

"Sounds fair, if it will work with the other language. 'Course it won't sound fair to a corporate lawyer. Want me to send Amanda?"

Harry laughed now, "No, I do want her to handle the trial though if there is one. This is just shouting back and forth and I can do that well enough."

"Amen to that, pal."

"Everyone has a skill, William. You're a better businessman than I. I've always been adept at speaking loudly."

"Hell, don't sell yourself short, Harry. Your one of the best at bombast the world has to offer right now. Anyway, good luck with it. Gonna have time to be amused?"

"I'll try to make the symphony tonight."

"Jamie always liked goin' there."

"She did and then accused me of stalking the solo violinist. God, she was nuts."

"We're pretty sure about that. You found company there?"

"No. I had dinner with a nice woman with a marvelous sense of humor, who says she loves music and dark movies, or I think that last part is right. Unfortunately she works for the publishing company so whatever companionship dinner produced needs to be over. I owed her a meal since she's done me a few favors."

"Film Noir, Harry, it's a genre. Look it up on the computer then you won't sound so stupid."

"What do you know about it?"

"I'm a lot smarter than ya think. Why does it have to be over?"

"I don't fraternize. If I see her more of her it would be. I have no way of knowing whether she'd tell her boss the next morning it was more than dinner and it wasn't consensual do I? I mean, I need to worry about those things."

"I suppose you do. It's why you need somebody like Martha."

"There's no time for that now, and I'm not sure I'm capable of it. You of all people know how badly that's gone in the past."

"Yeah, I do. How do you feel?"

"The headaches are dreadful and I seem to be getting forgetful. When I'm done here, Chris—"

"That her?"

"Yes, she's very good at booking flights, even enjoys it if what she says is to be believed, so perhaps she can make it easier. I'll try to give you a day or so notice when I have a better sense of the schedule."

"Do that. Doesn't matter much like I said. I'll alert Martha."

The maids were done so he lay down for an hour and when he woke just after five he finished re-reading a journal article on brain tumors and was about to go downstairs when the hotel phone rang. Odd, he thought, that hasn't happen since the days of Jamie Wells and her boozy late night rambles,

"Yes?"

"Harry."

"Chris? Why are you calling this number?"

"I'm in the lobby. Will you come down?"

"I can be there in a few minutes."

As he got off the elevator he saw her staring out the vast front window.

"Do you see anyone you know out here?"

She turned and looked at him and seemed to suppress a smile,

"Hello Harry."

"Is there something we need to talk about?"

"There is."

Harry sat down, "What?"

She looked at him steadily. "Having dinner together was fun but I'm not sure I should have asked. We both have rules about that sort of thing and people enjoy talking over there, and I don't I want to listen to it. I think you'd be wonderful friend, but others might read more into it if we're seen together and that would make both our lives difficult. I enjoy your friendship though. I hope we can keep that."

Harry sat thinking and finally said,

"I appreciate your friendship, too Chris, but you're right. I'd like to stop and say hello when I'm here and perhaps we can have a drink now and then in this very public place. Can you manage at least that?"

"I'd like that. I should have thought more before I asked about your health too. I understand your reluctance to talk about it with anyone, especially me. I just put it together and asked. I wasn't thinking and I'm sorry."

"It's all right."

She smiled, "Thanks for understanding."

"I do and I'm sorry that it has to be that way. I may need you to find me a better way back to Tucson. Can I call you about that?"

"Sure, call my cell anytime."

He walked her to a cab, "Don't worry Chris. We know what's happened. I find it petty and annoying that they decide it too."

"I just hope we don't lose touch, Harry. I enjoy talking to you."

"There's always that fishbowl." Harry said pointing at the lobby, "we can sit there and discuss life's vagaries anytime I'm here."

"Thanks. Call when you need to leave town."

Harry went to the symphony that night and found the music as relaxing as ever. He gave up waiting after talking to Elspeth a day later and went to Hamilton. Bill met him and they went downtown and ate lunch. When they went back to the house, Harry took a walk and told Bill he meet him at the basketball court.

As he rounded the corner, he saw Bill taking jump shots. He was still smooth on the court with soft hands and quick movements. He looked very young, certainly younger than Harry felt right now. He was a healthy, well off six foot five inch man with a wonderful wife and two great boys. Harry envied him that more now than ever. When he reached him they began one of their ritual games of HORSE, which all basketball players know as a game of matching shots with a shot for each letter. Harry and Bill speculated endlessly on the origins of the game, giving it the most absurd provenance they could imagine. They never looked it up because they really didn't want to know the truth and spoil the fun of it. Bill tossed the ball to Harry and asked,

"You said you were gonna be in the city two, three more days, where you goin' after that?"

"Tucson. I have to make a decision."

"The headaches still bad?"

"I'm told they aren't going to go away on their own. A Dr. Morris is giving me an opinion. Dr. Zuckerman will have a report from him which saves me a trip to Mayo Clinic."

"There's new stuff after the last tests?"

Harry picked up the ball, made a shot and said as casually as he could, "Yes and no. Paul, that's Dr. Zuckerman's first name, took my films to New York and had three other neurosurgeons look at them. He wants to remove what he thinks is a small tumor here," Harry pointed to his ear, "Morris apparently sees something that the others didn't."

"Jesus, Harry, that's horrible."

"Well, no one will know that for sure unless I let them go in and look."

"You are gonna let them, right?"

"I'm not certain. I still have questions. Zuckerman seems to be anxious to do it now but I want to know some things first."

They were walking back to the house now after Bill let Harry win,

"What do you need to know? I mean, you've had the tests and seen the film, right? There's somethin' there, huh?"

"Something, yes, but that's not the question. The headaches become intense when I'm working and need to focus under stress. Why? Everybody just shrugs and acts as if it's psychosomatic, just Harry being Harry and I'm nonplussed by that. I mean, they're my headaches after all so why isn't the information relevant?"

"Don't ask me, it seems logical. They gonna tell ya?"

"Zuckerman better or nobody drills any holes in my head."

"That might be kinda self defeating."

Harry turned and said with some heat now, "Not to me, William. First, no one knows if it's benign or malignant until they open my skull. It's a big surprise to all of us don't you see? Like Christmas morning when we were children. We'll all know when I wake up or if I wake up. Second, they're sure it didn't start somewhere else, which is what causes most malignant tumors in your brain. This one is small and likely benign so it's possible we could leave it alone. Third, they need to tell me if I'm going to be able to write when I wake up if I let them do it. If I can't write afterward, what's the point? You know I wouldn't consider that a life."

"You'd really leave it alone?"

Harry sighed, "Look, I read all the literature they gave me twice and all the articles I could find after that. I know the risks and I know the benefits of doing it or not. I'm waiting until I see Paul again to decide whether it will be worth it," Harry glanced at Bill, "Someone needs to know about all this and what may need to be done. I'm sorry it has to be you but you're my Executor and the only one I trust."

"Who else knows, you're not tellin' the publisher? Elspeth?"

"God no, the contract would at least be put on hold if not litigated and I'm not telling Elspeth any more than it's a personal matter for now.

All she'll do is worry longer. They each have reasons to want a book from me, not an illness, or a contract with someone who doesn't know his own name."

"What do you want me to do?"

"Hold my Advanced Directive for Healthcare. It makes you my surrogate decision maker. I'll leave it with you. Just follow my wishes if I can't. I've spelled them out as clearly as I can. The University Hospital has your name and address."

"Okay." Bill said quietly, "I know how all that works. Let me read it before you go. I gotta tell Martha, you know that, right?"

"Of course. I just don't want it shared further or even with her until I go tomorrow. There's still a chance that I may avoid it."

"I'm not so sure but I understand. You okay with everything else?"

"Not really. I have a great deal to worry me now, a book contract to keep, perhaps surgery, and I need a place to live."

"Pretty messy."

"I'll muddle through somehow."

"Well, I hope ya do pal, this is big league stuff."

"It is, but I'm supposed to be a grown man, aren't I?"

"Yeah, but sometimes you don't act that way and we both know that. This has to scare you."

"It does because it's so hard to understand. I mean, why? Why me? I just wish it didn't make me so angry."

"You need to decide. That might make you less angry. That and the fact that you needed to share it with someone. You can always call and yell at one of us if you want."

Martha's car pulled in the drive then and as it did Harry's phone went off. It was Elspeth telling him the VP and lawyers wanted to meet at ten in the morning.

"I'm in Hamilton, El. I can't possibly be back that early. I waited two days for them before I decided to take this trip."

"When can you be back?"

"I was planning on leaving tomorrow anyway, so I could get the early train. Will you see if they'll agree to a later time tomorrow?"

"Certainly."

"Do you have any sense of how they feel about this?"

"I think their first thought was that you wanted to get out of the contract, perhaps publish with someone else, but after they went over the language we proposed, they just seem confused."

"Drew has to agree to this. It isn't hard."

"Well, don't worry about it now, I'll call and see if we can move it. I'll call back as soon as I know."

"Thanks El."

Harry greeted Martha and was delighted to know he was going to get another home cooked meal. He told them about his need to get back early.

Elspeth called back a few minutes later. They would meet in the VP's conference room at one-thirty. He thanked her and as he was hanging up noticed it was a bit after five so he walked outside and dialed Chris's cell number.

"Harry? Are you in town?"

"No, are you in the office?"

"I'm just walking out, what's up?"

"I just wanted to say hello and tell you I'll be back tomorrow afternoon. If you can find a way to Tucson that will take the least amount of time in two days, I would appreciate it."

"Sure. Word in the building was you're causing trouble."

"El says the lawyers seem confused so I doubt we'll get done tomorrow."

"I'll look at the flights and see what looks easiest. You check out of the hotel?"

"No, I didn't. It was easier to leave that mountain of stuff there. Another thing to figure out when I get back."

"Don't get overwhelmed, Harry. Enjoy your friends now and then think about what you have to do after that. One thing at a time."

"That's so practical." Harry replied dryly, "I'll talk to you tomorrow and thanks."

He walked back. She was right, enjoy tonight, and think about the lawyers tomorrow. Just do one thing at a time. He stopped in the hall long enough to call Marion, told her what he thought his arrival day would be and she assured him Paul was in town for the next three weeks, so she'd set up the conference when he was sure.

When he got to the den he found Bill changing channels, unhappy and mumbling that he couldn't find a basketball game from the east coast. Without turning he said,

"You done with all that now?"

"For tonight. I'm going to have to get the eight o'clock train in the morning. Can you get me there?"

"Sure, we can get coffee on the way if you want. Who you been yelling at out there?"

"I wasn't yelling."

"Thought that's why you went out."

"I talked to the Doctor's office, Elspeth, and Chris about plane tickets."

"How's Elspeth doin'?"

"Nervous about meeting the lawyers. You know far more than she does so she's upset about having to do this amendment."

"You doin' that tomorrow?"

"In the afternoon, yes. We pushed it back because those twits waited until I left to schedule and wanted me there in the morning."

"Woulda been tough."

"Well I'm tired of their nonsense so they can eat donuts or whatever corporate lawyers do when not annoying me."

Bill snorted. "Sounds right."

"Who else?"

"Chris. She's looking at tickets for me back to Tucson."

"She know?"

"She's not completely sure why I go to Tucson. She's very nice and helps me when she can."

"Jeez, Harry, you got anyone out there these days? It's not like you."

"I don't have time for that now. It's fine. I hope to be writing soon."

"That gonna be hard without company?"

"I hope not. You remember the last time? I lived in the office for months at a time once crazy Jamie left me for her not so former husband. I'll find amusement this time I hope." He smiled, "I make friends easily enough. I mean I can't be a Carthusian Monk for a year or more."

"Don't understand how you live like that and then be the charmer I saw at the awards dinner."

"No you don't William, I doubt you ever will. While I write all I have is self-doubt, anxiety, and the awful fear of failure. Then I have to put a shine on my shoes and a smile on my face and sell it. I rather hope your line of work isn't quite so schizophrenic."

"It isn't and I don't envy you that, pal."

In the morning they got coffee at the Café and parked at the station with time to spare and drank it in the car.

"Do you ever see Anita?" Harry asked idly.

"Me? No, but I'm not in town as much as I used to be. Martha still sees her at that farmer's market on Saturday I think, although she hasn't mentioned her lately. She used to see more of her, ate lunch with her and she did some charity stuff when you first left and she'd called the house occasionally. Why?"

"No reason really, just curious. She was getting out a good deal when I left, even lunched with Amanda now and then. They seemed well on the way to being friends, yet Amanda never mentioned that. They're bright, beautiful, and single. It surprises me that she's not around, but maybe she's seeing someone over on the coast. That was where she was from."

"Maybe, it does seem odd now that you mention it. I mean she was in and out of the Pub and other places with her friends all last year. Now," Bill shrugged, "seems like she's just gone again."

"It seems strange."

"Yeah well, not to dwell on it. I'm sure there's an explanation."

"I don't plan to dwell, William, I was just thinking about all she said about my getting her back to a normal life, yet we have no evidence she has much of one now do we? I hope she's all right, that's all."

CHAPTER FOUR

It was five fifteen and they were still meeting. Harry's head was screaming for relief. The lawyers were talking to each other and appeared not to have heard a word he said all afternoon. The misunderstandings began as soon as the meeting started. The VP had been in and out all afternoon, giving the appearance of more important matters that needed his attention. Harry thought his behavior appalling. Having a secretary bring notes every so often and apologizing for having to leave was one of the oldest ruses he knew. Drew was the only decider here. The more he was gone, the less he understood. Harry was sure that, as much as he found the VP dense in some matters, they could have settled this by two if he stayed or these two weren't here.

The negotiation was, in Harry's view, specious and more fantasy than reality. They spent the afternoon arguing over verbs and clauses when he cared not a whit what the damn thing said so long as it meant that he had an additional six months to turn in a completed manuscript. How hard was that? The more odious one, Frank Burns, he of the sniffling sinuses, suggested loudly and as often as anyone would let him that Harry was in some way building an escape clause into his contract. He repeatedly made it clear he would advise simply writing the advance out of the contract if Harry couldn't agree to get a manuscript in when it was now due. The VP made only miscellaneous attempts to restrain him. The other lawyer, Al Davis, never spoke directly to Harry and seemed to study the language that El's lawyer had prepared with exceptional intensity all afternoon.

Harry tried everything to dissuade them. He was loud, bombastic, and obnoxious. He'd tried to wheedle them with flattery, suasion, and any other way he could think of, even suggesting at one point that Frank had a fine legal mind.

When he was asked again now why he wanted the time while the VP was gone, Harry was finally done,

"I told you. It is a personal matter and none of your business. It will cost this firm no money and the manuscript will be delivered. That is what the words on those pages you are looking at so intently say and yet you seem to be unable to process. I am done. I do not intend to explain this once again to technical draftsmen who have no authority to tell me whether this publishing house can accept an amended contract. I have one suggestion. It is my last. If you two can stand up and walk out and send the VP back in here alone in the next," Harry looked at his watch, "five minutes, I will make one last attempt to make him understand this minor adjustment. We are not re-writing the Magna Carta here, gentlemen, it is a simple request for a time extension at no additional cost. If you like, I will repeat that and you can write it down and hand it to him. Now what will it be?"

Harry was livid. If he didn't get some medication and away from these people in the next twenty minutes he was walking away and they could sue him while he lay in a hospital bed with a hole in his head. That would make for wonderful press for the publisher and would surely please the Board of Directors. He heard Davis mumble something to Burns and they left. Elspeth came and sat down next to him now. Despite how he felt, Harry managed a smile,

"Well, Elspeth, do you think they understand me or are we going to have to leave and face them in court?"

"I believe they understood when you explained it the first time. They've been advising Drew that you want to void the contract and perhaps publish elsewhere. You're not a favorite in the legal department."

"I'm sorry about that, but they never have behaved very professionally toward us have they? Last time it was about the tour expenses as I recall."

"Among other things, yes."

"I'm sorry El this may not be good for you and your clients. I know this place has courted you since we did well the first time. Surely if this gets nasty there will be a way to keep you out of it."

"Don't worry about me, Harry. I can send my people elsewhere, and based on this charade today, I may want to anyway."

The VP returned at that moment and Harry stood.

"I have your message Harry." He said quietly, "I understand it. It's late and I apologize for having been absent for much of this. Why don't you and I meet at eleven tomorrow. The lawyers can look at the contract for me and see where it might be amended before then. We'll clean up the language when you and I reach an agreement."

"Fine."

He nodded, "I'll see you here then. Goodnight Harry, Ms Henson."

Harry was having difficulty understanding. It was what he wanted in the first instance. Now, these many excruciating hours later, the VP was suggesting the solution could be reached tomorrow. He left as quickly as he could. He had to get back to the hotel and was as gracious as he could be in refusing El's offer of dinner.

He was lying on the bed in his darkened room feeling only slightly better. One more day of this he thought, Chris said take one thing at a time. He was trying.

He heard his phone but hadn't the energy to answer and slept another hour and woke to the sound of the hotel phone.

"Yes?"

"Jesus, Harry, are you all right?"

"Chris?"

"Chris. Yes, why, you have a bimbo scheduled?"

Despite himself he laughed, "I don't know any."

"Are you awake?"

"I am now. What time is it?"

"Seven thirty. Did you eat?"

"No. I'm not hungry."

"Are you capable of coming down here?"

"I think so. Can you meet me in the bar?"

"I could. The lobby is better. I don't want to sit in the bar alone."

"I'll be down in ten minutes."

She was relaxed in the same chair she sat in nearly a week ago. She stood when he came near,

"You look like hell."

"Thanks, I appreciate that. Actually, I feel worse than I appear."

Harry sat and tried hard to concentrate but still felt awful. He needed to sleep.

"You must have been in full voice today."

"Why?"

"You think that little shop of ours over there had no idea that the biggest selling author we have was in the conference room allegedly trying to leave for an unnamed New York publisher? It's a small place,

Harry. You were big news all day. The whole executive suite was on pins and needles. The VP talked to the Chairman of the Board more than once."

"Did he really?"

"I heard that from his secretary who came down to my floor during the day. All the rest were rumors."

"Well the VP was behaving badly all afternoon."

"Drew?"

"Yes."

"Do you call him VP to his face? He has a name."

Harry chuckled, "It started the last time around. I never refer to him by name in public because it annoys him. I do call him Drew in our casual conversations."

They were there less than twenty minutes talking about the Tucson transportation arrangements she made for the day after tomorrow and he was obsessing about the morning.

"You need to get to bed."

"I do. I'm still exhausted. I can't go on like this, can I?"

"Only you can answer that, Harry, what did your friend say?"

"He said to do what I wanted. Bill isn't often judgmental. He yells at me from time to time but mostly he lets me fail on my own."

She chuckled, "Doesn't sound helpful."

"Actually, it is. I trust him and we get along as well as we do because he doesn't try to get into my life too much. If I fail, he'll be there to help, but he's not much on preemption."

"You prefer that?"

"Seems so, I don't know what I'd do without Bill. He and Martha are nearly my family now. It was wonderful that I found them after moving there. I had no idea where he was after he went to Stanford."

"Sounds like he's good for you then."

"He is."

They were walking to the door now, "Tomorrow will be better. I just need to get the VP organized and pack."

"Sounds fine if you're in better shape than you are now."

Harry put her in a cab and went back to his room.

The morning meeting was friendly enough. He and the VP were friends in their way. Elspeth waited outside while they sipped coffee and walked through the amendment slowly. It was over by one o'clock when he agreed to sign an assurance that it was his intent to publish the book exclusively with them. He thought it paranoid of them to want that twice since it was already in the standard contract but supposed it was a sop to Frank or one of the VP's nervous superiors. When the language was clear, the secretary who was taking notes took it to legal so it could be added in the right place and he would sign it before he left.

The VP was curious about why Harry needed the time and he remained evasive, His health was never questioned, so he was able to be honest if vague by saying it was a very personal matter that would take some time. He apologized for asking for it on such short notice. The VP waved that off as if nothing much happened here in the last two days and Harry took Elspeth to lunch in the hotel dining room and filled her in. He was due back at two-thirty to sign the amended contract.

As they settled in, Elspeth said, "I wonder what happened in the last twenty four hours."

"I don't think the VP, or Drew or whatever we call him ever understood it, or perhaps finally understood I might really find a way out unless he got involved. He does pay attention to the revenue side. Sometimes lawyers just make it worse. In retrospect, I suppose I should have talked to the VP and let him tell the lawyers what we needed. In the end, it's what we did anyway."

"True, but they seemed so, I don't know, suspicious? Vindictive?"

"Well, I don't trust them and never been nice to them, so I guess they saw a chance to bite me back. If there is a fourth book, and I dearly hope there will be, I'm glad I avoided further commitment to them. Now that the world is digital, authors find less need for publishers who have no idea how to handle the new electronic age. Tours are being cut back, advances are smaller so the big money makers have no need for the big cumbersome publishing industry anymore and they are struggling to figure it all out."

"It is a new world. It will change more by the time you finish this book I suspect."

Harry nodded, "Yes it will, and I have some new ideas for the tour they won't like either. It isn't comfortable for boutique houses such as this one. After all, how many more Harry Logan's will they get?"

"Excellent question, but more of a reason to keep the one they have which perhaps turned it in the end. I hope it's over now and you can get on with whatever it is you need to do. Are you leaving this week?"

"Tomorrow."

"Your personal reasons?"

"Yes. Please keep a close eye here, I may be more cloistered than normal for the next several months, and I don't trust them."

"I have three other authors with them right now so I'll be nearby. Now I suppose we ought to get back. Are you comfortable signing without my lawyer seeing this?"

"It's about what he wrote anyway. I suppose we could make it contingent on that, but they may balk and I need to get away from here. Let's see what they have. I want that ridiculous pledge of exclusivity as a separate document. I hope I was clear about that. I only agreed so the lawyers would feel they got something for all their whining."

They were done by three and he was back in the hotel. The medication last night helped. He silently thanked Chris for taking care of things. He felt as good as he had in three days so long as he didn't think about tomorrow. One thing at a time, everyone said, and he was trying.

CHAPTER FIVE

Harry was in no mood to wait. Paul Zuckerman was in conference with another patient and Harry was showing little patience with the delay. Finally one of the Fellows came and took him down the hall.

"Harry, good to see you and sorry it's so late," Paul said as he stood to shake his hand. Harry nodded, and noticed that the full complement of physicians were in the room. I guess this is it, he thought. He sat near the screens with all his scans now posted. If it hadn't been so serious a moment, he might have found it funny that he actually was beginning to recognize the inside of his own head.

"How was the trip?"

"Unhappy."

"Did you say unhappy?"

"Yes. I only come to Tucson to see you and as much as I enjoy our talks, Paul, you rarely say anything that makes me happy when we're done."

Paul smiled, "Okay author, I get it. You've read Dr. Morris' report I'm sure, what do you think?"

"He seems to think it's worse than you do. I know something is wrong with me. As to what, I can't really say."

Paul grunted, "Well, you and I have only one more decision to make. I understand Stan Morris' concerns. I don't share them but once we are in there we will likely have a definitive answer to his question of malignancy. How have you been feeling?"

"I have some new issues. While I was working, I was having further short-term memory problems. The headaches are nearly continuous. I have some dizziness but only in the morning. My stomach is fine except when tired I have no appetite. As for my moods, well, I suppose you have to ask others that question. I'm an unpleasant sort on my best days and I may have simply outraged a few extra people because of my innate ability to do that or it may be because of my head."

He saw two of the Fellows smiling at each other. He was sure he gave them reason to agree when he was here last. He was sorry actually. This wasn't their fault.

"So those are all the new things in what, the past week?"

"They are all insidious in their onset so it's hard for me to tell. I mean the dizziness is there, but it doesn't last once I'm up," he shrugged, "I did notice the memory issue while I was at the publishers and it seemed reasonably serious in the sense that I was forgetting easy things, things I'd heard but the day before."

"Do you want me to walk through the procedure now?"

"We need to, yes. There is one thing first however. You may not see it as important but I've never felt I had an adequate answer."

Paul frowned and looked quickly at the others, "What? I wasn't aware of anything."

"That's because you were busy telling me what was wrong and not paying attention to what I said. I don't mean that as an insult, I assure you. Your job is to heal, convince others that they need healing and perhaps now and then you stop listening to what the patient is saying because you've already decided what should be done. What I say then may not seem relevant so we forge on, does that make any sense?"

"It does. I apologize if it happened."

"Don't, please. It's no one's fault."

"I take your point, Harry. What do you want to know?"

"I don't understand why the headaches and other symptoms become exacerbated when I work. When I was in Malibu, there were few headaches at all, and I was quite physically active without the benefit of very much medication. If there is something in my head that adds to the pressure all the time, why is the pain more apparent when I'm focused and working and under that sort of stress?"

"Do you remember I told you we knew you had this but that we didn't know why you have it?"

"Yes, you said that the first time I was here."

"Okay, this is like that. In some patients the ICPs are steady no matter what, in others, additional stressors raise them, so when we say we don't know why the pain is worse when you add mental stressors of one kind or another we mean it."

"So there's no reason why I have this symptom and others don't, it's something that is particular to me?"

"You and others, but not all others. If I say it could be anything or I don't know, it means no one has seen it enough of it or studied it well enough to attribute it to the specific condition. Patients report worsening pain under all sorts of circumstances and stress. We don't know enough yet to tell them the reason."

"Will that change if we remove it?"

"You're getting ahead of me."

"All right."

For the next two hours they went through it and then Harry had him go through it all again trying to get Paul to be as specific about each side effect and likely problem intra-operatively and post-operatively as possible. He had a ventricular meningioma that Paul wanted to remove. A shunt would be placed in the ventricle in the left side of his skull to stabilize the ICPs and that the chance of malignancy was, in Paul's opinion, atypical for this type of tumor. The postoperative period would include at least an eight-day stay in the hospital with heavy sedation for pain. Because of the insult to his brain he could expect continued but lessened head pain, drowsiness, dizziness, muscle weakness, and fatigue after discharge all of which would resolve with time. That assumed all went as perfectly as possible. If it did he would have no lasting neurological defects. When he felt he'd exhausted Paul's knowledge and patience, Harry nodded and sat quite still for a few moments realizing again just how alone he was now. That saddened him in a way he couldn't articulate even as it relieved him to know that his life was the only one that could be substantially altered.

"Thank you Paul, I apologize for the endless questions. I'm sure you have easier patients and the time you took is appreciated."

"Its fine," Paul said, "I appreciate your need to know. I wish all my patients were as exacting. I know you don't buy that, but I know this is hard for you, especially someone of your age and intelligence. I've never walked in your shoes as they say, so I can't know what it's like. However, this isn't my first rodeo either. I see a good outcome here, an excellent one barring any infection or complications. I'm confident as I can be without being in there yet. I think you'll be able to live with the results for a very long time."

"There is still one question I haven't asked, my elephant in the room as it were. Will I be able to write, not just my name, but books?"

Paul took in a breath, slouched in his chair, and let it out slowly. "I believe you will."

"You don't know though?"

"I can't know until I see it, can I? Where it's located tells me it shouldn't affect your writing ability and your memory won't be adversely affected long term and you'll return to a normal life, but if you want a guarantee, I can't give it. It could all go horribly wrong and the worst outcome possible will occur. Surgery has risks Harry. We've been over all of them—twice I think."

Harry gave him a small smile as he looked at him, "Yes, at least twice, yet you're always selling the best possible outcome. I read everything you gave me and more, Paul, and more than once, I assure you. You're not selling me a new car. You're telling me first, my chances of living, second, of regaining normal function, and third whether I can go back to work at what I love when you're done. If there is a significant doubt about the last one we can stop now because I won't be living if I can't write."

The silence grew in the room until finally Paul stood. "Look Harry, I can't promise you that, because I can't promise you what I'll find. So, is there significant doubt? No. Is there doubt? Yes, of course there is. You have to accept that just as I have to accept what I find. I believe it worth the risk or I'd say otherwise. You have to trust me. We do paint you the rosiest picture we can, what you'll get with the optimal outcome. However I'm not selling you this procedure, I'm just describing it, and the likely outcomes based on the hundreds like it I've already done. Now, I need a decision from you. I want it next week. I can schedule you in the following one. You're still an elective case for now unless your symptoms worsen markedly. Go talk to whomever you trust and let me know."

Harry was standing too. His head hurt,

"I know this is difficult Paul, and I'm not making it easier by asking for omniscience from you. I'll be in town while I decide. From your description of my postoperative period, it sounds as if it would be best if I were nearby when you're done for a bit as well."

"If you could stay near Tucson until we've seen a follow up scan or two after the swelling has subsided that would optimal yes, or you'll need to get here easily. Do you have friends here? Can my social worker help at all?"

"I'll manage for now. If that changes I assume the ever efficient Marion can get me in touch with the social worker." As Paul nodded, a thought struck him, "if I was in the Santa Catalina area would that be near enough? My geographic knowledge of this area is limited."

"Sure. That's less than thirty miles to the north of here even if you were to go up the mountain."

"There may be a place near there. Someone at the publishers recommended it."

"Where are you staying now?"

"The Tucson Inn."

"That's good. I prefer you close until we do this, assuming we do. Call the emergency number if your symptoms get worse or any new ones appear and we'll do it right away if that's your decision. We can't spend any more time waiting. You understand it certainly. I want you to tell Marion your decision no later than Wednesday. Sooner would be better since it would move you up on the schedule."

Paul walked him to the door. The office was empty. He shook hands and left for the hotel. Harry felt very much alone.

He tried to read some of the e-mail that was clogging his computer after he slept an hour. He took medication when he returned and he was falling asleep again periodically as he sat in the comfortable chair in his small suite. While he could read the easy ones, he was unable to reply to any. His mind wandered. He needed to make some calls, try to eat and get himself out if this mood. Maybe he'd make them tomorrow. If he was having surgery in two weeks he had a lot to do. He put the computer aside and wished briefly there was someone to talk to but no one was going to appear tonight. As he climbed into bed later he reminded himself that he was here and alone because he chose it. He needed to get used to it.

Harry called for room service early and ate breakfast on the little patio in front of his suite. He scrolled through the e-mail again and decided the best way to answer some of them was by calling. He'd call Bill and tell him the news today. He might try Chris today as well. It was getting warm now. His head had been bad all morning and the dizziness had stayed with him longer today.

He found the real estate listings Chris gave him and wrote down the address of the house she had told him about here. He would go Sunday if she'd tell him who could show it to him.

He'd thought of little except the decision since yesterday. It depressed him. He didn't know whether to go somewhere and try to cheer up, or just give in to it and go to sleep. He wouldn't talk to Chris in this condition. He knew he could share this if he wanted to and she'd be a willing listener. His problem was he wasn't sure he did or what to say. He called room service a few hours later, ate again in his room, and listened to the symphony while he sorted out his clothes. In the early evening, he called Bill.

"What's up, Harry, you out there in the land of cactus?"

"I came in yesterday and spent two hours, maybe three listening to all the reasons why Paul Zuckerman has a need to enter my skull. He was getting testy near the end. It was somber stuff."

"Bet he enjoyed that cross examination. You know what you're doin' now?"

"No, or maybe yes. I have a few days to schedule if I want to get it done the following week. I'm beginning to understand just how overwhelming this is going to be and it makes me tired."

"You think you still have a choice?"

"I'll always have a choice until they sedate me. I'm just not sure I want to live the rest of my life feeling this awful and not knowing why."

"Are the headaches worse?"

"They were terrible while the contract was redone. That was an ordeal and a story for another time. They aren't better now and there are other things. I'm forgetful, dizzy, and very tired although the last may just be because I'm depressed about having to go through all this."

"No fun in that or deciding either. You been out on the town at all?"

"I'm in no shape for that."

"Ah, get off your butt and get out and find somethin' to do. Jeez, you ain't gonna sit there suckin' your thumb for two weeks are ya?"

"No, I have enough to do, in fact that may be why I find it so hard to start. I mean, I have three suitcases full of things and I need to find a place to put them. If I'm going to have this done, and am reasonably sure I'll live through it, I have to find a place to do that."

"Where are you now?"

"The Tucson Inn, down the street from the hospital although you would never know the business district was that close. It has about twenty acres of small suites, all in the adobe style. They call them casitas. Very desert but very nice too."

"So no neon lights flashin' in the windows, huh?"

Harry chuckled.

"So where's this house you said you knew about?"

"North of here and up higher. Cooler up there Chris tells me. It's about twenty miles from here."

"Seems pretty far."

"Out here they think that's just down the street. I guess it's one more thing I'll have to adjust to if I rent it. I'll try to see it this weekend."

"Talked to Elspeth?"

"Not yet. If I decide I'm going to go through with this, I'll have to tell her more than I have. I doubt I'll have my cell phone in ICU."

"What about Chris?"

"I sent her a text when I got here. She knows where the house is although she has remained mysterious about it, only saying she'd tell me if I needed to know. I suppose I do now."

"She must be gettin' to know you. You woulda' asked her a million questions if she'd told you much more."

"Well, I would have asked how she knew about it, certainly."

"You two gonna' stay friends now?"

"I hope we can remain friends given where she works. She's a nice woman that I enjoy talking to and has been very helpful."

"That's probably about right."

Harry knew the next question wasn't a fair one to ask, but he asked it anyway,

"What do you think about all this? I've been going around in circles since I saw Paul."

"Me? What I always think of your decision making. You're putting off making the hard decision like you always do while you think about all the trouble it's going to be. You have to decide what happens here, nobody's gonna do that for you. You went and got the best advice you could. You can't just reject it. That's self-defeating to me. I know you want to get the book done, but can you just leave this and do it? That book will take what? A year, maybe two? I hate to get brutal about this but you may not live that long for all you know. I was hopin' you got over deferring stuff like you used to all the time. You did that with Agnes and Anita and probably most of the rest of the important personal things in your life. It's been goin' on since I've known you. Can't do that now."

"I know that, but this is a bit different isn't it? I mean, yes, I have to decide on the surgery, but I want to write this book, and I don't want to wait. That's what bothers me. I have the advice now, true, but I get to decide what happens next don't I?"

"If you say so. I'm not sure you understand how impaired you really are."

"I will not follow blindly the advice of a physician who can't possibly know how I feel." Harry snapped.

"You don't know what they know either, so that argument isn't worth having with me. You're talking nonsense now. You really think you can spend two years feeling the way you do and write a book? Really? I don't see it and can't agree with you. You tell me what I can do to help and I will, whatever you decide. You know that, but don't ask me to convince you not to have this done, because I can't believe that's a good idea."

"So I'm on my own then?"

"Come on, Harry, be smart about this. You have to sign the consent forms not me. I'm not deciding for you is all I'm saying and I'm guessing any friend would say the same. If things were different, Anita wouldn't have and you know it."

Harry was silent. Bill never intruded like this before. He always gave advice but Harry never felt their friendship was in danger if he didn't take it. He did now. Was he just being selfish and asking too much of his friend?

"Okay, I understand." Harry said quietly, "I have to decide, not you. This is very difficult Bill. I'm going to have a hole drilled in my head. Maybe I need help handling that."

He could hear Bill sigh, "Yeah and I'll help and the people there will too but you have to decide to do it first. I can't do that. You're facing the hardest decision you ever made. What it comes down to is do you have the operation or try to write the book the way you feel. I'm guessing you already know the answer to that, don't you?"

"Those really are the only things I suppose."

"The second option is gone and you know that. You keep saying it's an either or situation. If you're asking for my opinion, there's only one choice now."

"I need to look at it that way, then. I hate the idea. You know that, don't you?"

"It's why you keep looking for a way out."

"I'm in real trouble here, aren't I?"

"Sure you are, but it isn't going get better. If you have it done, you can say you did the best you could. You're giving up your cherished independence here, Harry. That's much worse for you than havin' holes drilled in you or anything else they could do to you. You hate it and I understand that. You just have to do it and get on with it. Stop fighting. The war's over."

Harry was silent. He knew Bill's logic was correct. He had to do this, as much as he hated putting his life on hold and his future in the hands of others, he couldn't keep this up. He sighed,

"All right. I may hate all of this, but I need to do it. I'll call the first of the week then and let you know when it'll be done. You working in town this week?"

"Most of it, but call when you want, you can always get me. If it's a rush, call Martha."

"I will. Thanks, Bill, I needed to go through it with someone besides the surgeon I guess."

"It's what I'm here for, I told you that. Now, get out of that room while you still can. Find somethin' to do. You need to stop broodin' about this. You're gonna do it now so get out of there and talk to somebody or do something, will ya?"

"I will. Love to Martha."

Harry dropped the phone on the desk and looked out the window. Bill was right. He needed to wake up and get on with this or he was sure two things would happen. First, he'd get annoying and evil and never do this thing because the public Harry would take over his life again. He was already trying. Second, he had to act like he hadn't died, at least not yet. He took a shower and resolved to call Chris as early as he could and went to bed.

He ate breakfast very early in the quiet dining room and he just opened the door when his phone rang. As he dug it out of his pocket he wondered who was awake enough to talk at this hour.

"Hi Harry," Chris said softly, "I was hoping you'd call, and then decided to call you. I'm up because I ate with boring Bernice and you can bet that wasn't a late night. You okay?"

"Better than yesterday. I talked to Bill last night."

"Do you want to talk? I mean we can if you want."

"Let's stop tip toeing here, Chris. You're trying to be gentle with me because you've already guessed this is awful. Don't. Just be Chris, okay?"

She was silent, "You're right I'm walking on eggs right now because I'm afraid to ask what I really want to know."

"You don't have to ask. I'll tell you. I planned to in an hour or so when I was sure you were up anyway. Let's do this first, though. I saw your notes on houses yesterday and I have the address of the house out here. I want to go see it. Will you finally tell me how I arrange that?"

"Sure. Call Claire Benson. I'll send you the number."

"Who is she?"

"I know her from my Arizona days. She handles properties there and has the keys. I'll call her when we're done and be sure she's around."

"You think I can see it soon?"

"Tomorrow if she's there."

"Suppose it's rented?"

"She'll tell you. You thinking of taking it?"

"Yes, if it's as nice as you say."

"That's going to be strange. When did you last live in a real house?"

"Nearly three years now, and yes," he chuckled, "it will be strange. I suppose I can't call room service can I?"

"You can, but no one will answer would be my guess."

He laughed, "Ah Chris, thanks for that. It may have been my first good laugh since I left up there."

"The least I can do is make you laugh. So what is it that's wrong? Are you going to tell me, or is this going to be like a root canal?"

"No, I wouldn't do that. There's a benign tumor and if all goes by the surgical handbook, I'll be in the hospital about eight days and I should be fine in a month or two. There will still be some headaches, weakness, and fatigue requiring me to rest. That's about all there is. I have to schedule it on Monday. I decided after I talked to Bill that it was the only thing to do much as I would like to bend the world to my will as I usually do."

Chris let him go straight through. Still there was no sound from her now. He heard her take a breath and let it out now and finally she said,

"I wish I was happy to hear any of that but I'm not. The operation sounds gruesome to be honest."

"It isn't a day at the beach."

"Let me call Claire then and have her call you."

"That would be a start. I'll call tomorrow if I see the place."

"Okay, I should be here or I'll have the phone if I go to the office."

"Fine, talk soon."

Harry was walking to lunch when Claire Benson called. She would meet him at noon tomorrow in front of the Inn. If the house didn't work out, he might like two others that were available next month. He walked the few remaining blocks to the Mexican restaurant that Marion recommended. He sipped at his sweet iced tea and was staring out the window when a young woman approached,

"I'm sorry to disturb you, but you're Harry Logan aren't you?"

She was a young, intense, rather short woman with blond hair, and very blue eyes who looked vaguely familiar, "Yes, I'm afraid I am," he replied with a smile, "and you are . . . ?"

"Nicole, Nicole Eagan. I'm sure you don't remember me but I interviewed you over in Phoenix when you were on your book tour."

"Hello Nicole, you looked vaguely familiar. Can you join me? It's good to see a familiar face."

"Sure I'd like that. Do you mind if Kate joins us? We just came in for lunch." She pointed at another table.

Harry looked up and saw another woman standing there waiting. She was strikingly beautiful, about thirty with wavy black hair almost to her shoulders who towered over Nicole.

"Of course not."

He introduced himself to Kate Beckett and they settled into the booth across from him and gave the waitress their orders.

"When was I there, Nicole? I mean, it was only one stop on a long tour, so I apologize for not remembering more. I remember what I do because I think Phoenix was my only desert stop."

"I understand. It was over two years ago. We did it at the studio at the ASU public radio station. I came here to get my PhD shortly after that."

"I think you'd actually read the book. Not a common thing among my interviewers." Harry said with a laugh, "and may have even liked it."

"Oh I did and you autographed it for me. Kate here read it too after you won the Pulitzer. Congratulations."

Harry waved his hand, "You're very kind, thank you. How much it's enjoyed by readers is the important thing. I assure you I appreciated the recognition. I just hope I don't ever believe it's the most important thing. Now what of you Kate, what did you make of it?"

Kate smiled what Harry thought was a wonderfully friendly smile and said in what he hoped was her normal voice which was quiet, soft, and musical, "Your minister is very perceptive. I agree with much of what he said about America which I found sad actually. So there was truth for me in your fiction."

"That's very nice of you. Are you in communications as well?"

"No, I finished my nursing degree here a few years ago and I'm taking courses in business. Nicole and I are roommates through the magic of the internet."

"Sounds like a diverse household then, are there others?"

Nicole laughed, "I take in strays for a year or two. My family owns a house here that I use and it pays their mortgage."

"Well that likely beats dorm life. Are you going full time?"

"I am," Nicole said, "I'm also at the public radio outlet here now. Kate is working and in school part time for her MBA."

The food came and they talked of little while they ate. He said he was here for personal business and Nicole asked about a new book.

"Kate," Harry asked when done, "what does one do with a nursing degree and an MBA, run a hospital?"

She laughed. It was a very soft and relaxed laugh. "Not right away Mr. Logan, I think being a nurse administrator would come first."

"Ah, I see. Do call me Harry please. I never use Mr. Logan it if it can be avoided. So what sort of nursing do you do when not in business school?"

"I work private registry."

"I'm sorry but I have no idea what that means. You must understand that I live in a cave for a few years at a time writing so many things elude me."

She gave a soft pleasant laugh, "It's a pool of nurses that take private home care cases mostly, some private duty, and shifts in the hospital if they need temporary help. I do mostly postoperative home care."

"I see. Do you like it or just paying the bills until you can administrate something?"

"It's all right. Post-op is good. Sometimes I stay, sometimes it's just a day job, or I do two patients at once if they aren't very difficult."

"Sounds like a complicated life, albeit a rewarding one."

"It's not complicated, just schedule juggling and odd hours."

"Do you enjoy nursing, I mean hands on nursing?"

She smiled and Nicole laughed and answered for her, "No she doesn't which is why she wants to push paper instead."

Kate protested, "That isn't true. I probably should have done something else, been something else but," she shrugged, "four years of school sort of locked me into this. I enjoy helping people though." She looked at him with a deadpan expression now, "Perhaps I'll try social work next."

They all laughed. "And you Nicole, still asking insightful questions of self important authors should they wander into town demanding to be interviewed?"

"Tucson isn't usually on their itinerary. I talk to local authors and artists occasionally. There are a number of them here, mostly painters and sculptors but a few writers. Only a few are nationally known. Right now I'm doing weekend mornings. We do an hour before we send it to the network and one before noon. In fact that's why we're here. I just got done and Kate finished a shift at the hospital this morning. We're headed home after this."

"I'm geographically impaired so far as Tucson is concerned so where is home? Do you live near the campus?"

"No, up the hill as we all call it. Near Catalina. Further out than I like, but much cooler up there too."

"I'm looking at a place up that way tomorrow. Not at all sure where it is. Some agent is taking me."

"I hope you like it there. I mean it is the desert, but cooler and greener than the valley here, I'll tell you. I wanted to ask before we go, are you going to be here next week? I'd love to have you on the show. Brett is the other anchor and we haven't blocked it out yet because our producer went out of town so it will be very late in the week before I can be sure."

"That's very kind. I'll try. I'm not sure of my schedule yet, but anytime I can pontificate into a microphone I'm always happy to do it. I'll give you my number. I'm just over at the Inn so you can call me when you know."

"Thanks so much, that's great. Here's the station number, you can leave a message for me if you can't do it. It was nice seeing you again."

"You as well. Kate how does your registry work?"

"They contract through the medical group handling the patient. Do you know someone that might need them?"

"Actually, I do. A patient of Dr. Zuckerman's."

"We work with his group all the time. His social worker, Barbara Lee, will set all that up. She's excellent. She's also quite beautiful. I think she was a model but I haven't heard the story, only the rumors."

He thanked them for joining him and paid for lunch over their protests. He waved as they drove off and he walked slowly back to the hotel.

He came back from the dining room about seven and decided to try Chris tonight. His head hurt but he wanted to see if she could help with a few things before he went to bed. He punched her number figuring he could at least leave a message if she was off somewhere.

"Hi Harry."

"I thought you might be out so was going to leave a message. Claire called and will fetch me at noon tomorrow. Whatever power do you hold over this woman anyway, are you ever going to tell me?"

She laughed out loud. "Sooner or later."

"What does that mean?"

"Not sure, I'll work on a better answer."

"You'd better."

"So what's up?"

"There are so many questions I need to answer. Maybe you can help with the process of who to ask what. I recall you believe yourself very good at process. I guess I need to talk to Paul's social worker, don't I?"

"If she's good that will take care of a lot it. Claire can help with cooks and cleaning people and things like that. She knows them all from the rentals she handles."

"Bill is my decision maker for health care since I lack blood relatives by the way. Is that going to present problems?"

"Better be sure everyone and I do mean everyone is clear on that before you start for the sake of HIPAA. They need to know who they tell what and that may get complicated since you have no family."

"What on earth is HIPAA?"

It's the patient confidentiality law. You have to tell them all that stuff beforehand. Just ask the doctor's office."

"How am I ever going to muddle through all this?"

"Because you're smart enough to figure it out. Just be sure you ask your inexhaustible questions of everyone at least twice before they sedate you. You'll do fine. Use a note pad. Write everything down and then carry it with you. It will work a lot better given your memory problems and the confusion of getting things done."

"How do you know about any of this?"

"I did most of it with my father when my mother died. After you see them you can ask me again if there's anything that isn't clear, maybe I'll know who else to ask. Meanwhile after you see the house let me know what you think."

"I will and thanks again."

CHAPTER SIX

Claire Benson was a small woman of near sixty with graying hair and a wonderful smile. She drove a smart little sports car entirely too fast and with little attention to the road as she pointed out various landmarks on way to Catalina. Route 77 was a commuter road down from the altitude where many people who worked in Tucson liked to live. They went through Oro Valley and continued uphill toward Catalina. The elevation here was over 3,000 feet and it was noticeable cooler than the valley floor. The terrain was rugged and according to the sign, about 7,000 people lived here. Small by Harry's standards, and he was surprised how close to Tucson it became rural as he defined it. After a series of turns off the highway they rolled into an area with eight houses some distance from each other, spread in an arc facing the mountains. The short stone drive faced an eight-foot wall with a carved wooden door set into it to the left. It opened onto a walled and tiled courtyard. The house was one story, flat roofed and nearly U-shaped, the courtyard was the center of the U. There was a modern kitchen, an eating area adjacent with a small counter with stools separating them, a small living space with a fireplace and an office beyond. The master bedroom suite was large, with a fireplace of its own and another much smaller walled terrace that opened from it. There was another large bedroom and bath. All the main rooms opened onto the larger walled courtyard in the center. There was an outdoor fireplace and teak furniture in it. It was a compact space, beautifully furnished. He saw no reason why he couldn't live there.

"Can I walk to town from here?"

"Well town is a hard thing to define here. The older section of Catalina proper is a mile north, but there is a shopping center a half mile from here. I'll show you as we leave. It has a small grocery store, café, and Mexican restaurant as well. I'm not sure what else is in there."

"There's no reason I couldn't live here. The view of the mountains is nice. Which direction does it face?"

"The front courtyard faces southwesterly so you never have to deal with the full sunset in summer, but you do get to look at the mountains."

"Chris says there's no lease."

"No. It's ready now if you like. You can go month to month as for long as you like."

"Seems a bit odd. I mean it's nice that I could take possession now, but leases are common here as elsewhere aren't they?"

"Yes they are. The other two I have are leased."

"Why is this different?"

She smiled, "The owner wants it that way."

He shrugged, "Fine with me. Let's look at the town before we go back down. Oh, there is a spare bedroom, is there any other sleeping space?"

"There's a Murphy bed in the office in that tall cabinet on the right hand wall."

"This courtyard access is interesting the way everything opens to it. I know nothing of these houses but Chris seems to know about this one and said it is quite cool in here as well."

"This is one of the few real adobe houses built up here in the last twenty years and yes, these very thick walls make the difference. The access to the courtyard from all the main rooms was a unique feature of the older adobe homes."

"Well, I'm not much on impulse, but since Chris has such a high opinion of it and the area, and the rent seems ridiculously low, I see no reason to look further."

"I can give you cleaning and household help references if you want them."

"Please do. Let's take a look at town and we can go sign whatever I have to and I'll try to remember where it is so I can find my way back sometime this week."

"I'll give you a map of the area."

"Good, I can start getting out of the hotel then."

"Wonderful, I'll have the utilities turned on and drop the extra keys at the hotel. Chris said you've been on the road a long time?"

"I have. This will be different."

When he called Chris, he demanded more information from her about the beautiful house and the mysterious owner and his or her eccentric rent scheme. He was not required to sign anything or give a security deposit only what he thought was a paltry one month's rent. He found it all very odd. She just laughed and said there were lots of crazy desert rats out there so anything was possible.

He stood in front of Marion on Monday morning. He was feeling better now that at least one thing was off his list.

He held his pad with all his questions and Marion was trying hard to answer as many as she could. While he hoped now to get this over, they were admitting him the following Thursday afternoon with surgery on Friday. It displeased him to wait that long. The HIPAA matters were indeed complicated and Marion was making some calls about them and hoped for answers about what they would need from Bill by the end of the week. After he learned he'd meet with the social worker at one he went out to find lunch. As he left the office he saw Kate walking down the intersecting sidewalk from the direction of the hospital toward an office nearby. She saw him before he could decide whether it was good for her to know he was coming from Paul's office. Out here she looked even lovelier. She had an athlete's build and stride. She was Latina and at least one other ethnicity. He wasn't sure which only that it softened her angular features and enhanced her dark good looks. She was dressed in the light blue scrubs worn by many of the nurses he saw around the grounds. They set off her large dark eyes and black hair. From her expression now, Harry wasn't sure she was happy until she smiled,

"Hi Mr. Logan. Sorry, I'm used to doing that, are you coming from Dr. Zuckerman's?" She still spoke in that same wonderful soft voice.

"Hello Kate, it's nice to see you. I was just talking to Marion for a bit. How are you? Working today?"

"I'm fine and going in here to get my next case, someone being discharged today by Orthopedics. Be with her two days I think. Where're you headed?"

"Lunch."

"Not in the hospital I hope."

He laughed, "I know better than that although not sure where yet. Where are you working, or is that a secret?"

She smiled and showed wonderfully white teeth, "Let's just say near home."

"Okay let's. Are you starting now?"

"No, later this afternoon. I have a class in a while. If you wait while I drop these papers off to make me official, I'll show you a restaurant near here and I'll be glad to buy today."

"That would be nice."

"I'll be right back."

They walked to a small place that had a bigger menu than the building. She filled the holes in the conversation by asking intelligent questions about writing while they ate. He found her a pleasant companion and was oddly sorry when she excused herself as they left and went to her class on the other side of the campus.

He went back to Zuckerman's office. At three minutes to one Barbara Lee Johnson walked into the room where Marion told him to wait. She was one of the most gorgeous women he had ever seen and was dressed as if she just walked out of a store on Rodeo Drive. He wasn't certain if he ever saw as much jewelry on a woman at work. She spoke in a silky smooth, well-modulated voice,

"Mr. Harry Logan, how wonderful to finally meet you. Dr. Zuckerman told me all about our most famous patient and Marion says you are one of the nicest we've ever had."

"Please Ms. Johnson, don't stop now," Harry said with a laugh, "It's a pleasure to meet you. I hope you will feel the same about me," He waved at his pad, "after we've been through all this."

She gave a wonderful laugh and sat gracefully in the chair across from him, crossed her legs shook her hair off her face and leaned back before she spoke again,

"That looks like enough notes for one of your books, but I'm sure we can get through it."

For the next two hours they went back and forth. She stopped him now and then to make a call, schedule someone, or clarify something with one of the nurses. She never hesitated or slowed down or was overwhelmed. If it was something she would take care of, Harry didn't doubt she would. If she didn't see a reason to be concerned she said so and he was, he quickly learned, to accept that. Nothing he said, or the way he said it, fazed her. Her expression of pleasant good humor never changed no matter how gruesome the question or irritated he became. He thought she was wonderful, and for Harry, a onetime practicing misogynist, to admire a woman's abilities that much was remarkable. She made it seem so much easier, took a huge burden from his mind, and crossed many questions off his list.

He talked to Bill a long time for them that night. He told him about Barbara Lee who still amazed him and talked out all the fears he'd harbored since the headaches began. They talked of the Hamilton days and how much his imperiousness cost him. They talked about Agnes, the wonderful young widow and good friend of Bill's that Harry lived with for a time and treated so badly she left him. He never found time for her problems as he thrashed around trying to solve his own and desperately trying to find a book inside him. He found it hard to think about how selfish that was even now. Bill conceded that Harry was different now, no longer universally boorish, loud, bombastic, and self-centered as he was when he and Bill reconnected in Hamilton after so many years. In private now he was much more the articulate, funny, and dramatic Harry, traits learned from his policewoman mother and less his father's son, the Colombia University professor of English literature who never took off his loud imperious public persona once he tragically lost the love of his life and who wove a similar one for his only child in the years he raised him. Harry was a gentler man now having managed to finally understand the need to be both Harrys. He could still be that spoiled child who wanted to control his world. The difference was that he knew it.

In two hours they covered a lot of old ground and Harry felt better for it. Bill was a wonderful friend and he was relying on him now more than he thought he should.

"So what day did you say the surgery was?" Bill asked finally.

"A week from Friday. Seems too long yet I doubt I'll abandon the hotel. Paul thought it better being in town and it is easier."

"Yeah, it ain't like you're gonna put a car in long term parking and come out a few days later all shiny and new."

"No clearly not. I'll need something other than a rental car sooner or later I suppose."

"Be better to wait until you know you're gonna' drive one."

Harry chuckled, "Yes, there is that, isn't there? Well, I'd better go. I said I'd call Chris a few hours ago. She'll give me hell."

"I'd pay to hear that. A woman given' Harry hell while he apologizes? This really happens huh?"

"You'd be surprised. She's quite rude as well."

Bill laughed, "Okay, better get on to that then."

"Take care and give my love to your lovely wife. Thanks for staying on so long. I guess I just wanted to talk about the old days since I have no idea what the new ones are going to be like or if there are any. I appreciate it."

"Ah, just hang in another week or so and get most everything moved. Can't be much you're gonna have to do in life that's gonna be worse than this."

"I surely hope that's true, William."

Bill chuckled, "Call me when you need to and be sure to fax me whatever I need to sign for the privacy thing."

"I will." He dropped the phone and found some water. It rang before he got back.

"Hi. Just going to call you."

"Where've you been Harry? Damn, you said you'd call me after work. It's after nine."

"I told Bill you would give me hell so go ahead. I was telling him about today and the house, we got started in on a lot of the old baggage I've carried most of my life, and we just kept going. I'd apologize, but since you just finished scolding me I'm not sure I will now."

"All right be that way, it is annoying you know that, don't you? Now what have you got left on the list?"

"Not a lot. Claire gave me some references for help. I'll deal with that once I get up there again and you said she'd have good ones. The surgery is not until a week from Friday. I wish it were sooner, but I suppose I can find useful things to do between now and then."

"Good. Any specific questions?"

"Barbara Lee actually answered many of them. She is unusually good for that line of work and is also gorgeous which seems oxymoronic."

Chris laughed, "Some reason a social worker can't be both good and beautiful Harry?"

"No, but she's beyond that. There must be a story there somewhere."

"Maybe, you think you're going to hear it?"

"No, but as stories go, it can't be more ridiculous than your not telling me that you own the house here all this time."

"How do you know that?"

"I guessed mostly. I knew you lived down here and there were too many other coincidences. When I asked you or Claire, you were both evasive. You're usually easy to read and honest. It really is a lovely place. Did you find it when you moved here?"

"No, I built it, or my father and I did. I was hoping he'd stay there after I left but he loves being with his war buddies over in Anthem so he left. I really need to sell it one of these days. I used to get back in the winter, but haven't for quite a while."

"Why not rent it? Surely you can get far more than what I'm paying you."

"I could and did for awhile, but tenants just beat the place up so I don't. Your rent covers the mortgage so don't worry, I'm not giving it to you free. My father gave me the money to build the place. All the neat stuff in it is his doing. I just did the paint and the furnishings."

"Well, you're very good to let me have it. I think I'll like it there. The experience will be unique."

"I hope you meant what you said about being solitary when you write. Not much happens in Catalina."

Harry chuckled, "No I suppose not, but I'll find things to do. Be a nice place to be while I get through this part anyway."

"I suppose it will."

"I need to take some pills and sleep. We'll talk again soon. If I think of anything, I'll e-mail it to you."

"Just call Harry. I don't mind. I'm around. Good luck this week and call me if there are problems at the house."

Harry's week was busy. He had an appointment with one of the Nurse Practitioners to talk about his postoperative hospital stay and she gave him a schedule for the clinics he needed to go to for pre-operative testing. He went to the house twice, ferrying his clothing out along with things he bought in town. He walked the property and through the rooms again being sure he was familiar with where everything was. He really did like the place. He interviewed two people Claire recommended as cleaning and cooking help and decided on Elena, who did both and the one he liked best. He made sure she understood he was going through a hospitalization and would need her all day through dinner the first month or more. She was a cheerful woman about fifty-five who lived north of there and had her own transportation. Her husband drove her the second time she came. He was Joseph, a small, muscular man who offered to work hourly fixing things and keeping the native plants hacked back and the courtyard clean. Harry was glad for the help and readily agreed.

He wandered around the hospital complex getting x-rays, blood drawn, his heart tested, and another brain scan for a baseline and all the other things he needed to clear him for surgery and was back at the hotel most afternoons. His list of things to be done was diminishing. By Friday night, he had the weekend free and thought he might explore the area where he was going to live if he had the energy. He was very tired now, his head hurt and he was writing everything down or dictating notes into his phone to be sure he didn't miss anything. He still was very frightened of facing all this alone. He knew he chose that, and wasn't depressed about it, just frightened.

He talked to Bill two more times and Martha for a short time as well. He had a brief conversation with Chris about two or three things at the house but the rest of his time was spent either getting ready to move or going to the hospital or resting. He was frankly tired of the wait but tried to stay as positive as he could even as he failed. He and Bill finished a call about nothing more than Harry's angst on Friday night,

"I'll talk to you next week. I have a message from a Nicole Eagan, a woman over at the radio station. I need to call her."

"Interview? You doin' those?"

"One maybe. She worked in Phoenix and interviewed me there when I was on the tour. One of the few who actually read the book. She's at the University here now getting a doctorate and working at the station on weekends. She wants to do one either tomorrow or the next day."

"You feel good enough for that?"

"No, not really, but it will kill a couple of hours and she's a nice kid and I'm finding having something to do everyday makes this less tedious."

"If she's cute, take her to dinner."

"She's not my type and I'm drawing the line at thirty these days and she's south of that. Her roommate is a very beautiful woman of the appropriate age, but I don't see spending time with her in my future."

"Where'd you run into these two?"

"We were in the same restaurant, Nicole remembered me, we all ate lunch together and I ran into Kate again on the campus one day and had lunch."

"That doesn't have to be all, does it?"

"I suppose not, but Kate is an innocent bystander. A nice friendly sort, but I'm sure a busy woman with work and a real social life. I mean, you and I can't go to the Café every morning and have you scream in pain while I explain in minute detail how badly I need to see her again as in the old days now can we?"

Bill's laugh was loud and long, "No we can't and that's a pity Harry. Have fun on the radio. You always loved that stuff."

Harry laughed too, "Yes, I did, and I will now. I can get just as pompous and acerbic as I want and nobody will get mad at me."

Nicole was all charm when he called and she asked if he could do a segment with her tomorrow at eleven. She apologized for waiting so long to call, but with her producer out of town all week they were doing the blocking now. He said he would do it, found out where the studio was on campus and agreed to be there at ten so they could talk. He wandered into the garden, chatted with two businessmen stranded in Tucson for the weekend, and ate with them. He went to bed after a look at his lists and checking his messages and memos. After a heavy dose of relaxant he was instantly asleep.

He and Nicole talked in a small room off the studio while Brett handled the local station breaks. When they went on the air, she asked good questions about the last book, the awards, what he'd done since, and the next book. She drew a parallel to his nomadic preacher and his lecture tour which pleased him. She was very thoughtful and professional for her age with a very pleasing radio voice and a nice sense of on air timing. As he left the booth she offered him lunch if he'd wait until she and Brett did the last fifteen minute segment. The producer stopped and asked if he'd be around if they needed some literary reviews. He said he would in a month or two and Nicole knew how to reach him.

They went to a small place just off the campus which was not bad all in all on this quiet Saturday afternoon. Kate appeared nearly silently with that lovely smile on her face and a book in her hand. He was pleased she'd joined them but couldn't say why. She just finished a class. Nicole waxed rhapsodic to her about what a great interview he was and how she missed the national authors because they were so polished, glib, and witty. Kate objected thinking she was insulting the locals and Nicole tried to explain what she meant and was, from Kate's responses, failing. Finally he offered,

"Perhaps I can try Kate. Do you mind, Nichole?" She nodded and he turned to Kate, "She's not voicing a lack of appreciation of their talents as artists or writers, Kate. It's just that when some over confident loud mouth like me comes through, Nicole knows I've already done nine or ten cities in eleven days, and it's a bit like talking to a tape recording. I know what I want to say. She doesn't have to pull it out of me, as she likely has to do with the less experienced locals. Most of what she'll ask, I've been asked before. Touring is an art form all its own. If the interviewer took the time to read the book as she did, I'll know it immediately and give a better interview. We send a one or two page summary and a biography and we're lucky if most read all of that. We know that, so we treat that interview quite differently. We get the message of what makes our book excellent out as best we can. In Nicole's case, she's good at it and understands the nuances so is taken seriously. If you're ever bored enough to listen to one of us hacks, note how we end the interview. It'll always tell you how delighted we were to enjoy six or eight minutes of intelligent conversation or how glad we are to be done with it."

Kate gave him that soft laugh, "You make it sound like a game."

"Let's say it's a dance."

"Meaning?"

"Some people are more fun to dance with than others, have the same rhythm, you understand what I mean. Some don't so it's less fun. Nicole is a good partner so it's fun."

"I take it there quite a few interviewers who didn't dance very well," she said with a twinkle in her large dark eyes.

Harry laughed, "More than you could ever know."

"Want to share?"

"I think not." He said and they all laughed.

"Thanks again for doing the show Harry. It was great. Stu said he asked if you'd do some reviews. Since you agreed I guess you're going to be around."

"I am. I now reside, or will in a few weeks at 1432 Franklin Circle, near Catalina."

"That's just up the highway from us."

"Is it that beautiful adobe in there?" asked Kate.

"Both of you know the neighborhood, then. Yes, it's about a half mile from the little shopping center before you get to town and yes, it's the adobe. Do you know it?"

"Yes. Very few real adobe houses are built anymore. I had a client on Franklin for a few days once. Did you buy it?"

"No, just renting, why?"

She shrugged, "No reason, I didn't think they rented."

"They don't often and only with mysterious terms with which I won't bore you. It's lovely though. I've been moving in slowly. Be up there most of tomorrow. Come by, if you like, I'll let you peek inside."

"I'd love to. Nicole thinks I should have taken architecture. I enjoy looking at the native style buildings here." Kate said.

"You should have, you know all about them and you know how it bores me." Nicole said.

Harry laughed, "Are there many different types? You needn't answer that, Nicole may nod off."

"There are actually, and yes, let's keep her awake, she's driving."

They parted in the parking lot. He refused the ride back to the hotel saying he would walk across the campus because he needed the exercise. By the time he reached the hotel, he was tired and his head hurt. He enjoyed the morning and the company for lunch. He liked broadcasting, felt good about the interview, and hoped he could do more as he had in Hamilton. Perhaps Todd could find a few of his old contacts and he'd have something to do when the editing, the clerical work, as he always called it, began to bore him.

As he lay down he knew he was assuming a successful outcome. He had to of course or he would go crazy between now and the end of next week. He needed to tell Elspeth on Monday and he wasn't looking forward to it. He really didn't know how she would react but he hoped she'd be as positive and supportive as she was when he had so much trouble starting *Country*.

Early Sunday he took more things he bought in town to the house. It was a pleasant day up there. He picked up a few things at the small shopping center he'd leave there today. He gave Elena and Joseph the job of getting whatever she'd need. She obviously was here with the things one never thinks about until you don't have them. Joseph came by in the late morning. He was quiet, quick to smile, and seemed a gentle soul. He gave Harry the receipts and Harry paid him. They sat and made small talk in the courtyard. Joseph had a nice sense of humor, was a war veteran, but aside from training and the war, was here all the rest of his life. He had the leathery skin of a desert native and that sense of indeterminate age. He said he rarely even went down into Tucson now except to see his son who went to the University. Harry could tell he was very proud of him.

When he left, Harry wandered the house again, marveling at the bright colors inside and the airiness of it despite its size. He sat at the desk and wasn't happy with where it was. He wanted it nearer the door to the courtyard. He added it to the list on the yellow pad as something Joseph could move. He looked around the room, thought of a few more changes, and was startled to hear the large bell that served as his doorbell at the courtyard gate. He went out of the room through its own door. He opened the heavy oak gate and Kate was standing there smiling.

"Kate, how nice to see you." She was wearing the standard desert dress of sandals and khaki shorts, and with them a white peasant blouse.

"Hi. I was coming back from town and came by because you said you'd be here. I have something for you if you're interested."

"Come in, come in, what do you have?"

She was proffering a book to him, "It's about the types of houses out here in the southwest. Lots of pictures, I thought you might want to look at it since you sounded interested."

"I would, and I am, thank you for remembering." They were walking through the courtyard now towards the main door that led to the living area.

"Do you have time for a tour?"

"I'd like to take a look, sure. This courtyard is exquisite."

"It is, isn't it? I won't have to ask you to excuse the mess. I haven't been here enough to make one."

She nodded, "Odd isn't it, unless you're visiting a compulsive hoarder, there's rarely much of a mess to excuse, is there?"

Harry laughed, "Not the usual way one thinks of it but you're right. Here's the living area, there is an office on the other side of the wall. The kitchen is there to the left. You need to tell me about these bright colors and the other details."

As they made their way through the house she commented on all the details and explained what mimicked the original adobe houses. They talked about the main courtyard and its walls which Harry found odd at first but now thought wonderful because of the privacy and the unique access to it from all the rooms.

"Think of it as a fort," she said, "they protected themselves from the wind and wandering coyotes, wolves, mountain lions, and the rest." She laughed, "Even bandits in some cases. Whoever did this really did a nice job. Of course with this beautiful interior there is no resemblance inside to the old adobes except the arches, colors, and doors and the fireplaces did look much like these. The courtyard was the main living space for the family. They cooked and ate here. If there were smaller children, they would be out here most of the day because the inside was so small. These thick walls are wonderful. I wish we had them, you may get away with only a little air conditioning."

"My fondest hope actually. I hate sleeping in it although this is from a man who endured some of the best and worst hotels and motels the country has to offer in the past three years. I still prefer being without it."

She smiled as he offered her a seat in one of the teak chairs.

"Thanks for helping me understand the place. My last house was an old Craftsman I restored, so I do have an interest in the details of various periods. I've never been out in the desert so am wholly ignorant of these types. Perhaps if we talk of the various ones now I won't sound as ignorant."

She laughed softly, "So long as Nicole isn't around we might enjoy that."

"Yes, that. Well, she might need a good nap. Now, which way are you headed, I seem to have forgotten."

"I just came up the hill, but I had the book in the car and you said you'd be here so I thought I'd bring it to you."

"I'm glad you did, Can you stay a bit, or do you have plans?"

"I always need to study."

"Can we have coffee or something at the café over there on your way? I assume you ate lunch?"

"No actually. Did you eat?"

"No, let me grab a few things and lock up. Stay there and enjoy the view. I'll be right back."

They ate at the small restaurant, mostly empty this early Sunday afternoon. He brought the book in and she sat next to him and pointed at pictures of territory houses and other examples. She was very serious about the subject, but was quick to laugh when Harry asked about some of the absurd ways the settlers thought they could live once they began to build above ground. When they were done, she said,

"As I remember you're leaving for a while."

"The end of the week, yes, not certain for how long. Why?"

"We could go over to the National Park if you are here a while when you get back. There are a few excellent replicas there of original houses. Not all, but the adobe and two or three more. You might enjoy it."

"I'd like that very much. Would you really take me?"

"Would there be something wrong with that?"

"No, no, I just meant you're busy with work and school and your social life."

She smiled, slouched down, folded her arms, and looked over at him with a small smile, "My schedule is flexible, if erratic and my social life isn't very complicated. I can be a difficult woman to spend time with."

Harry laughed loudly, "I'm sorry, I wasn't making fun of you. I enjoy the way you say things. You're very good with words. I do find it preposterous however that the men you know are that selfish. Even one as awful as me would understand."

She shrugged and laughed, "Its fine for now. Besides, my white knight may come along and it would be terrible to miss him."

Harry looked at her and said with mock solemnity, "It would, Kate, it surely would."

She said more cheerfully as she sat up, "I should get going. I could bring the whole household by and warm the place once you move in."

He chuckled, "Would that be fun?"

"Depends on what you wish for. I live with a bunch of young kids like Nicole."

They were walking to their cars by now, and he was laughing at that when she said,

"I'm not sure when you'll need it, but I'll give you my number. When you want the tour, call."

"Thanks, I'll want to get the book back to you, and I do want you to show me the houses. Should I give you mine?"

She smiled, "Nicole has it."

Harry nodded, "We'll do it when I'm back."

"That'll be fine." Then she waved and was off. Harry watched her leave and then drove to the hotel.

"Elspeth, how are you? It's your favorite author."

"I thought you might have lost your phone, Harry. I mean I do love those banal e-mails you've been passing along, but it's about time we talked. Where in the world are you?"

Harry laughed. "I'm in Tucson Arizona."

"Why for heaven's sake, what's out there that could possibly interest you?"

"Actually, it doesn't interest me at all. I'm here by necessity. It's why we changed the contract."

"Your personal reasons?"

"Yes, I want to tell you the rest of it now. You know I've been complaining about headaches for months so I decided to get an opinion as to whether it was just stress and travel or if there was something more. Well, there is. I'm going to have a bit of surgery here at the end of the week."

"Oh Harry, I'm so sorry, is it serious?"

"All the tests are good so if it goes as planned, I should only be hospitalized a week or so and a month or two of recovery—I'm told the brain is very fussy about such intrusions—and then I should be able to resume my usual annoying behavior."

She was silent for a bit.

"Is it something that is going to be a lifelong problem?"

"No one seems to think so. If it goes as the textbooks say, I should be fine once it's over. However, now you understand why I wanted the extension. Given that my recovery time could be a bit longer and that I can't be sure the procedure will go exactly as planned, I needed more time to be sure I get the manuscript done."

"Of course. This won't affect your writing then?"

"Not long term barring unforeseen problems. I should be writing again soon enough. I saw no reason to tell you all this until I was as sure as I could be as to what it was and I was finally convinced that there are long term considerations if I didn't do it."

"I really don't know what to say, Harry, I mean you did say it was serious and personal, but this isn't something that ever crossed my mind. Are you sure you want to continue the book?"

"Quite sure. After all, I write. It's about all I know how to do with any skill isn't it? If I can't do that . . . well, I'm not fit to be a relationship counselor certainly. We know that."

Elspeth laughed, "You're taking this better than I thought, Harry."

"Yes, well, it's been a process. My friends have been helpful. I'm not depressed about it, just a little more anxious than usual. It can't be delayed any longer. I just don't have the energy to live with these headaches anymore. I need to feel better and the writing will come. The health clause in the contract will protect us both should anything go wrong. We need to assume the best outcome of course. Meanwhile, I've rented a house here and plan to stay. It's a charming adobe up the hill from Tucson in a town called Catalina. I'll go there afterward and have hired some help. It should be fine."

"What do you want me to do? I mean, can I help in some way?"

"Thank you, El, stay in touch with Todd about press matters if you will. I'll give you Bill Powers number, you remember him from New York I'm sure. He'll be my contact while I'm hospitalized and in the days afterward. If there is anything, get in touch with him."

"When are you having the procedure?"

"Friday. I'll be there through the next week at least. I found a wonderful couple to cook and keep the house. Now, please don't worry about me, I'll be fine. Call Bill if you have anything that needs a decision. He'll be in touch with you over the weekend. You're on the list of those that need a call."

"I'm so sorry about all this, Harry. I'll say a prayer that it goes well."

Harry was surprised that she prayed at all,

"Bless you Elspeth, take care and we'll talk when I can."

"Get well, Harry, that's the main thing."

"I know. I'll check mail through Wednesday night if you think of anything."

"Just get well Harry."

He was happy with how the call went and decided to take a walk before he did anything else. The headache was dull today. The forgetfulness was serious now and he was worried more about that than the pain. It was warm even in his proper desert sandals and shorts yet he wasn't in the mood to sit in his room alone. He needed to see other faces. He was a sad, frightened man right now trying hard not to think of the fact that he could be very impaired or even dead by Friday night. It haunted him, despite his protests. Most nights now, he woke often, worried much, and tried to accept it. The house, the preparations for "after" were a stage he was preparing, one he hoped he would be on, but feared he wouldn't. The recuperation period seemed a very long time. He resolved that if he got through this, he would work hard to shorten it.

He wasn't headed in any particular direction, but found himself down near the University. He decided as long as he'd walked this far, he might as well eat and at least see other people. As he crossed the street a compact car stopped and when the tinted window came down, he saw it was Kate.

"Hi, where are you headed?" She said.

He walked over and she gave him a big smile,

"Hey, I was going to find some lunch. What brings you down?"

"Paperwork for a patient later today. Going to eat myself, want to come?"

"That would be nice, thanks."

"Get in. It's cooler in here. I recall your views on air conditioning but it can't be avoided in a car." They drove to a place on the other side of the campus.

"Hope you like Mexican food. This is the best around."

"I don't know it well. I'll find something."

Once they were inside she ordered, suggested he try what she was having, stirred her tea and looked over at him,

"What are you up to?"

"Very little actually. I was walking from the hotel because I like to walk and needed to get away today. Did you say you were on your way to work?"

She nodded, "a night shift. I need to get the paperwork done and be up there by six."

"You manage to stay awfully busy and I see what you mean about an irregular schedule."

"Well, the bills have to get paid. It's also nice to eat every day."

Harry chuckled, "Yes, there is that. Do you go to class everyday as well?"

"No, just three days a week for now."

The food came and Harry found what she suggested quite good. His limited knowledge of southwestern food kept him in the taco and enchilada part of the menu. This was an egg and red sauce concoction. His memory hadn't retained the name and he was embarrassed to ask her to tell him again. As he finished he watched her as she bent over her food. They'd talked more about houses while they ate and now she was trying to catch up with him. Her long black hair obscured much of her face now but he found the long wavy fullness of it quite lovely. He was glad he'd run into her. When she finished, she slid down in her chair and sipped her tea. It seemed a position natural to her.

"Was that good?" she asked.

"It was, thanks for recommending it. I'm a little tired of tacos."

She laughed that soft laugh, "If you stay out here long you'll need to learn to enjoy Mexican and Tex Mex food. Up the hill there are some places with very good Anglo food, but not many down here. Although I'm sure the Inn has its share."

"Yes, the menu there is light on Tex Mex."

"You have to let me buy this lunch, by the way. May not get the chance to pay you back for a while."

"You needn't do that."

"I owe you for yesterday."

He smiled, "So we do this by turns, is that it?"

"I can't just hunt you down and have you feed me every day. That seems wrong."

He laughed, "Why? I enjoy our lunches."

She looked up with that deadpan look on her face, "So I should just drive up and down Elm Street until you appear in front of the Inn and blow the horn?"

"Are you needling me?"

"No, just saying."

He smiled, "It would be easier to park across the street and lie in wait."

She laughed now and he noticed again that twinkle of amusement in her eyes, "lie in wait. There's no one else I know that would put it that way."

"That's because you don't get out enough. We talked about that."

"We did," she said cheerfully as she stood and took the check, "and I explained why. Now, I have to go get my paperwork. I'll give you a ride back." She looked at him with that deadpan expression again, "Maybe I'll check out the parking."

Harry laughed. Her sense of humor was a nice distraction. He enjoyed this talk of inconsequential things.

As he got in the car he said, "You realize that we'll have to eat lunch again? I can't let it end on your turn."

"So you agree about doing it by turns?"

"I think keeping track of turns is good."

"So it would be my turn to talk now?"

"It would, yes. Why, is there something you wanted to say?"

"No. I just want to understand the rules."

Harry chuckled, "I doubt we'll need many."

"Here you are."

"I appreciate the ride. How late will you work?"

"All night." She turned and looked at him with that expression again, "It's what nurses do."

"Right, thanks again for lunch. Take care Kate."

He reached his adobe casita again that was home for now. Despite the heat he found a chair in the shade on the veranda. He slouched down and closed his eyes against the pain to no effect. He had no plan or purpose. Before the sadness of that thought could take hold, he stood, and went in to check his notes and called Bethany, the very small blond Fellow with the wonderfully sensual voice whose duty today was to ask him how he felt. One of them did every day. He wasn't very positive, telling the truth as he saw it as always. She wasn't any less professional or more sympathetic despite his whining and asked him to call emergency if he felt any worse as they always did. He heard the tone of a call waiting, told her he needed to go, and picked up the call. It was Bill.

"Hey Harry, You okay?"

"I suppose. Let me do this while I'm looking at it on my list and before I lose you to a client. On Friday or Saturday, whenever you find out my diagnosis, there are a few calls I need you to make, that okay?"

"Sure, was gonna ask about that."

"Call Elspeth Friday if you know anything. Leave a message to have her call back if you don't get her. Give her the news live though, don't leave a message."

"I know how to do it Harry, just tell me who and the numbers."

"I'm sorry. There's Chris, I'm sure she'll be trying to get through on my phone. I'll text you her number when we're done here. I'm not sure I need anyone else to know except you and Martha. El will talk to Todd and they will take care of the literary crowd once she gets the news and will handle the press nonsense with him if there is any."

"Martha wanted me to ask about Anita."

He sighed, "We're not even sure where she is now, are we? No, there's no reason."

"I didn't see one, but you might've so she wanted the question asked."

"Thank Martha for her sensitivity. When it's over and if Martha sees her she can tell her what happened. I just don't want her being sorry this happened to poor old Harry now or then. You can tell Amanda and anyone else there when you think best. I'll leave all that to your judgment."

"Okay that'll be fine. What about Carlton in LA?"

"He can wait. I mean if I'm dead or dying I suppose I'd want him to know, but there's no hurry. Call him sometime after I'm stable assuming I ever am."

"I gotta say your attitude is impressive today," Bill replied dryly.

"I'm sorry. Tell Chris to deal with the realtor. They're old friends. The bank is The First National of Tucson. No one else knows that but my banker in New York. Elspeth will let the publisher know if there's a reason to stop their checks and Chris can sort things out with Claire. I'll send you all this in an e-mail on Wednesday."

"Okay. Got that. Anyone else?"

"My new housekeeper and her husband need to know when I'll be coming if I am and surely if I am not. You need to let them know a few days before I go home, assuming I do. She's Elena and he's Joseph. He's Anglo, so talking to him will be clearer. She speaks excellent English but I'm not certain how well she grasps concepts. He has your name and expects the call."

"What about your new friends out there?"

"No, I saw Kate today at lunch and she thinks I'll just be gone for a few weeks."

"You lied? You never do that."

"I didn't really lie. I told her I'd be missing a few weeks. I will be."

"Is this the older one?"

"Yes. She's the nurse and part-time MBA student. That's nearly all I know about her, except she really likes old houses, is very beautiful, has a wonderfully quiet voice and a quick wit, and we seem to both eat lunch at the same time of day."

"So is that everybody?"

Harry sighed, "Yes, I think so. You have my lawyer's number if it goes badly. That should be all."

"Okay, call me if you need anything and on Thursday before you get admitted. I sent the paperwork for HIPAA back to Marion and the other administration people over in the hospital. That should take care of that."

"I'll check on it with Barbara Lee when I see her. Thanks again for that, for all of this. I know you have very little time to be fooling with my nonsense but it can't be helped right now."

"No worries, Harry I got time. Still have more to do?"

"I'll go out to the house tomorrow. Staying here is maddening."

"Gettin' out sounds good. Be sure you don't push it. Too late for that."

"I won't. I can't frankly. I'll talk to you Thursday."

When he was done he called Chris. He wanted to be sure that she was as comfortable as she sounded. There were times when he talked to her that he wasn't sure.

"Chris?"

"Harry, I wasn't sure I'd hear from you."

"I thought I'd just say hello. I just finished up with Bill and have most everything done."

"When are you checking in?"

"Thursday sometime in the afternoon. Bill will call you when he knows something on Friday or Saturday depending in how it all goes. He has your number."

"Okay. I can't say I'm happy for you Harry, but the wait must be hard."

"It is. Perhaps the hardest part of all this so far. I've been busy but feel terrible all the time so there's no joy in any of it. I hope to get out to the house tomorrow to get rid of the rest of the things here."

"You get through all your notes?"

"I will by Thursday morning. I hope I didn't forget much."

"It'll be fine. You sure you don't want any help? I could come if you want. I do know Tucson."

"No but thank you. You have enough to do there and a life to live. I do want to thank you for the house and all the advice. You seem to be my third friend now. I hope you don't mind that."

"I don't mind Harry. I hope we'll talk when we can after this is over without any tricked up feelings. I do have a life to live here. I know that and I need to get on with it."

"Then let's see how that works."

"Call me if anything is screwed up at the house, okay?"

"I will. Now I need to go. It may be a while before we talk but Bill will know what's happening."

"Okay. I wish this wasn't true Harry, I really do, but you're doing what you have to and I'm glad of that."

"Then go eat with boring Bernice, she may need you."

She laughed, "Bernice always needs someone."

It was late when he woke the next morning. When the room stopped moving he took a long hot shower. It invigorated him. He went in search of his yellow pad first and then food.

He called Zuckerman's office to report his condition, absorbed the usual admonishments, skimmed the newspaper, and drove up to the house. He took what he wouldn't need while in the hospital and when he pulled in the drive he noticed the difference in temperature and was pleased. He walked to the gate and saw Joseph's truck was parked on the street. The gate was unlocked so he called out when he got inside. Joseph's head appeared over the edge of the roof.

"Good Morning, Joseph."

"Hello Mr. Logan, just finishing up here. Elena's inside. I'll be down in a minute."

He went in the main door and called out, "Elena! It's me, Harry."

She came out of the kitchen, "Oh Mr. Logan, I was making sure there are enough pots. Joseph wanted to work so I came along."

"Do you have what you need?"

"I think it will be fine, I could use a big iron skillet. I will get one."

"Fine, thank you. I'm glad I found both of you. I want to pay you for your time before you both leave."

"No, that is not necessary. It will wait."

"No, I insist. When I first come home, I don't know how I'll feel."

Joseph came in then and he paid them and told Elena to be sure to get whatever else she needed. He wrote Bill's name and number down for Joseph and reminded him he was the one who would call. Joseph collected his ladder and both wished Mr. Logan luck. He was sure they would never call him Harry.

He sat in the courtyard for a bit and drank a bottle of water. There was a wonderful breeze, and he read through Kate's book, which was more interesting than he expected. It was early afternoon when he walked around the house, locked up, and decided to eat up here before he went back. As he pulled into the shopping center it was after one. On an impulse he called Kate.

"Hello, Kate? It's Harry."

"Where are you?"

"I was talking to my new housekeeper. Are you down in Tucson?"

"No, I'm up here until later. I was debating whether to go to the library or take a nap."

"I'm sorry. I should have known you'd be busy. I was going to ask you to have lunch."

She laughed quietly, "Okay, then ask me."

"How about lunch?"

"Sure."

He chuckled, "I have your book and many questions."

"Good. Where?"

"I'll be in the Mexican place. Come in when you get here and thanks."

She laughed quietly as she ended the call and he went in and found a booth. He had the book open in front of him but was deep in thought about just how awful life would be very soon when she entered silently and slid in on the same side close enough to lean lightly against him. He looked up in surprise. Despite her sad deadpan look her eyes told him she was amused,

"You need to stop saying thanks for buying me lunch."

"It was short notice."

"I don't need notice." She smiled now as she moved away and looked at the menu.

"You're off today?"

"Going back at six. Doing twelve's on this one," she saw his frown, "Twelve hour shifts, sorry for sliding into the argot of my other life."

"You mean you have to go to work at six this evening?"

"I do. I did yesterday."

"Then you should be asleep, shouldn't you?"

"I wanted to see what you learned," her eyes twinkled again, "besides I was hungry and didn't have to lie in wait."

He laughed, "Where do you get all your energy?"

"What I do isn't hard. I'm not building walls or writing lines of computer code. The patient I have is easy and there's only one more night," She shrugged, "I'll survive, trust me."

"Do I have a choice?"

"No actually."

The food came and she answered some of his questions between bites. They sat pouring over the book while they drank sweet iced tea for nearly two hours afterward. She was quite good at explaining things and had a ready answer for his questions. He enjoyed talking to this nice woman about old houses. There was no bombast, entendre or word games, they just talked. He stumped her on a question about roof materials and she was re-reading a section about it because he said it was confusing. While she read, he looked at her profile and thought she had a most wonderful face. Her long neck and her dark skin were set off by her yellow sleeveless top. She was even more sculpted then he noticed before. He was sure she was an athlete, or was once. She looked up quickly and caught him appraising her,

"What?"

"Nothing, just wondering."

"Are you going to tell me or do you want to hear the news I have about roofs?"

"It's your turn and you were good enough to read all that."

She explained it all simply. He found her skills at explaining the nuances of these houses impressive. He was about to say so when he decide it seemed gratuitous and he wasn't sure how she would take compliments about her talents. It was a feeling not knowledge, so he simply thanked her for clearing it up.

"So what was it?" She asked.

"What?"

"That you were wondering."

"Oh, sorry. If you were an athlete."

She smiled, "I was. Can you guess what sport? You're either a basketball player or maybe soccer. I can't decide."

He looked at her in surprise, "How can you know that? Did I ever say I was an athlete?"

"No, but your hands are large, you're light on your feet and tall and you're obviously someone whose stays in shape. So which one?"

"Basketball. I wasn't quite good enough to play in college, but I've been a gym rat all my life and I still play. I don't understand how you knew though."

"Just observation. They teach us that, you know."

"Yes, you medical types would learn that, wouldn't you? I could only guess about you since I have no such skill. Besides being tall, you just seem to have the build for it."

"I was a volleyball player, so you were right about the body type. I played a very long time."

"Do you still?"

"No. I gave it up after the last Olympic trials. I played some of everything all my life, but nothing now. I enjoy walking, but never go near a gym because I hate it after all those years of nearly living there and my job is physical enough."

"You like it, nursing I mean?"

"There are things I'd rather do. I like buildings, their history, and the shapes of them. I like the symmetry of walls and gardens and admire those that create them."

"Why not change then?"

She shrugged and said quietly, "I think about it. I should have five or six years ago. I didn't and it's late to start over."

"Please Kate, you are by no means an old woman, you may work another what, forty years? Do you really want to be doing something you don't like all that time? How late will it be if you don't change?"

"You're making an intellectual argument out of it now."

Harry laughed, "I am, I suppose, but it is intellectual in a way because this," he pointed at the book, "fascinates you. If it were me I'd want to know more."

She looked at him quite seriously for a minute as if deciding something,

"You see my problem then. I'm about done with the business courses I can take without going on for an MBA and my dirty little secret is that I hate it. I'd like to take architecture or something like it but it would be committing to another degree and even with my credits it might be years part time. Nicole and all the kids at the house know what they want and I should have figured it out when I was their age too."

She was quiet and turned to look out the window. Harry wasn't sure what to say. He felt that way once too. Then he got lucky and found writing and a publisher. If not he could easily be a sad, paunchy tenured professor somewhere teaching literature to people with no interest in it. He knew he couldn't fix it for her and felt she'd said all she would about it now.

"You'll figure it out. You're surely smart enough."

"Do you think so?"

"I don't know you at all Kate, but you don't seem the type to live unhappily."

"I have a problem with decisions. I make them quickly enough but often without enough thought. Deciding something this life altering is hard for me."

Harry wondered if she really was a happy person. He thought of her as pleasant, quiet, reserved, and happy but maybe she wasn't. She seemed to be struggling. It was water too deep for him today, however, so he mentioned the time and her need for sleep. They gathered themselves and went out into the late afternoon.

"Don't worry Kate, everyone has doubts. I've enough to fill that valley over there. You'll figure it out."

"I shouldn't complain. Just tired I guess. I enjoyed talking about the houses with you."

"Anytime you're upright, awake, and have money we'll do it again. It's your turn and I still want the tour."

"I haven't forgotten," she said as she got in her car, "But you go away, or go missing, or whatever words you're using now soon don't you?"

"I do, but we'll probably have lunch when I'm back. We seem to get hungry around the same time."

She laughed softly, "We do, don't we? Thanks again."

"You need to stop thanking me, Kate." He said seriously.

She smiled, getting the joke, "Call me when you're ready. I'll be hungry."

"Get some sleep." Harry said as he shut her car door.

CHAPTER SEVEN

By noon on Thursday the scribbles on his pad said it was time to go. He called Bill and was at Dr. Zuckerman's office at two. One of the nurses walked him to admissions. After a dozen redundant questions from the clerk and the clacking of her computer keys he was banded at the wrist like a tagged bird with all the vital facts of his life embedded in the barcode. In his room a nurse took his vital signs and the rest of the afternoon was lost to the inevitable health care shuffle and the pain in his head. Barbara Lee swept into his room looking as stunning as ever and went through his Advanced Directive again, assured him the hospital had the paperwork they needed, and promised to talk to Bill and that she would see him when he came back from ICU. At seven-thirty a tired Paul Zuckerman came through in his OR scrubs with an exhausted Fellow in tow,

"All your questions answered Harry? Anything you need?"

Harry sighed, "No, you need to answer the big question but that's for tomorrow."

"It is. To be trite, sleep if you can. I've ordered something to help. You'll be in ICU at least a week after it's over. I'll have a result from the biopsy for you when you wake up. We'll send it on for more testing after the initial reading by the histologist here but what we see tomorrow is usually what the final reading will be."

"It could change?"

"It's unlikely. Don't worry about that now. Let's get it done."

"I'm very tired of all this."

"I'm sure you are. You have at least eight or ten days here now. I'm not going to tell you it'll be fun. It won't. There'll be a lot of confusion and some pain because of the insult to the brain, but we'll keep the latter under control. Now, let me get them in here to prep your head so you can get something for sleep. One of the Fellows will come up in the morning with the OR transport people. I'll try to send Bethany. I know how much you like her."

"I don't know her. I love her voice though."

Paul chuckled, "You'd love the rest too," he shook his hand as did the Fellow, "trust us now Harry, this is what we do."

By the time he slept he was bald and resigned to whatever the consequences the morning would bring.

He sat in his robe on the love seat in the courtyard. He was out of the hospital for nearly two months now and beginning to feel like Harry Logan again. For most of the past week he was nearly free of pain although still tired and weak.

The house was quiet, Elena having gone shopping, the nurse dismissed after three weeks. Bill was here again until this morning to be sure he was doing his exercises and to take him to his appointments. He'd come unannounced the day of surgery, stayed with him through the first few weeks and then he or Martha were with him until this morning. Harry only became aware anyone was there near the end of his twelve day ICU stay when he was finally conscious and coherent for a few hours. Bill made and took all the calls from Elspeth and Chris and Carlton and updated Martha until she arrived. Harry's phone was still turned off. Anyone he knew reached him though Bill and he was without curiosity about the rest.

His malaise now was the result of completely surrendering himself to the will of others for so long rather than any physical impairment. Bill warned him when he went home this morning that he needed to exercise longer and start taking control. Harry knew he was right of course but was having trouble finding the motivation. He didn't know why. It was as if he was owed this time wallowing in self pity and almost enjoyed it. He knew he needed to start doing normal things. It was the only way to get control of his life.

Yesterday, Bill took him to Tucson to have another follow-up scan and they'd found a car to lease. It sat in the drive now. There was no reason why he couldn't dress and go anywhere he wanted. Yet he didn't care if he did and it puzzled him.

The scans since the surgery were "fine." The histology report on the reasonably well, but not completely encapsulated tumor was "almost surely" benign and the recovery of his sensory, motor, and memory skills seemed complete. The staining of the tissue was done now for a second time since the initial histology report was inconclusive. While that was a concern, it was not deemed a problem to worry over.

Harry decided to take some medication to be rid of his minor headache. Being pain free was liberating and he supposed when the fatigue was gone he'd feel more motivated. But he needed to work at it. His head looked like a furry cue ball now and he while Bill kidded him mercilessly about it, he actually enjoyed the coolness of it on warm days.

Most days now Harry was glad he'd gone through the surgery. The nightmare that was his time in the hospital was receding. Only on sleepless nights now did he remember the very frightened Harry rolling down the darkened halls to the OR squeezing the hand of the lovely Bethany while she reassured him even as she surely smelled his fear, or the confused Harry in the chaos of pre-op and the one who remembered a long period of feeling only movement or being moved and the sound of voices he couldn't identify or answer asking him if he could do something he couldn't. Only now and then was he the Harry who heard the voices of people he knew but to whom he couldn't speak, no matter how desperately he tried.

When he woke Bill was there, he was sure he heard his voice before he knew it for certain and he wanted to tell him how glad he was. He heard other voices too. Was that Elspeth? Chris? Martha? Kate? He was sure he heard them all as he wrestled with the pain, disorientation and confusion. After he left the ICU he was certain he heard Kate's soft voice while he slept telling him to get well and yet he didn't know. He knew Martha was there to make him laugh as he regained his ability to speak. Nurses came and went, Fellows stopped in seemingly around the clock. There was no day or night. They asked him things, gave him medications, took pressures, and rolled machines around in such confusion that he merely surrendered to it. They were doing the necessary, getting him up to walk, to sit, helping him do things he still couldn't while weakened by the insults to both his brain and his body. He asked Bill about the voices later and he said that he and Martha were there and any other voices he heard were from the drugs or his imagination. It was a horrible memory he wanted to leave behind.

Harry knew he needed to keep moving if that was to happen. He lobbied Bill to leave, knowing he had far more to do than sit here and remind him to do his exercises and walk with him. He needed to lengthen his walks, his exercise regimen, and ready himself for the eventuality that people were going to want to see him and talk to him. He needed to be the other Harry Logan again. There was a book to write and he needed to get ready to do it. Now that he had the car he could drive up to the café and drink coffee, eat lunch, something. He knew he looked like hell, that he was thin and bald but no one cared. He couldn't afford his previous vanity if he was going to get through this. No one knew him here so what did it matter? He sighed heavily. His recuperation wasn't going to go well unless he made the effort. He recalled that resolve he had in the idle, pain ridden days before all hell broke loose. Where was it, he wondered? Where had he left it?

He made his way into the office and turned on his phone. He checked for messages. There were far too many texts from Chris and he resolved to call her. There was a voice mail from Bill saying he was nearly home and that he would talk to him over the weekend. There was one from Wedgie wishing him well. A few acquaintances who knew nothing about this business called the last several weeks to talk. He was surprised by one from Kate. It was short, simply saying she was off work while school was out and to call when he got hungry. He quelled his obsession for privacy. If Kate or others knew now it couldn't matter. It happened. It was done. It was part of his history and he needed to make it that way so others would as well.

He dressed after he showered and went back to the computer. He opened the e-mail. Two were from Charlie, a long one from Elspeth, and much of the rest literary news he couldn't care at all about right now. He scanned the relevant ones. Charlie was just telling him he had another book right now and would be busy so not to expect much turn around if he was working. He wrote a quick note to Wedgie telling him all was well and he was healing. He let Charlie know he had nothing yet and would be in touch. The one from Elspeth was a lovely one wishing him well. It was so sweet his eyes were wet when he finished. He was told this new emotionally labile state was a result many experienced after surgery due to the sedation. He didn't like the vulnerability he felt when it happened.

Bill saw it as had Martha. They saw it as natural enough and said it was good that he showed more emotion.

Elena was back and he knew lunch would be soon. He walked out the gate and looked at the car. The lease on the BMW was cheap which, along with Bill's love for the brand, is why he took it. He opened the door to the superheated interior, pushed the start button, turned the air conditioner on, and closed the door. He walked the length street as he had with Bill twice a day in the past week and resolved to keep stretching it this week until he made it to the highway. He got in the now cool car, drove it to the store and bought a paper. While he ate, he made conversation with Elena who wasn't talkative ordinarily but responded easily to questions. It was probably what he liked most about her besides her wonderful cooking and pleasant helpfulness. She was wonderful with Bill and Martha and more than happy that there were more people around to cook and care for. Elena enjoyed cooking for more than just one. Joseph said little, but if Bill or Harry needed a hand he was always available. He'd needed them both, but needed to decide soon when to have Elena just come late in the day to cook so he would increase his need to do more for himself. He announced his nap and went to his room. He did well this morning but needed a plan to do more.

He woke an hour or so later oddly refreshed. He went out on the terrace off the bedroom where there was shade and looked at the phone again. Kate was still on vacation so he pushed the number resolving to drop the call if she didn't answer. He wasn't even sure why he was calling except that she'd asked. She got it on the third ring,

"Hi, you're making calls?" She said in that soft musical voice, "Word in the village had it that you went missing in some extraordinary way."

He chuckled in spite of himself, "Really? It was rather ordinary actually. It's good to hear your voice."

"Yours too, although ordinary circumstances don't really describe your disappearance. How are you feeling?"

"I'm fine. Why the question?"

"You wouldn't remember, but I stopped to see you after you left the ICU. Your friend, Bill is it? He was there."

"How did you know to look for me?"

"Well, HIPAA notwithstanding, nurses learn who is in what room on the floor we work. I was on yours for two evenings doing private duty for another patient after you came down from the ICU so I stopped one afternoon to see if you were awake. You weren't."

"You said to get better."

"Something as suitably sympathetic as that I suppose, yes."

"I remember. I was sure it was your voice. I tried to answer. Bill said every nurse looked alike to him so he was no help when I asked. It was nice of you to do that."

"Well it wasn't hard." She laughed softly, "I was being paid to be there, after all."

He laughed, "You still have that way with words don't you. As to your question, I'm mostly fine. Tired too often, but since you know more about these things than I, that's not a surprise to you."

"No, it isn't. Are you out walking? Doing exercises?"

"I am. Drove today as well."

"So you're recovering?"

"Yes, gaining weight and I feel better every week. The scans are clear although it wasn't as tidy as Zuckerman advertised. I suppose I was the last one you expected to find sleeping in the hospital."

"Truth?"

"I deal in nothing else."

"Really? Maybe we can talk more about that. I suspected something. You looked pretty awful the last few times I saw you and I never believed your earlier story about a friend seeing Dr. Zuckerman either."

"You're excellent powers of observation at work again?"

"It wasn't very difficult with what you gave me."

"Well just to be certain the record is straight I never said I had a friend seeing Paul, I said that I knew someone who was seeing him."

"So it wasn't meant to mislead us?"

"It was meant to deflect you from further inquiry."

"Yes, but hardly the truth. Now, are you ever coming out that lovely house again?"

Impulsively, Harry asked, "Are you still on break and vacation?"

"I am, yes."

"Would you eat with a tired man with a nearly bald head? Bill left today and I need to start getting out of here."

She said quite seriously now, "Are you sure you're up to that? I mean, I don't care if you're nearly bald, I just don't want you pushing yourself for the sake of eating with me."

"Why not? I enjoy eating with you and while I may have forgotten a good deal, I know it's your turn."

"It is. Suppose I come by tomorrow about four? If you're awake and up to it, we'll eat somewhere."

"Fine."

"Just listen for that bell of yours." she replied.

She sounded happier and Harry was pleased. He hoped she was out of her funk. He'd enjoy talking to her again.

After one of Elena's wonderful dinner he went out to the courtyard. The fireplaces were all gas with faux logs, so he lit the one out here and sat down to enjoy the nice evening. The dark shapes of the mountains were merging with the sky when he pulled up Chris' number. He hoped she wouldn't yell at him for not calling sooner. He was tired. He answered El's e-mail and written a very long thank you to Bill and Martha after he spoke to Kate.

Chris got it on the second ring,

"Harry! Are you okay?"

"Here Chris, just in a bit of a shambles is all. Bill explained that."

"He did, but I wanted to talk to you. Do you feel better?"

"I'm getting there. Today was the best day I've had. Bill is gone. Elena is still here all day until four or five and does my dinner before she goes. Don't be angry with Bill."

"I'm not. He answered all my questions. I just wanted to help and couldn't from here."

"You already helped. I'm living in your desert palace here."

"Do you like it?"

"I do. I'm sitting by this nice gas fireplace in the courtyard, its quiet and the house is quite beautiful. You did a great job with it."

"You can thank my dad for all those neat touches. Is everything working?"

"Joseph has it ticking like a well oiled clock. You'd think he owned it."

"It needed someone like that. Unless you stay there forever, I really do need to sell it."

"I doubt I would thrive here forever, but it's a nice experience, will be nicer when I feel a bit better and get out more. Have to see how it is to write here too. Haven't had an original thought in two months."

"What's the plan?"

"Eating well and getting back to normal is all anyone recommends. Elena is taking care of the first and I'm beginning to get motivated. Maybe next week I'll start going out for coffee. Make a friend or two, something. If I keep Elena for dinners only and to clean, that will make me less dependent too."

"What about the doctor, what's he saying?"

"Oh, what doctors always say. It wasn't quite the tidy little job he hoped and he believes he got it all."

"Is it . . . I mean . . . could it still be bad?"

"The head scans are clear so there's nothing to worry over now."

"God, Harry, I'm just glad you seem to be doing so well."

"A week makes a big difference now. How's life up there? No talk of me I hope?"

"Not since you were here, although Charlie seems confused as to why you aren't calling."

"I had a note from him and answered it today. When I feel better I'll talk to him. It'll be a while before I'm up there. I plan to have hair by then."

"Oh my God, you're bald!" She gave that wonderful throaty laugh. "Send me a picture, please? It sounds hysterical."

"It's a bit like a furry cue ball now. I actually like it in this climate. Be fine in a few weeks. No, no pictures, you would taunt me forever."

"I would. You're so sensitive." She laughed again, "it's fun to picture you bald."

"Glad it makes you happy."

"Don't be petulant. I'm mildly amused, okay?"

"I wasn't being petulant. Its fine that you're amused by it, mildly or otherwise, just forget about a picture. Now, I need to go, it's late for me and time to wrap myself in a blanket. I hope you're having some fun."

"I am."

"Good. Take care Chris, glad we got caught up."

He was tired. He was pleased by what he'd done today but also worried about sustaining it. He needed to stop being tentative. As he yawned his way into the bedroom he hoped would be awake enough to go to dinner tomorrow. He was curious to hear if Kate made any decisions or was just floating along in what he amateurishly diagnosed as a depression. She seemed so pleasant and peaceful this afternoon. He fell asleep as soon as he was in bed and never finished the analysis.

It was cool and unusually overcast in the morning. He was up at seven with effort, but slept well. He drove to the small market for a newspaper and was home before breakfast. He was still on his feet at ten, was pain free, and felt he should walk before he lost the will to do it. He made it nearly to the highway and back, Elena brought him a bottle of water after his exercises and he sank into a chair in the courtyard determined to read the paper. He dozed fitfully until lunch while he fought to get through the crossword puzzle. Once he ate, he fell on the bed and was asleep in a moment.

By three he was up and feeling better. Elena was happy to go home early with no dinner to cook and just after four the bell rang. Perhaps because she dealt with illness all the time and was mostly a stranger he felt comfortable that it was Kate. There wouldn't be any sympathy from her. He was anxious to see how she was. He was startled that he felt anything at all, but decided he just missed talking to someone besides Bill. When he opened the gate her dark eyes twinkled in that way of hers when she was amused or happy. Her hair was even longer than it was when he'd seen her last. It became her, and he thought again of how stunningly lovely she was. She had a big smile for him.

"Kate, it's wonderful to see you. You look lovely in that color and you are even prettier than I remember."

She laughed that soft laugh, "That's quite a greeting. You really do need to get out and see other people, but thank you for the compliment." She leaned into him in something resembling a hug, "You look good yourself considering," She rubbed his head and laughed again. "I like your hair."

"Do you want to sit in or out?"

"Out."

"Do you want anything?"

"Not really, no, maybe later. Why don't you stop being solicitous and sit down."

He chuckled, "I do sound like an overwrought host. It must be my solitary life."

"You said Bill left the day before yesterday, didn't you? Does one day make you a hermit?"

"You're going to needle me aren't you?"

"No. but I'm not listening to any pathetic nonsense either. You were headed there."

"I wasn't."

"If you say so."

"Are you needling me?"

"Perhaps. I'll leave you alone after we settle the matter of the line you tried to give me on the phone."

"All right," he sighed, "Let's get these issues dealt with so you can decide if we can still eat together."

She gave a wonderful laugh, "you just swept me in here like I was Cinderella and you think this will go so badly now we won't be able to eat together? You worry me."

"Well, you may be Cinderella or Florence Nightingale for all I know about you. I thought we ought to get whatever is on your mind out of the way before I start asking questions. I do a lot of that."

"So it's my turn?"

"Yes," he said as he went to the kitchen, "Do you want some water since I'm getting it?"

"Please."

As he came back Harry said, "Now, as I recall I offended you in some way before I went in the hospital."

"You made a big deal out of your honesty on the phone and I said you weren't then."

"Oh that. Well, I defended the remark didn't I?"

"Yes, badly I thought."

"I think you should consider the context. I never saw you before in my life, had no reason to believe I ever would again, and saw no reason to tell you and Nicole why I was here. I mean, what would you have done?"

"What would I have done?" She smiled, "If it were me, I wouldn't have been talking about it at all."

"Yes, well, there is that."

"I wouldn't ask a total stranger about home health care either."

"Hmm, so you're not giving me this one?"

"No, it wasn't the whole truth."

"Okay, how about a bad choice of words? A slip of the tongue?"

"No."

"Then not the whole truth."

"Now was that hard? There was something else I wanted to hear more about, wasn't there?"

"Only that I said I never lie and you were going to make me tell you more about that. I think I just did."

"Yes and no. I'm not really giving you a bad time about that day. I do understand your question was innocent enough but you said you always tell the truth. I assume you mean about bigger things than whether or not you're seeing a doctor when talking to strangers."

"I abhor lying or being lied to if that's what you mean. I don't lie about anything important. What I said to you and Nicole didn't seem important since it seemed unlikely I would talk to either of you again. I may omit something, but I don't make things up."

"Have you told anyone you loved them when you didn't?"

He looked at her and frowned, "Where ever did that question come from? It's a very odd one."

"It is odd, but have you ever done it?"

"No I've always believed it if I said it."

"Have you ever been married?"

"No. Have you?"

"No. Is it still my turn?"

He sighed, "Yes, just take us wherever we're going here."

She smiled, "I was making a point. That's as terrible a lie as there is."

Harry saw that she was more serious than not,

"It would be an awful thing to say unless you meant it, but it isn't always true is it? I mean, people delude themselves into believing they're in love all the time. So one might say it and then regret it or realize it wasn't love after all."

"Yes, but you're drilling deeper than me. I just meant the words are tossed around now in such a superficial way. You're talking about something more serious."

"I am but it's the only context I would use the words. I don't say it as a way of expressing simple affection or because I like someone or something they did."

"Yet we hear people use it that way all the time, don't we? I think the words have meaning."

"I'd agree, but many wouldn't."

She smiled, "It's a riddle then, isn't it?"

He shrugged, "I suppose. I never gave it as much thought as you obviously have. And why have you?"

"I'm not sure I've thought much about it at all. It came up at the house this morning. Someone tossed it out about their latest infatuation and it struck me as superficial so I questioned it. Next week or month they'll mean it about someone else. It's silly. No one gives it any meaning," she looked at him, "since the characters in your book understood the burden it carries, I wanted to see if that's how you felt or if it was just in the fiction you write."

Harry wondered how they ended up here but decided she'd made an interesting point.

"Do you have anything else?"

She smiled again, "No, I'm sure I will, but you can have a turn if you like."

"How long is the school on break?"

"Another week after this one."

"Do you always take time off work when you don't have class?"

"No, I usually work full time to make extra money. I'm just tired of it all and decided I didn't want to be a nurse this week. I've wanted to get a way and think."

"About a different career?"

"You remember then?"

"Was I forgetting things with you as well?"

She nodded, "The day I was here you asked me where I was headed, and there were a couple of times at lunch."

"It doesn't sound like I succeeded in deluding anyone."

She gave him that deadpan look he remembered,

"I'm a trained professional."

He laughed a genuine laugh. "Was it obvious to others do you think?"

She shrugged, "I don't know, Nicole didn't get it, not sure who else you were talking to."

"Myself, mostly. Are you always so good at this?"

"I'm really not that good. I mean, I just remember things. At that last lunch you really looked unwell and distracted."

"Well I apologize for that, what's your thinking on careers now?"

"You didn't persuade me to change, just made me think more about it. I still am."

"I didn't try to persuade you if my memory is anything at all. I wouldn't try to do that. But are you going to share?"

"Are you interested?"

He looked over to see if she was kidding. She didn't smile. He said quietly,

"I'm curious, but you needn't tell me." He shrugged, "I'm certain you know better listeners. Life is mostly about me anyway when I'm not in this quiescent state."

"So I if I want your opinion about anything I should ask now before you get better then?"

They both laughed.

"Now, do you need anything before we go? Do you want to check my vital signs or anything to be sure I'm up to this?"

She was smiling and shaking her head as she stood.

"Good, then I'll drive and you tell me where we're going."

They ate at a place in Oro Valley and they managed to laugh a good deal mostly because of that almost unexpected wit of hers. She could look as sad as anyone he'd ever seen and an instant later manage a quiet, funny remark. He liked the way she had about her. She was a comfortable person to be around. As he pulled back in the drive he was both delighted she'd come and as tired as he was, glad when she said she was leaving.

She stood next to him by her car, "I'd thank you for dinner since it wasn't your turn, but we banned thanking each other for meals, didn't we?"

"If I remember it right, we banned thanking each other for asking each other to meet for meals which is even more convoluted. We might as well ban thank you altogether. It was good of you get to come and get me out of here. I really need to do it more. Let's say I'm grateful, okay?"

"Okay."

"If you're without plans one day while you're off now, will you come by here for lunch and tell me more about what you're thinking about doing?"

"Can we eat in the courtyard?"

"Of course."

"Can you do it tomorrow around one?"

"Yes."

"Do you want me to buy since we skipped my turn?"

"No, Elena will make lunch."

She got in her car and gave him a happy smile, "Listen for the bell, then. Goodnight."

Harry was at his desk scribbling a chronology and filling in character's names for the book on his yellow pad. The house was silent now. He'd changed Elena's hours a week ago. She only cooked dinner and something for the next morning now. She came to clean on Thursday mornings. The bell at the gate rang twice and he heard footsteps. He saw Kate when she came even with the door.

He turned, "Hey you."

"Hi."

"I'm ready if you are."

"Good."

He dropped the pad on the desk. "Be right there."

He threw some water on his face and when he reached the kitchen slid onto the other stool at the counter. She was already eating.

"Not much ceremony in this now is there?"

"Is that more of your innate sarcasm or do you really mean you don't care that I'm already eating?"

He leaned gently against her for a moment, "I don't mind, it's comforting somehow."

"What does that mean?"

"After twelve days of lunches and having dinner here twice there isn't much need for formality, is there?"

"It's impolite not to wait. My father used to start ahead of everyone and my mother'd yell at him."

"Oh well in that case, it has to be genetic," Harry said seriously as he took a bite of his deli sandwich. It was, as were all the things she brought, terrific. He had no idea where she got them. She wanted to write the names down for him but he'd put her off since he thought if he knew the names she'd stop coming and he enjoyed having her company for lunch the past two weeks so he just gave her the money every other day and hoped it would continue until she went back to work.

She stopped eating and looked at him in that deadpan way while she drank her tea,

"So you've researched this? Do you have data? Perhaps you have a Journal article or two I can read?"

He nodded vigorously while she spoke and when she was done he said,

"Yes, Yes of course. It's all right there. Wikipedia, I googled it. There were footnotes."

She left the stool, trying hard not to spit tea or laugh and failed at both. She got a paper towel in the kitchen and turned as she wiped her chin and leaned against the counter, still laughing in spite of herself. Harry looked at her trying his best to look bored.

"What's the score?" She asked finally.

"I have no idea. I think that gives me four points, although I should get a bonus for forcing you to leave the counter."

"There's no rule about that."

"There should be."

"We can make one."

He shrugged, "We can if you like, but I think we have enough rules for this as it is. I'm not as competitive about it as you."

"No, I'm more amusing."

"You are actually, but more competitive too. That's why you're winning. Now come back here and finish, and then tell me what you've been doing all morning. By the way, I love your new blouse. Great color on you."

"I'd thank you if I was allowed."

"Know you would." He said as he finished the sandwich and picked up the huge dill pickle slice. She sat down and finished in silence. Talking with her mouth full was another of her mother's admonitions and she still mostly abided by it.

When he was done he turned and faced her. He still couldn't get over how much he enjoyed listening to her and having her here. She was so different than he expected. He was enjoying all this time she was giving him. Her daily appearances were something he looked forward to and he was as comfortable with her as if he'd known her a very long time. She seemed to enjoy it. She was a good listener as well as being a very witty and intelligent woman. He knew something of her now as she did of him. Her father was dead, and she'd clearly adored him. Her mother, whom she never talked much about, re-married and lived in Texas now. She was born in Phoenix, grew up in San Diego, and went to school here. Except for the time spent traveling to play volleyball she'd lived here all her life even after her mother left. These things about her life were woven easily in her conversations in the afternoons they'd spent together. He was sure his time with her was fleeting. She would go back to her work and her real life soon. She was surely doing this because she liked doing for others and he needed doing for right now. He was grateful for that because she made him do things and go places he wouldn't on his own and he needed to be pushed right now. That he found her amusing was nice, but she was likely as comfortable with everyone as she was with him. One day he might ask why she came, but he was enjoying their conversations and nonsense games and he didn't see a reason to spoil it with any other expectation of her. He knew all too well what expectations did for Harry Logan and none of it was good.

She drained her glass now and turned on the stool to face him, their knees touching as naturally as it was something that happened all the time.

"What?"

"Nothing, watching you, that's all. Thinking Harry thoughts."

"Harry thoughts."

"Do it all the time."

"You know that sounds nuts, don't you? You probably shouldn't say it out loud."

"It seems all right to say it to you."

"It is. I may even know what it means."

"How?"

"I seem to know what you mean most of the time."

"You do."

She shrugged her shoulders, "Can I sit in a real chair now?"

"Pick one. I'll be out in a minute."

Harry cleared away the paper and glasses. Her abrupt subject changes were part of her way and didn't bother him. He wasn't sure why because in others he found it annoying. She was on the love seat in the courtyard when he came out and he sat next to her.

"Were you working when I got here?" She asked.

"I was starting to, yes. I was just doing a chronology and naming characters. I may get it done soon."

"Did you walk today?"

"I did Florence, thanks very much for asking, you can put a gold star up on the board for me. I did my exercises and made it to the highway and got a newspaper and I wasn't falling down when I got back."

"I grow less fond of that nonsense the longer you do it. Are you aware of that?"

He nodded, "Yes, you've protested my excessive sarcasm before. If you're that sensitive about it, you need to get over it."

"Florence. I mean that's just silly. You're wittier than that."

He laughed, "Am I?"

"Do you want to hear about this morning?"

"I'm waiting for you to start."

She made fist and hit his shoulder and said softly,

"The better you feel the worse you get."

"I warned you. I'm really an awful person. Now, what did you do?"

"I went to the National Park Regional Office and talked to the Director. He told me about what he did and what other work there was in agronomy. He even offered me a temporary job next fall if I wanted it. It was fun. I wasn't moved to take the job or enroll in agronomy but he was very nice and took a lot of time to show me around."

Without thinking he said, "If that's what you were wearing, I'll bet he did."

"Stop that, can you?" She said sharply.

"I wasn't being sarcastic Kate. I meant he likely thought you as beautiful as I do."

He heard a sharp intake of breath. He'd done it now. They were supposed to sit here and just talk amiably as they always did about life in general and weigh the pros and cons of her career change. He never said anything like that before.

When he looked at her, she was staring at him,

"Do you mean that?"

"I do," he said, not expecting the question.

Her eyes sparkled and she smiled before she folded her arms and slouched down in that way of hers and continued softly,

"So that's agronomy. Tomorrow I'm going to talk to one of the professors in the architecture department. I am working at this."

Harry left it as she had, "Are you glad you took the second week off to think about it?"

"I am. I find talking to you helpful. I told you I often make the wrong decisions on my own. You made me think it through."

"I'm sure you could have figured it out on your own. So what happens after tomorrow?"

"I'm not going back to school. I've had enough of business school. I don't want an MBA, I'm sure of that now. I'll work for now and make some money for whatever I decide," She shook her hair from her face, "I'll tell the registry I'll only take post ops and not work in the hospital. There are too many competency tests to stay current for that. There are some for home nursing too, but fewer and I'm current now. If I decide to do this, I want to go to school full time. How does that sound?"

"Astonishing."

"Why?"

"Because it's as close to a decision as I've heard so far."

"It won't be easy. It could be as much as four years of my life."

"You aren't being sent to prison, you'll have more time and intellectual fun don't you think?"

"Yes, but I still have to figure out the finances for school and how I live without an income. Do you think it's the right thing?"

"You need to decide that, not me. Don't get ahead of yourself. You need to talk to the architecture school first and decide if that's what you want. I can't see how this is going to take four years though given how many credits you have already, but you need to find out. I do have one thought. You said once you have a fascination for the symmetry of gardens, that sort of thing. Have you thought about landscape architecture as a possibility?"

"Not specifically, it does make sense, because I do love all that. I'll ask about it. Every once in a while you're helpful."

"That's just cheap flattery."

She laughed.

Elena came in the gate, so Harry guessed it was near four. She greeted them with a big smile. Kate stood up and stretched,

"You want to take me for a walk?"

"You bring your leash?"

"No, just be sure I stay out of the middle of the street."

"Do we have a destination?"

"I need tea."

"So we know what that means. Can you stay for dinner?"

"I'd like that."

"Let me tell Elena."

"I'll tell her. Go change your shoes."

He came back out and heard Spanish being spoken and a laugh. It was Elena's laugh but not her voice. In a moment Kate appeared and they walked up the gravel path. This was only the third time she stayed for dinner. He still didn't feel comfortable about what happened earlier but she acted as if nothing was different. They walked back sipping tea and talking about nothing special.

After three more months, Harry felt better than he had in years. His scans were clear. The biopsy was ruled inconclusive, which bothered Paul but he assured Harry there was nothing to worry about since he was sure he got it all.

It was early summer now and it was warmer, but as Chris predicted the adobe was nearly immune.

Harry pulled in the drive. He was at the hospital for the latest scan and now he was anxious to work. The early chapter drafts were coming now. He was writing quickly. He wanted to send these re-drafts off and take a break. Six new drafts of chapters would keep Elspeth and Charlie busy until he went up there. The telephone conversations were fine but there was a disjointed feeling and he wanted to ask Charlie more about the protagonist's motivation. The book was moving fast but it was missing something. Elspeth said little but he could tell Charlie was concerned.

He did a few interviews by phone to keep the literary world from wondering what happened to him and his name in the right places and he taped a piece with Nicole Eagan for a mid-week show here at the AU station about authors in the desert. The NPR network picked it up and Nicole was thrilled. He was as happy for the exposure as she. He checked the time and went into change now. Kate would be here soon. She worked last night and was bringing lunch. They fell into a routine that was quite different now that she was working again. By some mutual agreement they still ate a meal together nearly every day. It might be lunch as today or dinner or breakfast depending on her hours. He met her somewhere now more often than she came here. He still enjoyed talking to this witty and, as he was quickly learning, brilliant woman. She seemed to still enjoy seeing him. They never asked anymore as to whether they would eat together, only where and when. He was attracted to her and he'd like it to be more than eating together but his discomfort with what happened that afternoon months ago kept him from it. He wasn't sure yet how much he cared for her romantically, but she surely seemed more than a comfortable companion now. It was a nice friendship and he wanted no expectations of her to distract him from the book. He sighed and pondered the riddle of that as he sat at the desk and typed brief e-mail to both Elspeth and Charlie.

He was checking the typos when he heard her footsteps. She hadn't rung the bell, but chose instead that stealth entrance she was good at and knew amused him whenever she did it. She was behind him now,

"Hi," she said in that wonderful soft voice as she put both hands on his shoulders and massaged them lightly.

"Hey. Glad that's you."

"Did you think it was someone else?"

"No, but you manage it so quietly I wonder sometimes. Happy you're here," he said as he reached up and put his hands on her wrists. She gave them to him without resistance and let them come down across his chest. Her head came down on his shoulder.

"Happier than usual?" She whispered.

"Just more demonstrative perhaps, do you mind?"

"No, I enjoy demonstrative happiness." She pressed her face against his neck and then stood up straight again and squeezed his shoulders.

"Are you finished?" She asked.

"Just sending these off to Elspeth and Charlie."

"When did you get back?"

"About an hour ago."

"How did it go?"

"The scan was fine. I bet you give wonderful back rubs."

She squeezed his shoulders tight and let go,

"I would give you one if you ask."

When he stood and they were standing very close and he said softly, "You could have offered sooner. Seems you should have when I was so debilitated."

"That's pathetic."

"It isn't, just a fact. What did you bring?"

"Chicken from Harrisons."

"Is that the place I like?"

"It's the only place I get chicken, so it better be."

Neither moved or showed any intent to do so. "It's in the kitchen?"

She smiled, "It is. Hungry?"

"I'm enthralled by the smell of berries at the moment. Is that your shampoo?"

"Yes."

"Could I get a better sense of it?"

She gave a soft laugh, "You could."

He leaned over her now and put his face in her hair and then somehow they had their arms around each other and kissed.

When she leaned away, her eyes twinkled. "I'd say thank you if it was allowed," she said very softly.

"So would I."

She left through the office door and went across the courtyard and he followed after he'd pushed the send button. When he reached the kitchen she was putting the food on plates. He leaned on the island counter.

"Kate?"

She stopped and looked at him.

"Do you know what happened in there?"

She smiled as she turned back to cut one of the sandwiches and said quietly,

"If you mean literally, we kissed each other. As to what it meant, I'm not sure."

He watched her in silence as she sat next to him and began to eat. He decided she wasn't going to say more about it, so he changed the subject,

"What time did you finish?"

"I was home early. She was sleeping and the next shift came early. I was up in time to audit that class this morning. Interesting stuff."

"What was it?"

"Bridges and their stress points."

"Oh, wonderful. Surely sorry I missed that."

"Don't be sarcastic, I learned interesting things. For example, a garden bridge is built in the same way as any other bridge, did you know that?"

"It's not something that would have entered my mind."

"Well it's true. You could look on the internet if you want."

He laughed, "I would never check to see if you were right."

"You laughed."

"I did."

"I have 23 points."

"You're merciless about this."

"That's how I got to the Olympic trials."

"You and Bill should play basketball sometime. Be something to watch you two super competitors. You'd probably win."

"I'd try. Is it my turn now?"

"It is."

"Are you happy with the book?"

"I'm not sure. It's early yet. It was harder the last time and I worry now that I'm working so quickly."

"So you're undecided?"

"It always worries me when it goes quickly. The last time was awful," he shrugged, "this time it's coming more quickly. My editor is a bit confused at the moment and that's never good so there's something missing. I'll get there."

She tossed the wrappings away and they walked through the courtyard and for some unspoken reason through the gate. They did many things like it without words, things that seemed natural to both, as if they were sharing a mind. It confused Harry when he tried to sort it out but he found comfort in it, so he gave up trying. She said once she knew what he was thinking and he wondered if she felt the same thing.

They were nearly to the corner still talking of the morning class and how much she liked architecture when he stopped. Today was unusual for at least one wonderful reason. It was time to find out if it really was different.

"I want to ask a question."

"It was still my turn, but you make it sound important so go ahead."

"It may sound strange."

"Why would that be unusual?"

"You're needling me. This is serious."

"Then stop doing the introduction and ask the question."

"I have this sense that much of the time we just seem to know what the other wants. We don't ask if we'll see each other. You tell me your schedule and we eat together somewhere or other without any sort of invitation. We just say where and when and show up. You once said you know my thoughts, my Harry thoughts. We do many things without words, without asking permission, as if it's implied or something." He smiled, "That's more of the preface I suppose, but what I want to ask is does it seem the same to you?"

She stopped and looked at him a moment and then turned back. She didn't say anything. He didn't know how else to say it or whether it offended her. They went through the gate and she sat down. She pulled her knees up to her chest, and looked out over the mountains.

Finally she slid down in the chair and her long hair fell over her face. When she looked up at him, she shook it away, and there was a serious look on her face. She spoke as softly as ever,

"It's always been that way with us. It bothered me at first. It didn't seem . . . I don't know, right or something." She smiled now, "we act like kids who grew up together mostly. I mean, we talk about nearly everything, make up games, and make each other laugh, and we do just show up without perhaps knowing why except that we'll enjoy it. Yet I've wondered about that other attraction too, the one that surfaced today. That seemed natural too. I've always been such a conventional soul with the usual romantic tendencies. I meet a guy. He becomes a friend or I date him. What I mean is I've had friends and interests romantically, but never in the same person. I thought it was how it was supposed to be." She stopped and was quiet a minute before she shook her head, "It isn't like that with you. This doesn't have a category. I don't know what I feel. You're someone I like to be with very much and one I'm attracted to in that other way too. I don't want those feelings to change us but knowing we both have them makes it nicer. When I'm with you, I'm happy. Not because of anything we say or do necessarily, I just know I am." She looked up at him with wide eyes now, "So yes, I understand what you mean, I just can't explain it any better than you can."

Harry didn't know what to do next. He was so relieved she didn't reject his premise and seemed to share it he wanted to leave it alone. Perhaps for once in his life he ought to let it be and not discuss it to death. Finally he said,

"It seems strange, doesn't it? I mean that we can't explain it better. We've never tried to make it anything yet it is something. I don't want to change it, that's not why I asked. I wanted to know how you saw it especially after what happened earlier. It would be nice if we just went from here. Is that all right?"

She smiled and her eyes twinkled as she sat up now, "You already know the answer to that."

"Do I?"

They both laughed, perhaps nervously and then she poked him, he poked back and it all seemed fine again.

She leaned her shoulder against his, "You have anything else today?"

He smiled, "No, it's better if I don't start asking a lot of questions. You know how awful that can be."

She laughed softly and pushed him away.

CHAPTER EIGHT

In the heat of a late June morning he was on his way to the airport. He would soon find out if Chris was still good at booking flights. She swore to him as late as yesterday that this new connection was going to be fast. He'd threatened to expose her to all of Arizona as a slumlord if it went badly. She stuck stubbornly to her opinion, and because he could avoid leaving his car in Phoenix he was willing to try flying from here.

He asked Kate to house sit and lured by the quiet coolness and the promise of dinners from Elena, she agreed. He planned only a week, and hoped he could stay within it. These were only first drafts but there was much to talk about with Charlie. Bill was in the city this week too, and Elspeth was delighted he was finally coming.

Kate was busy. While still working full time, she was getting ready for separate exams for the school of architecture and they were highly competitive. He was sure she would get in without trouble despite her doubts. While they were more openly affectionate it wasn't much more now than before they talked. It was still comfortable and uncomplicated. She came to the house this morning on her way home from work. As he left he squeezed her shoulders and kissed her on the forehead.

"Is it all right if I miss seeing you?" she asked smiling.

"Do we have a rule against that?"

"Not that I know about." She looked sad for a moment and not in the way she did before saying something funny.

"It'll be Friday afternoon before you know it. We both have a lot to do." He said quietly.

He sent her, Chris, and Bill a text as they pushed away from the gate and he settled back now, feeling very much like the old Harry Logan. He found it hard to comprehend all he'd gone through since the last time he'd left Tucson.

He gave Charlie all the reasons why several difficult passages were narrative while Charlie argued for dialogue. Harry said there was too much dialogue already and the story needed to move along. Charlie said it would move along better if he would find another character to help get some tension in the early chapters. Harry was about to issue a broadside attack on the whole day of ceaseless nit picking when he decided to raise it with Charlie in another way.

"You've done all my books, I need an honest answer. Is this as good as *Country* was at this stage?"

Charlie looked out the window and then back, "It's rough, but it's compelling."

"Should it be smoother, I mean, this early?"

"It should be doing more. You're protagonist is just wandering around and I don't know why everyone hates him so much."

"You're not supposed to know yet."

"I should at least know why he's evil if he's going to move the story along. I can tell he's a bad person, but I'm not sure why. It isn't in here."

"Okay, okay, I see your point, what would help?"

"Have him do more. If he's evil, have him do evil things or at least say them. We can get to all this dialogue with his wife and his back story later. This is a process Harry, you know that. You seem to be trying to get from beginning to end too quickly and filling it with endless detail. Get the plot in and the details will come."

He sighed, "I guess I'm trying too hard and that's no way to write. I know that."

"Stop writing then, what's the rush? You've been through one draft up to chapter seven and now this. It took a long time to pull this much out of you the last time. Slow down, write chapters, edit, and edit it again. Take a breath now and then."

"I find that hard to do."

"Try. This is good, but you're capable of better. If this was a first book," he shrugged and rolled his eyes, "I'm not sure we'd be here."

As he left, Harry thought that may have been the most advice Charlie ever offered verbally. Usually it was just questions in the margins or short nasty comments on e-mail or in one of their meetings. He sat in the lobby at The Universal now, waiting for Chris and wondering what the problem was. Maybe he only wrote well when he was unhappy. When he saw the auburn hair that could only be Chris's coming through the door, he went to meet her.

"Hello Christine."

She threw her arms around him,

"Harry, it so good to see you. I thought I never would again."

"So much drama Chris? Really?"

"You were so sick and gone so long."

"You're being melodramatic. You know I'm fine. We talk on the phone enough don't we?"

"We do, and I'm sorry. I told myself I wouldn't do that. It's just that you're here now and it's different."

Harry looked at her. If this was going where he thought it was he needed to deal with it now.

"We settled that. That isn't going to change this week. It's as we left it."

She looked up at him a minute, "I'm fine. I've seen you now and know you're as healthy as you sound."

"Did I tell you how nice you looked?"

"You took no notice of my clothing as you usually do. I have a right to be upset about it too. I changed so I wouldn't look like some floozy you brought in off the street."

"You're the best dressed woman here."

She sipped her scotch, "God that is still the best ever. I am not, so stop the shameless flattery."

Harry laughed. "By the way, the plane connections were quite decent."

"Decent? Decent? They were better than flying from Phoenix. You didn't have to wait at all so come on, admit it. Decent, really. How rude."

"Okay, they were good. It is a long way though."

"Well, you could fix that now couldn't you? Do you have to be that close to the surgeons now?"

"No, I could move, but your house is nice. I like it and I've made a few friends there now, so I'm not the same orphan I was. It's a very relaxing place actually."

"Yes it is because nothing ever happens there, that's why you get so relaxed. I lived there, remember?"

"Nonsense, there are rabbits and road runners and all sorts of things all around the place."

"You're easily amused if rabbits and birds will do it. What about this woman you tell me you're having lunch with all the time. What's with that?"

Harry didn't really want to go into it,

"Kate. She's very nice, has a wonderfully quick wit and I believe she's brilliant although I have no empirical evidence. I enjoy talking to her. I'm writing now, so my time with her or anyone is limited. She may be busier than I am actually. What of you? You've managed to get past dinner with boring Bernice. You told me there was someone although it sounded exceedingly complicated."

"I get out."

"That's it? You get out?"

She gave that big throaty laugh, "There is someone, but I don't want to talk about him."

"Fine. He isn't coming in here to beat me up because we're drinking together, is he?"

She laughed again, "No, he's in San Francisco this week."

"And you won't speak of him?"

"No, we're having another expensive scotch. Wait, what's in your glass? Is that scotch?"

"Water. I haven't had any scotch since my surgery."

"You gave up scotch?"

"I was told to for a time. Then I couldn't taste it. I actually don't miss scotch as much as I thought."

"Oh my god. I never thought I'd drink with you and you'd be wholly sober. There's no fun in that."

He waved down the waitress, who nodded and went to get new drinks,

"I'll try to hold my own."

She sipped at her new drink. "When are you leaving?"

"I'll be home, if I can use that term, by Friday night."

"You getting a lot done with Charlie?"

"Yes and no. Charlie is unhappy right now. Gave me a proper lecture today."

"Charlie? Our Charlie? He gave you a lecture? Really. I'm supposed to believe that? How do you find these traits in Charlie that I never see? Charlie never lectures anyone. He listens, he smiles, he nods, and he writes notes. That's what Charlie does. You make this stuff up just to annoy me."

"There were many questions in that outburst, Chris, which do you want me to answer?"

"Tell me why Charlie is unhappy."

"He isn't moved by my prose."

"What does that mean?"

"He thinks I'm rushing somewhere and have no real destination."

"I'm still not getting it."

"Oh it's all right, it can be fixed, but I'm struggling with this book now in a different way than I did the last time. He's seeing lots of draft chapters and seeing them fast but he's not getting the thread of the story. My protagonist's motivation eludes him—Charlie not the character—and it bothers him. To be fair, it's beginning to bother me. I likely needed more time before I started. He thinks it would be better if I slowed down."

"Interesting theory. I thought you just drove straight through once you started."

"I did the last time, but until recently I haven't felt strong enough to just hammer at it until I can't think and then fall into bed or eat out of frying pan and then go back at it until dawn. Sleeping was my vocation for two months. The fatigue was still bad when I started. The fact is I don't want to write that way now either. I suppose I'm tentative."

"Are you afraid of it?"

He sipped some water hoping the question would go away.

"Harry?"

"What?"

"Is it that or something else? Something's bothering you. I know you well enough to know that so don't get all puffed up and yell at me. I'm trying to be useful here."

"I know. I don't know what's wrong, honestly. I don't even explain it well. Hardly the Harry of times past who would lecture you without prompting. I'm writing fast but not well. I'll see what Elspeth thinks. She's always been honest in the past but she's holding back for some reason. Perhaps it's because she thinks I'm still sick, I'm not sure. I send her the chapters and that used to mean a call if it displeased her. Now, she usually doesn't, and I send it to Charlie who then is less happy than he usually is. I'll see her tomorrow."

"Is there anyone else you'd trust to read it while it's being written?"

"I've never shown my work to anyone. I've always been passionately possessive of my work. I once dated someone back in the awful Harry days who suggested she could fix whatever it was I was lecturing her about at the time if I'd only let her read it. She worked in real estate, thought it was a brochure for an open house or something. It made me furious."

She chuckled, but said seriously, "You're too private Harry. I mean there's this public Harry and you say he sells the book, but from what you've told me, he was around some the last time."

"He was early on certainly, but I'm not him anymore. There should be a life for me besides writing. I've said I'm without the social skills to do that but I seem to have the urge to try. Maybe that's the problem."

"We all need something in our life besides work."

Harry thought about that. "Maybe. Bill can tell you how my eventual isolation was what led to *Country* getting done. After I ruined all my relationships or they failed me, he used to come and pull me out of the office to play basketball. My life became the book, and while it resulted in my life being in chaos, it was the way I managed to write the better part of it."

"That sounds pretty abnormal, but be clear about it, what scares you, that you're taking time to enjoy life or that book isn't right."

"Both. I worry that I won't be able to focus well enough to write the way I know I can."

Chris shrugged, "You may need to find your Zelda somewhere. Might be good."

"I'll think about it. I'm sorry. I didn't mean to get into all this."

"You're down Harry. Friends are for when you're down. I'm just suggesting things here."

"I know, and I appreciate it. Perhaps when we talk I can bounce some things off of you. Would you mind that?"

"I'm not sure I can help, but bounce away. It doesn't sound as if Elspeth is helping much right now." She looked at her watch and stood, "If my opinion counts, I think you need to think more and write the book as it comes. Stop worrying on it like prayer beads. Write when you feel moved to do it. You have time. Use it. Now, go to the symphony and have a few hours of Zen or whatever it does for you. I'll see you before you go."

The symphony was curative. It made him as peaceful as watching the fireplace in the courtyard. He went back to the hotel feeling better.

He woke early, walked a mile or so around the city, and ate breakfast. He wasn't scheduled with Charlie until the afternoon and he was catching up with what seemed like endless calls from literary friends, outlets, and magazines. He did an interview for the style section in the Los Angeles paper. It was the usual vacuous nonsense that she would somehow shape into a puff piece for the next edition because she needed copy and a byline. His name would be there though, and that was what mattered to him.

His caught up to Kate. She was quiet and brief on the phone always. He summed up his day to come,

"So I'll go back to work with Charlie after my lunch with Elspeth and hope for a dinner with Bill. Are you working again tonight?"

"No, I'm studying. I work tomorrow. There's so much to read for these tests. It's nice and quiet here. I use the courtyard in the evening. It's a wonderful place to get work done."

"You could do that whenever you wanted."

"Not when you're here."

"All right, do it your way. Have you seen Nicole?"

"We've talked. I wanted to ask if it's okay if she comes for dinner."

"You don't need my permission."

"I do if it's in your house and cooked by Elena, don't I?"

"No, I said to treat it as your own while I was gone, so do, please."

"I'll ask her then and would say thanks if we did that sort of thing."

"Without question," he said and laughed, "enjoying the adobe?"

"It's very nice. Around dinner though, I wonder why you aren't home."

"Is that a euphemism for missing me?"

"That word means something I would say if I was being less direct about what I meant than I wanted to be."

"It does. Are you reading the dictionary as part of these tests?"

She laughed her soft laugh, "It's what the word means isn't it?"

"It is."

"Then no, I meant around dinner, I wonder why you aren't home."

He laughed, "All right fine."

"If I missed seeing you, I would just say it."

"I'm sure you would."

"I miss seeing you."

He gave a huge laugh, "You really should be taking the exams for English majors."

She said softly, "Will you be home on time?"

"Unless there's foul weather. Wish it was sooner."

"Don't wish that. You have work to do. You'll be here soon enough. You always tell me about focus. Go have lunch with your agent and say hello to Bill who could know me but doesn't because he thinks all nurses look alike. His loss."

He laughed again. "When will you be home tomorrow?"

"Very early and then very late. You needn't call. Friday is only two days from now."

"I'll text when I have a chance."

"That'd be better. Get your work done."

He met El in the lobby. Her greeting was so effusive he was sure the prodigal son received a lesser welcome. They settled into the regular dining room for lunch. He really had to get her out of this "I'm so glad you're well" state of mind and back to being the excellent critic she once was. He told her about the new symphony which she hadn't heard and she expressed her dismay with the opera company and hoped they would find a new director. She was being encouraged to run for the board next year.

"You must run, El. You've held season tickets for years now and know nearly everyone there."

She waved her hand, "Well, we'll see. Now, how's your week going with Charlie?"

"Reasonably well. I see him later today and we'll grind through the rest until Friday. He's having some trouble with context. Frankly his concerns perplex me. I wanted to ask you what you thought. After all, you've always been my best critic."

"What's Charlie's concern?"

"He thinks my protagonist is having trouble finding his way early on and doesn't do enough to move the plot."

She was silent a moment and ate some salad before answering,

"Well, there are some issues. I know you went back to the book as soon as you were able and the early chapters were done quickly. You have a lot of detail considering most is only in first or second draft."

"It may be that I was too hasty. I wanted normalcy and being unwell was annoying. Christine was right in a way. I should have spent more time with it. I thought about the last one a long time before I was really working hard at it. My fatigue keeps me from staying at it long and I need to be able to do that at times to make sure I don't lose the thread of the plot."

She was very serious now, "Surely you can fix it."

"I'd better, hadn't I? I'm working differently now. I try to focus for some hours of the day and then get away from it. You know it was a marathon when I was finally moving on *Country.* I worked until I was exhausted."

"I don't want you to live in some awful garage again for 20 hours a day, Harry. Don't rush it. You seem to just want to get done."

Harry looked up. The question was worthy of thought, but not discussion with Elspeth. Finally, as he finished an excellent fish filet he said,

"I see the problem El and I wanted to see if you and Charlie agreed. I would ask you a favor though. You seem to be letting me off easy this time. If I sent you chapters that offended you in the past, you were usually on the phone to me straight away."

"I may have been reticent until now because of your health, Harry, but if you'd slow down a bit, take a break to think it through or whatever it is you need to do, it might help me as well."

"I need to look it all over again when I get back. Would doing another draft from the beginning help you?"

"Well, that is drastic, but there's far too much going on in the text right now. If you think that would be best then do it."

"All right, at least that's a plan of sorts."

"They'll be watching this one, as you know all too well, Harry. I needn't remind you that mediocrity after winning the Prize will be treated by the critics as failure. Don't be upset about what you're hearing from Charlie. The puzzle will come together. We know you can write. That isn't the issue. Right now, something's missing. Take the time to think it through. You'll find it and it will get better."

"Perhaps I should start talking to myself again."

She laughed, "There's no need to become the village idiot Harry."

"There has to be something that will get this moving. Charlie is going to give me some suggestions today. I asked him to write some things down."

"I don't see any need to hold your hand these days and I have a new client this afternoon who is working with Christine. She's a little tentative, so I want to be there."

"Is Chris doing well with your authors?"

"She has in one case, yes, very well. Have you seen her?"

"We had a drink last night."

"I find it hard to believe that you two got to know each other well enough for that."

"We got off to an unusual start certainly, but she apologized and seems an insightful woman. I enjoy talking to her."

"Charlie and the others seem to like her. Thanks for telling me, it may make my afternoon more pleasant."

As they walked, she wished him continued good heath, and promised to take a harder look at his new draft. They parted with a brief hug at the elevators.

His afternoon with Charlie was short. He left at three to teach a class. He gave Harry the specifics he asked for yesterday by producing three single spaced pages of "notes" he came up with overnight. Harry wasn't happy at the extent of them but Charlie said they were just things to think about.

By four he was finishing his walk and talked to Bill who was somewhere in the city. He was just out of a meeting and said he'd meet Harry at six thirty in the lobby. He looked over Charlie's "note" and at the chapters he was worried about. He saw several of the problems and was pounding on his laptop redrafting when the hotel phone rang. He saw the time and knew it was Bill. He picked it up and said,

"I know we said the lobby, William, but I'm working. I'll be there presently."

"Hurry sport. I have to go back." Bill replied.

He went downstairs and saw Bill in a corner of the bar.

"Now what's this business about hurrying, William?"

"I need to take these people to dinner, but I'm free until eight. This is what happens when you catch me in the city."

"You work too hard."

"Nah, just when I have this bunch in one place. I'm tryin' to make them see it my way. It's a struggle, I'm tellin' ya. Come on let's sit."

Bill had his favorite local beer, and he had water on the rocks.

"No scotch?"

"I'm still not drinking. I couldn't taste anything and now," he shrugged, "I think I still like scotch but don't like drinking it alone."

"Nobody drink scotch in that dust bowl?"

"Yes, but I'm not eating with people who do so far as I know. That reminds me, Kate Beckett sends her best. She said you could have met her if you didn't think all nurses looked alike and it was your loss."

Bill chuckled, "She really say that or is that your paraphrase?"

"She talks like that. Her exact quote was even funnier."

"You two are getting pretty tight."

"It's been nice to have her around since you left. I thought she was just doing good works, but it's gone on so long now I'm not sure what it is. I need to find out more when I get home."

"She gonna move into the adobe?"

"Only when I'm not there. She's house sitting now so she can study and eat Elena's wonderful food. This isn't Agnes revisited, William. I'm working and you know how horrible I can be. I refuse to get into that situation again."

"Ya mean you care about her? Thought that was against the rules when you were writing."

"It is, yet I miss seeing her. Mostly we go out and eat now or she shows me things in the desert I would never find on my own. It's comfortable and I do care for her. The book will get done and this will get done too if it's supposed to. I refuse to listen to a lecture from you about deferring the hard decisions."

"Jeez Harry, ya lost a lot of friends and a potential bride or two in the past 'cause you couldn't do that."

"I'm painfully aware of what happened in the past, thank you. It's not going to happen again. It will stay the way it is or we'll move on. It may or may not become something more but the book will get done too. It isn't doing well right now and I need to know why. It has nothing to do with her. Perhaps I just wanted to make up the time I lost. Nobody likes it. I'm not sure I like it. It'll have to get a lot better."

"You writin' a bad book?"

"One without an apparent point to anyone at present. There's a lot to figure out."

"Sorry to hear that. Not yellin' and screamin' about it are ya?"

"No. I don't think telling everyone how I would fix it ever helped much."

"It didn't stop ya before. You were pretty annoying most of the time."

"Well, I don't want to be now. I'm glad I came this week. Elspeth seems over her funereal mood now that she's seen me in person and promised to be more critical, Charlie has given me some ideas, and Chris has given me some things to think about as well."

"You see Chris?"

"Last night. We were in here before I went to the symphony."

"No more'n that?"

"No. She's seeing someone here. It's what she needs."

"You Harry, what do you need? You're done with Zuckerman. Why not move closer?"

"I actually like the quiet and the lack of community involvement there for now. There are still follow-ups with the doctors and I want to understand this business with Kate. She's going back to school full time soon. She wants to be an architect. She thinks she'll like that better than nursing people back to health."

Bill checked his watch, "She sounds interesting. Now, I gotta go herd my cats. If I was less sure this was gonna be good when I get it organized, I'd go back to sellin' full time. Pullin' all this together is interesting, though. When you comin' back?"

"I have no idea. Be off and do good works. I'll call. Be home soon?"

"Yup. Stay well Harry, you look better than ya have in years. You ready to play some ball?"

"Nearly. If you ever come back there you may have to beat Kate. She says she plays."

"She an Amazon or somethin'?"

"No, William, if you were paying attention, you'd know she is a very tall, dark haired, well-muscled woman of remarkable beauty. She was a finalist for the last two Olympic Volleyball Teams. She may be more competitive than you are."

"Jeez, you play her yet?"

"No. I haven't felt strong enough until now. I'll let you know how that goes."

Bill laughed, "Do that. I don't need to be humiliated by some woman volleyball player at my own game. Now I gotta go, sorry about dinner."

After another full day with Charlie, he stopped and thanked Chris for the plane reservation help and ate at the hotel and worked late on the redrafting. He was seeing more of the problems now. When he rolled away from the gate on the six-thirty flight he sent a text to Kate to say he was on the first leg and slept most of the way to San Francisco.

He made notes the rest of the trip. He was trying hard not to believe he was as lost as he was the last time. He couldn't get lost now, he just couldn't. There was a story here, it needed work, and he could do it. He refused to fail now.

He called Kate from Phoenix. She was working south of Tucson but would be at the house when he got there. Her car was in the drive when he pulled the bell twice. She opened it and they wordlessly fell into each other's arms and held on tight for a long minute before he let her go. He could feel the heat in both of them and it scared him a little. Not now, not tonight, he thought, this is just loneliness and lust and it needs to be more than that.

She walked him into the house. He threw his bag on the bed and found her waiting in the living room,

"Hungry?"

"Not really. I'd kill for tea."

"Would you?"

"Figuratively speaking Kate."

She went and got it. "Thought you might miss it. Walk me out and go to bed. You look beat. I'll see you for lunch. Chicken or Mexican?"

"Surprise me."

She looked at him a long moment after she put her things in the car and seemed about to say something but then kissed his cheek and was gone.

Harry was at the computer by six. He slept soundly and woke with an idea. He came in to write a note about it and then decided to find where he wanted to put it in the new draft. Once he found it, he decided to try to do it and now it was near ten and he was still here. Aside from the coffee he made earlier, he hadn't eaten yet. He got up now, took a shower and dressed, drank the rest of the coffee and was looking at the next chapter. He knew what was wrong with it, just not certain how to write it better. He'd try later. He heard the gate but no bell and saw Kate cross the courtyard and move quietly to the other side of the house. He found her as she put the food bag on the counter.

"Hey."

"Hi, are you working?"

"Drafting some new ideas."

"I can leave this and read if you want to keep going."

"No. I've done what I want for now. I was in there early."

"Why?"

"I woke up with an idea and then just stayed at it. Now, I have a proposition for you."

"What?"

"Given you're competitiveness you'll like this."

"Are you going to tell me or just talk about my less charming personal traits?"

Harry pointed as he sat down, "If I guess what's in the bag, the score goes back zero. If I don't, you get 20 points so the score will be around fifty to five."

She smiled, "forty four to seven, actually. Is this a trick?"

"No, a proposition."

"Never had one like this."

"I certainly hope not."

"So, what does it take for you to win? Do you have to tell me what each of us is having?"

"No. It's all still sitting there in a plain brown bag. So I have to guess Mexican or chicken since those were the choices last night, right?"

"Yes, but how can you know?"

"Doesn't seem I can, does it? You want the bet, or proposition or whatever or not?"

She looked at the bag, folded her arms, walked over, and looked at the other side. She looked at him, back at the bag and frowned,

"There's no way to tell."

"Come on, you're just afraid to lose. Are you in or out? I'm hungry."

"Oh all right, I'm in."

"Mexican."

"How did you know?"

"I applied your deductive method."

"No. You cheated."

"I'm shocked, shocked I say, that you would think I would do such a thing."

She laughed, "Then tell me how you knew, Inspector."

"I just came back from the northwest and I haven't seen a tortilla since I left so I knew you would bring Mexican today because you have no idea what I've been eating for a week but you were sure it wasn't Mexican."

She laughed again, "That's actually good."

He looked at her in mock seriousness, "In addition, you just laughed twice so I'm winning."

She put the plates down on the counter and came around to join him. They talked about the trip. Then without looking, she pushed an envelope across the counter. "These came while you were gone."

He opened it and took out the paper, read it, and put it back and left it on the counter without comment. It was her SAT scores from a few months ago. She was in the 96th percentile. Yale and Harvard took people like her.

He said seriously, "Best you could do?"

"I had a headache."

He was trying hard not to laugh. She was silent.

"Would you have done better if you didn't?"

"Maybe."

Harry sighed, "Well you're going to have to live in the 96th percentile the rest of your life."

"I killed them, huh?"

"Yeah, you did. A few hundred points higher than me. Creep."

She finally gave up a soft laugh, "You work on this while you were gone?"

"No, and my lead won't last. That said, those are fantastic."

She shrugged, "I'm older, been to nursing school too, so if I'd done badly I'd be embarrassed."

"That's not the way those tests work, you know that. You can give me that 'aw shucks' business all you want, you're still brilliant."

He drained his glass, and swiveled to look at her. She still had her head down finishing the last few bites. As he watched her the thought struck him that he didn't care if he ever finished the book if it meant she wasn't in his life somehow. He didn't know what he did to deserve having her want to be here with him and to miss seeing him when he was gone. It came over him so swiftly it startled him. His eyes were wet and he left the counter abruptly to do something about it. When he came back she was sitting on the sofa with her feet on the table,

"Are you going to tell me why you're upset?"

He looked at her. "Upset?"

"Yes, you were when you got home and you are now. You want to talk about it?"

"My editor has problems with the book. I asked Elspeth about it. She does too but was so worried about my near death experience she's let it go instead of talking to me. I'll fix it, am now. It's why I was up early."

"No."

"What do you mean no?"

"You weren't up early because you had some big 'aha' moment."

"Come on, Kate, I'm annoyed for sending Charlie substandard work and having my usual pre-book neurosis that's all. Can this wait?"

"No. I think we need to talk."

"About what?"

"Us. We need to understand what's going on here."

His heart jumped. What did she mean? He was silent because he was afraid to ask the next question, afraid where it would lead. He was angry with himself now. He didn't want Kate to be confused. She seemed a part of his life now and yet the book was more than that. The tension was palpable last night and even more so now. Finally she broke the silence,

"Are we going someplace?" She asked quietly.

"You mean in life?"

"I didn't mean to the grocery store, did I? You knew what I meant, don't be flippant."

"I wasn't being flippant. Your question wasn't clear."

She stared at him and said nothing.

He sighed, "We need to talk."

"Are you sure you want to? It doesn't sound that way."

"I'm sorry, I didn't mean to snap at you, but there's a tension between us right now I don't understand. Can we talk about it?"

"What's left to know?"

"How we feel Kate. I want to know, don't you? Can we try to understand this?"

She was quiet again and he dropped onto the sofa.

"You're right. It's uncomfortable. We're both holding back for some reason."

"Then talk about it. It's better than stumbling around, isn't it?"

She sighed, "It is. Since I brought it up I should go first."

"You don't have to do that."

"No I started this with my cheesy book so I should have to go first."

"It wasn't cheesy. I was glad you brought it and you came with it."

"Yes, well, that's fine, but at that point we were just being nice to each other. After that, you were beat up after surgery and I came because I was off, glad to have you to talk to, to help me make my decision, and thought you'd like the company."

"I did."

"Stop interrupting me."

"Go on then. I was trying to help."

She ignored him and continued in her soft voice,

"We said most of it when we talked before. Nothing's happened to change that. We spend a lot of time together and it's all so comfortable, or it was until just now. We laugh a lot and still act as if we've known each other all our lives. I've never been this close to anyone. Yet there are those other feelings too, the line we've never crossed. We both felt it last night. I like those feelings and I want to be free to share them yet we're suppressing them and I don't know why."

She turned, "When you went away, I missed seeing you and wanted you back here. Not abandon everything, just come back when you were done. I think you felt the same. Then last night . . . well, I'm glad we didn't give into it because it would've been like some creepy romance novel and I never want us to be like that."

She stopped and looked away again. "You need to tell me how you feel. You're reticent about saying anything because you don't believe you can handle a complicated relationship and write a great book. It shows now. You're unhappy with the book and you may be unhappy with me. I'm not as verbal about these things as you are, but I'm having trouble too. I want to pass these exams and get the very best scores I can yet there are times when you get in the way of that. Academics are competitive for me but hard too. Writing is focused hard work for you, so we need to figure out how to do all that and have this be good for both of us or just get out of each other's way."

She stopped a moment, "If it's not right for one of us then we need to say that. If we're okay with it as it is, we need to say that too. If there's more . . . you have to tell me. I'm not going guess."

She stopped, took a deep breath, and slouched down in that way of hers and he knew she was done.

Harry sat thinking about what she said. She cared for him as much as he did for her. That's what he heard. He stood and walked in front of her thinking about what he wanted to say. She was watching him with that sad expression. He sat down on the floor and looked into her face and said quietly,

"When we first met, I thought of you as a very smart, beautiful woman whose company I enjoyed. We kept running into each other, or calling, or showing up. It was nice, without motive, and we shared interesting conversations. It just happened. Then after my surgery you started coming here and needled me about getting back to normal. You said when I first met you that you liked doing things for people so I saw it as only that. I had no idea it would become what it is now. It seemed quite natural. I was getting well, you got me out of here and made me want to do things and you were rearranging your life. Then one day something happened, surfaced you said, and it was more than just conversation for both of us and it makes us happy in a different way," He shook his head, "I don't know how we got where we are now Kate, we just did."

Harry stopped to think and she said,

"What happened at lunch?"

"I was looking at you and thought how glad I am you're here, that you miss me when I leave, and how I won't let the book come between us. It startled me that I felt so strongly about it."

He stopped, took a deep breath, and looked up to keep from tearing up again. He shook his head and sat next to her before he spoke,

"I don't need to think about how I feel. I just need to be a grownup about it."

"What do you mean?"

"It's what Bill and I always used to argue about. I defer things. I'm very good about rationalizing. It's why so many important things in my life slipped away while my writing consumed me. When it happened, Bill would ask me why and I'd always say the same things about how writing is solitary and how insecure I am while doing it. I've made myself believe that my life is so different, so chaotic that I can't balance the professional and personal parts of it. Well, I'm going to have to learn because I won't defer now. You're too important to me. Neither of us thought this would happen. It just did and now if it's in any way up to me I don't want it to end or just have it be as it has been either."

He stopped. They were silent a long time. Finally he said,

"What do you want Kate?"

"I want that too."

"I wish I'd realized how it was affecting you, I just didn't, I'm sorry."

"I'm not very good at saying what bothers me. I need to do better." She held his arm now and looked at him, "You can't give up on the book because of us. I won't let you do that. You'd feel awful, I'd feel worse, and we'd be over in a month. You know that. I'm not quitting either. I'm working on a new career and you have a book to write. We need to find a way to do both and be whatever it is we are together too."

Harry knew this was a woman who was working hard to find herself, to find a new professional life. She knew what she wanted and if he was going to keep her he was going to have to give back. There was no room for the old Harry here, the one full of obsession and pomposity. If that Harry came in the house, she'd leave. There would be zero tolerance for prosaic dissertations on why he didn't get his work done or why his was more important than hers. They both had a professional passion quite different from the other. He needed to remember that and give her the room to excel at it and not resent it.

They went for a long walk and said very little, both lost in their thoughts. When they came back to the courtyard she agreed to go to the Tucson Inn for dinner in gratitude for her house sitting and to celebrate her SATs. As she was leaving for home to change Harry said,

"Kate? You know I'd thank you if I could."

She smiled and put her arms around his neck and kissed him, "You'll find a way."

CHAPTER NINE

She wore a simple ice blue straight-skirted sleeveless dress with a single silver chain at the neck that set off her hair and dark skin. Her full wavy dark hair was down below he shoulders now. In his opened collared shirt with a summer blazer, he felt underdressed to be taking this vision anywhere.

The manager remembered him and made room for them this busy Saturday night. They drove up Elm Street and gave the BMW over to the valet and came in laughing and holding hands. She was gracious and comfortable. He wasn't surprised although he'd never given a thought as to how this woman of the desert, lover of plants, old houses, and long walks in the arid landscape would take to this sort of world. She fit in with grace, elegance, and the same enthusiasm here as she did on their walks through the cactus. She was enjoying it immensely, not as an adventure, but as something she liked doing and it didn't surprise him at all.

She agreed to have a scotch with him and as she sipped at it she wrinkled her nose,

"Why haven't we had scotch before?"

"I didn't think you drank liquor."

"I didn't know you did either."

"I haven't since my surgery. This is my first. Scotch and I have been having an affair for a very long time."

"I like it."

"You're enjoying this, aren't you?"

"Very much. It reminds me of the times my father used to take us to dinner. It was always somewhere that required being dressed like this. I'd thank you for the memory if I was allowed."

"Was it something you did often?"

"We'd go to the Officer's Club or somewhere once a week. Taught me the few manners have."

"I hadn't noticed you were devoid of manners. I did mention I love your dress?"

"I'm not devoid of them, I just haven't exercised the ones I need in a place like this for the past few years because it would cost my rent money to eat here, and no one offered to take me. And yes, you've talked about my clothes since I reached the house so don't start that again. What did you expect me to wear, pink shorts and a purple tank top?"

He gave a long laugh, "No, of course not. It's just that I haven't seen this Kate before. She's as lovely as the other I see all the time."

She looked at him with that twinkle in her eyes, "That's very nice."

"I can be that way now and then."

"And what else are you like? Around me you're always nice. Sarcastic and too full of questions, usually, but never anything else."

"Oh, I'm too loud and arrogant much of the rest of the time. Nicole can tell you what I sound like on the radio. A loud voice and a careful choice of vocabulary has largely been my way to get others to see things my way since my mother died. My father was the one who taught me that behavior and assured me it would serve me well. I suppose it has in its way for more years than I care to remember."

"Why are you different now?"

"I'm not sure. Bill and others helped me understand there's another Harry in here, one that knows how to act with nice people like you and enjoys it. I can take that public persona off now when I don't need it. Maybe I just finally grew up."

She smiled as finished her scotch. "I want another one."

"You sure? They get lethal at some point."

"I've had a few." She deadpanned.

Harry chuckled, "I expect you have. Now," he said as the drinks came, "shall we toast your enormous intelligence and my gratitude for watching the house?"

She smiled, "neither is necessary. Staying at your house was the easiest thing I've done in a long time. The peace and quiet was great and Elena's food is wonderful. Let's just toast understanding everything better."

"Fine, I can surely drink to that. Now you can read a menu or listen to me since I know it by heart having lived what seemed like a few years of my life here before my surgery. I can recommend something in beef, pork, or fish, but nothing Mexican."

"That sounds right. Good Mexican here would be antithetical."

"It shouldn't be but it is."

They ordered and talked more about life before they met. He described Charlie Winchester at her request and she laughed at his eccentricities. The Inn manager stopped by and greeted them both effusively. They debated sharing a desert but decided to pass it up for brandy and coffee. Kate seemed to glow. He'd never seen it in her before.

"I enjoy being here." She said dreamily and then laughed, "It doesn't have the charm of chicken sandwiches at the kitchen counter, but it is nice."

Harry chuckled, "By the way, you said you play basketball, didn't you?"

"Of course. I've played all my life and even a year on the high school team so I know the rules, why?"

"I told Bill that you two should play if he ever comes down here again. He's more competitive than you are, although that seems improbable. He's afraid you'll humiliate him. He wants me play with you so I can tell him how good you are."

"I haven't seen you play."

"Its how I let off steam when I write."

"You have a ball?"

"Somewhere."

"There are courts in Catalina. You could get in a game there."

"Will you play?"

She laughed, "Not in a game, I'm not good enough for that."

"I'll bet."

"When it cools off we could walk there and get all the exercise we need."

"It'll be a long walk back."

"Is that a problem?"

He laughed, "If you do it I'll do it."

"That a motto or something?"

He signed the check and patted her hand. "If you like."

She smiled, "Are we going?"

"When you're ready."

He woke in the near light and heard water running. It stopped and it was quiet again. He was almost asleep when he felt the bed move and opened his eyes to her smiling face and her twinkling eyes,

"Hey."

"Hey yourself."

"I missed you."

She kissed him and laughed, "You did not. You were asleep and didn't even know I was gone, so that line won't work."

"Are you staying?"

"Oh yes." She fell on top of him and he wrapped her in his arms.

"Kate—"

"I know."

They were drinking coffee much later and deciding whether to eat breakfast or lunch.

"The most democratic thing is go out and eat whichever we want."

"I'll vote for that." Harry said.

He ordered a huge breakfast and she ate lunch. They were working hard to keep distance between them while making small talk.

"How many nationalities are you?" Harry asked.

"My mother is Mexican American and some Indian. My father's mother was Hawaiian, probably some Samoan too and his father was from somewhere in the Midwest, Illinois I think. They met when he was in training."

"Here?"

"No, Phoenix. He was in the Air Force at Luke. We moved back there from California when he came home the last time. My mother had an aunt here in Tucson then. After he died we lived over here. When she remarried she moved to San Antonio and I stayed to finish school."

"Do you like Tucson, is that why you're still here?"

"Like it? I suppose. I never thought about it much. I could easily leave. I never had reason to stay after school really. I never developed strong ties here after my mother's aunt Maria died, perhaps because of all the traveling the team did. There was lots of work for nurses and I wanted to do more with school, so I never left completely."

"Do you see your mother?"

"No. We stay in touch but that's a long story and not for today. Are you really going to eat all those pancakes?"

"Why, do you have some moral objection?"

"I think you're showing off and will fall asleep when we get back."

He leaned up against her and whispered, "Can we take a nap?"

"Stop that. Don't do things like that when we're in public."

"Oh all right."

She laughed without thinking.

"Four to nothing," he said.

"That's not fair."

"It is."

"Is not."

"Now you sound like a fourth grader at recess. You're behind and you hate it."

"I do."

"It won't last."

"Fine. Just hurry and eat the rest and let's go."

He grabbed her hand and pulled, "Come on, I'm done. Should I get some tea to take with us? Never mind, I can tell by the look on your face that was a dumb question. Do you have money?"

"No."

"Why? It's your turn."

"I know, I forgot. I'll get it next time. Now please, can we just get out of here? I'll meet you at the car."

He bought two bottles and settled in the passenger seat. She frowned when she saw him but went around and got behind the wheel.

"What's this about?"

"You only care about me because you covet my car, I know that, and I accept it. You can drive."

She laughed, "You're nuts. I get to drive, what? A half mile?"

"Go into town first if you like. You need to learn the switches and things."

"I'm a fast learner," she said as she pulled it into gear and went down the road that went back to the house.

They were in the living area and she was lying on the sofa. He slouched in a chair watching her. He knew this day was only a wonderful interlude and there was the work of figuring out how to manage two full schedules and their time together He got up and went over and sat on the floor next to her head and leaned on the sofa arm.

"Figure it out?"

"What?"

"You're thinking about how to do this."

"It's going to be hard."

"If we let it be. I don't think we should. I know you're concerned about it almost to the exclusion of all else right now. You said there was time."

"I did, but time is relative."

"Do you have books in the car?"

"Yes."

"Here's the first decision we just made. They stay there. You working tomorrow?"

"No, I have a home care case down in Bisbee for two days starting Tuesday."

"Good, so that will be the end of your nursing career until after the tests. After Wednesday, you're going to be in a quiet place studying with the concentration you need for six hours a day until the tests are over. Don't care where that is, it's up to you. I'm not doing any more chapters until I understand what's wrong with the ones I have. I may do them all over. I'd like to quit Friday afternoons and have the weekends for us while we can. What do you think?"

She said quietly, "That'll work for now. I can pay the bills without working for a few weeks. I'll work out the rest when the tests are over."

"Good, now stop. We have to take this one step at a time. In this case one person and one problem. When do you take the test?"

"In three weeks."

"Okay, you have three weeks, which is 15 weekdays. Is studying six hours a day enough?"

"If I can concentrate, yes, that's enough."

"Good. So that wasn't so hard, was it?"

"I still need to find a place."

"You mean the same place?"

She nodded, "Yes, Nicole's is more a boarding house than anything. There are people in and out all day. I can't work there."

"And you can't do it here?"

"No."

"Can you reserve a carrel in the library?"

"That's a thought. I'd have to call and check. It's expensive though for the kind you just lock and leave."

"It would be like an office."

"It's a good idea, maybe better than that, but I'd have to work to afford it."

"Would you let me loan you the money? I would let you loan it to me if I needed it to write."

"It would solve the problem. It has to be a loan though, I won't let you just pay for it."

"We can arrange whatever terms you like if it means you won't work while you do this."

"A loan then."

"Call and find out. Try now, there's probably somebody at the desk today who knows whether there are any available." He tossed her his phone.

Ten minutes later she learned there were plenty during the summer, got her name on the list and she could do the paperwork on Monday. She wore her happy smile when she tossed him the phone,

"That's fantastic. You're good at this."

"I enjoyed solving the problem for you."

She stood now and stretched, "What do you want for dinner?"

"I have no idea I just ate a few hours ago. You can decide if it needs to be now."

"I want to get ribs while they still have them."

"Take my car so you can say you really drove it."

Harry lay on the cool floor when she left thinking of how nice the last twenty-four hours were and how he hoped he wouldn't screw this up.

He smelled the ribs before he opened his eyes. She must be part cat, he thought idly. Maybe he could stay here a little longer if he was quiet. In a minute or so he felt a bump against his ribs. When he didn't open his eyes right away, he felt another, harder this time. She was smiling down at him and laughed as he shook his head.

"Why are you kicking me?"

"I want you to get up."

"I'm not sure kicking me is good."

"You'll get over it."

"You wouldn't want me to kick you, would you?"

"No and I won't kick you again if you don't fall asleep on the floor in the middle of the house. I want to walk before we eat. You have the strength for that?"

"Of course."

"I'll meet you at the gate."

They walked for more than an hour and her enthusiasm for natural things even here in what seemed like a vast wasteland amazed him. They ate ribs and drank Tecate beer by the fire outside but didn't try to solve problems or make plans. They shared stories about their pasts and present and laughed until they finally gave in to their stronger urges.

It wasn't much different from other nights they'd eaten here except she didn't go home.

He said goodnight to Elena and Joseph at four on Tuesday afternoon four weeks later. Kate's exams might be late so he went to take a shower.

In the weeks since he got home the book began to make some sense again, yet he was still ambivalent. He talked to Chris twice and she tried to help him understand it. They had a long conversation one evening about the protagonist and his inability to move the story along. Harry was reluctant to accept what he would have to write to do that. The sadness of it, the brutality of what needed to happen to make the story plausible bothered him. She thought he liked his characters too much and needed to get over it. They were there to move the story not become his friends. She thought he enjoyed writing conversations fraught with possibilities and then the conclusions became too complicated. He didn't agree with all of that, but talking to her helped. Not his Zelda, surely, but a very perceptive woman he was glad could talk to with the added benefit that she'd read a sparse outline of the book.

Elspeth, returned to her editing and questioning with a bit more enthusiasm. She thought there was more work to be done, but urged him to review the plot and characters, and be sure that he understood how to make the story worth telling.

He was editing as much as he was writing. He took walks very early and went to the Café for breakfast and talked to a local or two he'd come to know. He came back by a circular route he and Kate discovered so he could see the long eared rabbits and roadrunners scurry around the arid landscape. He often sat on a huge rock downhill from the house while he thought something through. None of his issues with the book was the fault of his time with Kate and he was glad of that.

She'd buried herself in her books. These tests were peculiar to the school of architecture. They had their own rules which she understood fully but he only knew they were hard and important. She was ensconced in what she called her "neat little office" in the University library. She was home by five every day. She came by or met him to eat some nights and then went home. He knew she never stopped thinking about the tests. She was so competitive he knew it was hard for her. When she came on weekends, she was less relaxed and more distracted the closer the tests got. Maybe it was all those years of sports competition he didn't know about. Things between them remained without friction or anger although he was occasionally baffled by her distraction and need to work so hard. The compulsive Harry found little in her ways to annoy him. She was so direct and funny and quick to object or let him take her on when there was an issue that it was nearly impossible. He hoped it stayed this way.

She took the test Monday and today. She was distracted over the weekend, stole a few hours to review here Saturday afternoon, and went home early Sunday. Elena made her favorite enchiladas for tonight. Kate said she wanted to stay tonight when they talked on Monday. As he dried off, he knew somehow she was here, in the courtyard probably, drinking Tecate or Corona from the bottle if he had to guess. He went out after he dressed. She sat staring at the mountains with her back to him and her feet up. The bottle dangled from her hand.

"Hey."

She turned slightly and met his kiss and gave him a smile, "Hi. How was your day?"

"Better question is how was yours. Glad it's over?"

"I am. Did you work?"

Harry sat now and sighed, "I did. You burn all your books?"

She laughed, "No, actually, When the test was done I went over to library and looked at them, left the carrel just as it was, locked the door and left. Felt good for some reason."

He smiled, "Are there things in the car?"

"Not anymore, while you were singing that horrible song in the shower, I put them in the closet."

"It was an aria in Italian. You look tired."

"I am, but I'm okay. There was a party at the house. I don't enjoy going back and finding the children all trying to get drunk by seven."

"Does that happen often?"

"No, and I usually don't care but I wasn't in the mood to have some twenty something hit on me tonight. I called Nicole and she'll throw them all out when she gets there." She had that deadpan look and a twinkle in her eyes as she finished quietly, "the guy had attitude, and I probably should have beaten him to a pulp. The little dweeb looked easy."

He laughed, "Then he's lucky you were in a good mood because I'm sure you could have."

"Speaking of beatings, that basketball of yours got air in it?"

He nodded, "I was down there this morning for an hour before it got warm. Why? You want to play?"

"I want to shoot baskets before diner. I've been sitting too long."

"I didn't think you did sports anymore."

"Well I don't want to do anything serious. Get the ball and put on the right shoes. I'll meet you in the car."

They shot for about forty-five minutes and she seemed awkward, as if she hadn't done it much or at least not in quite a while. It was fine with Harry. He didn't need another competition with her. Maybe she really wasn't good at it.

She happily praised Elena's thoughtfulness for all the food she left while she ate her enchiladas as fast as her gracefulness would permit. She washed off dishes while he walked out into the courtyard. He heard her trying to sneak up behind him and turned to catch her up in his arms. He was about to laugh but she wrapped arms her around him and kissed him with such fervor it surprised him.

She fell asleep as darkness came and he watched her. The last month was hard work and an emotional rollercoaster for her. She was an important part of his life now. It wasn't love, but it was more than before and he was still afraid he would find a way to ruin it, to make her want to be anywhere but here.

She sighed and opened her eyes looking surprised and not entirely happy when she realized she'd slept. She whimpered and reached for him.

He took her hand, "Its fine Kate, you're beat. Sleep a bit more, I'll be here."

"Hold me."

There was an odd, almost authoritative tone in her voice. This was far from a typical night for them and he wondered why she was clinging to him so fiercely. He put his hand in her hair when she finally laid her head on his chest. In a few minutes her hard grip relaxed and her breathing became rhythmic and he knew she was asleep.

He dozed until he felt her stir and reach for him again with an almost frightening urgency. Later, he was drinking tea on the sofa when she came in wearing a robe and a smile.

He looked at her as she sat in the chair across from him drinking the tea she'd gathered off the counter.

Finally, as the silence lingered he said,

"Talk to me."

"About what?"

"Are you all right?"

"I am now." She said it very softly, "I was so wound up. There was all this energy in me and I needed so badly to let it all go. Shooting a basketball didn't do it."

She stopped and smiled shyly before continuing in a near whisper, "I don't really understand, but it wasn't going to wait. I've never felt that before."

Harry said quietly, "It's been a long month, Kate. The exams had you tied in knots. When you've been here you've been distracted, especially the past two weeks. I doubt it's been out of your mind once. You needed to let go."

She laughed softly, "That sounds like Freudian nonsense."

"It's not Freudian at all. It happens. Just think of it as sigh of emotional relief that's all."

She said in a very small voice, "It was just so . . . I don't know, intense? Is that the word I want?"

He smiled, "I don't know but it's nothing to feel bad about. It was fine with me."

She laughed her big laugh and landed against him on the couch. "Was it?"

CHAPTER TEN

Summer was gone. The monsoon season came and went with its short fierce period of torrential rains. Kate was accepted at the University and working harder than she ever had in her life according to her. It was the end of mid-term exams now and she'd nearly moved into the carrel in the library. Harry doubted she'd ever give it up. She said it was a wonderful place to work between classes and after and often stayed into the evening. She was on campus nearly all day, something she'd never experienced as a part-timer. The give and take she found there stimulated her and she was happy.

He was proud she'd worked so hard to make it happen both academically and financially. She was adamant about funding it. She found a scholarship and with the remainder of her survivor's benefits she was breaking even.

Harry had been gone twice since summer. He was struggling and he found seeking out Charlie helpful for a time. He had a book he wasn't excited about and he'd rewritten most of it four times yet it was wrong, off somehow, and he couldn't find the answer. He wasn't ready to admit it was a bad idea but he wasn't happy with it. Some of the dialogue was fine, he loved the protagonist and his wife, yet he fretted about the rest. He worried over his skill to get it done, an unlikely thing for the ever confident Harry. He was nearly at a dead stop for perhaps the first time since his self-inflicted writer's block of years ago while writing *Country,* There was still lots of time to submit the manuscript. Many of the chapters were in fifth draft and yet he had little confidence in them. He thought it was still a good idea and a good story but he wanted more than that. He had no illusions about it being the same critical success as the last book, but it had to be good enough to keep his readers and the critics happy or it wasn't worth doing. When he talked to his literary acquaintances in New York, he remained upbeat and for all they knew he was breezing along. When he gave interviews he stayed with the plot line. He could expand or contract that to fit the minutes needed. That was easy. Yet he couldn't fill the holes in what he'd written and finish the book.

Kate asked how it was going now and again and he would answer vaguely and move on to other things. She spoke of her joy at being back in school learning about something she really enjoyed but rarely about the details. While Harry was glad she showed no persistent curiosity about his writing he was sure she knew he was struggling and he knew she was as well. Neither of them was sailing along at the moment. He was firm in his resolve not to return to the Harry that walked around telling her how he was going to fix it. Kate would be on her first break when these exams were over and he was looking forward to it. He hoped a week with no work would clear his head and a week with Kate would make him happy, and perhaps he'd see it in a new light. Yet from experience he knew it might do nothing at all.

Since school began, they managed all their weekends together except one when he was in the northwest. He saw her during the week for an early breakfast when she could or dinner occasionally or they ate lunch if he was in town. Their living arrangements were the same. Kate showed no inclination to move and he was surely in no hurry to change her mind. He was at his desk from eleven until dinner. When Kate wasn't there, he'd go back to it for a few hours after he ate. He couldn't blame her for any loss of focus. He was focused. Unfortunately he wasn't sure he was focused on the right thing.

Dr. Zuckerman and his band of Fellows were seeing him every three months now. He was strong, yet for the last two months was plagued by headaches for two or three days at a time at irregular intervals. He couldn't correlate them to weather, work, or travel. They were as mystified as he was. The scans were clear so they waited for the next one. At his last, they said Paul suggested he call if a headache came and they would do an MRI while he had it and see if anything was different then. It nagged at Paul perhaps as much as it did Harry. While they were very mild compared to anything he experienced before surgery, they were reminders of a time Harry wanted very much to forget. Kate knew nothing of them. The scans were clear so he was always able to tell her that and so far as he knew hadn't been foolish about advertising his pain out loud. He tried not to think of it. A recurrence was too horrible to contemplate. The pain that woke him frightened him but since there was no etiology, he kept the fear away by blaming it on his problems with the manuscript.

On this Friday he was again re-writing the pivotal house burning in chapter eight near five thirty when he heard the bell ring twice. Kate did it so he'd know she was there. He kept going, knowing she would find some amusement until he appeared. She never came in the office now unless he called to her. She was respectful of his work time as he was of hers. An hour later he thought again he had it solved and shut the computer down and went out to find her. She was asleep on the sofa.

She took two of her exams today and he expected her to be tired. It had been a long week and she had one more on Monday in perhaps her hardest course. She worked far too hard at perfection in her grades, something that no doubt came from her sports career. Perfection was no more likely in academics but she refused to accept that. There was more work than he expected and it puzzled him. First semesters were hard he knew, but she seemed to have far more to do than he ever experienced. She was always vague about specifics, and he never asked her to spell it out fully. He went into the kitchen and set out the food Elena had left for them and came back. He sat next to her and put his hand on her shoulder,

"Hey."

She took in air, rolled over on her back, and opened her eyes.

"Hi."

"Dinner."

She sat up, stretched, and went off to wash her face. He sat down and waited for her. She appeared in a few minutes and smiled,

"Looks good. I'd thank you for getting it ready if I could."

"No doubt. How'd the exams go?"

"Horribly. Too many equations about metal fatigue for my tastes."

"You want to wait to eat?"

"I would but I'm afraid I'll fall asleep again."

"You can always go to bed. I'll tell the people to keep the noise down and make your apologies."

She was toying with her food and he could tell she was as close to asleep as she could be on her feet. She frowned,

"What people?"

This was as tired as he'd ever seen her. He tried again,

"At the party. No need for you to stay up for it. I'm sure they'll understand."

"Who?"

"The people we invited."

"I don't remember planning a party."

"Fine, just eat something then and go to bed."

She yawned and took a few more bites, she drank her tea and yawned again,

"I'm sorry, I can't eat anymore. Save it for later. I have to sleep for a while."

She walked slowly to the bedroom. Harry ate the rest of his, wrapped hers, and rinsed the dishes. He looked in the bedroom. She lay across the bed sleeping soundly with all her clothes on. He got her half awake while he helped her undress and put her to bed. He went back to the office to see what he could do with chapter nine. He finished half of it around eleven thirty, went out into the cold night, and paced around the dark courtyard thinking about the house fire again and looking at the sky full of stars. When he went in, she never moved as he came to bed. He'd see what she remembered about the party joke tomorrow. He hoped she didn't get up early. She needed sleep and he worried because she shouldn't be that tired. She was trying so hard, he was afraid she was losing the ability to let go.

He was up early on Saturday. As she slept, he took a walk, and when he came back she was still in bed. He re-read the fire scene and near nine, he went to check on her. She was an early riser even in the worst of times. He debated leaving her, but knew she'd be unhappy if he didn't try to wake her. He shook her gently and she murmured something and her eyes fluttered open. She sat up with a moan. He handed her coffee.

"Hey."

"Hi, what time is it?"

"After nine."

"Come on, what time is it really?"

"Drink the coffee."

"It can't be that late." She sipped the coffee, "Mmm, this is good. I wish I could thank you."

"You can be grateful. Do you want to stay there longer? It's all right with me."

"No, I want to get up. I need a shower and I don't want to waste the day sleeping. Did you eat?"

"A bagel a long time ago. Tell you what, you take a shower and I'll get something."

"Can you, please? God, why did you let me sleep this late?"

"I wasn't in control of that, was I? I'm still wondering how you managed to get here last night."

She made a disgusted sound, gave him a peck on the cheek, and went to shower. Harry went to the café and was back in twenty minutes. He was heating the food when she came in the kitchen, wrapped her arms around him from behind, and hung there while he put it on plates. She ate with pleasure this time. They said nothing until they were done. As he finished, he looked up and she was watching him,

"I'm sorry."

"What for?"

"For leaving you alone last night."

Harry waved his hand in dismissal, "You were beat. You remember anything at all?"

"Some. You tried to feed me, talked some nonsense about a party I was going to miss about which there were many witty things I wanted to say, but I couldn't get my mind to work."

He chuckled, "You remember driving home?"

"I remember leaving there and getting here."

"That's not funny Kate."

"I know. This is over Monday."

"You going to study today?"

"Yes, but not right now."

Harry nodded as he sipped his coffee.

"When?"

She kept her head down now, "I need to leave before dinner."

He looked up quickly. She'd never done that. Yet there were never mid-term exams before either. He wasn't happy because he wanted her here at least for dinner. Finally he grunted, stood, and walked outside. The sun was bright but the temperature was pleasant. He kept going out the gate. He knew being angry was futile. She was working too hard yet nothing he could say now would change that. By the time he stopped thinking about it he was surprised to find himself leaning on the rock he sat on mornings. He stared at the mountains wondering why this was bothering him so much. Was he just being selfish Harry? Just because he wanted her company didn't mean he got it. He walked back and met her as she came out the gate with a question in her eyes.

"Let's go over to the houses in the Park. It's been awhile since you gave me a dissertation on early Arizona architecture." Harry said.

"You sure that's what you want to do?"

"We can eat in town and you can take your car home on the way and I'll drop you off on the way back."

By six thirty he was home and wandered around before he went inside. They spent the afternoon looking at huge saguaro cactus and the rare birds she always seemed to be able to find. They ate in town and talked as easily as always yet there was a distance to it. She seemed distracted and Harry thought maybe a little confused as to what was important right now. It was an odd day. He knew he needed to give her room to do what she needed to as she did for him yet he felt unimportant to her right now. He kept reminding himself that his need to control was showing again. He didn't control her, didn't want to, yet there was enough of the old Harry still in him to resent her absence because he knew it was her drive for perfection that made her leave. It was part of what he liked about her, but when faced with an inconvenience to him it bothered him.

It was dark before he came in and ate the food she hadn't last night. He was thinking again about chapter eight when she called,

"Hi."

"Hey, you take a break?"

"Yes. Look, I'm sorry about tonight, but I need this exam because I haven't done well in the course so far. I needed the time tonight."

"You told me all that today at least twice."

"I know, but I feel bad about it."

"Stop it Kate. You're spending too much time worrying over this. I understand what you're up against. Things will get in the way now and then."

"It's just hard for me to expect you to understand."

"I understand that you have a lot of work. I'm not sure why, but I never studied architecture either."

"This semester is hard and there are some extra courses I took because they were available."

"You picked up extra courses? Why? You knew it would be hard to go back full-time. What's the hurry Kate?"

"I didn't think it would be as hard for me as it is. When these exams are out of the way it'll be better, promise."

"Don't make promises about things you can't know. It may not get better, but we can talk about it another time. How long is your break after Monday?"

"A week. I want to spend most of the week doing nothing."

"Are you coming here Monday?"

"I'll be there before dinner. Are you working tonight?"

"Yes and no. I'm thinking about the house fire in chapter eight that I either made too serious or not serious enough."

"That's awful."

"Perhaps. It was necessary and I'm not certain how gruesome it will be yet. I may re-write it yet again. Anyway, I need to think it through and I'll find a basketball game tomorrow. Sometimes the high school kids give the old man a break."

"You're probably too good for them."

"I doubt that. Get some sleep tonight."

She sounded lost. He knew this was hard and now that he knew about the extra classes he understood better why she was struggling. She was brilliant but even the brilliant could be overloaded. He shook his head to clear it and read for two hours, checked his e-mail, answered a few, and took a shower and went to bed. His head hurt.

He woke at seven to a clear fall day. He did a telephone interview back east very early, went for the paper, and finished the crossword puzzle. He went up to Catalina, got in a half court game with some high school kids. After his team won the fourth, he waved to the next kid waiting to get into the game and came home. After a long hot shower, the headache he'd had since last night was still with him so he called the beeper number and the Fellow on call got back to him thirty minutes later. He managed to get him on the MRI schedule at seven the next morning. Harry said he'd be there if he still had pain, or he'd cancel if he didn't. The rest of the day was spent reorganizing files and backing up the latest chapters off the computer. Kate called before dinner. She was brief, distracted, and without apology. He didn't keep her. He told her he was going out in the morning. She showed no curiosity as to where or why.

He was still in pain and hadn't slept well when he got up Monday morning. He went down to Tucson and had the MRI. He was back at one after eating at the café and picking up tea. He was sure Kate wouldn't want to do much so he hadn't made any plans. He wandered into the office, but still had no idea how his protagonist felt about burning down his house with his mother in it so left it for now. It was after three when he heard Kate's car. His head was clear now and he hoped he'd have good news from the Fellow before the end of the day. He met Kate as she came through the gate. She was smiling and kissed him, but looked as if she hadn't slept.

"Is there anything in the car?"

"Yes, but it can wait. I need to put my feet up and drink some tea."

"Are you hungry or just thirsty?"

"Thirsty. Some of us ate after the test. Everybody wanted to dissect it. It was terrible."

"It's what you get taking a tough major with extra courses. You can stop talking now if you want."

"I feel so edgy I thought the air would go out of me when it was over."

"We could try the remedy you favored after the tests last summer."

"Not that sort of edgy, just nervous or something."

Elena came in then and they talked in Spanish for a minute or two about what he presumed was dinner before she disappeared into the kitchen.

"What's for dinner, you two get that far?"

"Sorry, yes, chicken."

"Good. Now, give me the glass and I'll get you more."

When he took the tea back, Kate's eyes were closed, but she was still awake.

"Got a question."

"Hmm?"

"Are you here until tomorrow?"

She looked at him and frowned, "Yes, why?"

"Because you never said. You won't make it until dinner now, so go in and sleep until then. You're pretty useless actually. I doubt you can have a conversation, so go."

"You don't mind?"

"Of course I mind. I don't understand why this is so hard or why you're so tired unless you were up all weekend. We'll get to that later. Here take this with you," he pulled her up and handed her the tea, "I'll see you at dinner."

"I just need an hour."

"Sure you do. We're eating at seven and I rather not do it alone."

She nodded and walked in the bedroom door, closing it behind her.

He wondered how long it would be before she snapped out of it. He knew what tired was because he was that way when he wrote all night. He never saw her this way before. He knew she was working hard but she had since he'd known her and her energy always seemed boundless. She was always up for anything and he didn't get it. Her study habits couldn't be that bad, she'd done well this summer and fall until now. More likely it was staying up all night to deal with the self-inflicted pressure of taking more courses than she needed and trying to be first in the class. She was in a hurry to get on with her life, he knew that but if she kept this up she'd never get that far.

His phone rang and he hurried in to pick it up off the desk. It was the Fellow. He said the radiologist read the scan and he wanted Paul to look at it. He was due back in the morning and he'd see it then. Harry pressed him, knowing by now that he didn't always get the full story from the MDs in training the first time, but he stopped there, just saying that Paul would call when he'd seen it. Harry thanked him and hung up. He had a terrible moment of foreboding as he looked at the dead phone. That wasn't the call he expected. If it was clear, there was no reason for Paul to see it. The radiologist and the senior Fellow could decide if it was clear and he was sure she was there on a Monday afternoon. He sat down at his desk and stared out the window. Something was there, there had to be. He felt cold. His eyes filled up. He stood, taking deep breaths trying to fight it. It couldn't happen again. It couldn't. He refused to believe it. He walked outside and glanced at the bedroom door. What would he tell her? He went out the gate, walked to the rock, and sat on it until it was nearly dark.

There was no sign of Kate when Elena left at six. He spent over an hour rationalizing the telephone call and convinced himself it was just the most junior Fellow being overly cautious. He felt fine. Kate stirred when she felt the bed move as he sat down and turned toward him. She wasn't fully awake as he reached for her hair,

"Hey."

"Hi, it's dark."

"It's nearly seven."

"It can't be." She pushed him away and rolled on her back. "I hate this."

"Take it easy Kate, it's all right."

She raised her voice for the first time since he'd known her, "No it's not all right. I just can't do this, I don't know how." She looked over at him, "I hate it, and I can't do it anymore. I can't."

She stared briefly at the ceiling and left. He went to the kitchen and she came in as he was getting dinner.

"I'll do that." She said quietly.

He watched her move with her usual efficiency yet she was silent and her frown seemed permanent. He wondered how long she'd felt the things she just said and what they really meant. She put the plate in front of him began to eat. He asked if she liked it and she only nodded and didn't look up. They ate in silence. Harry remembered the silent meals he'd eaten in his last days with Agnes so long ago. He caused those and vowed it would never happen again yet it was now and he hadn't done it. He was angry now. He wasn't sure what she hated he knew he hated this. When he was done he took his plate and tossed it in the sink with some force. She looked up, startled at the noise it made. He poured himself a small scotch and came back. He pointed at the glass and said,

"Do you want one of these while you talk to me?"

Her tired eyes held his a moment,

"About what?"

"Just tell me what you're thinking, what you meant before. All of it."

"I'm not sure I can."

Harry sighed and shook his head as he sat down,

"You know, Kate, back in the bad old days I lived with a wonderful woman. As it fell apart, we'd have dinners in silence like this one after I lectured her about the lack of progress on my book and how terrible my life was. You could hear a pin drop. Even though I was the cause of them, I hated it," he took a drink and looked at her, "I still hate that silence. I forgot how much until just now." He looked her in the eyes with what he hoped was a neutral expression and said as evenly as he could, "You need to tell me what's wrong. We can't survive silence. You can ramble as much as you want, I don't care, just don't be silent because if you are you may as well not be here."

She looked at him a long time. She still looked very tired. Finally in a very small voice, she said,

"I should go then."

"Is that what you do when things get difficult?"

"That's not what I meant."

"What did you mean?"

"I don't think I can explain it."

"Why?"

"It's too complicated."

He looked at her, "Clarity won't come from avoidance, Kate."

"I know but it's just . . . I can't . . . I should just go."

He drained the glass as he stood. "If that's what you need to do."

He took her plate into the kitchen. When he looked up, she'd left the table. He leaned against the counter. He knew she hadn't left yet but there was little doubt she would. She never said things she didn't mean and he wasn't going to try to make her stay. If she didn't have anything to say, she was probably right to go. He heard the gate close and walked to the door in time to hear her car go up the street. He hated this, yet he didn't feel he'd done anything to cause it so he wasn't going to feel guilty about it. Either she'd tell him what it was or she wouldn't. He was angry because she wouldn't talk to him and that she didn't find him before she left. If she was so unhappy and confused that she could leave him standing in the kitchen without a word and go home, he wasn't sure what they had here. He went through to the office and sat looking at the computer. He couldn't work now. There was too much to think about. The woman he didn't want to live without just walked out of the house in silence and his doctors saw something in his head today that could be horrible. Given that, his fictional protagonist's torment about setting a house on fire seemed unimportant now. He wanted to talk to Bill but didn't try. He was always calling with problems he needed to solve himself. Besides, soon there might be more serious things than a silent Kate. He got up and reclaimed the scotch bottle and his glass and sat in front of the fire trying to understand.

He failed.

Paul Zuckerman called at eight Tuesday morning,

"How do you feel now, Harry?"

"Fine Paul, why?"

"This MRI has something. Not sure what it is, but we need to be. Can you come in?"

"When?"

"Come in now and have another MRI since you're pain free."

"Do you want to see me?"

"We can talk later this morning. I don't like this. I'll put Marion on," Paul said abruptly and put him on hold. He sounded as upset as Harry felt when he got the call yesterday. Marion told him to get the MRI first and they would take him as soon as he could get there. Harry was sitting next to Paul looking at the MRI images before noon. Just coming in here reminded him of the most frightening time of his adult life. He waited for Paul to tell him what he saw because to his untrained eye there was nothing to see but the inside of his skull as it looked since after the surgery.

"Thanks for coming Harry. The same people who saw the tumor before surgery have or will see both these films now. There's something here. Can you see it? The biopsy was never ruled conclusive so it's possible there's a malignancy. It's at or near where we removed the tumor. Stan Morris thinks that's what it is, as he did in the beginning. I'm baffled because the scans have been clear until now, yet something must be raising your ICP's."

"I don't see any difference except perhaps a shadow. What does it mean?"

"The most likely answer is a very low-grade malignancy. What I can't understand is where the hell it's been on all the other scans, why it showed up now. We should have seen it after the swelling subsided."

"Is it from somewhere else then?"

"I doubt it. It could be new which would explain its absence until now or something I didn't see then yet is now apparent. We need to run the other tests to be sure and as soon as possible."

"I'm in the middle of the book Paul, on deadline now, I can't just skip in here and have 'the other tests', as you so elegantly put it. Authors do work every day despite the fact that most everyone thinks we're a bunch of dreamers."

"If it's what Stan thinks it is, you're going to have to do something soon."

"I can't just stop writing and see to this. What I do takes continuity."

He nodded, "I understand, but you need to find a way."

Harry thought that over. Was it possible that this was going to happen again, perhaps be worse? If it was malignant then he would be out of the contract yet he could die from it eventually. He couldn't delay finding out very long or he'd have problems with the publisher as well as his head. He snapped out of his trance,

"What do you think it is?"

"I don't know." He waved his hand at the film in disgust, "For all I know there's something wrong with the machine and this is a shadow. I wouldn't want to get comfortable with that, however. I want the tests done. We need to know why you have headaches again."

"How many days?"

"Two, there'll be much the same as the last."

Harry was silent. He needed to know.

"Tuesday then."

Paul nodded, "I'll have Marion schedule them. I wish I had better news, Harry."

"I suspect you're no more wishful than I am Paul."

CHAPTER ELEVEN

Elena came at four as usual on Thursday and seemed disappointed that Kate wasn't there. There was still no word or sign of her and while he was doing his best to suppress it, he was worried about her. The week was nearly gone. He dismissed the idea of calling. He didn't care about the protocol of who should call who he just wanted to be sure she was all right but didn't want to talk to her voicemail which was what he was afraid would happen.

He worked through the afternoon as he had all day Wednesday, stopping only briefly for an early dinner after a distracted goodbye to Elena today and went back to the office until after ten. He was getting there. The plot line was clearer and if he could only decide the right way to do chapter eight he might have a way to the end now. He went out to the courtyard and watched the stars when he stopped at eleven remembering that this was Kate's week off and the hope last week that it would just be fun. It was gone now and he had a new problem quite apart from her. He knew he was thrashing around, not solving anything or even thinking logically. Yet he couldn't. Paul's news this week was more than he could handle, and without Kate he felt lost. He was trying hard to stay focused but was losing the battle to thoughts of Kate and the nightmare of another tumor. While his health was the most important thing, it wasn't where his mind wandered most. It bothered him that being involved with her was taking him away from his work this much and he was very involved now whether she was here or not. Some of the anger he felt was because he let it happen, he'd let her become so important when he knew the book should be his main focus. He walked around the courtyard trying to shake his confusion. He missed her terribly yet he needed to stay with the thread of the plot until he his protagonist was headed in the right direction. Kate wasn't here. She said she hated it and couldn't do it anymore. Harry didn't know what "it" was, but surely they were at least part of it. From what she told him of her past, she would bury herself in her work now and forget they ever met. Whatever he felt for her wasn't going to change her and now more than ever he needed to concentrate on the book. She wasn't here and he needed to get used to it. He went in and answered the e-mail he'd been avoiding, edited the chapter drafts he'd re-written this week until nearly three, and went to bed.

He slept badly and woke at six Friday feeling no more focused or decisive than he was the night before, only angry that he wasn't better rested and knowing why. He got some coffee and resolved to decide chapter eight for good and went back to work. By the time he was certain the very first draft of it was better than the other six versions he'd tried, it was close to noon. He went back after lunch in hopes of concentrating the rest of the afternoon. The more devastating version of the chapter still made the most sense and he decided to leave it. He was sure Elspeth wouldn't agree but would have that argument when the time came.

It was after two when he sent the chapter to both Charlie and Elspeth convinced he was right and would wait to see what they made of it. He was about to go back to work when he heard the bell. There were two rings. Only Kate did that. He leaned back and looked out the door into an empty courtyard. There was no sign of her despite the gate being unlocked. He supposed it could be someone else and walked out. He saw her through the wire square in the gate standing in the hot sun with her head down and her arms wrapped tightly around herself as if she was cold. When he opened the gate she looked up at him without expression or a word.

"Why didn't you come in?"

"I wasn't sure you'd want me to."

Harry didn't know what to say. She looked drawn and her eyes told him she hadn't slept. He stepped back and beckoned to her. He let her pass and walked with her across the courtyard. As they reached the kitchen, she stopped at the counter and sat down. He poured some iced tea and brought it to her. He handed it to her. She nodded and drank it.

He leaned an elbow on the counter, still facing her and asked,

"Are you all right?"

She drank more tea and spoke without looking up,

"No." she said in that same forlorn whisper she'd used at the gate and he was sure he'd never heard before today.

He stood next to her and looked at the haggard dark eyes staring over his shoulder, so different from the ones he always saw. They were flat, lifeless, with circles beneath them. He wasn't sure where this was going. He had no idea what she was thinking. He wasn't sure he was happy she was here or that he wanted to know and was startled at the thought of that given what they meant to each other.

"Why are you here?" He said quietly.

She took a deep breath and looked up at him,

"I'm sorry. I didn't know what else to do. I . . ." she stopped and stared. There were tears in her eyes now and she lowered her head. She raised it again and tried to continue, "I'm sorry. I never meant to hurt you. I'm . . . I can't talk and . . . I'm . . . miserable . . . I'm sorry."

She stopped and began to cry.

"Kate—"

He voice was muffled, coming now between sobs,

"I left you. How could I do that? It was terrible to do that . . . to you . . . to us . . . I didn't want to . . ."

"Kate, stop. Tell me what's wrong. Can you do that?"

Between sobs she only managed to nod her head.

"What is it?"

"I just left you standing there." She said it in a tone of disbelief as if she hadn't heard him. She cried for a long time and then slid off the stool and pulled him to her so quickly the force of it startled him. She whispered almost fiercely, "I'm so sorry. Can you ever forgive me?" she said, "I just need to hold you now. Will you let me, please? I'm sorry . . . I'm so sorry."

He heard a short burst of Spanish and Elena's laughter in the courtyard. Nothing was clearer except how sorry she was because she refused to stop saying it the while she clung to him. She was sitting in the courtyard as he came out. Her color was awful and there were still those tired, lifeless eyes,

"I sent Elena home after I helped her get dinner," she said it so quietly in a voice not quite her own again that he barely understood her, "We do that when you're away. Was it all right?"

Harry walked over, leaned down, and kissed her the top of her head, "Sure."

"Do you want tea?"

"No. I want scotch. I'll get it." He said. When he came back he sat next to her and sipped his drink,

"Are we going to talk?" He asked quietly.

"I want to. I have to, no, I need to tell you things that are going to be very hard for me to say and I need to be sure you understand. Can we just sit here for now?"

"All right. Just don't tell me again how sorry you are."

She stared off at the mountains. Harry wasn't sure what to expect. He still knew nothing about why she left despite the fact that she'd been here more than an hour. Nearly five minutes passed now before she turned back and began to speak in the same whisper as before,

"Any relationships I had with men when sports, the game, and then the Olympics were the most important thing in my life were short and superficial. Since the last Trials I've remained good at making other things besides men important in my life. If a relationship lasted more than a month and became mildly complicated because anyone wanted that but me, I found a reason to be busy doing something else and made it go away. The world would go around a few times while I buried myself in whatever I was doing and whoever it was would be gone and my life went on."

She stopped now and looked away. Harry waited,

"It's been difficult for me since I left the team. I was certain I finally made the Olympics that last year. I'd been with the team nine years waiting my turn and I wanted it so very much. I was sure I deserved it. It was my life's dream, my whole reason for being and yet they took it away in one short conversation and never said why." She shook her head, "Someone decided. I don't know who or why because they never explained it and perhaps that was what hurt the most. For nine years I was a good sport, a good teammate, and yet no one had the decency to tell me why they left me off, why I wasn't going. I hated them for that and when I left I quit sports altogether, doing it, or even watching it. I'm still trying to prove them wrong, to prove it wasn't my fault. I swore then I was going to be the best at whatever I did so that no one could ever do that again. If it couldn't be volleyball it would be something else. I'd prove they made a mistake. It's quite irrational, of course, but can you understand? I doubled my course load this semester because I believed if I worked hard enough I could do it. Why not? I was just proving I was the best. Yet there was us too, and unlike the past when I would have made it nothing important and let you go, I couldn't. You mean too much to me, more than anyone I've ever known. We couldn't explain it to each other when we tried, but we knew it was special then and it's more than that to me now. I need you in a way I've never experienced before. Yet now I'm halfway through my first semester, staying up all night studying, scared to death of failing to be the best in the school of architecture and making you angry with me for perhaps the first time. I tried to push you away even though it's the last thing I want. I'm buried in my books making you somehow less important despite caring for you so much now it scares me. I'm afraid that I'll fail to do my best but even more afraid you'll decide you've had enough of me and this need for perfection. It's what I spent nearly a week thinking about. I worried that you'd never forgive me. I tried to understand how to fix it and I can't, not by myself. I know I need to change if I want you in my life and I very much want that. I just can't do it on my own. I need your help."

"Do you really believe we can make this work?"

"I want to believe it. I came because I want that. I want to tell you all the rest too if you want to hear it, to hear why I'm so obsessed."

"What do you want me to do? I mean, if you tell me but what do you want me to do with that knowledge?"

"Help me the way you always have. I need to find a way to get all this work done, and never let this happen again."

"That can't be done in silence Kate."

"I know that. I tried to let go and leave you as I would have done in the past and I spent the week regretting that. I never beg. You know me well enough to know that. I never have, not for anything. But I will beg you to help me if that's what it takes."

"Tell me what you meant when you said you couldn't do this the other night, that you hated this." Harry asked, "Let's leave the rejection and your obsessive need for achievement aside for the moment."

"I can't keep straight what needs my attention and when. I don't seem to be capable of doing both. School seems too important now. You don't matter less, but I can't seem to find the time for both. I can't balance it. That's what I hate, what I can't do."

"Maybe school needs more time now."

"I don't want that. I want a different life than that if you agree to stay in it."

She's more like him than she realizes, Harry thought. Nothing else came from her so he spoke softly now,

"When we decided there was something special about us, we agreed we'd find a way to do the work that made each of us happy and be together. We did and it worked for a while but it isn't now, is it? When you first went back to academics this summer you were comfortable coming here weekends with occasional time away when I was gone. Neither of us was working as hard as we are now. Now time is a problem. You clearly made it worse by doubling your course load in a difficult major. You're in a hurry because you think you got a late start at what you really want to do with your life. I understand that, but you have to live with that decision now. It means we'll see less of each other. Neither of us will die of that. We'll just miss each other a little more. There's no guilt or shame in it and it's not something to hate. It's the way it is, the way it has to be right now. It'll change again next semester and as I get busier and we'll need to adjust to those things too. You took on too much. Your impossible quest for perfection makes life hard for you but have to either change or live with consequences of that. You've brought all your baggage here more and more since you went back this fall. You're distracted, tired, and seem to be coming here weekends out of the mistaken belief that you're obligated to do it. You're not. You need to come when you want to be here, can be fully here, if this is to work."

She was watching him while he talked, "How do I just put it away? Not have it distract me while I'm here?"

"Come on, Kate, think. You're surely smart enough to answer that. You need to decide whether you can spend the weekend here and enjoy just being here or whether you'll be distracted because you need some or all of it to study. If the answer is study, stay home. Don't drag yourself over here exhausted just because it's Friday or after an exam because you said you would. You aren't making either of us happy doing that. Spending the whole weekend together was never a requirement, just how it worked for us early on. Just come one night, or only have dinner, stay a few hours and leave. I'll understand that for now." Harry paused and looked directly into her tired eyes, "If you come half asleep, eat in silence, annoy me, and hate yourself for trying to push me out of your life, I won't have to understand it because I won't live like that no matter how much we care for one another."

She was silent for a few minutes and then left and came back with her own scotch. She sipped at it and he waited. She put the glass down and said quietly,

"I am in a hurry, but I didn't expect that to affect us. We did say we'd have weekends together while it worked and it did long enough that I suppose I thought it always would. I didn't see this coming. I was exhausted the other night and knew I would be terrible company but I felt it'd be unfair to you if I didn't come. It was wrong. You've a right to expect as much of me as I do of you and didn't give you that. From what you say, I haven't been giving you that for a while now. I wasn't even aware of it until this weekend when all I could do was fall asleep, whine about how hard it all is and say I couldn't do it and leave you without so much as a goodbye when you got angry. I may never forgive myself for doing that. It was incredibly selfish."

She sat there thinking now so he went to get dinner out of the oven. He still wasn't sure they could fix this even given all she'd said. He understood now that her feelings for him were much deeper than he suspected, but whether that really mattered, whether it could all go bad again if she became distracted, forgot the priority she was trying so hard to give the relationship now was a question he couldn't answer. If it happened again, he knew all he would feel was worse.

She came in the kitchen now,

"Let me help. We need to keep talking."

He leaned back against the counter and watched her,

"How can you be sure it won't happen again?"

189

"I can't, can I? I've never asked anyone to forgive me or help me and all I can tell you is I want to change and I know I have to or I'll ruin what we have. I never want this to ever happen again." She tried to smile as she wiped her hands and leaned back with her arms folded, "I know what I'm capable of, how terribly selfish I can be and I know it isn't pretty and need to change that if I'm to keep you in my life. What surprises me is that you've know that and yet you must still care or we wouldn't be talking. My less attractive personality traits are a given to you. You understand me in some way no one else ever has and you don't tap dance around trying to change me. You help me understand, make fun at my competitiveness, talk back to me when I need it and never seem angry. You never try to run my life. You're always willing to talk it through, you just don't tell me I'd better be different or else. You're not threatened in any way."

They were sitting down eating now,

"Why ever would you threaten me? Is that what you felt you've done to the other men in your life?"

"I probably did in some way. At least the few I knew well enough. They needed to control me or control the relationship in some way I think. I'm not really sure."

"Not much caring in that sort of behavior but perhaps the wish to do that came from your apparent need to have it your way."

She stopped eating and looked at him,

"Do I do that with you? Try to have it my way?"

He looked up, "Yes, sometimes you do, but I don't just let you, do I? Perhaps my own obsession for control in my own life makes it easier for me to understand why you do it. We're a lot alike in that way." He stopped and looked at her, "I spent the week trying to work and I admit there was a part of me that wondered why I let us get so involved. I've told you how hard relationships were for me in the past when I was writing. It hasn't been hard with you until the other night despite how distracted you've been. I admit to thinking that it might be better if you weren't part of my life right now. This week seemed like the bad old days, albeit for different reasons."

"Different how?"

"I wasn't trying to be controlling or obsessive or ceaselessly lecturing you about how I wanted things to be. You were in the way of my progress for different reasons. You distracted me and intruded while I worked because I was worried about you. I missed you and I thought you'd gone, left as you've done before with the others," he looked at her and finished softly, "and I wasn't sure how I would manage that."

She stared at him a long time,

"I'm not leaving you unless you want that. I was wrong. I regretted it before I was home. I just didn't know how to fix it."

Harry sighed, "All right Kate, look, we are as we are. You didn't make me happy leaving. Given how we've always been it was probably the worst thing you could have done because you know I always try to talk through everything with you. You didn't leave because you wanted to hurt me. I know that. I have no reason to compete with you and your professional life and no wish to control it or you. I'll try now and then. You will again too. We both know that. But that's part of the Kate I met and have come to care so much for. I'm not interested in some ersatz version of her. We'll both have to work at this to get it right. That's what life is, isn't it, trying to get it right? We have mostly. We'll be all right if we keep talking because it will happen again if we stop and neither of us wants that."

They were eating again and she smiled now for the first time since she came,

"That's a very different way of looking at it than I've heard before."

"Well it's the way I look at it. If you like it, then we'll try to sort through the rest of it."

"I'll talk as long as it takes to understand it if you'll let me. I want to get this right."

Harry stopped eating and sat back and smiled,

"I know. Or rather, I know that now. I'm glad you're here."

When he came out of the bedroom the next morning, he heard Kate in the kitchen. She was wearing one of his shirts and making coffee. She looked rested despite the fact that they'd talked until very late. The sparkle was back in her eyes. She smiled her big happy smile when she saw him,

"Hi."

"Hey, I thought you might have made another run for it."

She laughed softly, "No chance of that. If someone runs for it now it'll have to be you. It's your turn. You want coffee?"

Harry chuckled and kissed her, "Are you offering anything else?"

She said sweetly, "Not right now."

"Coffee then. Just let me know if it changes."

She sighed and jumped on a stool, "you need food, don't you think?"

"I think we both do."

"Can we change the rule on thank you?"

"Why?"

"Because I want to."

"And if I don't?"

"We don't have to beat it to death, but sometimes we need to say it."

He nodded, "How do we decide when that is?"

"It'll be up to me."

"Really. Why?"

"Because I thought of it."

"Well then it makes perfect sense to you, doesn't it?"

She stood up and put her arms around his neck while he sat, "Just listen, please? I need to thank you for letting me come back and for spending most of the last day and night listening to me because there's never been anyone who did that, not even my mother. Thank you for how you handled all of what I said. I've never been that honest about my life before or said most of those things out loud. You helped me understand as you always do. I'm not worth the trouble that took, but you've deluded yourself into thinking I am." She kissed him, "Thank you."

He laughed, "My God Kate, you just said it three times and that's not beating it to death?"

"I needed to."

"You don't need to thank me for letting you come back. You were never really gone. I'm not delusional either, at least not about you, but I'm glad you feel better. We'll keep trying to get it right. Just keep talking. I'm sure there's more."

"There is, but everything looks much better this morning."

"Good. You look better too. You do wonders for that shirt."

"I'm not going to say it again."

"Say what?" He asked innocently.

"Do you want to go for a walk after we eat?"

"Can we walk to the park and shoot baskets?"

"You have the strength for that?"

"I can do it if you can do it, but as wonderful as it looks, I think you better wear more than my shirt."

Three hours later they were walking back. She wanted to play a game after they warmed up and as he suspected by the way she moved on the court this time she was much better than he thought. He taunted her about hustling him the last time, talked trash, pushed her, and only managed to win by six points. She certainly didn't quit on the court anymore than she did at anything else. They tried pushing each other off the path and laughed about it the way back.

As they reached Franklin Circle he asked,

"Are you staying tonight?"

"I want to."

"Let's shower and get some water then and we can settle whatever else may need it for now."

He was sitting with his feet up when she came back from her shower. She took a drink and settled in next to him with a huge sigh,

"You ran me out of my shoes up there. It felt good to work that hard. I think I need sports again. Getting that competition out of me on the court is good for me."

"It undoubtedly is but the last time you couldn't hit the backboard and today you turned into someone I didn't recognize. Don't ever give me that big smile and 'aw gee maybe I can keep up' stuff again."

"I wasn't hustling you. I said I could play when you asked. I just hadn't in a long time and wasn't all that interested the last time. If you hadn't pushed and fouled so much I might have beaten you."

"Don't talk nonsense. Next time I won't feel sorry for you and you'll be bawling like a baby."

"You think so, huh? We'll see how that goes, sport. I will beat you one day. Believe it."

He laughed, "You talk as tough as you play. Is that how you stayed single this long?"

She laughed that soft laugh, "What man wants to marry that?"

"All right, we'll leave basketball for now but just understand you don't scare me at all. Now, what do you need to get done before you go back to school, when? Tuesday?"

"Yes, I need to do some work tomorrow. The syllabi are out for the rest of the semester and I need to correlate the book chapters. I didn't do any of it while . . . when I was home."

"Will you hike up on the mountain with me on Monday?"

"Sure."

"Sounds fine then."

"Really?"

"Really what?"

"Are you going to ask why I won't stay longer?"

"You just told me why," he shrugged his shoulders, "so that's what'll happen. You leave tomorrow and come back Monday. When? Afternoon?"

She nodded.

"What else?"

They sat there in silence for a few minutes before she spoke very softly,

"Just be sure you understand what I say now, please?"

"I'll try."

"I've never been with a man as often or as long as you. Staying more than I do now, no matter what I feel, would seem as if we're headed toward more of it. I can't do that."

He looked at her and frowned. "More of it? More of what? You mean living here? Why do you think I would want that? Did I ever give you that impression?"

"You ask why I can't study here, things like that. Sometimes it sounds like you're hinting at it."

"Well, I'm not. Given all we've talked about since yesterday, I'm sure it would be a very bad idea for both of us. Now, do you mind looking for some food? I know Elena left some."

She gave him a hug and went to the kitchen. Harry sat and thought how unfair it would be to say anything about next week now. He wasn't sure what to do. She'd be in school and perhaps he could just have the tests and not tell her until he knew what the results were. He could, but there was no honesty in it. She'd been brutally honest about herself and most of her life in the last twenty-four hours because she said she wanted him to understand her. Many things she did and why she did them made sense to him now. He didn't care any less for her, perhaps more. He was sure she told him all of it as honestly as she could. He sighed and went in to eat. He had to tell her before Tuesday. He owed her that.

CHAPTER TWELVE

He was sitting in the courtyard late Monday morning when Kate came in and stopped in surprise when she saw him.

"Hi. You just come out? You look cold."

"I'm fine. Are you early?"

"I am. It was easier than I thought. That one course is still horrible. I just hope I get my exam marks soon so I know what I'm up against." She stopped and frowned, "I'm sorry, that was more than you needed to know, wasn't it. Are we still going up on the mountain? It'll be windy higher up."

"Let's not then. No point in freezing up there."

She went in the house and he stared out at the mountains from the doorway. He'd spent an hour out there wondering how to tell her. He hated most everything about life right now except her. He'd tried to reach Bill earlier and failed. He needed to talk to someone. He didn't want this on Kate now. She was still trying to figure out how to act around him and worrying about school already. He knew after the debacle of the past week she would try hard not to show it, but it was as inevitable. He met her with a smile as she came back.

She looked out,

"Can we walk? It isn't that bad."

He took his jacket from the hook and crossed the courtyard rapidly while pulling it on,

"Come along then."

She laughed and followed, catching him as he went down the drive. She tried to get in front so he held her arm. She stopped and turned to look at the rabbits as they neared the end and he went ahead of her but she chased him down and they pushed at each other trying to be the first in the gate. They were still laughing as they reached the house. He lit the fire and threw her a bottle of water as she landed on the sofa.

"That was enough. It's getting cold."

He sat across from her and drained the bottle he'd brought, "It is. Guess winter is back."

"Did you work?" She asked.

"Some. I tried to reach Bill and couldn't. Just thinking mostly."

"That your whole day, then? Just redial Bill's number and think?"

He chuckled, "No. I worked with Elspeth earlier this morning but for some reason I couldn't find Bill."

"Maybe they went somewhere. Do you need to find him for a reason?"

Harry didn't say anything.

She laughed softly, "You going to tell me or is it secret guy stuff?"

He said quietly, "No."

"What then?"

Harry stood and went into the kitchen. He needed to tell her but he knew it would end the afternoon of relaxation when he did. She followed him,

"What is it? Something's wrong, something's bothering you."

Harry looked at her, "I saw Paul Zuckerman."

"Why? You weren't due for anything."

"No."

She frowned now, "Then why did you see him?"

Harry walked back with more water and she followed,

"Will you tell me, please? Why did you see him?"

He sat and looked directly at her and spoke as evenly as he could,

"For the last few months I've been having headaches that last two, maybe three days without any pattern but with some increase in intensity. Nothing's been on the scans so they asked me to come in when my head hurt and they'd do an MRI while it did. They did one Monday and Paul called Tuesday and wanted another MRI then since I was pain free. We talked."

She stood very still watching him and spoke very quietly, "Why?"

"There was something there that made him unhappy."

"Something."

"Yes, something. You know how this goes, he wants more tests. The same people that he consulted before the surgery are looking at these films and Paul refuses to give an opinion until he does the tests."

"Are you going to have them?"

"I don't really have a choice do I? I'm on deadline and the book will require nearly all the time I have left if it's to get done."

"So you saw him the week I was . . . wasn't here?"

"Tuesday."

"Really. And you let me come in here and pile all my twisted emotions and deranged thinking on you while this was hanging over you and you never said anything?"

"We had problems to solve. I hope we did that. The tests aren't done so I don't know anything, do I? There was nothing to do then or now but speculate."

She stood over him now with her hands on her hips and raised her voice in exasperation,

"That logic amazes me. You amaze me. Your world is supposed to be all about you. That's what you always tell me and yet you let me talk for a day and a night about me and you had this to worry about? I'll never understand that, never. How could you do that? Why didn't you tell me?"

"Don't be upset Kate. You're still a nurse. You know the tests will tell us if it's anything to be concerned about."

She still stood over him staring down at him. He knew she couldn't argue with that.

"When are you having them?" She asked.

"Tomorrow and Wednesday. They'll admit me as a boarder since there's sedation the first day."

"Tomorrow. Why didn't you just wait until you were in the hospital and call me?"

"Don't, Kate. It's fine, they're just tests."

"It's not fine. I know what tests you're going to have so don't patronize me. When do you have to be there?"

"Before nine. I'll drive. They aren't debilitating."

"No."

"I'll be fine."

"No, I'm taking you."

"You'll be busy your first day back, I said I'll be fine."

"I don't want to talk about it. It's not debatable. I'll take you and leave early Wednesday and bring you home."

"There's no need for that. I've done this before. You need to get back to your classes."

"No." She said firmly as she leaned over him and looked at him very seriously now, "are you okay with this?"

"No, I'm angry, but I have to do this much, I mean I have to know, don't I?"

She sat down now,

"You seem so calm. I never saw you except for a few lunches before your surgery but I thought you'd be more upset."

He leaned forward in his chair, "Don't confuse my demeanor with my feelings right now. There was never a conclusive biopsy, and we both know what it could mean. But yelling about how unfair that is or speculating about what it is isn't going to change that today. I've done the waiting before. I will now."

"Does he think it's malignant?"

Harry raised his voice now, "He doesn't even know what it is yet. Leave it alone, please. I'm not happy that he saw anything, but I'm not going to hang out the black crepe until I know more than I do now."

"You really feel that way?"

"I haven't any choice except to whine about it to you and I won't do that. Now, are we going to watch the sunset and then eat or just sit here and have a wake before anyone is sure what's wrong?"

"Don't make a joke of this, it's serious." She said sharply.

"I know that better than anyone, Kate. I wish it were different, but it isn't and we can't change that today, can we? So watching the sun go down and eating with you sounds better than talking about this any longer."

She stared at him a minute and then tried to smile, "You're right. It does."

After dinner they walked outside and she pointed out the different constellations, a pool of knowledge she possessed due to her pilot father's fascination with them. When they got back she picked up her purse, and was quickly on the way out. She stopped when she reached the door,

"Don't get used to being alone. I need to talk to Nicole and get my clothes. I'll be back."

"I thought you were going home to read. I don't need to be in that early, you can come in the morning."

"I can leave from here. You want to watch *Casablanca?* I have it at home. Know it by heart."

He laughed, "I'd like that."

"I'll be back in a little while."

He watched her drive off and went inside. He knew she was worried but given her training he hoped she knew it was fruitless despite being upset at him for not telling her until now. Bill's phone went to voicemail again. As he stared into the dark, it struck him how few people he needed to tell about this. Being the loud imperious Harry served him well over the years, but it didn't make him many close friends. It bothered him now to think about all those years he was so very sure he was right and the only one who knew the truth.

He was staring out the window feeling sorry about the mess he might have to face now when he heard her come in.

"Hi." She said as she wrapped her arms around his neck, and held on tight. When she let go she stared at him as if she was going to say something. Her eyes were tearing up.

"Come on Kate, we don't know anything yet." Harry said quietly.

"I know. I'm okay. I even stopped for popcorn."

He was thinking about how much fun she'd made it as he checked in the next morning. As they stuffed themselves with popcorn, she talked to the characters in the movie, giving them all stage directions, telling them what they should do or say next. She was purposely wrong and it was remarkably funny. He was laughing so hard that if he hadn't known the story so well he would have to see the movie again to know what happened. He'd never seen this child like side of her wit before. It was wonderful.

She knew he needed her now and she gave him that. She wasn't being kind, it was more than that. He sensed now she decided something in the chaos and reconciliation of the previous ten days but he didn't ask what it was. She would tell him when she was ready.

He submitted to the tests as before and would see Paul again on Friday. Bethany came by to check on him before he left. She was now, he knew, the senior Fellow, but surprised to learn she also was a reader of his books. Kate drove him home and stayed for dinner. He was beat up from all the poking and prodding and intrusion of the testing but otherwise fine. She helped Elena cook and laughed with her and asked endless questions. They sat and talked quietly of little things until late. He tried to thank her but she overruled him and demanded he call if he needed anything. She never mentioned school.

Marion and the rest of the office staff tried to amuse him. He wasn't in the mood to be amused only anxious to know the test results. Bethany called and scheduled the conference time but gave him no indication of the results. He let her off with thanks because he knew Paul was the ringmaster of this circus and he'd be the one to deliver whatever news there was. He smiled at that. He supposed a Neurosurgeon's ego was at least the size of his own.

He was ushered into the office thirty minutes later. Paul wore his green scrubs and looked tired. He never wore them in the office if he could avoid it and forbid his Fellows to as well. Harry asked him why once and he said that patients were more comfortable hearing his sort of news from someone in street clothes. Harry saw it as the eccentricity of a thoughtful man.

"Hello Harry," Paul said rising and offering his hand, "Sorry Brian and I still have these on, but we did an emergency case very early and the conference schedule backed up so I'll apologize for the wait as well."

"Hello Paul, you look like hell."

Paul chuckled, "I appreciate the concern, author. Now, let's see if we can make up some time, although with you I'm just hoping for lunch."

"I know I wear you out with questions, although were the roles reversed, I believe you would be as exasperating as I am."

Paul laughed a genuine laugh, "True, we do seem to share a propensity for minute detail. Brian, give us both films at once please," Paul said briskly then as they walked to the other desk and sat down.

"Okay Harry. The one on the left is the first, the one taken when you had the pain. The other was when you didn't. See any difference?"

Harry still saw a very small shadow on the first one. "Yes, here," he said as he pointed at it, "I still see this shadow here on the first, but I can't find it on the second."

"Nicely done. This spot here, much harder to see than that one, is the same. It may or may not be part of the first tumor. It could be that or its new or the old one has recurred. A new one is so rare as to be nearly statistically impossible. A recurrence due to a low grade malignancy is extremely rare as well, but whatever it is it's there and we need to do something about it."

"Would that explain the inconclusive biopsy?"

"It fits but it may just be something I didn't see when I was in there due to the incomplete encapsulation."

Harry thought Paul was being rather off-handed about all this and wondered why. He was sure he had a plan. Finally Harry said,

"So what do you want to do about it?"

"Radiosurgery will take care of whatever it is. It's painless but there are several days of treatment in a row. The neuroradiologists will tell you how it works and how many they think best."

"You mean you don't need to go in there again?"

"No, I think radiation would be best now. No matter what it is it will do the job. I want you to talk to Jim Griffin. He's the best there is at this. He'd be the one I'd want if I needed it."

"Then I suppose I should ask him about how all this is going to work."

"That would be best. I can tell you that the worst of it will be the fatigue afterward. It lasts the longest. Any radiation runs the risk of raising the ICPs again, but the shunt should handle that or there are steroidal medications. He can be more precise."

"What sort of confidence do you have that it will work and I suppose just as importantly, how will I know?"

"I'm confident. It's minute and if it is a low grade malignancy, it's hardly on the scale from what we know from the tumor. You were vigilant about symptoms so it's very early in recurrence if that's what it is. Talk to Jim. Marion is setting it up and he and I have already talked. He wants to do it right away."

"The second part of the question. Should I wait and ask him?"

"That also would be best. This is still a reasonably new therapy, so there are some long term things to watch for and some that can occur a few weeks or months after treatment." Paul looked at him with a crooked grin, "I'm sure you'll have him go over all that more than once."

Harry smiled, "So we're done?"

"Talking, yes," Paul said as he stood, "We'll be glad to follow you for the aneurysm and check-ups while you're living here. I know you'll miss Dr. Stark, but I can't help you there because in three months she's finished here."

Harry chuckled, "I only need to talk to her now and then. Her voice has curative powers."

Paul laughed. "Be nice if such a thing was possible in this business." He shook Harry's hand, and told him he'd check with Dr. Griffin to see how it went,

"I have your last book, by the way. My wife loved it and I'm trying to find time to read it."

"That's very kind."

"All the best with the new one. I know this screwed up the schedule and I feel a bit responsible for that."

Harry waved a dismissive hand, "Not something you could influence it seems. I'll make sure you get a copy of the new one. I'd recommend sleep, but won't because I'm sure you have other things to do."

Paul laughed out loud as they left the office, "I'm afraid that will have to wait. Thanks for being so agreeable. See Marion and she'll give you the information for Dr. Griffin." He turned and barked as he went down the corridor that connected with the hospital, "Let's do this Brian I'd like to eat dinner at home tonight." The junior fellow hurried to catch up.

Harry went to Marion's desk and she told him Dr. Griffin would see him at one. He got directions to his office and as he walked out he sent Kate a text. He asked her to call and set out for the restaurant where they often ate down here. When he got there, she was standing by the door smiling,

"How'd you know where I was?"

"Where else would you eat? Knowing what you're thinking saves time."

They found a table and he gave her a quick summary of his meeting with Paul. She didn't know Dr. Griffin, but he bet she would know a great deal about him before the day was out. She thought it sounded encouraging. He said he'd wait and see. One thing at a time he reminded her.

"You're not as pleased about avoiding surgery as I thought you would be."

"There isn't much to be pleased about is there? I may or may not have a malignancy. I have to have a procedure I know nothing about and I have no feeling yet for how it will affect my work. I need to move the book along, Kate, there's a lot left to do and much of my work will be up in the city soon."

"You need to be healthy, isn't that important?"

"Unfortunately it is, but I can't stop for this. I have to work. It would be like asking you to drop out of school. I'm sure we'd argue about that."

She was quiet and stared at him for a minute,

"Go see what he has to say and we'll talk tonight."

"Can you stay for dinner?"

"I'll stay the weekend if it's all right. Things are slow, just a lot of reading. I can get a lot done here before my late class."

When they walked out she uncharacteristically held his arm and kissed him in public and whispered, "I'll miss you," before she melted into the crowd in the street.

Dr. James Griffin was twenty years older than Harry. His mien was professional and clinical. He possessed none of the warmth of Paul Zuckerman but he was didactically efficient and knew what he wanted to do and how. They discussed how the Cyberknife worked, and how it would remove the "miniscule remnants" of the tumor. He wanted to start on Thursday. He recommended they do the maximum five treatments which meant he would be treated everyday through Monday. There would be a scan a week later. Harry was free to do whatever he could tolerate. The only preparations were x-rays he could have now to be sure the frame for the precise radiation beams would be positioned correctly. The treatment, while only fifteen minutes, took preparation so Harry should plan to be here at least two hours each day. Seven o'clock was as early as he could take him. Harry had the x-rays, came back to the office and wore Griffin out about the risks and then had him tell him again about any possible long term effects until he felt he knew all he could. Griffin never raised his voice or lost his temper and was clinically professional to the end. Paul must have warned him. When Harry finally stopped, Griffin said,

"There's a number for you to call if you need to change anything. Elsa handles all that. I think you'll be fine when this is over, although remember to be aware of the fatigue. You're young and in excellent shape so I don't expect it to be debilitating for too long. We'll do the MRI in a week and then some cognitive tests in three weeks or so. Do you have someone at home? You can't drive the days of treatment, or try to do much."

"Yes, thanks. Paul told you I'm on a deadline I believe. Is it a fair assumption that I'll be able to work soon?"

"You can as soon as you feel up to it. You'll tire very quickly but go at whatever pace suits you. The brain doesn't enjoy being disturbed as you learned from your surgery. We need to see how you react. One of the MDs will ask you about all that each day. I'll look at the results and talk to you again when you return for your scan. Elsa will call you to set that up. If that's all, we'll see you Thursday morning."

"If I have any questions before we start, may I call this number as well?" Harry asked.

"I hope you will. Elsa will give you the packet of references and articles you asked about."

When he came out into the bright cool sunlight he felt a bit better, yet wanted to know more before he became too comfortable.

He was home around four and read the material Griffin had given him. Once started, there was a variety of side effects. He'd see what Kate knew about all that. He talked to Elena about coming all day again beginning Thursday and perhaps working over the weekend and she was willing to do it. He asked if Joseph would be around next week and she said he was coming Monday or Tuesday.

He called Bill and told him. He and Martha were over on the coast and there was no cell phone reception all week,

"Damn Harry, you ever got anything but bad news?"

He sighed, "Not lately, no. I'll avoid the hospital this time at least. It's hard to tell how ill I'll be."

"When does it start?"

"Thursday very early and they're going to do five, so I'll be done Monday."

"You got help?"

"Kate's close by. Elena will go back to full time and Joseph is around. Kate's good about being here, but I can't ask her to stay, school just started again."

"Why not? Ya need her don't ya? Or are you two growin' apart down there with her school and the writing?"

"We're doing fine, William. She's just busy. She'll be here over the weekend."

"That's been goin' on a long time, why is she still livin' somewhere else?"

"Because we want it that way. I don't want her living here and she prefers that as well. I'm having enough trouble writing as it is. She's here weekends. It's fine."

"Sounds pretty rational. You serious about her?"

"There's time to decide. We're both very busy and I have this to deal with right now."

"Busy is no excuse. Busy is what life is Harry. One of these days you're gonna' run out of that precious time you're always talkin' about."

"I know. I need be healthy though."

"Be good if you could stay that way too. You need me to call anybody?"

"No. I needed you to know because you have my Directive and they have your name as the last time. Let's see how it goes. I'll call you next week."

"Call me Wednesday. Sooner if the schedule gets changed. And text me Kate's cell number when you hang up now."

"I will, and by the way, never get near her with a basketball. I have to work very hard."

"Damn."

Kate rushed in at six apologizing for the time and went straight to getting dinner out of the oven. She was a fount of information on Dr. Griffin and the efficacy of the procedure while she did. She looked at the references while they were eating. When she was done she sat back,

"Well, this isn't going to be fun. You're going to be tired, have no appetite, and feel terrible for a while. It will get worse every day until it's over and then slowly better. The first day you'll think you're fine but by day three or four you won't want to eat, be sure you have the flu, and want to sleep most of the time."

"Where did you read all that?"

"I'm a nurse remember? I also have a computer and I know people. Two nurses and one of the docs I know are working in radiosurgery now so when I called around to get more than what the computer had on Griffin, I found them. He's a straight arrow, Stuffy sort, but very good at what he does. He practically invented this stuff." She smiled, "I can be useful now and then."

"You're always more than useful. I'm glad you could find out that much."

"Just don't thank me. It isn't a thank you situation."

"I wonder why I agreed to let you decide that."

"Doesn't matter now it's my rule," she said as she finished in the kitchen and came back and sat on the sofa with him. "Now, what else do we need to do?"

"Do?"

"Do you need to talk to anyone?"

"I told Bill and you. He and Martha needed to know. He's listed as my next of kin and has my Health Directive. That's all for now. He has your number, by the way, and I'm sure he'll call you soon. I asked Elena if she could go back to full days and she can. I said I'd let her know Monday about the weekend. I'll talk to Joseph on Tuesday."

"About what?"

"He'll get me there and back."

"No."

"Don't start that Kate, you have enough to do without working around this every morning for a week. Go to class, do what you need to do."

"I need to do this."

"Come on Kate, you don't have the time for both."

"I know that."

"Meaning?"

"Meaning I'll call Elena so she doesn't cancel any plans for her weekend. She should come back full days but not over the weekend. I'll come here Wednesday night. When Elena's here during the day I'll go to class. Two days are over the weekend and I'll be here then. You're done Monday and I'll see how you feel. You're not staying here alone until I say you can."

"Now wait," Harry protested, "you can't do that. What about all the work you'll miss?"

She leaned close and spoke softly in his ear, "I can do it because I want to. Being perfect in academics isn't the most important thing for me for now, caring for you is. So that's how it will be."

He didn't know what to say. She was so certain, so in control, as if it was the natural thing for her to do.

"You know, I thought I figured you out and now you do this. You're supposed to be a selfish competitive high achiever with little concern for anything but your work and in a big hurry to be a success," he smiled, "you know, as awful as me. Now you want to watch me sleep." He shook his head, "I'm never going to understand you."

"You have most of me right, although I've thought a lot about all that since we talked it all out and I don't like that woman much." She shrugged, "I'm trying to do what you said and forget being disappointed about missing the Olympics and remember how much fun I had with the team and how lucky I was to be allowed to try. It makes me much happier," she smiled, "I still to want to succeed at everything I do. Being sure you're all right is what I want to succeed at right now."

Nicole dropped her off on Wednesday night and on Thursday Bill and Martha called from the airport in the afternoon. Harry only heard her end of the conversation. She and Bill were talking like old friends while Harry was dozing on the sofa more from the early rising than the treatment when she came in and told him how great she thought it was that they'd come. They stayed for two days and as Kate had predicted he'd felt reasonably well, especially with the house full of noisy, laughing people to cheer him up. Bill and Martha left early Saturday, satisfied he was in good hands. When he came home from his treatment he felt like he was getting a cold and he was more tired than he'd been the previous days. Kate got him to eat something and insisted he go to bed. She stayed and talked before he slept.

"If you only have two friends, those two are as good as you could ask for, you know that don't you?"

"I have three counting you or maybe four if I count Chris. There are wonderful though. Bill's like a brother, I told you that."

"He cares like one."

"As I do for him. You enjoyed them, it seems."

"They were so nice to me. He called me last week and it was like talking to an old friend. I still can't believe they just showed up. He never mentioned they were coming."

"He did the same when I had surgery. He's incredibly busy and I'm not sure how they find the time."

"You'd do it for him, wouldn't you?"

"Of course. I hope I never have to, but I would."

"It not hard to tell how much he loves Martha. The look in their eyes when they talk to each other is like a neon sign."

He chuckled and coughed, "He's loved her uxoriously for a very long time. Never been afraid to show it either."

She leaned over him. "Here, drink some water and try to sleep. I'm going to study for a few hours. Call me if you need anything. Oh, and here," she handed him an envelope, "read this before you fall asleep. I got it Thursday." Then she was gone. He opened the envelope. It was her mid-term grades, a 3.4 GPA while taking two semesters at once.

He saw Dr. Griffin on Monday after his last treatment and would go back in a week. He felt ill most of the time now and Kate remained, using the spare bedroom to study. Late Monday while he was trying to get a piece of chicken down Harry asked when she was leaving and she said she'd go to class while Elena was here and come back before she left until she thought he would be all right alone. He tried to protest but she rolled her eyes and gave him that deadpan look he knew so well. She made him go back to bed when he nodded off on the sofa and she stayed with him until he slept talking quietly about how this was the end of it now and how he shouldn't try to rush back to the book. When he woke in the morning, she was gone. He lay there thinking of how wonderful they all were to him and how little he'd done to deserved it.

CHAPTER THIRTEEN

Kate stayed over two weeks and was finally satisfied he was without any side effects other than fatigue. He went back to writing. The fatigue dogged him and he slept when he had to and worked whenever he woke no matter what hour of the day or night. He spent three weeks that way and saw Kate when he could. Often it was for an early breakfast or a late dinner. It was much as it was when she was working. She was baffled as to why he felt the need to get up in the middle of the night to write, but never did more than wonder about it and he never said anything about it unless she asked. Surely a different Harry than the last time who would have shared how hard it was with anyone who would listen. He felt better about the plot now. Charlie was happier and Elspeth was relieved when they saw his progress in these revisions.

Kate worked just as hard through the rest of the semester and when she missed a weekend, she'd come by for a walk or stay a few hours, or he met her on her way back. She seemed happier not to be expected to have a routine. Their caring seemed stronger but gentler too, more as it was in the beginning, a conveyance of thoughts without speech, and comfort in just being together.

She managed her finals without incident mostly by staying in the library most of the time and away from the house until they were over. She had Christmas and all of January off between semesters and planned to work so she would be ahead of her bills. Bill and Martha wanted them to come to Hamilton for the holiday. He needed to work in the city so he asked Kate if she'd go and stay with them while he did. She surprised him by eschewing work for the first two weeks without hesitation. He put her on the train for Hamilton when they reached the city and he stayed four days before the holiday to work with Charlie.

She and Bill played basketball nearly every day. She was on a mission to beat him at least once before they left. She teased him mercilessly and Harry never doubted that she would win, although he never convinced Bill he should be concerned. He was on the phone late one gloomy afternoon when she came bouncing in laughing. Bill was walking behind her looking annoyed. Harry laughed so hard he had to end the call. She'd won by a point. Bill just shook his head, turned on his beloved sports channel, and sank into a chair wiping his face with a towel and mumbled about how dirty she played.

He went back to the city for four days the following week. There was still some work to do, but the final draft was nearly done. They found it hard to leave Hamilton, or more specifically Bill and Martha. Kate tagged along with Bill to work for a day while Harry was gone and went with Martha to a charitable function or two. She declared Amanda one of the brightest and beautiful women she ever met. She also decided she was insanely funny after she listened to her take on Harry with unusual vigor one morning over coffee about Wagner's *Rings,* opera in general, and why they'd never married. Kate declared it all wonderful and said she wanted to come back again.

She registered for her classes when they came back and worked night shifts. Just as last time it was going to be an exhausting grind because she stubbornly refused to lighten her load. Her GPA for the first semester had stayed well above 3.0 and she was dug in about doing it again. He argued with her, reminding her of the consequences last year. She insisted it wouldn't happen again now that she knew her limits and his expectations. In the end, he let it go. If she failed to live up to her standards of perfection she needed to learn that on her own. If that affected them then there would be consequences they might not be able to control but he wasn't going to try to bend her to his will. He respected her and what she was doing too much for that.

Harry would have the book done soon and talk of how to market it was in the initial stages. Elspeth agreed that with all the electronics and remote capabilities available since his last tour, he could do much of it from no further than Phoenix if the publicity department could grasp how to set it up that way. Aside from the obligatory trips to New York and Washington and LA then, he thought he could do the other interviews close to home. They were thinking it over.

Over the two weekends before school began they went hiking and enjoyed the last of the respite. Kate was ready to get back and he was going to be in the northwest most of February. He would miss her but she said it couldn't be helped because it was part of his job and needed to be done. She could be as rational as she wanted to be, Harry thought, he'd grown too used to having her with him now and he didn't need this test.

As the month ended she came one afternoon with sandwiches. It was warm so they ate in the courtyard. He knew she wanted to talk when she refused a walk after lunch and brought some water back with her when she got rid of the lunchtime leavings.

"I've reconsidered walking but let's do it before dinner. I need some advice right now."

"I hope I have some."

She slouched down in that position she took so often when she had serious things to say,

"I want to change majors."

"Now? Just like that?"

"Next year. I saw my advisor and he agrees that I'm wasting my time with all this steel and rivet stuff. I'm never going to build a building or a bridge, except in someone's garden. I need to know more about the plants. I'll have the basic structure courses by spring."

"So you're settling on landscape architecture?"

"I really think I'll enjoy it, but I need to know the plant material. I'd like to own a nursery some day but concentrate on landscaping. I get the symmetry, the Feng shui, and all the brick and mortar materials now but I don't know the plants well enough. All the business and computer courses I've taken will help me run it but botany would help me know the varieties of plants. It's grounded in biology and I have lots of credits from nursing school in the physical sciences. My advisor guessed I might be a junior or better depending on grades and credits. I wanted to know what you thought of the whole idea before I went off and tried anything."

"It's a great deal to think about. Would you want to transfer as well?"

"I've thought about it. It might be a good idea to go somewhere more temperate to learn the plants since I have no intention of trying to do landscaping here but it would be a lot of trouble so let's leave that for now, what do you think of taking botany?"

"I think it makes sense."

"I'd rather change here and see how it goes. I need to talk to more of the botany people."

"Is there a way to shorten this up? I don't mean doubling your courses again, but perhaps someone in administration can help in understanding the credit transfer issue. You need to ask more questions than you have. Talk to as many people as you can while you re-think it. Universities are strange places, like corporations really. There are many ways to get where one wants to go but you need to be sure you've asked the right questions of the right people. Often the alternatives are mysterious to the advisors. The administrators will make the final decisions anyway."

"Be easy enough to do. I will. Bill and I were talking about all this up there and he introduced me to one of his clients who has that huge nursery out by the main highway. You know the one?" He nodded and she continued, "He and his wife run it and were very helpful. I guess he helped me decide it's what I really want to do. He thought having a degree in botany would be best. Besides the finances, I can't just rent a place and start a business. I have a lot to learn so working for someone is going to have to be the first thing. Most states have work requirements for the certification of landscapers. He even offered me a job for the summer to be sure I like it as much as I think I do."

"You did get around when I was working, didn't you?"

"Do you mind?"

"No, no, of course I don't mind. You're thinking seriously of it as a career."

"I need to talk with more people here about how long this will take. There may be something I've missed or someone I didn't ask. Maybe I could work up in the northwest this summer to see how I like the business."

"You'd go because Bill and Martha are up there and you met some nice people?"

"If it was for three months, yes, I think what I'd learn would make it a legitimate reason. The fact that they are there and you'll be in and out of the city makes it reasonable, doesn't it?"

Harry frowned, "My time up there will depend on the book, remember, so don't I don't know about that yet. Hamilton is an easy place to like though."

"It is."

"That's your decision, of course. I do think you could graduate earlier, but you need to find out."

"Okay, I didn't expect to get this done today. You helped me think it through and I have a better idea what I need to do."

By late February Kate was moving through this semester with far more ease than the last although her obsession about grades and the stupendous course load she was carrying kept her in the library late many nights. She was more relaxed now and so far shown the capacity to turn it off when they were together. Harry began what seemed like endless trips to the city. It was more difficult to get there and back quickly from Tucson. Chris was still a marvel at finding flights that he wasn't even aware of and he insisted she was the wrong profession. She protested that she wasn't cut out for the chaos of booking cruises and adventure vacations for seniors and children.

It seemed that he was in the city more than he was home and hated being a hostage to the process now as he tried to schedule an early summer release date and met resistance to that and his desire to do as much as he could from the affiliates in Phoenix rather than travel as much as he had the last time. The publisher wanted to hold the book for a big fall release and he thought this book was better as a summer book unlike the more introspective and allegorical *Country*. It wasn't clear to him why doing the tour remotely was so difficult for them to understand, but he was becoming convinced that since they'd done little of it, they didn't know how. The pre-tapings and the use of affiliates and the need to have two stations involved and the other technical details were such that he frankly didn't think they understood how to manipulate it. It would be much easier for him but less straight forward for them. They knew how to book a station to a date and program, get him on a plane and find a hotel and then send him on to the next place. That was what they'd always done. There was a need for that in the media markets in New York and other east coast cities as well as Los Angeles and San Francisco, but he saw no need to crisscross the country when he could be here and still give it the time and attention it needed.

Time was moving quickly now. They argued over précis material and Charlie nitpicked edits to the largely completed manuscript. He spent all his weekdays and many nights polishing and trading pages back and forth.

Kate was surprised at how much time went into publishing a book beyond the writing. Like most of the world, selling a book wasn't something she'd given any thought. The collaborative work that went into setting up the tour, deciding a release date and where one went to have the most impact was a revelation to her. The publishing and the selling was something quite different from his time of near solitude while writing.

Kate still stayed at the house during his absences. She brought Nicole "home" with her many nights for dinner now and continued to enjoy her time with Elena. While he missed her and she missed him, they accepted that. It would be no different if they were living together or said vows. As long as each wanted to be what they were passionate about, separation was necessary for now.

He met with the publicity people for nearly a week about the tour and when the book would be released. They only reluctantly discussed the former except in broad terms until the latter was settled. Harry was frustrated by their enchantment with the idea of a fall release and remained adamant that it be a summer book. The end came when they decided Thursday morning that they needed to talk to the VP. He left after he made it abundantly clear as only the public Harry could, that so far as he was concerned, two weeks was long enough for them to ponder it.

His plane was late leaving and weather delayed his connection. He was now scheduled for a very late arrival in Tucson. He regretted he hadn't the time for a drink with Chris this trip. He sent her a text and got only a curt reply. He decided that she was either tired of his excuses or found better company. He sent one to Kate during his layover. He asked her to call if she could. His phone soon rang,

"Hey."

"Hi, I'm at the library and when I got your message I thought I'd get some fresh air and call back while you were still there. You may not get home before dawn at the rate you're going. Why so late?"

"Oh, a little of everything. Rain, the plane needed to be fixed before we left up north and I thought I might miss this one. The weather has everything delayed." He sighed, "Have I told you that I hate this going back and forth?"

She laughed that wonderful small laugh, "You've mentioned it."

"I shouldn't complain. You're being good about not whining about what you're going through, I don't know why I feel compelled to do it tonight."

"It's okay. You've been on these trips all month. The travel can't be much fun. Did you get a lot done?"

"Some, we can't agree on a release date. They're taking it to the grand Pooh Bah to ponder. The little cretins are incapable of independent thought apparently. I'm beginning to feel like a hostage to their problems and I'm unhappy when that happens so feel free to yell at me if I get pompous and annoying."

"You don't often."

"You've never been around when I was going through the publicity process. You may find I have some less than angelic characteristics for a while."

She laughed again, "That sounded pompous."

"I'm sorry Kate. I just want to be home. I miss being there."

"I know."

"How're you doing?"

"Busy, but coping. My exam is very late tomorrow and I don't like that much."

"I don't either. Although at this rate I may get home after you do. I won't wake you whenever I get there."

"You better wake me. We can have breakfast too if you can manage to get up early. I need to come in to take care of some things."

"I'll be up. This is the last mid-term isn't it?"

"Yes. Are you going to be here?"

"I'll refuse to leave if I must."

She chuckled, "We'll see how that goes. There's a play on campus this weekend, are you up for that?"

"What is it?"

"Ibsen, *A Doll's House*. Nicole and her latest asked if we'd go."

"Fine, I haven't seen it since college. We'll have to do that. What else?"

"I found out more about changing majors. I'll tell you about it when we have time."

"Is it what we've been talking about?"

"Some new wrinkles. I better get back. Aside from the exam that needs attention, I'm freezing."

"Then get inside. I'll see you before dawn I hope."

"I miss you."

He chuckled, "You say that a lot now. It started when I was sick. I'm not complaining, I'm just not certain why you always do."

"I know why." She said softly, "see you before morning."

He hung up wondering what she meant. It was something nice anyway and it made him smile. Surprisingly his flight left soon after and he was unlocking the courtyard gate at two. She'd left the outside lights on and he tried to be quiet. He needn't have. She was awake to welcome him home.

He stood with a coffee cup in his hand at six thirty the next morning watching her car go up the street. He smiled at how cheerful she was when he knew this was another grind for her that would last well past eight o'clock tonight. At least it was over for a week then and she was coming back here.

His fingers hurt from holding onto the phone. He was on it all day. He did laundry, unpacked, and ate lunch while he talked. He talked to El who relayed information to the VP's office. He talked to the PR people twice and it appeared they were coming around to his view on the earlier release date. How the tour would be done was yet to be settled.

Elena came and he spent some time talking to her. He hadn't much lately and wanted to be sure she was still happy with all the comings and goings. She was pleasant and direct as always. She was voluble about the beautiful "Katarine," as she called her, whom she now clearly treated as the daughter she never had. She enjoyed having her stay there and teaching her to cook. After eating her wonderful magic chicken recipe he took a shower and sat down to read his manuscript vowing to go straight through without so much as a margin note if he possibly could. He always did it before publication. He wanted to know what it would be like to pick it up as a first time reader. He knew Kate's exam was in the early evening so he had no idea when she'd get there. He was halfway through and fighting the impulse to edit when the effects of his late night and early rising overtook him. He left the lights on and went to bed. He was just falling asleep when he heard her come in and the shower running. He rolled over and smiled. It was nice to have her come in like this and he wondered what it would be like if it was this way all the time. Then she was there with a whisper, smelling of berries and soap.

They went to dinner and the play Saturday with Nicole and her date. The production was very well done and as he watched he knew Ibsen wouldn't be enamored of Kate and her need for a life of her own any more than Torvald was of his Nora. They were out late and by lunch Sunday they were still browsing the paper, neither seemingly in any hurry to do more than that. She was issuing idle threats now and then about beating him at basketball, but he knew she wanted to talk about her new plans, so he settled in for what he hoped would be a quiet day.

CHAPTER FOURTEEN

"Now," he said as he returned to the courtyard after a trip to the kitchen for snacks, "are you ever going to tell me about these, what did you called them? Wrinkles you've introduced into your plans are, or do we have secrets now?"

She laughed, "They aren't secret. I'll tell you now if you want."

"Then why don't you do that."

She made a face at his sarcasm,

"I went back through everything I knew about changing majors again at least twice and talked with everyone I could find on campus who knows anything about it including an assistant dean and the provost's assistant. There is, as you have always suspected, a quicker way to get my degree. With all the credits I have now and one more semester at the same rate I can qualify for a bachelor's in botany in December if I change in September. That's the plan now wrinkles and all."

"That's remarkable."

She chuckled, "I'm working on succinct."

It meant she'd be done in less than a year and getting a job to do her work requirements. Where she'd go was a question, but the book was done and leaving Tucson in December wasn't a problem assuming he was going with her.

Harry looked down at her, "There had to be a way and I knew you'd find it if you kept asking. Will it break your heart not to have a degree in architecture?"

"The department I get my degree from was never an issue. I just want to be trained well enough to do what I think I'll enjoy more than being a nurse and I think I found that. If I haven't, I can always go somewhere else for the rest of the architecture. My grades are decent enough."

"Yes, I'd say the 3.4 GPA you're carrying with all those courses is decent. Stop being so humble." He smiled at her as she watched him from her favorite position with her hair over her face, "maybe they want you out of there so they can re-adjust the curve."

She laughed softly, "It impressed them."

"I'll bet it did. Just remember you owe me for that carrel."

"You worried about your money?"

Harry laughed, "I'm not sure. You're a pretty sketchy character. Everyone knows that. You doubled you class load every semester and never mentioned botany to me so who knows what you're capable of now?"

"I didn't tell you because it didn't matter."

"I'm not sure I buy that. We deal in honesty around here."

"You knew I was taking extra courses."

"I did, we talked about it back when you registered and you characteristically refused to listen to reason. I told you then if you couldn't handle it you needed to find that out on your own. I'm sure you are delighted to get your degree at the end of the year. Now tell me about the rest of the wrinkles."

"How do you know there's more?"

"I know."

She sighed and stood and then sat on the armrest and looked at him, "Just stay with me here, please, because I know what I want to do, but it means leaving here this summer, and I'm not sure how it will work."

"Does it involve a man in Hamilton named Caruso?"

She slid onto the cushion again, "Did Bill say something to you?"

"Whatever does William to do with this? I know the Carusos were enchanted by you and would employ you, you told me that. You thought it was wonderful and I'm not surprised you'd think of going up there."

"I called Bill while you were gone. He talked to Mr. Caruso to be sure he was serious. He was and he offered me a job. I thought he might have told you."

Harry watched her now as she searched his face. He knew she was looking for a sign of how he felt. He couldn't refrain from frowning because it would complicate his life enormously. He still needed to finish the negotiations about the book's release date and the tour. Kate didn't know that because she'd never asked what his plans were for the summer. He was annoyed that she was planning her life on her own again, but getting angry at her was pointless. He needed time to settle his plans but also knew by the tone of her voice she needed something now.

"Okay. All things being equal, it might be a good place to start. Bill would have discouraged you if he knew a reason not to work for him. It's a nice opportunity to be away from here in the summer if that's what you want."

"I think it would be fun to be up there and I'm sure I could learn a lot from them. Would you be able to get away from the city when you're there?"

"I won't be in the city if the timing can be worked out. I'm still negotiating with the publisher about the release date and the final manuscript approval, so there's no point in talking about my summer since nothing about the promotion of the book or even when it will be released is certain. If it works out as I hope, I'll be on the east coast first and then LA. I hope to do the remote interviews from Phoenix in late spring and summer. There are sound business reasons why I want to publish before summer but it isn't something I get to decide now. They own a good part of me if I want them to promote the book and these aren't only my decisions now."

"I thought you could work from the city and we'd be together weekends."

"Well, it's a real possibility it won't work that way, Kate. If you work forty hours a week there all of the late spring and summer I may get up there a few days when I hope to be dong the interviews from the affiliates in Phoenix. Even if I arranged to do those from the city, it still would be difficult since our work schedules would be quite different."

She slumped down on the love seat again and gave a big sigh,

"I thought you had more control."

"I don't, but maybe we can figure it out when I know more."

She was silent now and he knew she was disappointed.

"I'm afraid we'll have to leave it for now Kate. When we get back to it we ought to discuss the fall as well now that we know you're going to finish so soon. It's a lot to talk about."

She was silent for a long time,

"How would you feel about my being gone all summer?"

"I don't know. There was no reason to think about it until now."

"Could you live with that?"

"I would have to, wouldn't I?"

"And you're not sure when the book will come out and can't plan any of the summer now?"

"That's the way it is now, yes. How and when it will be promoted are decisions made by the publisher. I don't control the promotion of the book. It depends on them. I do as much as I can to influence it, more than most I suspect, but some things have to be done on their schedule. It's what was so contentious up there all week, by phone Friday, and will be again for at least another trip. If I can get them to do it early I hoped you might go on part of one of those trips at the end of the semester. You won't if you're in Hamilton."

"Going to Hamilton seems like a great opportunity."

"You have to decide that."

"I know."

They ate in town so they wouldn't have to change. Kate said she wanted to clean up the carrel tomorrow so would go home and to the campus in the morning and would be back with lunch tomorrow. He knew she was unhappy that her plan posed problems. Yet he wasn't happy either since she did it without knowing his plans. It hadn't stopped her from trying because she was being the solitary Kate who was in charge of her life again and impatient to move on and liked the idea it of it being as soon as summer. Hamilton made sense to her. It didn't for him. But it didn't sound as if that mattered.

He was staring into space with his manuscript in his lap at eight that evening and hadn't come up with any alternatives for Kate. He wasn't happy with what he was reading either and quite impulsively he called Chris,

"Harry, what a nice surprise."

"Are you busy? I'm sorry it's so late."

"It's okay. I'm just sitting staring at a television program that I fail to understand because I'm not paying attention."

"Would you rather concentrate on it or talk?"

"Depends on what Harry wants to say."

"First to say I'm sorry we've been missing each other. I know you're busy with better things than our cocktails. But it's always a good evening for me."

"We've both been busy. From what I hear you've been in and out all month."

"I have. Edits with Charlie and the inevitable pre-publication battle with the dolts in the PR department. I wish they'd hire someone there as smart as you."

She chuckled, "They aren't stupid, Harry. You just don't like them because they make you do things you don't want to do. You want to control all that."

He chuckled, "True enough. They must detest it every time I publish since we have to find some way to get the publicity done and I'm always trying to tell them how. Do other authors complain about these things as much as I do?"

"Some. There's a lot of general complaining now about how we're cutting back. They don't think the publisher is doing enough for them."

"I'd do it all electronically from the courtyard here if I could."

"Well, it may come to that and you're way ahead of most of them because you already thought of alternatives. Now, did you just call to whine about publicity or was there something you needed?"

"I wanted ask a question and a favor if you have time."

"I always have time for you."

"Please Chris don't toss roses on the path. That isn't true. You've been avoiding me when I'm in the city. You rarely even answer a text these days."

She was silent for a minute, "Truth is I have. I decided having you stop to say hello, having lunch across the street now and then, and booking flights for you is all there's going to be with us. Sitting around over cocktails isn't the best thing for me if that's all there is, especially with you."

Harry said softly, "sounds like you've thought about it."

"I have."

"I'm sorry Chris. Selfish Harry was only thinking of himself. I don't want you to be uncomfortable."

"It isn't your fault. I still think you're wonderful and that's part of the problem, isn't it? Its fine as it is. We have a mutual admiration, I know that, but that's all we'll ever have."

"All right Chris, so long as we stay in touch. Can we do that?"

"Sure, now what do you need?"

"First a favor. Would you to read my book?"

"You'd never ask."

"I am asking. I know you're very perceptive or Elspeth wouldn't be so happy with your work with her clients and I need some perspective. I don't want you to read it with a blue pencil in your hand, that's Charlie's job but I'd very much value your opinion. You talked me through some of the roughness early on and I'm sitting here looking at it now and still having trouble believing it's done right."

"Isn't that what you have Elspeth for?"

"Yes, as an agent. I'm asking you as a person I admire, isn't that your status now?"

"Come on Harry, this is serious. You want me to read your book before it's published and tell you if I like it? Just as a reader?"

"I do."

"You told me no one has ever read even any part of a book of yours before publication beside your agent and editor."

"I've never even talked to anyone seriously about one of my books until I bounced a few ideas off you this time."

"But you want me to read it?"

"Look, Elspeth's begun to believe my press clippings and I don't think she's ever felt she could be as hard on this one as she was in the past because of my surgery. Besides all that she was never enamored of the story and sometimes that gets in her way. I don't fault her for that, but it doesn't help me much."

"You're sure about this?"

"I'll take that as a yes and overnight the latest draft to your house tomorrow. Read it at home. Then none of your eleven rules or however many you have now will be broken."

"I'd be glad to help if I can. It's scary though."

"No it isn't, just be as honest as you always are, as you were just now. That's all I ask. Now can we talk about your house?"

"Did something bad happen?"

"No, no, it's fine. Joseph is watching over it. I'm just thinking some things through. You said I could stay as long as I wanted. Are you still okay with that or do you want to sell it?"

"I'm not in any hurry. I don't need the money right now. Why the question? You want to stay?"

"No, much as I love the house I don't love the desert enough to make it home. I'm trying to answer some questions about the summer and fall. If I left for three or four months this summer would that be a problem?"

"No, you could close it up for awhile and I'd be fine with that. Where're you going?"

"I'm just asking questions for now. I'll be gone for good by January certainly assuming no further health problems."

"How's that work with Kate?"

"She's found a way to graduate in December and wants to spend this summer working in Hamilton. I'm trying to see if I can find a way to make it work."

"That won't be easy if it's a summer book. Charlie tells me it's what you want."

"No it won't, but I just heard all this today."

"Have you two decided anything?"

"I don't know how she feels if that's what you mean."

"How do you feel?"

"I'm not sure Chris except that I care for her a great deal."

"And she's not saying?"

"No. The only man she's told she loved was her father."

"Really? She's thirty isn't she?"

"Yes."

"And never told a man she loved him? That's pretty remarkable."

"The words mean a lot to her."

"She's a pretty unique, then."

"She is. I'm not sure how she sees us."

"Well, one day she needs to say how she feels."

"I know. We're getting to a point where it's going to take that or being apart a good bit. I'm ambivalent about the latter."

"It'll work out if it's supposed to Harry. It's better to be sure."

"I know. Thanks for agreeing to read the book and for being honest. Both mean a lot to me."

"I'm glad we have things straight. I know how much you value honesty and it needs to be that way for me too. I'll call when I finish the book."

Harry had too much on his mind to sleep well. He took a walk and drank coffee and sat thinking while the sun rose.

The book was done. While it was troubling him, if Chris thought the story worked as it was, he'd to go with what was there. The tour still needed to be set. The earlier the better appealed to him because he saw it as a good summer book and saw no benefit in doing the pre-release interviews he'd done the last time. They knew who he was now and he wanted to talk about the book, not himself.

Kate wanted to get on with her new career and she didn't want to wait any longer. Hamilton was logical because she liked it, knew Bill and Martha, and had a job offer. That was a decision she'd made for herself. She'd surely made no attempt to make it theirs. It gave him an empty feeling to know that she was so sure about wanting to go that she'd consider going without him. From what he heard yesterday, it seemed to mean more to her than being together this summer.

All that aside, he had a book to sell. Harry was sure the VP wouldn't go against his wishes on the publication date. Drew trusted Harry's instincts and he'd let him publish when he wanted. He was certain of that. How the tour would be done was another matter. Drew would leave that to the others and while Harry was reasonably certain they would see it his way in the end, he couldn't be sure. For all he knew now, he might be on the road all summer doing the usual circuit of interviews and signing books. He didn't know yet because the decisions were largely theirs although he would surely do all he could to influence them.

Assuming that his inability to follow her to the northwest for three months meant they still had a relationship Kate was the only reason for him to come back here in the fall. He didn't know if she'd thought about that. She didn't know anything about what he would do after the tour. They never talked about it. Until yesterday he was sure she was going to be in school another year. Getting her degree this soon was such good and recent news to her that she was moving on without thinking of them now as the old Kate would. Their relationship was on plateau, was for months now since his last illness. Deciding how much this meant might work in Tucson but he didn't see it being done in the separation caused by a summer job in another state and the confusion of a book tour. He was sure she never considered staying here and taking a semester in the summer to make her fall load a normal one because she was enchanted by the green hills of Hamilton. Once she learned she could graduate in December she'd likely thought about going there to work first because it was going to be her new life and she was in a hurry to try it out.

As he emptied the coffee pot, he knew Kate wanted to be a landscape architect with that singularity of purpose that defined her. He had no quarrel with that. He had the same feelings about being a writer. He's annoyance was with the way she was planning her immediate future without knowing his. Harry was querulous in the best of times with most everyone, yet he was trying to figure out a way to accommodate this now when it only involved a summer job. He couldn't do it and perhaps it was because he was tired of trying. If she wanted this to last longer than this spring she needed to decide whether he was important enough to her to make her own compromises.

He put it all away for later at eight o'clock, called Elspeth, and explained again how two stations needed to coordinate with each other in order to do a taping or a live feed. She was having trouble grasping the concept. She agreed with Harry's reasoning about Drew and the publication date. She would be in the building today and would see if a decision was made.

Todd called with three media requests. One was from NPR with a national Saturday show and the other two were print requests and would be done by phone. He said yes to all. He needed the visibility now.

He heard the bell. He grabbed up a copy of the newest manuscript, addressed a mailer for it to Chris, and brought it with him when he came out.

"Hey, do you have a nice tidy work place now?"

"It's clean but still has too much in it."

"Offices always do."

"Well, it will have to do for now. What are you up to?"

"I talked to my landlord after you left last night. Woke up too early but tried to sort out some things."

"What things? I didn't know there was much left to do."

"There's quite a bit actually. Besides what we talked about that still need to be settled, I still have context edits in the manuscript and the rest of the minutia that besets me at the end of the writing. It's time consuming and I hate it but it needs to be done. I talked to El about the tour. The remote part of it is complicated and confuses her. She was going in there today so she'd see if they'd made a decision about the publication date. Todd called with interviews. Two are print so done by phone and easy enough. The other one I agreed to is for NPR on the weekend so I need to go to Tucson on Thursday and tape it."

She looked at him a long moment as if she were taking that in,

"That's a lot considering what you told me yesterday."

"It's always busy until the book is in print and the tour is set. Most of it is clerical work, but it needs to be done right. It will slow down then until the reviews get done."

"How do you do an interview by yourself?"

He chuckled, "I don't. I can hear him or her in the headset. Besides, the engineer is there so you can pretend he or she is the host if you like."

"Then you do that, I'll do plants. I don't have to pretend with a plant."

"Oh, this is just me being the overbearing gasbag I'm capable of being on a moment's notice. Did you get a point for that chuckle?"

"Of course."

"Do you know the score?"

"It's seventy one to forty two."

"Really?"

"Really. That bother you at all?"

"No, I accepted your wit as superior long ago. Good sandwiches by the way. Now, I need to do something. Want to come?"

"Sure, where?"

"I need to overnight this to Chris and then my day is done. Do we have plans after that?"

She swiveled on the stool and looked at him,

"We need talk some more about the summer and fall."

"I thought we didn't know enough to finish that."

"We need to straighten some things out."

He nodded and they walked to the car.

They were back in a few minutes. She refused to participate in his playful shoving at the gate so he knew she was distracted.

"Okay," he said as lightly as he could, "what do we need to straighten out?"

"We didn't do very well yesterday, or I didn't."

"You didn't get done if that's what you mean, you were still planning and there was more I needed to know. You got a lot done. You know when you'll finish now and it was up to you to find the answer to that."

"I asked the questions that brought me to the surprising result of leaving a year sooner than I thought. I did the asking and found the answer but you and I decided how to go about that in January."

"I suppose we did."

"The problem wasn't when I'd graduate. That's wonderful so far as we're both concerned. It was the summer. I had an idea of the publishing schedule you wanted since you've told me but I ignored it and where you might be because of it and expected you figure out how to be in the northwest. I decided that was the only place I could work and I needed to go there. I never thought about how we'd manage. I wanted you to work it out. I was being that Kate who only cares what she wants again. I've tried hard not to be her but I was again, wasn't I?"

"How you spend the summer is you're decision."

She stood and came over and sat next to him and slid down letting her hair fall in her face. "No. It's our decision. It was wrong to make it mine and it makes me angry that I fell into that again so easily."

"Do you have an alternative?" Harry asked.

"I don't. If I don't go to Hamilton, I don't have a plan."

"You want to go don't you?"

"I did until we talked. It was fun to think about it since I can see the end of school now. You think its nuts but just haven't said so."

"I can't tell if that matters, Kate. It didn't yesterday. You thought it was a great opportunity then and as I recall asked if I could live with you being gone."

"Yes I did and it was an incredibly selfish thing to ask of you."

"What do you mean?"

She sat up and looked at him,

"Do you seriously think I'm leaving you for three months? I miss you enough when you travel. Being with you is a big part of what makes me happy. How am I supposed to be without you all summer?"

"You thought it would be all right yesterday."

"No." She said so loud it was nearly a yell, "I wanted you to figure out a way to make it work and it doesn't. There's nothing to figure out, nothing to fix." There was exasperation in her voice now he'd never heard before. "My leaving won't work. I can't just do what I want and not take what you have to do into consideration." she looked at him with those wide eyes, "I'm sorry. I didn't do that, it's wasn't right."

"What do you want to do then?"

"Work out the summer together. You've been accommodating me and my career since the day I first came through that gate. Don't do that now. Decide this with me and don't assume you aren't part of it. You always are. We need a solution, and I don't have one now. You can't just keep saying that we'll figure something out. I need more than that from you. Let's talk about it. Don't try to work around me."

"All right."

"Good, now let's talk about what might work."

"Can we start with not going to the northwest?"

Kate sighed, "It was a bad idea for more reasons than I can count. The logistics alone are impossible, so let's talk about something else."

"Did you consider going to school this summer? Are there courses offered then that you need?"

She looked at him with a frown now, "I'm not sure. I was going to take them all next semester and was so busy planning my fun job I never looked. I never thought about going straight through."

"You'll have a break between spring and summer and then again after summer semester. You'll be off what? Two months each time? That's hardly straight through. If they give me what I want, I can try to schedule the eastern trip after your exams this semester and we'd get to do some of the tour together if you want. If I get the idea of using some or all the remote feeds from here agreed to, I'll be as close as Phoenix much of the time you're in school for the summer session."

"So you and I can take a trip together and then while I'm in school we'd both be here?"

"I won't be here all the time. I'll be over in Phoenix on an irregular schedule much of July and perhaps early August after the trip. I'll be back and forth and do the print interviews from here. None of that is decided yet, I could end up traveling for six more weeks but that's what I hope it will be."

She was staring at him and said quietly,

"Do you see why you can't let me walk in here with my blueprints and then just try to fit in? It never occurred to me to stay in school this summer. I don't even know why."

"You know very well why, Kate, the first thing you thought about when you got the stupendous news that you could have your degree in December was to do landscaping with Mr. Caruso. It was fun to think of getting your hands dirty and live among all those trees. Going to Hamilton was likely the first thing you decided and it became the most important thing. Cutting back on your classes to make this a bit easier never crossed your mind."

"It was the first thing. I was so pumped up about going up there I never gave anything else a thought."

"Well, why don't you see what they have? Maybe you can take half of them."

"I will. This is so annoying. I mean I never thought of that and I never thought about what you would need either. I knew you'd be working. I didn't know what you'd be doing exactly but I just went ahead anyway and yesterday wanted you to find a way to be there. Why don't you get angry at me when I do that?"

"What would be the point of that? We've both been on our own a very long time Kate and we act as if we still are now and then. We talked about that last March. You did it yesterday. We should be able to figure things out without anger even when our old solitary selves try to take over again. I wasn't all that understanding either. I was annoyed that you'd dig in like that but giving you a lecture about what might happen to us or any of the other awful things I know how to do wouldn't have changed your mind. You needed to understand it wasn't possible."

"It's more patience than I deserve. You were right to assume I was leaving and it didn't matter if you couldn't yesterday. But you never raised your voice. You tried to work through it. You always let me try to find my own way. It's why I trust you so much. Now, what should I do with all time I'll have if I'm only in class two or three hours a day after this semester?"

"I'll leave that to you. You'll think of something you."

She smiled, "I "m sure I will. I just hope it isn't anything we have to discuss it for two days." She sighed, "I'm sorry. I just got excited. I should have waited for you to get home."

"We found a way for now, at least until I know what they have planned for me. Anyway, I'm sure it will be more pleasant for you to go at a normal pace the rest of the way."

"It'll be different. Can we talk some more about the fall? I have no idea what you're doing then. You've never said but I never expected to be finishing then with an easy course load either."

Harry nodded, "I won't be writing. I never go right to the next book. That will take a year or two at least. I may lecture as I did the last time or do some media work from here or write reviews. There are opportunities that come up on a book tour depending on the success of the book. I can't even guess about that now. All I can say for certain now is that I'll live here."

"That sounds vague and complicated."

"It is vague. I don't know how complicated it will be. Perhaps it will be something that I can do from here, but things happen once a book is published. I can only control some of it. We'll talk about it when I learn more and try to avoid the trouble that we had with the summer."

"I hope so."

Harry watched her now for a minute. He needed to say this and he supposed now was as good a time as there would be,

"We'll both be leaving this winter, Kate. This arrangement we have is fine while we're here and you're in school. I'm not sure how it will work once we're beyond that. We need to think about that."

She slid down again and folded her arms, "I've thought a lot about it already. But when I do something like this and get it so wrong I worry. I don't want to disappoint you. I want to get it right."

"There's right and perfect Kate. You always want perfect and there is no way to have that. Right is the best you can do."

CHAPTER FIFTEEN

Chris called Thursday afternoon. Harry frowned when he saw the number since it was still working hours and wondered why she would call now,

"Hi, are you still at work?"

"No I'm not."

"Are you ill?"

"I took the afternoon off so I could look over the book again before we talked."

"You're finished?"

"Of course I'm finished. I didn't move my lips. I read for a living. Don't be insulting Harry, remember, you asked me to do this. We're going to talk about it now if it isn't a bad time."

"As it happens no. I suppose we can do it now."

She gave one of her huge laughs, "Jesus, Harry, you don't act this way with Charlie or I'd know it. Why are you afraid of this?"

Harry sighed, "Never mind. Just let me sit down and then you can tell me what you think."

She chuckled, "You act as if I'm going to give you a failing grade. I gotta say Harry, you're strange."

"Of course I am. You knew that before you saw the book. How long are you going to torture me before you say something about it? This is death buy a thousand cuts."

"All right, stop all the nonsense now. Let me tell you about your book."

"Yes, yes, fine."

"It's a very good book, Harry and it may be a great one. It's far better than you've been saying. I don't see any reason to be uncomfortable. Your protagonist is unbelievably evil certainly, yet you made me love him in some odd way too. You style is still elegant and the story is a very good one."

"I can say you liked it then."

"You may. It's simple and powerful. I can tell you if I was editing it, except for some transitions I wouldn't change much."

"You're very kind Chris and I hope the critics see it as you do. Do you have a problem with the fire?"

"No, I'm not sure why it bothers you. You had to write it that way. It's the pivotal point. It needs to be as horrible as it is. You aren't changing it are you?"

"The version you read is as I wrote it the first time. Elspeth argues that it's far more graphic than necessary but Charlie seems all right with it so far."

"Then leave it alone. Go with your instincts. We can go over the other things if you want. I have time. There are some places where I thought the reader might have trouble following."

"Yes, please if you will."

For the next hour they went through the chapters. He was thanking her again for how much she'd helped when she stopped him,

"Please, we're done, Harry, okay? I'm glad it worked out because I know how afraid you were to let anyone see it."

"It was very helpful, Chris."

"Good, then publish it and sell as many as you can because I need my job and the more you sell the more likely I am to have it."

He laughed, "I'll ask Charlie about some of the clarifications. He has this copy and may well have picked up some of them. He enjoys inflicting this sort of thing on me as late in the process as possible."

She laughed one of her big throaty laughs,

"Well, aside from these transitions, he can't get too fussy with this."

"Now, I owe you lunch for doing this, so I'll see you in a week or two."

"You will. Have you decided about the summer?"

"Yes, I won't close the place down. Except for the one trip that I'm trying to plan so that Kate can go with me, she'll house sit as always."

"What's she going to do?"

"She'll take some of the classes she needs here this summer and is looking for a job."

"What will you do after the tour is done?"

"I'm never certain about that. These tours always have opportunities depending on how well the book does. I don't want to stay on the road for two years again but a lecture here or there would be fine."

"I hope it all works out."

"Well, we'll see, time is moving on and decisions come with that. Now, I need to let you go. You've been good to give me all this time."

"I enjoyed it actually. Hard to believe I thought you couldn't start with that outline of yours and get a book this good. I may have to re-think my obsession with process."

Harry laughed, "Take care Chris, have some fun."

"I'll do that, promise. Luck, Harry."

He breathed a sigh of relief. He was glad he'd given it to her. It was an impulse, but she was the right one. He didn't know why, but she made him feel comfortable with what he'd written now. Maybe the book was better than he thought.

When Harry prepared to go on the road with *No Free Country* he was overwhelmed by the need to succeed, so much so that he lost track of nearly everything else in his life. He wanted it so badly he could hardly breathe or concentrate on anything else. When the book did so well, he knew he was going to be gone for months to make the most of its success and it was clear he couldn't do that and maintain his life in Hamilton as it was. He'd weighed the cost of that and chosen.

Now he'd experienced that success, a frightening illness, and found Kate and he refused to ever want success that badly again. He loved Kate. He didn't know when he first knew that, but he was sure of it now. It wasn't amorphous. He wasn't ambivalent. He would finish the last details of the book and sell it as well as he could but he'd not sacrifice what they had for the bright lights this time. He would be the gracious and grateful author if the reviews were good but he wouldn't wheedle invitations to every literary party for months afterward just to be sure he was well remembered. He didn't need to weigh his feelings for Kate. She meant as much to him as his writing and certainly more than how than how well he was remembered. He wanted there to be only one Harry

Logan now. He still saw a frequent author yet there was room now for that other Harry and he wanted to be a partner in her life if she'd have him. He wanted that as much as anything to do with writing and if it meant selling fewer books or never winning another award he didn't care. He no longer wished to make a Faustian bargain for the Nobel Prize. His life had to be more than that, more than the writing and selling of books. The old unhappy self-promoting Harry was gone, removed perhaps by the collective efforts of a skilled surgeon, a radiation beam and the help Anita and Bill gave him in realizing he needed to grow up. He wasn't the man on the train platform anymore. The bombast, pomposity, and ego were still there when he needed them to cow some simpleton or make his point or sell his book, but he didn't feel any need for them in his personal life.

Throughout April, he was pulled to the northwest. Kate was happy in school if only because it was the last semester with a backbreaking course load. She was working the system to get her courses for the summer. They ate whatever meal they could together and she was grateful for her house sitting duties while he was gone because she had a quiet place to live. She was in the library some weekends since her last break. What time they'd been together was happy, but it never seemed enough.

He knew Elspeth wasn't going to be able to finish the promotional tour without him there. The remote setups, the virtual part of the tour weren't clear to her yet and Harry was becoming increasingly frustrated trying to explain it to the PR people from here. They agreed to meet again to try to resolve it and he was back on the phone with Chris trying to find a flight that made sense on a Sunday. There was a little work to be done with Charlie as well as the tour schedule. He knew it wasn't possible to get all that done in one week so he left the return open. He was annoyed since all signs pointed to a free weekend for Kate but he needed to do it if everything was going to stay on schedule. He was fiddling with the last margin notes for Charlie and he was surprised when the bell rang twice. Instead of respecting the boundaries of his office, she literally bounced in a moment later with a happy smile, that wonderful laugh, and planted a kiss on his forehead.

"Hi."

"Hey, I wasn't expecting to see you until tomorrow."

"Is it okay? I tried to call but you were on the phone."

"Of course it's okay. I was on the phone all day."

"Business?"

"Yes, why?"

"Because you ignore the tone and never look at missed calls when you're shouting at someone up there."

He laughed. "Is that true?"

"I can't tell you how often it's happened."

"I'm sorry. The conversations were pretty intense. The bad news is the technical things are confusing everyone and I need to go up there and finish the itinerary next week or the book will be delayed. The good news is that unless Charlie has unearthed new things to hector me about, the book will be ready when I come back."

"It's really done?"

He smiled up at her, "It is. Now why do you have that big smile on your face? There's something you can't wait to tell me. I'd apologize, but I believe it was my turn. Tell me now or you may hurt yourself."

She laughed and hugged him from behind his chair, "I have all good things. I got all the courses I could for the summer. There are two that are only offered in the fall that I need but that will make the summer easy and," she spun him around in his chair and laughed again, "I have a job at a nursery starting next week."

"A nursery? Next week?"

"It's very part time for now. Just Saturdays but it will be more in the summer and with the reduced load I'll have lots of time. They're very nice. It's owned by the family of one of the women who has a carrel near mine. Isn't that wonderful?"

"It is Kate, its perfect."

"I remembered that Karen said something to me about her family's business when I was talking about changing majors, so I asked her today and she was nice enough to help so my summer is settled."

"That's wonderful. Can you stay for dinner and chirp some more about all this?"

"Yes, but that doesn't seem fair."

"Life isn't fair right now, I'll get over it. Have you been home?"

"No, why?"

"There's lots of food and I thought we might see if Nicole was hungry."

"That would be nice. I'll call when we're ready to eat."

"When are we eating?"

She leaned over him and whispered in his ear,

"Later. You need to help me with all this happiness I feel and we aren't playing basketball this time."

"Oh my," he said as she pulled him out of his chair.

Late Sunday morning, Kate drove him to the airport. She wanted to wait with him but he insisted it was futile to stand around an airport if you weren't the one leaving.

On the way, she was trying to cheer him up,

"Don't be miserable, you haven't stayed a weekend for a long time and I have enough to keep me busy. I have the nursery Saturday and can't wait for that and there's lots of studying to do."

"I surely hope this will be the last long one. Don't forget to send me the dates for your exams this week so I can try to schedule one of the trips after they're done."

"Are you sure you don't want me to park and wait with you?"

"No, please, I need to wrestle through security and standing around watching me do that while you wish you were in the library won't make you happy."

"I'm not going to ask how you know that, but I'm glad you understand."

He leaned on the driver's side door after he took his bag out of the trunk,

"Be careful while I'm gone, please. I'm sure you and Elena have much to catch up on when you see her tomorrow."

Kate held onto his arm very tight and looked at him steadily,

"Get it all done this time. I need you here." She leaned over and kissed him, "I'll miss you."

Harry straighten perplexed by her intensity,

"I'll call."

She gave him one of her happy smiles, waved and raised the window as she pulled away.

The Regent was comforting and quiet. He always knew he'd come back here sooner or later and had several trips ago. He talked to Kate after he ate and read his notes for Charlie and readied himself for a week or more of being the full time public Harry. He wanted to go to Hamilton this weekend if he were here, but wanted to see how the week went before he called Bill. He went to bed still wondering how serious Kate sounded tonight.

The three days with Charlie weren't as contentious as usual. He accepted the things Chris found, made two suggestions about short re-writes and asked him to explain once more his reasoning for making the house fire so graphic. He grunted and accepted it in the end. Harry asked what he thought of the rest as they finished. He smiled and said wryly it might be a good summer read.

There were meetings with the PR people scheduled for the next two days. The real decision makers likely wouldn't be there since they usually absented themselves until he was tired of arguing. He would be here for some part of next week in any event to be sure he and Charlie were done and there was a resolution to the way the tour would be done as well. He hoped the meetings were civil. His outbursts and sarcasm were bothering Elspeth more now and she was impatient with him occasionally because she didn't fully grasp how it worked despite knowing what he wanted to do. He would catch the four-thirty train to Hamilton Friday. He and Bill had spoken briefly and would be glad to be there rather than here. Playing some basketball and talking appealed to him more than anything in the city.

After a quiet dinner on his own he called Kate,

"Hi."

"Hey, busy?"

"Not now. Nicole left after we both stuffed ourselves. My car is worrying me though."

"Do you know what's wrong?"

"Not yet."

"Well, you have mine for now. We can make another deal like the carrel if it's serious."

"Be nice not to have to do that. I'd rather be in debt to you than a bank but I'm hoping it might be simple. I only need it eight or nine more months. It seems a shame to spend much money on it."

"Take it for an estimate before you do anything else. It might be easy. If not, maybe we need to talk about it."

"I'll do it in the morning. Nicole's going in early so she can follow me and bring me back. I'll call her."

"See? That wasn't hard, was it?"

She laughed, "No, but I needed your opinion before I did anything because your money might be involved."

He chuckled, "Okay, I get it."

"What are you doing?"

"I'll see the PR people tomorrow and Friday. They just can't get this done and all this electronic business is confusing Elspeth. She's upset because I'm being so adamant and I suppose my outbursts are making her impatient because she wants it finished. I'll be at Bill's on Friday night. I'll need to see Charlie one more time next week. I rewrote two things this week that made him happier."

"It's such a strange process. I'm not persistent enough to manage all that. It reminds me of business school."

"It's the way it usually is. It'll get done."

"Well, don't expect me to ever really understand it."

"I don't expect you to understand it any more than I understand how to hybridize a rose."

"Do you know when you'll be home?"

He sighed. "Next Friday unless there's some miraculous breakthrough. They'll change things the day I leave and I'll have to work on it from home but some of that will be dependent on the stations and not their fault."

"Why is a publicity tour schedule so hard to figure out?"

"It isn't. I made it hard now because these remote interviews are a relatively new way to do this and you have to first get the programs to agree and schedule it very differently. Most authors don't do much of this yet and don't necessarily get this involved. The PR people here send them off with a plane ticket and an itinerary, and they're thrilled. They're a traditional bunch here and don't really understand the concept yet. I told Chris they probably began to drink heavily when they knew I was ready to publish."

She laughed, "They probably did. Be sure to say hello to Bill and Martha. I wish I were there. Maybe you can manage a day or two of fun."

"I hope so. Bill seems to have a need to beat my brains out on the court. Probably in reprisal for your humiliation of the poor man."

"He's easy. He just talks all that big college jock trash."

"Just remember that you haven't beaten me yet."

"Your day's coming sport, I will beat you, never doubt that. They'll be calling you drum when I get finished with you."

He laughed loudly, "You're really getting competitive about this."

"Well yeah? You get me all pumped up when you taunt me that way. It's good for me, though. I'm enjoying sports again. I even saw part of a game on television the other night and I enjoyed it. Now, I need to get some reading done. Call me from Bill's so I can talk to them. I miss you."

On Thursday he went in very early and up to the executive suite where he hoped to find Drew. He was always in early if in town and it wasn't uncommon for Harry to pay his respects this way. It occurred to him on Wednesday night that some of the problems with the tour might be due to resistance from the decision makers so he thought he'd see what Drew knew about that. Drew was smart, always knew what was going on in his shop, but was easy to read because he didn't keep secrets well unless they threatened his authority. They chatted amiably. They did actually like each other well enough personally. Drew knew Harry was struggling with his travel this time and he sympathized on the occasions he'd seen him in the last year. He said he'd heard yesterday that he and Winchester were done with the manuscript and asked about the press date.

"Yes, well, the press date is a bit of a sticky wicket right now. Thanks to you it will be a summer book but I have the PR people confused I'm afraid. You recall we talked about the availability of so much electronic media these days that I thought your people might look into the idea of what I called a 'virtual tour' to save author travel and that I was anxious to try."

"I do remember," Drew replied, "I did a good bit of reading about it and thought it was excellent. I asked the PR people to look into it after that. There was a short presentation here some months ago that I sent back for revision since the cost comparisons needed to be clarified. I must say I haven't heard anything about it since," he made a note and continued, "are there problems?"

"Not problems really. It seems a hard concept for them to grasp for scheduling purposes."

"Why?"

"Well, you surely don't have all morning to hear the horrid details, but there are issues of timing quite different than plane schedules and hotel reservations. Much of this is new and I understand why it seems confusing."

"I don't see why it should be," Drew leaned back, "tell me, what you think you need to do as a traditional tour now? I mean those places you really have to go rather than do remote interviews?"

"Well, the east coast stops, New York certainly, and Boston. Washington still needs personal time as well. Los Angeles needs to be included and San Francisco too because of the demographics. Those are also the best media markets. The signings garner press in those places and the reception opportunities are best. I believe the rest of the electronic media can be done from the affiliates near any author's home. The print media isn't a problem. One can talk to them from anywhere. Signings in the small cities is easy to set up and cheap, but of little value now."

Drew swiveled in his chair, thinking. "Sounds efficient. Just the savings on plane tickets and hotels would be substantial if most could be based at home. Why is it difficult?"

"It requires a different approach. Tapings or live feeds need to be coordinated between the affiliate one is using and the show and the show's home station, that sort of thing. There is cost associated with that of course but I believe it's less than the traditional ones and will become cheaper over time. I don't mean to be disrespectful, but your PR shop is a traditional operation. That's my opinion, of course," Harry chuckled, "and as you know very well, it's never a humble one."

Drew laughed out loud as he stood and walked around his desk, "No Harry, yours never are but you raise some interesting issues for us though. It's good to see you. When are you going home?"

"I'll be here at least next week or until this is done. I'd very much like to make it my last trip before publication and the tour. I'll meet with the planners in PR both today and tomorrow."

"Well, I'm sorry we'll cost you a weekend here then, but perhaps it can be wrapped up soon. Let me ask Greg and Abigail to be sure one or both of them are going to be there today and tomorrow. None of the planners can approve a tour or make a final decision on your concept."

"Thank you Drew, that's very kind. I don't want to interrupt anyone's schedule and they may well have it on their calendar."

Drew furrowed his brow, "Perhaps. I didn't hear about it, but you may be right. Thanks again for coming up." As he walked him to the door, Drew asked, "Have you seen Miss Morgan this trip?"

"I did get a chance to stop and say hello earlier in the week. Elspeth tells me she's a most perceptive editor and that the other editors like her very much. Some of Elspeth's other clients have worked with her. You're quite lucky to have her. Elspeth isn't easily impressed having been an editor herself. Now, I've kept you long enough," Harry said and extended his hand, "it was good of you to see me as always."

Drew smiled, "Always a pleasure Harry. Thanks for the feedback. Have a good trip home. I hope the next time I see you will be in New York at the reception."

Harry smiled and walked to the main elevators.

As he boarded the train for Hamilton, Harry felt better. The concept was done now and they would finish the taping schedules and affiliate coordination next week. He hoped to have the "electronic itinerary" as he explained it to the always dense Greg and the brighter, yet more unpleasant Abigail, done by the end of next week. Unexpectedly to all but him, each managed to come to the meetings and approved the plan and the expenses. He knew this was a difficult time for many PR departments because they lacked the skills to 'transport' a voice but not a body to studios all over the United States and beyond. Yet the technology wouldn't ignore one industry no matter how much they wished it. There was no choice but to learn it as Harry did.

He watched the passing trees and the rolling hills and smiled, remembering the fun of the last trip when Kate was with him. He hoped there would be more. His time in the desert would be over soon and they would both move on. He'd be much happier if he was sure they were going together.

"Harry, you look wonderful," Martha said as he stepped off the train, "I'm so glad you were able to come."

"We missed ya, Harry," Bill said as he took his bag, "you gonna give me a game this time? You look great."

"I'm fine William and delighted to see you both."

"Ya shoulda' brought Kate. I may miss her more than I do you now. Coulda' watched you lose to her too."

Harry threw back his head and laughed. "When I do lose to her, William. I did ask her to play as hard as she did when she trounced you, but alas, I still prevail."

"Hey listen pal, one point ain't a trouncing. Get that straight, hear me? That was luck. And you ain't prevailing this weekend. You'll be beggin' for mercy when I'm done with ya."

"Oh, Bill, stop all that and let's get to the car." Martha said, "How is Kate, Harry? Is she really going to get her degree this winter?"

"She's fine and she is. There wasn't any way for her to leave right now. She does miss seeing you. She demanded I call from here so she can talk to you both."

"She's a remarkable woman Harry."

"I'm reminded of that every time I see her."

After Martha's wonderful dinner Harry and Bill wandered outside, tossed the ball to each other, and occasionally up at the hoop while they continued to catch each other up. Bill's re-organization of the region was complete and things were running more smoothly. Harry gave him a short summary of his week and they laughed over the consequences of his meeting with the VP. He grumbled about the fact that he was there another week without Kate.

"Aw quit bitchin' Harry, least you get to see her. Everybody up here's been askin' me where she went since after Christmas. The woman's got charisma."

Harry laughed, "Really? They've been asking for her?"

Bill nodded, "She met a lot of people while she ran around with Martha when you were working and then she tagged along with me. She's funny, curious, and a very smart woman who seems to remember everything about everyone she meets forever besides being just memorable for her looks."

He laughed again, "That's the first I heard about any of this. She said it was wonderful here and she seems to remember everything about it. She is funny and she takes on knowledge like a sponge takes on water."

"Your gettin' terminally attached to her Harry, I can hear it, how come?"

"Meaning?"

"You told me those involvements were over. Hell, Chris came and went like a one-night stand, but you've been seeing Kate, what, a year? More? I thought you were done with all that. It's what ya said when ya came back to sell the house."

"Things change. I've changed. Maybe being sick changed me. I'm not sure. I wrote the book with her there and she made it easier for me. Oh, we've had our moments of dissent and exasperation, yet few of anger. It was just a friendship that neither of us thought would become more. Now it has. I seem to need her," he shrugged and threw the ball up at the hoop, "and I have to find out if she needs me."

Bill grabbed the ball as it came down and held it and stared at him, "You mean she's the one?"

"She needs to decide if I'm the one for her. I know how I feel about it."

Bill laughed, "The vainglorious Harry Logan is lettin' a woman decide?"

"Does that frighten you as much as it does me, William?"

"It's frightening 'cause you aren't beggin' her like the Harry I thought I knew."

"I did that before didn't I? How'd that work out?"

"Badly, but I never thought that would stop you from doin' it."

"I can't beg Kate. We decide a great deal together but she's very much her own person. She says she cares a great deal, but she's never said more than that."

"You ever ask?"

"No. She'll say how she feels one way or the other when she's ready. It's the way she is." Harry pushed up another shot and watched as it dropped through the net and said quietly. "My problem is I find it hard not knowing."

"Really."

"Yes really, why do you find that a hard concept to grasp, William?"

Bill grabbed the ball, bounced it hard a few times, sat on it and looked up at Harry,

"What I grasp is that you're in love, that's what I grasp. You both are. She glows when you're around and you do too when you talk about her. She can't wait to tell you stuff or see you. That was how she was here when you were in the city working. She may like all of us, but you're the one she kept saying she needed to tell all about it. Why is it hard for her to admit that?"

Harry leaned against the basket support and spoke quietly into the near dark,

"Oh I don't know. She's more competitive than you are and can be as arrogant as I am. She's been her own person all her life. She lived with an older relative all through high school even though her mother was still in Tucson. I don't know what that did to her, Bill. I had my father until I came here. She's essentially been without a parent since she was what? Thirteen? Fourteen? We've never talked about the circumstances surrounding all that but there must have been many things she missed, don't you think? Learning compromise and sharing certainly were two. It can still be all about her once in a while. She was profoundly affected by the failure to be in the Olympics as well. She works harder than she needs to because she refuses to fail at anything as important as that was to her ever again. She's found it hard to share decisions and balance what she wants with the needs of a relationship. She's more like me in that way as well. She's never shared much of her life or emotions with any one before me so far as I know. She's never told a man she loves him and she's over thirty years old. She will one day, but when she says it, it will be forever. I can't ask her to have it be me because I can't decide that for her."

Bill watched him for a minute in silence, then stood up and started for the house as Harry fell in alongside, "Don't worry Harry, she loves you. She'll say it. It may be hard, but she will."

Harry sighed, "I hope you're right. I surely don't deserve such brilliant and beautiful woman but I hope you have it right."

As always the weekend went far too quickly. He and Bill played hard games twice on Saturday and while he stayed close in the first, Bill couldn't miss in the afternoon no matter what shot he took and beat him badly. He wasn't sure he wanted to tell that to Kate, but was sure Bill would. He called her Saturday night and she talked them both. He caught the train the next day and nodded and smiled when Martha demanded he bring Kate next time. He surely hoped he would.

He stood in the doorway watching Chris standing in a pool of light, bent over her desk leaning on her hands and read the pages they straddled with such concentration that she never heard him. He smiled. Editors were alike, he thought. Their powers of concentration always impressed him. He cleared his throat and her head came up,

"Harry! How long have you been standing there? I didn't know you were still in town."

"I was watching you work for the last several minutes. I've never seen that before. As to the second part, sadly I am. I came back from Bill's on Sunday and wanted to say hello."

As he came into her small but tasteful office she gave him a brief hug,

"I'm glad you came by. I hear from Charlie that you're done. He asked me Friday whether I was going to read the final manuscript. I didn't laugh but it was close."

Harry chuckled, and sat across the desk from her, "What did you tell him?"

"If I had time, but that I was sure you and he had it right."

"Ah, nicely done Miss Morgan. By the way, have you seen the VP lately?"

She smiled as she sat down now and cocked her head, "Funny you ask that. Drew walked in here with Crampton last Friday. First time ever. You could have knocked me over with a feather. He said he'd been hearing good things about my work and wanted to thank me and shook my hand while Crampton did a little dance behind him and bowed obsequiously as he left. Never did figure it out. You know anything about it Harry?"

"Me? Heavens no. I'm sure he's quite correct of course. Perhaps one of the agents said something to him. Elspeth may have."

"So no good words from you then? You were up there Thursday. Everyone here knows when you go up to the executive suite," She smiled, "this is a small world, Harry."

"Well, we did have one of our courtesy chats and I may have said something. I can't recall."

She leaned back in her swivel chair and her impish eyes sparkled as she twirled her glasses in her hand, "Can't recall? You can't recall? I'd say that's miraculous Harry, you likely recall the first words you ever said."

He threw back his head and laughed, "I may."

She sat forward, crossed her arms on the desk, and looked directly at him. "Thank you for that. You're wonderful. God, I hope Kate knows that." She said very softly.

"You're welcome but you deserved it. El tells me you work well with her clients and you surely helped me, albeit off the clock. Now, enough mawkish conversation. Are we having the lunch I owe you before I go?"

"I'd love to, but doubt it would be a good idea. You're a hot topic here now that you're ready to publish. Even if we ordered in to my little world here, they would talk about it for a month."

"It's really like that?"

"Sadly, it is," She said.

"Well since someone has been extolling your excellence to the VP we wouldn't want to do anything to sully your newly burnished street cred would we?"

She laughed, "No, we wouldn't, but I appreciate you're asking."

Harry stood, "It's sad you know, friends should decide these things, not these," he waved his arm in the direction of the outer office area full of cubicles, "yahoos out here."

She sat and stared at him, "It's not sad, it's wrong, but it's how it is."

"I'll bet the heads were bobbing up and down when the VP walked through there."

She stood now and laughed one of her big throaty laughs, "Oh my, yes. That was delicious."

He laughed, "Take care then Chris, we'll talk."

"We will and thanks for everything." She hugged him again and kissed him softly on the cheek.

On Thursday, the last program and network affiliate he wanted to schedule agreed to an interview from Phoenix for their afternoon show and gave a tentative date, Phoenix was able to give him a taping date three days before, and it was done. He knew some of these dates were fiction. The commitment was what mattered and they would adjust them as time went on. He was on all the calendars he wanted to be now and they could be rearranged or deleted depending on how the book sold. What he'd wanted was proximity to home for two months and he had that now. Elspeth was elated that the book was done and the schedule was set. On the way to the airport he sent Kate a text that he would be back for dinner if the weather was good. When he changed planes in San Francisco, they spoke briefly. He wanted to take a car service home but she insisted on coming to get him. She prevailed by simply uttering that decisive "no" of hers and refusing to debate it no matter what he said.

He read the tentative travel itinerary on the plane. If the publishing date held, he and Kate would have a week or more in the Washington D.C. area after he trained down from New York and he only needed to do three days work there. There was time for her to come to New York too, but he'd leave that up to her.

CHAPTER SIXTEEN

It was still brutally hot when he landed at five thirty. He was surprised to see Kate standing in the terminal as he came out of the security area. She always met him outside. She stood perfectly still until he reached her.

"Hey," he said simply as he reached for her hand.

She was staring at him now with a small smile and that twinkle in her eyes,

"Hi," She said softly. She put her arms around his neck, kissed him, and seemed to be trying to squeeze him to death,

"I needed to come in here and meet you." She whispered after a minute. She kept a tight grip, not letting him pull her away. She'd never before allowed that much affection in public.

When he managed to separate from her he saw that her eyes were wet,

"Are you all right?"

They still stood facing each other. There was still a smile in her eyes despite the tears,

"Yes." She took a deep breath, "and we need to get out of here." She took his hand and seemed to pull him to the parking garage. He threw his bag in the trunk while she got in. He slid behind the wheel and looked over at her. She was staring straight ahead,

"Will you tell me what's going on, please?"

"No." She said with a smile as she looked at him, "It'll wait now." She took his hand as they pulled out, gripped it tightly and whispered, "Don't worry about it."

Harry was confused as he drove the busy highway up the hill but there was enough traffic at this time on a Friday night to make him concentrate. Kate looked out the side window and spoke only occasionally. It was comfortable but without their usual playfulness. He turned into Franklin and glided into the drive. Her car was there. He started to ask about it but she opened the door and got out so quickly the words never made it out of his mouth. She was in the gate before he opened the trunk. He sighed. This couldn't be good despite what she said, he thought. Something happened, was happening. He rolled the suitcase in and leaned it against the wall in the bedroom. She was standing with her arms folded by the love seat looking at the mountains. When he came over, she kissed him with more meaning and then buried her head in his shoulder. She wasn't crying, but he knew by her breathing her emotions were very near the surface,

"Are we going to repeat this all evening? I'm not complaining, but will you tell me what's going on?"

She took a step back and looked at him. Her dark eyes twinkled and she smiled as she held his hands,

"I'm having trouble."

"I see that, Kate. Why is it so hard?"

"I need to say something and I'm . . . I'm finding it hard to say it out loud."

"You're fearless. What could possibly be so hard for you to say?"

She laughed softly, "I wasn't sure I'd ever say it, but," she put both her hands behind his neck. "I want to now."

"Then say it, please. You're torturing a tired and amorous man."

She gave that wonderful soft laugh and, still looking directly at him with smiling eyes said as softly as ever, "I love you. I love you Harry Logan. I'm as sure of that as of anything in my life. I love you so very much."

Harry pulled her gently to him. All he could say was, "I love you too, Kate."

She gave a little laugh and said quietly from his shoulder, "I wanted to tell you so many times but something always got in the way. I was so very sure after you let me come back and I wanted to tell you then but you were sick and I worried you'd think it was said in pity or something and you wouldn't want that. Then there was all my bad behavior about the summer that made me worry that I wasn't capable of the sharing it takes. I just never seemed to have it right. It seems so melodramatic now when you've just come home and I'm sorry, but when I saw you come off the plane I just knew I had to say it now whether I have it right or not.

It couldn't wait any longer and if it isn't the perfect time to say it I don't care. It feels wonderful to have finally told you how I really feel."

They laughed, walked, and competed in their foolish games as always the rest of the weekend, but there was something else, an absence of doubt, a consent that wasn't there before. Her admission that she was no longer the only one in her world and his relief that he wasn't alone in his took all the doubt away. They repeated the words often, as if in wonder in what she humorously referred the rest of the weekend as her liberation and when Sunday came, she gave no sign of leaving.

He found it hard to let her go in the early morning light on Monday. She promised to be back that afternoon yet he missed her the moment she left and all the rest of the day. The real world would rush in soon but for now there was no one but Kate and it seemed for Kate no one but Harry. Her whispered words of goodbye were no longer how much she would miss him. The code was gone and she was free to use the words she said she'd meant all along. The week went quickly. She stayed every night even when she was late. It was a wordless agreement that they needed this time together now. It was her way of professing that her need for him equaled her need to finish what she'd begun.

He was sending a fax back to the city and to Todd with revisions to the schedule when she made one of her silent entries late Friday. He never heard a sound, only felt her arms go around him from behind as he watched the printer kick out his copy,

"Hi," she said softly.

"Hey, I swear you're part cat."

"I may be. I missed you."

"Are you still in love with me or have you reconsidered?"

She kissed him and laughed as she let go, "It's lasted a whole week, pretty good huh?"

He chuckled, "What are we doing tonight?"

"Oh, I don't know. I'm certain there is some heavenly meal in there. Do you want to go out? You've been home all week."

"You work tomorrow so we aren't going anywhere that requires effort. I'd like to eat at the Inn tomorrow night. What do you think?"

"I told them I'd miss this week. I want to be here tomorrow and dinner sounds great."

Harry smiled, "Well, you'll have clean finger nails at least. It was nice of you to take the day for me."

"It's for me too," She said softly and then laughed, "Why are we still standing next to the fax machine? You're finished for today aren't you? I didn't knock. I thought that rule was repealed now that the book is done."

He smiled, "It is, just stay away if I'm shouting into a phone when you get here."

"Fine. If we're staying here then I'm taking a shower and we can eat when you want. I have another Hitchcock movie that we can watch tonight."

"Take your shower. We'll have a beer and think about eating."

"There's something you want to talk about," she said.

"I'll see you in the courtyard."

"Are you going to tell me?"

"Go, I'll see you in a few minutes."

She poked him in the ribs and left.

Harry handed her the bottle of Corona when she sat down. She sucked on the lime, took a drink, and sighed, "Is this going to be hard?"

He chuckled, "Why?"

"I don't know," she said dreamily, "It just seems everything's been easy since last Friday. I'd hate to see it end."

"Have real life intrude?"

"I suppose that's it. I worked really hard this week but I never felt like my feet touched the ground, you know? Nothing's been hard since I finally told you the truth."

Harry threw back his head and laughed,

"I don't know why you're still available. Someone should have swept you up years ago."

"I didn't want to be swept up, not by anyone I knew before you." She shook her head, "I never liked a man as much as you and then I fell in love with you back there somewhere. I'm glad I love someone I know so well and like so much. Now, do we really need to talk or were you just going to grope me before dinner?"

"That sounds like fun, but we have some business first. You're coming east to meet me in about six weeks and you have to make some choices, so listen for a minute because you have to decide. I'll be in New York for four weeks. You can do one of two things. Fly there and meet me for the last week and we can take the train to D.C. for three days of work there and then have seven days to do whatever we want. Or, you can forgo New York and fly into Washington and we'll have the ten days in D.C. or around there. Got it?"

"This is after my exams?"

"Yes. Your exams are while I'm gone."

"Okay, I have it. Now what?"

"Which do you want to do?"

"All of it of course, it sounds wonderful. I haven't been to New York in years and we can see the Blue Ridge Mountains while we're down near Virginia. I always wanted to do that and maybe see Gettysburg."

"Are you sure you want to do all that? It would be nice to have you in New York because there's the publisher's reception and a number of social events the last week. It would be nice for me if you were there."

"If my exams are done and it's where you'll be, then I'll be there."

"Chris will do your flight when I give her the information. I'll try to get you into Newark. It's easier to get to Manhattan from there."

"You're sure I won't be in the way?"

"God no, we'll have the mornings and early afternoon to ourselves I hope. There is a reception or something every night that week in New York. Lots of standing around smiling and talking and too much rich food to eat, so you can miss any part of it you like."

"I'll be fine. Where do we stay?"

"Mid-town, SoHo, somewhere. I have the name inside. I was there the last time, lots of wonderful food."

"I have to bring real clothes then?"

He grinned, "You might want to dress for the parties or to eat at Per Se."

"I could get used to that."

"The D.C. week is easier and we'll have more time. Just three radio and televisions interviews are scheduled and there's some signings there but all in those three days."

"Okay."

"So you'll do it?"

"Of course I'll do it. Why wouldn't I?"

"No one ever has before."

She said more softly, "Well I'm going, and on the next one, too if there is one."

Harry smiled, "I'll talk to Chris once I'm sure what day you leave and you can talk to her if things change. Now, do you have anything before we eat?"

"It doesn't have to be before we eat but we need to talk about the future pretty soon. At least I do."

"Are you referring to forever?"

"That too."

"You need to talk about now, because we're breaking the rules. While I'm delighted you're here every night, you're getting uncomfortable."

"How do you know these things?"

"We agreed you wouldn't live here and it's been a week now."

She turned and looked at him, "It was different when you were sick but I can't do this now no matter how wonderful it is because I don't believe in it. It's not wrong, just wrong for me."

"I know, so we have to make some choices. Be better if we didn't have to make them now because it's busy, but as Bill says about this sort of problem, life is busy. We have to fix it."

"Can we?"

"Of course we can. You have to tell me what you want to do though. After all, it's your marriage too."

"I may never say that word. It scares the hell out of me."

"Why?"

"Because I've never used it in a conversation about me and wasn't sure I ever would."

"Do you want to talk about it?"

"Yes, I want to. I just won't do it very well. If you're not hungry yet, I'll get another one and we can try to do it now."

"Bring me one."

He was pacing when she came back and as she handed him the bottle he put his hand on her shoulder and said seriously. "Here are the only choices I know. Go to city hall this week and we're married and you stay here. We could do it again more formally if you want after the tour. The other is to wait. Leave things as they were until after we have a wedding in the summer or fall. You have to tell me which one. I won't decide. We won't decide. You will."

She looked at him silently as she sat down,

"You ready for all that?"

"If you promise to be as nice to me as you've been all week, I am. But you can go home Sunday and I can live with that, too. I know this is hard for you. I won't ask you to do something for the sake of convenience. If you want to take a deep breath now, I can be happy just knowing that you love me because I know what that means."

She looked up and smiled, "both make sense and are fine in their way as your solutions always are. Can it wait until tomorrow? I want to think about it."

"Sure. Now, can we eat and watch the movie?"

She laughed, "You'll love it. This is the best one. Glad I saved it. It's got airplanes and all sorts of great stuff. Do we have popcorn?"

"We did when I left. I haven't been here so you'd know better than I would."

"I remember now, Nicole and I ate the last of it."

"That's very unfortunate, Kate."

"I'll heat dinner if you'll go to the store."

"Are you buying since you ate the last of it?"

"Come on, that isn't fair."

"It is. We may even have a rule about it."

"Oh all right, there's a five with my keys and stuff in there. Just be sure you spend it all in one place."

They ate and then watched the movie. Harry was laughing so hard he was in tears as she jumped up and down, threw popcorn in her mouth and at the screen and pointed the way for poor Gary Cooper to get out of the way of the plane and yelled all her other misdirection. He tickled her without mercy all the way to bed.

He was up at six on Saturday watching the sun come up on what would be another warm day when she found him out on the back terrace. She went to make coffee while he showered and dressed. He found her in the same place, slumped down in a chair, sipping coffee, and staring at the tile through her ever longer wavy hair,

"Did you bring me some?" Harry asked.

"No. I didn't know when you'd be back."

"So is this is how it's going to be now, is it? First no popcorn and now this?"

"Don't be pitiable. It's very unbecoming. It will take you, what? Two minutes to get coffee if you just go in and get it and stop whining about how unfair it is."

Harry sighed audibly and did an exaggerated shuffle into the kitchen, smiling. When he came back there was a bagel in one hand and he held a tray, waiter-like on his shoulder with the other,

"Did you bring me one of those?"

"What?"

She pointed at his hand, "A bagel. Did you bring me one?"

"I didn't know you wanted one."

She laughed softly, "So this is how it is?"

"Who's being pathetic now?"

She groaned and shook her hair over her face again.

Harry laughed and put the tray down, "Here, there's cream cheese there too. Thanks isn't required."

"Correct, or correct in this situation."

"I think we should abolish the thank you rule. It's arbitrary and annoying." He said as he ate.

She sat up now and faced him while she spread the cream cheese. He poured her more coffee from the pot off the tray,

"That's true, it is. What would you suggest?"

"We could ban it again. It would be easier."

"It would and I wouldn't have to referee anymore."

"Fine. I'd thank you for agreeing, but now I can't."

"No you can't, even though I know you want to."

They sat silently for a few minutes both lost in their own thoughts.

"Why is Kate up so early? Want to tell me?"

"You were gone and I didn't want to stay there without you."

"That isn't all. Tell me what you were thinking about."

"I was thinking about your proposal."

"Did I propose?"

"Well, it wasn't what I dreamt about when I was a little girl growing up. You know, when the handsome prince came and swept me up on his white horse and took me away, but I'm reasonably certain that's what it was."

He chuckled, "I was trying to solve a problem, not really proposing."

She looked over at him deadpan, "The implication of both your solutions was that a proposal was required."

He chuckled now, "It wasn't really meant to be a proposal, Kate. I'll only propose if I'm certain you'll say yes." He leaned back smiling, enjoying this now as he sipped his coffee, "I mean you told me it would be forever if you said you loved me, but there was never a promise of more."

"You thought I meant just loving you forever?"

"I don't know, do I? You never said."

Kate remained expressionless, "You took that literally, did you?"

"You mean that wasn't what you meant?" He asked innocently.

She shook her head, "You really are insane."

He went over and sat on the terrace in front of her and she looked down at him.

"What I offered yesterday was a way out of an inconvenience. I'd want any proposal to be more memorable than that."

"You would."

"Yes I would," he said. He put his cup down and looked up at her silently for nearly a minute and finally took her hand,

"Kate, will you marry me?"

She touched his face and said very softly, "Yes."

He held up the small felt box, "Will you have this then?"

She put her hand to her mouth and gasped.

Her hand was shaking when she opened it and her eyes became very wide, "Oh my, you really meant memorable, didn't you?"

"Can we try it on?"

She gave that soft laugh he knew so well now, as he slid it on. She held her left hand in her lap and kept her head down looking at it, crying softly for several minutes. Finally, she looked at him. The twinkle was there with the tears,

"It's the most beautiful ring I've ever seen. It even fits. How did you know? I mean when . . . Oh never mind just come here."

Their engagement dinner was fun and Kate went home Sunday night. She settled it. They would be married during her break before the fall semester. They would live as before for now because she wanted that and in his way so did Harry. His mother's ring on her finger was enough.

The next weeks went quickly and were full of work for both of them. The inevitable itinerary changes came and he adjusted his calendar to them. His focus now was the New York and Washington trip. He would do Boston in those weeks as well. Todd called with an invitation from Harvard's Department of Comparative Literature in Palmer House. His alma mater took little notice of his career until now and he was quietly pleased by the attention. There was time for only one day there in the fourth week and he hoped he could do it justice. Kate would be in New York then and when he told her about it she wanted to go. She said that while she could hear him talk anytime, she always wanted to say she went to Harvard.

He called Bill and Martha to give them their news the day he gave her the ring. He never heard them happier and Bill agreed to be his best man whenever he needed him. Elspeth was equally pleased when he told her later that week. She'd not known of Kate until now but was happy he 'finally found someone' as she put it, perhaps since her best known author might now have a less disorderly life.

Late one Friday he was about to call Chris about plane reservations. He hadn't talked to her since he'd been back. He felt their relationship changed since she read the book and that evening in her office. He was comfortable with it and hoped she was too. They were colleagues and friends now, close ones, but not as close as they might have been personally.

"Harry, it's been a while. You okay?"

"Fine Chris, are you busy?'

"Busy. Well yes, in the sense that I'm still rattling around in my office, but not doing anything I'd rather do than talk to you."

"You're a kind woman."

She laughed, "I am and I wonder why that's so overlooked, you know?"

"Are you feeling underappreciated these days?"

"I'll get over it."

Harry's voice became serious now, "Is everything okay?"

"My boss is annoying me but the other editors are great. Word has it he may be leaving so maybe that's why he's such an angry bird these days."

"George is leaving? Is he retiring or going elsewhere?"

"Not sure. Rumor is he's being pushed. I only know for sure that he's being annoying."

"I'm sorry to hear that."

"No need, a nice man is taking me to the coast for the weekend tonight and this will all be here Monday. Now, what's on Harry's mind?"

He chuckled, "Well, he's glad to hear your dance card is full this weekend and he wants to send some plane information if you're still willing to book flights."

"Sure, I won't get to it until Monday, but glad to do it. You really should learn, you know, it isn't hard."

"You have a certain flair for it I'll never acquire. I'll e-mail this as we speak and you can look at it Monday and call me."

"When are they?"

"During the tour. It's for Kate and you need to charge it to my personal account. I want to get Kate to Newark and a car service for her into New York. Since I made the last leg in D.C. longer we both need seats back here on the date I'm giving you too. Harvard asked me to give a lecture, so I need two shuttle tickets to Boston the final week in New York too."

"Okay, I see it now. Damn, Harry, you're going to be busy. Boston twice, huh?"

"There's a lot. The media schedule is all tentative the first weeks until the Times and others review the book. The readings are down but the signings are up as are the receptions. The schedule is tight until I get to Washington."

"Kate's meeting you in New York? Does she understand she's going to have to drink cocktails and eat dinner with the VP if she does that?"

He laughed, "She does and looks forward to it. I'll see how she feels once it's done."

Chris let loose one of her big throaty laughs,

"Okay I have it all now. I'll do it Monday and call if I get confused. I saw your hard cover today. Yours should be there in the morning. You need more?"

"Can you ask them to send five more? I owe my neurosurgeon one and some of his help. After all, this book may be their fault."

"Come on, Harry, I've read it, remember?"

"Well, we'll see. I assume the jacket blurbs were done. Elspeth and her agency people handled that this time."

"Yes, actually, there were ten and all nice. Compelling I think would be the word of commonality."

He laughed again, "Well there are worse things than being compelling. I hope the critics get that far. You're in particularly fine form this evening I must say, it must be the weekend."

"There is that. He's very hot did I mention that? Speaking of weekends, is Kate there?"

"She will be in an hour. She had a late class."

"She still only visiting?"

"For now. She finally told me how she feels so that will be changing."

"She said the magic words?"

"She did."

"What are you doing about it, Harry?"

"Hoping its forever Chris. There's a wedding in August."

"Really! Congratulations. How'd all this happen?"

"She just said it when I got home the week I last saw you. I proposed the next weekend and she said yes."

"Aw Harry, that's sweet."

"It was actually. I hope you'll come. Once we figure it all out, we'll tell you when and where."

"I wouldn't miss it. After all, you're living in my house."

"At least until she's finishes in December."

"You made my day better, Harry. Now, I'm leaving here for some fun. I'll be in touch about the flights and I sent an e-mail while we were talking to get your books. Congratulations again."

"Thanks Chris, have a wonderful time this weekend. Talk soon."

Chapter Seventeen

When his book arrived, it gave him that nearly sensual pleasure he always felt when he held a new one of his own in print and made him smile for a week. He promised Nicole an interview for Arizona Public Radio before he left when he gave her a copy. He went for one more MRI and a physical to be sure whatever headaches he might have would be from the travel and tension, and not some new surprise. He gave Marion a copy and she said she'd get one to Bethany, now practicing near San Francisco. Paul laughed at the inscription in his and thanked him genuinely for remembering him.

Harry spent the first of his last two weeks at home talking to everyone he knew it seemed and many he didn't. He talked to his lawyer in New York who would draw a new Will and one for Kate and amend his Trust Fund and dealt with the myriad of details that would need doing by August while he had time now. He told Kate she needed to plan a wedding and that any wedding she wanted was fine with him. She said she and Nicole were on it and if that was all he needed to know she'd tell him the rest while they were on vacation.

The schedulers were moving things around in New York because of station conflicts and associate producers who couldn't keep things straight. He was ten days from leaving now and he was pleading in vain for a "lock" on the number of interviews. The book would be reviewed on Sunday by the New York Times and he hoped the others would do it then too or at least before he left. He was still surprised by how calm he was. There was none of the desperate anxiety he felt the last time when he was his full public self before he was even on the plane. He was a different Harry Logan now than the frantic breathless one before the last tour with great expectations for the book. He wasn't sure what to expect now, but found the lack of expectation a refreshing change from the past two tours.

He remembered that he characterized the early reviews of *Country* as "promising." The interviews helped and when it reached the best sellers list the mainstream press picked up the allegorical social commentary and decided it was "important reading" which was why it did so well. He was perhaps more relaxed about this one since it was meant to be a good summer read and while it surely had a message, its timing would land it on more beaches than bed stands. Once he knew what the Times said they'd be adjusting the New York tour the first two or three weeks either by cutting down or adding to the schedule.

He found himself sorting through his better clothes Friday afternoon and thinking of all that happened since he last did this. When he finished, he sat in the doorway of the office making check marks and drawing time lines on his yellow pad. The practice became habitual after Chris suggested it before his surgery. He would be away six weeks and at least three of those would be tempered by the good humor Kate would bring. He hoped she wouldn't be too put off by the Harry she'd see out there in his full public suit. He knew he would be wearing it most of the time until their vacation and she'd not really seen him in it yet.

He was still puzzling over the questions yet to be answered next week when she came through the gate. She was unaware he was watching from the doorway. She looked tired. She was working hard with only two weeks until exams and he knew there was a lot on her mind and a great deal more for her to do after that. She would meet him and then come back to a job, a summer session, and her wedding. He wondered if he was asking too much of her just to make his own life more pleasant. As she looked up and saw him her face brightened,

"Hi."

"Hey, you look tired."

"I am and I still have to work tomorrow. That won't be hard but I'd rather not."

"Hungry?" Harry asked

"Sort of, maybe it'll keep me on my feet a few hours longer."

"You can sleep if you want."

"No, we're not going there again. Ever."

Harry took her books and bag from her. He wrapped a hand around her neck and massaged it and chuckled softly, "No happy memories in that."

"Not one. Now take me to the kitchen and we can talk while I heat dinner."

"Do you want me to carry you?"

She laughed finally, "No. In fact, can you put that stuff in the bedroom for me? I'll try making it on my own."

"You make it sound like a ten mile hike."

Harry dropped the books on the table in the other room, the bag in the bedroom and found her looking in the oven to see what Elena had left. He came up behind her and wrapped his arms around her when she stood up,

"Are you all right? You have too much to do."

"I'm fine. Finishing the semester is hard but I've done harder things than that."

"I worry about you," he said as he let her go.

She laughed and poked at him with the wooden spoon, "you're supposed to worry about me aren't you? I worry about you."

"Has our love survived another week?"

She frowned and leaned against the counter,

"You ask that in one way or another a lot. Why?"

"Reassurance I suppose."

"You'd know if it hadn't."

"How?"

"I would call, say I wasn't coming, and your ring is in the mail."

"I should think that would do it."

"Well that's not going to happen but I still want to know why. Are you that insecure?" She laughed, "God, don't tell me I'm finding this out now."

"I just wonder why you love me now and then."

"Meaning?"

"Meaning I never thought you would so I don't know what I did or said that made you decide."

"It wasn't any one thing. You were just you. You helped me understand myself and get over most of my selfish independence by being secure enough in your own life to help me figure out mine. There's a lot more, but why can't you just accept that I love you for who you are? Why does there have to be a big 'aha' in everything for you? You know it happened in a most natural way for both of us. Why do you question that?"

"I don't know. I never experienced anything like it."

"Well, I've never been in this neighborhood either, but I'm happy I am and don't need to replay the reasons every day. Are we going to have a variation of this conversation all the time?"

"Does it bother you?"

"That depends. I don't want to have to enumerate all the reasons why I love you every day. We know we love each other. We need to say it often so we don't take it for granted, but I don't want to examine it all the time."

"You're right, I'm sorry. I'm just being needy and I never thought of myself as the needy sort before. It's a horrible trait."

She smiled as she put the plates down, "Now, what's really wrong?"

He smiled, "Oh, nothing really, I expect I'm feeling useless. This has to be all about me right now, you know that and I find this waiting hard. I watched you come in tonight. You're tired and I know you worked a lot harder than I did today and it bothers me. I talk on the telephone, act busy, and have too much time on my hands. I've done this three of times now and the last week or two is always terrible because it's a suspended time. I can't make it move faster because someone else's schedule controls it and I can't be happy until I'm selling the book. It's an odd time for a pause and I wonder why more isn't going on since it took so much work to get this far."

"You don't control much about your work right now and you're unhappy about it, that's all. You think you've done enough writing?"

"No," he shrugged, "maybe I just don't want to go through all the bothersome parts of it again soon. Like I said, I have too much time to think."

"Well you're working life as I know it would never be described as normal."

"No, it isn't. I mean I wrote the book, did all the rest and I'm just waiting for the other shoe to drop now. I have two weeks to just think it over."

"That would be hard for you I think."

"I suppose. I feel useless since there isn't more to do."

"You're being too hard on yourself."

Harry shrugged.

She was watching him silently now with that look that told him she was thinking,

"Maybe you need to think about all those offers you get to teach and lecture and do something else for a while. Do you really expect to be able to drag a book out of your head every two or three years? That's very hard, I think."

"It is. Yet the good ones do it, and do it well. If I think I'm one of them I need to believe I can too. Harper Lee and a few others managed to be famous and rich by writing one book and becoming a recluse, but the rest of us just labor on thinking we have something important to say or another good story to tell. You know, there was a time when I saw myself as the mysterious author who would only appear every five years or so when another book was published. It was what I had in mind when I moved to Hamilton. A nice small city where I could do things like be on the Library Board and the Playhouse fund raising committee and being an author would be less important to the people there and me. It was that way some of the time there and perhaps I need that again."

"Then do it. While I run my business you can be the town mayor for all I care. When I come home I want you there, that's what I want. What makes us happy professionally has always been different. It'll no doubt stay that way. I just want us to always share the personal part."

He laughed now as he cleared the table, "do you think we can do that?"

"I'm up for it. You're the one who's unhappy."

He sank into the sofa and sighed, "Ah Kate, I don't mean to sound so woebegone. I have you and the rest will work out. I just need to get this book hawking done and settled into some routine that doesn't have me guessing when I'll see you again. I'm leaving for three weeks and you're working very hard to get this semester out of the way and do all the rest you need to do now. I guess it makes me wish life was simpler for you."

"It isn't. I'm not sure it will ever be for either of us. You and I aren't the type."

"No we aren't."

"Then cheer up. You're leaving and you don't want to, I know that. It doesn't make me smile either. We'll both be working hard though and it's the way we've always gotten through it."

"I know. I'm just restless because I can't do anything but wait for the critic's reviews."

She dropped down next to him and leaned against him,

"You could try relaxing instead of obsessing about your lack of control."

He put his arm around her, "I'll try. Is there anything you need to talk about?"

"It can wait until you aren't so confused."

He chuckled, "I'm fine."

"Let's leave it anyway. I'm too tired. You'll have so many questions my head may blow up. We'll get to it before I leave. What about you?"

He chuckled, "Cars. We need to talk about cars."

"I hope it's about yours because mine isn't worth thought much less talk."

"That's why we're talking. The lease is up on the BMW and I think it would be good to for us to have it so I want to buy it out."

"Makes sense."

"It does, but buying out the lease would make better sense if we do what I think we should do."

"Which is?"

"Is yours still good enough to sell?"

"Since I did the repairs it's all right. I'm just not sure I trust it to last through the fall with all the driving I'll have to do. Around here a sick car is the last thing you want especially in the summer."

"Then here's what I think we ought to do. I'll buy the BMW out of the lease and you take it. We'll decide what to do with it when we go next winter."

"You're giving me your car?"

"You love my car."

"Of course I love your car, but I can't just take it."

"Why? You'll own half of it soon anyway."

"It just seems . . . I don't know . . . like a gift or something. Is this is how it works? I get to have your stuff?"

Harry threw back his head and laughed, "You really never have thought much about being married have you?"

She said softly but sharply, "Don't make fun of me."

"I wasn't making fun of you, Kate. I wouldn't do that. You just have such a wonderful way of putting things. Yes, you get to have my stuff.

Will you agree to take the car? We'll leave the title as it is until August. You're already on the insurance."

"What will you drive?"

Harry shrugged, "I don't know. I'll talk to the dealer and figure something out. The important thing is the BMW has hardly been driven and you need it. I'll worry less about you while I'm gone now and this summer if you take it."

"So I get a new car and live here for three weeks with my own cook and handyman. Then when we come back from this fantastic trip you're paying for I can keep the car?"

"Well, after we come back from the trip we're both going to live here after a few months, so think of it as trial run. You need to see if you can possibly live in such squalid conditions for that long."

She shook her head and laughed her first big laugh of the night.

"I'll try my best."

"Now have we taken care of the cars?"

"Except for the part where you don't have one, but you uttered the famous 'I'll figure something out' at some point so I'll let you deal with the consequences of that and I would thank you if I could."

"There wouldn't be any reason."

She kissed him and stood up, "Yes there would. Now, I'm going to take a shower and go to bed early."

"You sure?"

"It wasn't up for debate."

"We have things that aren't debatable?"

"Apparently. You just gave me your car without one."

He chuckled, "Can I ask a question?"

Kate groaned in mock exasperation as she turned in the doorway and leaned on to the frame for support, "For heaven's sakes, yes, what is it?"

"Can I come with you?"

They were both up at sunrise. She had two hours before work but refused to tell him what she wanted to talk about. He gave up after coffee and threw her a jacket. They went out into the early light and walked aimlessly for an hour talking about the logistics of the next few weeks and her plans for "their time in the mountains" as she called it. When they got back to the house he handed her the keys. She started to protest and he shook his head and waved his hand for hers. She gave them to him, kissed him, and waved goodbye as she pulled away.

When she was halfway up the street he called Chris,

"Hi. Did it work?"

"She agreed to take it, yes. Now what's this man's name again and are you sure he'll take this thing without a title?"

"His name is George Little and we were in love once so be nice to him. He said she can bring the title to him next week but he'd only take Kate's car if he can sell it. If not, you're on your own. He has two Benz's and an Audi. They're all trade-ins. He'll give you a twelve month lease on one and will take it back sooner if you leave and waive the penalty fee as a favor to me. Is she there?"

"No, she went off to work in her new car looking like she was born to it."

"You're a generous man Harry."

"It did make her happy."

"Well yeah? It would make me happy too."

He laughed, "Talk to George then, maybe he'll help you with that. Now let me get this done so I'll be back before she is and thanks as always."

"Happy to help. Call me next week and tell me how it went. Oh, and take the Audi if you like it. It's a great car."

George was most accommodating and he was reading on the sofa when she came in and sat next to him. He looked up,

"Hey, how was the nursery?"

"It was fun."

"Do you want to walk again, or have you been on your feet enough today?"

"Let's just walk down to the rock. We can talk there. First though tell me where you put my car."

"You drove your car."

"Stop it. My little car is gone and there's another one out there, where is it?"

"I drove it to the dealer early today to buy out the BMW. Since you said it was left it to me to figure out I did. I leased that one for a year and if I don't stay he'll take it back sooner because it's a year old trade in. I couldn't turn that down."

"You still haven't said where mine is."

He tossed the book on the table, "Your former car now resides on their lot on Speedway Boulevard waiting for some transportation impaired person to buy it. George thought he could sell it. You need to sign the title so I can give it to him this week, unless you'd like to say goodbye, in which case George will be happy ogle you. I took out all the things I could find of yours, but I may have missed something."

"You did all this since I left here? When did you decide to give me the BMW?"

"I don't know. I thought about it because I was worried about yours after it broke down the last time. But you had to agree to take it. The dealer is an old boyfriend of Chris' and she asked him to do a short lease for me as a favor. I didn't see the Audi or know if he'd buy your car until I went down there today. When he did, that made the decision easy. I wanted to save you the time—which you don't have—and trouble of selling your car. As it happens, it's enough to pay off the loan on your library carrel unless you need the cash."

Kate stared at him without expression as only she could,

"You know, you tell me all the time what a horrible person you are. Bill and Martha have stories about you when you lived up there that curl my hair. Yet you do these nice things for me I never expect. How am I supposed to understand that? Twenty-four hours ago I was driving a little compact wreck and now it's gone, and I have the kind of car I've wanted my whole life, you have a new car, and I'm debt free? Is that how it is?"

"You have the essentials, yes." Harry smiled, "mine is a year old too, but we won't quibble."

She still looked at him in the same way. Finally she said very softly, "I don't know how ever I found you."

Harry chuckled and kissed her cheek, "It was at lunch one Saturday afternoon."

They walked down the hill and Harry tried not to think how much he would miss just having this time to talk in the next few weeks. He hated the idea of leaving her here. All he did today was make some sense out of the cars and she was as amazed and happy as a child. He was amazed that she could be moved by something he thought so simple.

They sat and looked at the hills until she finally said,

"I need to tell you the rest about my mother and me."

"Why? I know the basics. You stayed with her aunt after she left and before college, what else is there?"

"A good bit, actually and I need to tell you all of it because you've told me everything about your life. It isn't pretty, but you need to hear it so you know where all my skeletons are before the wedding just in case you want to make a run for it."

"Come on Kate, I think we're past that point, aren't we?"

She sighed, "Well, it bothers me that I never told you all of it and now there's a chance we may have to see her this summer. Nicole has some strong views about her being at the wedding, and I may go along if you agree. I told you I don't see her but we're in touch now and then. I talk to her maybe twice a year now, remember her birthday, Mother's Day, that sort of thing. There's no closeness in it now and I'm not even sure whose fault that is anymore. I was a very angry and confused child when I moved out and I was happy to have her out of my life then. I was so young when I lost my father and then I left her. I mean there's never is a good age for either of those, but a pubescent girl misses having one or the other to help her, I can tell you that."

She stopped and hopped down off the rock and walked away a little and turned back with her arms folded, "She was seeing someone when my father was overseas. I was too young to know it. He lived in San Diego. When my father came back and we moved over here, there were weekends when he was off flying and her aunt would come and stay with me while she went somewhere. My father died about a year later and we came to Tucson. I started high school and was really doing well in sports. We stayed with her aunt until the guy showed up. I knew him of course but I was young and naïve and didn't understand. Anyway, they found a house here soon after and we moved. I didn't want to live there, I didn't like him, thought it was wrong, and it got really nasty. She and I yelled at each other all the time and he decided to get into it on day and try to fix it for us. One shout led to another and when it was over I knew what happened and I left. Her aunt let me live with her until I went to nursing school and then I stayed in the dorms when I wasn't with the team."

She sat again and stared at the hills, "She tried hard to get me to come back all the while she was here. She married him before they left and asked me to come with them. I was even more stubborn then than I am now so I wouldn't."

Harry nodded and waited. He knew she wanted to tell him everything because she knew he'd bury her with questions if she didn't.

She took a deep breath, "After that we talked once in a while, but less often now. I still believe she only married him because she thought that would somehow make it right. I needed you to know everything, to be as honest as you've been with me. Just understand, she may come to the wedding but we aren't spending the holidays with her and don't include in all your questions now anything about reconciliation, because that isn't going to happen either."

She stopped and looked at him. She had that sad look on her face he hadn't seen in a long time. She never really had a childhood, had she? Just sports and school and a missing father she'd loved very much and a mother she felt left her for someone else. Harry didn't fully understand why, or who was right but he didn't think talking about it would make it any clearer. She was happy now. They were happy. Wasn't that what mattered? Finally he said,

"I don't have any questions, Kate. If you want to be closer to her, it will be because you want that. You understand what happened and haven't shut her out completely."

She was watching him and looked surprised when he stopped talking,

"That's it? Nothing about what an awful child I was? About why I need to give her a chance because it would make us happy or more complete or some other nonsensical psychobabble?"

"Not from me. I don't know if any of that would be true. Your relationship with her is your business."

"Her aunt made it her business until the day she died. Most of the other people in my life made it their business too."

"I understand why her aunt would, but I have no right to tell you what to do about her. If your relationship with her is to change, it will because you want it to, not because I or anyone else thinks it's a good idea. We can talk about her again if you like, if not, that's fine too."

She stared at him for a long moment,

"I wanted you to know."

"I'm glad you told me. You can do what you think is best about the wedding."

She smiled now, "You never stop surprising me, you know that?"

"I hope I never do."

She took a deep breath. "I doubt you will. Now, can I look at your car? If I like it better, can I have it?"

He laughed, "Come on, let's go."

CHAPTER EIGHTEEN

Harry's last week home was pandemonium. The New York Times review was e-mailed to him and Elspeth early Saturday evening. He gave it to Kate without a word. By the time she was halfway through it they were both laughing in both surprise and happiness. It was far more enthusiastic than he'd imagined it would be.

The phone began ringing and by afternoon on Sunday, Todd and Elspeth were swamped with new interview requests. Reviewers were putting *The Miscreant* on their "summer reading" lists and it was on the fiction bestseller list after it was reviewed by the media in New York, Los Angeles and Chicago. The PR people up north were juggling the smaller signings and interviews to make room for the new network radio and television requests the first three weeks. He barely had time to pack and he found himself hoping he'd survive it all. He demanded the schedule stay as they had it for the final week in New York and yet they still added three more receptions. As Chris would put it when he finally talked to her from the airport in Denver, his wish might be their command these days since he gave the publishing house another huge seller, but there was too much to lose if they didn't put his success to use.

Leaving was awful. While he was elated that the reviewers were enjoying the book far more than he hoped and affirming his belief that it was a book meant for summer, leaving Kate, even for three weeks, was made harder by the enormous amount of time he needed to devote to the chaos before he went. They hardly had time to say goodbye.

When he reached New York, he smiled his way through the days and nights as the interviews rolled on. He had two very successful books in a row. It was far more than he ever expected. This book had great commercial appeal and his glibness in interviews and previous awards made him what he knew was called a "good get" in the media world of both the morning and nighttime radio and television hosts that traffic

277

in author guests. He was exhausted from a lack of sleep but soldiered on with a smile because he knew this would likely never happen again. When the delighted Elspeth arrived, she told him that the 'trades' declared him the hot literary interview of the spring. He smiled knowing it would be true only until the next new thing came along. Kate arrived on Sunday for the last week and renewed his energy. She looked so incredibly lovely and was so charismatically gracious to all the important, the innately pompous, and the chronically stupid people at the literary parties and receptions that she made everyone feel better for having met her. She was a delight it seemed to all that met her and surely the tonic he needed. She delivered remarkably humorous and perceptive summations of the day before over breakfast each day in her quiet witty way. Her latest game was trying to name their worst moment of the night before.

There wasn't time for sightseeing until Washington other than a quick tour of Boston the evening after his lecture at Harvard. The weather was wonderful, the monuments and museums a delight, and finally they had their week in the country. They explored the Blue Ridge, learned something of the Civil War, met some wonderful people, and were sorry when it ended.

Kate came to San Francisco and Los Angeles with him two weeks later for four days of signings, interviews, and receptions in each city. She met "Wedgie" who she thought hysterical for his accent, but appalled by his language, insane friends, and flashy wealth. She also admitted he was wonderful too for how he cared for them while they were there. She fell in love with San Francisco and wanted to come back again after school was done. By early August the remote interviews and his commuting to Phoenix was mostly over and she was getting ready for her summer session exams and still talking about how much fun she'd had.

Were this the Harry Logan of a few years ago he would have been a strutting peacock in the social circles of New York for the next several months, milking this new success and blustering his opinionated way through every important and semi-important event to which he could inveigle an invitation hoping to be remembered when the literary awards were handed out in late fall. Instead, he was enjoying quiet evenings in the desert as often as he could with the woman he would marry in less than a month's time and gladly taking phone calls from whoever in the country wanted to talk about the book, satisfied that it was enough.

As August ended the carousel music changed again as the wedding was upon them. Nicole and her friends did a magnificent job of getting it done and helping Kate through it. The ceremony was larger than he expected and was held in an architecturally significant mission in Tucson.

Her mother came and seemed both proud of Kate and glad to have been invited. She and Kate spoke pleasantly enough and she thanked Harry for making her "little girl" so happy and left soon after the ceremony was over. Many friends from her nursing and campus life were there as were two former teammates, something she found especially touching. He was delighted so many came to share the day. Elena and Joseph were at the service and Harry insisted Elena not work until Tuesday evening. She nodded, smiled, and exchanged a burst of Spanish with her Katarine and laughed as they hugged each other.

Elspeth looked as stunning as ever and flew on to Chicago after the much smaller reception that Carlton, Chloe, and even Paul Zuckerman and his wife managed to attend. Chris, Bill, and Martha were booked on the same flight home on Sunday. When all the others were gone, the five of them and Nicole returned to the house. Chris complained about all the "damage" he'd done and Bill's wit and Martha's wonderful laugh could be heard into the early morning hours while Nicole regaled them with stories about Kate during what she'd referred to as "the living hell" of the wedding preparations. They all found a place to sleep at some point and went out for breakfast before they made their noon flight.

Kate was free of work and school for two weeks and didn't want to travel. She said she only wanted to come back to the house she would now be able to call home. As they came in the gate Harry wondered how many times he'd heard her ring the bell there since the day she brought him the book on early southwestern architecture what seemed now so long ago. They leaned on each other for support and neither said much as they sat in the courtyard, tired after a long week with too much to do and a too many late nights. All they were able to do for a while was utter an occasional bit of remembrance of the week which made them laugh too hard and blame it on their exhaustion.

Finally Harry staggered to his feet, and headed to the kitchen for something to drink. He suggested she take a nap.

"I'm not going to sleep now. I'm only doing this once in my life and I might miss something. Bring me anything that doesn't contain alcohol."

Harry nodded and returned with water, announcing it was the last available.

They sat quietly for a while with their own thoughts until she finally said,

"I'm glad they stayed. It made it even better."

Harry sighed hugely, "It did, and it was all very nice. I'm still finding it hard to accept that we finally did it."

"We did. You could watch the video. Apparently there is one and we starred in it." she deadpanned.

Harry chuckled.

"I need to thank Nicole again. She was fantastic through all this. I'm going to miss her when she goes next month."

"She'll do well. Glad the network had the wisdom to hire her."

"Well, you made her sound like she should be the new morning anchor while you were there. I hope she can live up to that."

"Oh, they didn't care anything about what I had to say. They hired her because of the work she did. They know how good she is."

"It still was nice of you to do it."

Harry shrugged.

"Bill and Martha seem like family to me now."

He nodded, "They are in some way. They're surely happy you're here to keep me from doing anything stupid."

She moved closer and whispered,

"I'm glad you waited to tell me about the rings," she held up her hand to look at them, "I need to say thank you because I know how much they mean to you."

"Thanks aren't generally permitted as I recall, but we can make an exception for them. She'd be proud that you have them."

"It's amazing that they fit. I still can't get over it."

Harry nodded and said quietly, "I told my father when he gave them to me that I'd marry someone fit to wear them. It was metaphor of course. I was as surprised as you were that they did physically. It's a bit of kismet, isn't it?"

She hugged him, "I like to think that. I'm glad you trust me with them."

"I trust you with everything, Kate, even me, and that's very different from that callow loudmouth I was not so many years ago. Much of it is your fault."

She sighed deeply and put her head on his shoulder.

Finally he said, "Should we just sit here until we both pass out? I'm not clear at all about the time. This was quite a ride."

She sat up with that twinkle in her eyes, her energy somehow renewed, "We have to eat something and find something else to drink. It's a long time to dinner. Elena is bringing it tonight. It's what she said to me at the church. She's cooking enough for tonight and tomorrow at her house since you made her stay home. She thought we might starve, since I'm still such an amateur. She's wonderful."

"Well, she adopted you at some point, so why wouldn't she be wonderful to the daughter she always wanted?"

"We had fun the three weeks you were in New York. She taught me a lot when you were traveling. Be nice to cook with her whenever I want now."

"What do you want to do while you're off?"

"Only whatever needs to be done. I'm glad we're not traveling because I really am tired. We can go somewhere after I graduate. You told me there were lots of things I'll need to read and sign and you have to go down to the school and organize your teaching this semester now that you surprised me yet again by deciding to do it. Except for moving the rest of me in here I have nothing I want to accomplish except to get some rest. Maybe we can talk about where we'll go when we leave. We don't have to be two crazies running around here with our hair on fire now, do we." She laughed softly, "Does that sound too married?"

Harry threw back his head and laughed, "It sounds wonderful the way you put it."

"It's still very hard for me to believe I'm really Mrs. Harry Logan."

"Well, it makes me happy."

She pulled him to his feet,

"Tell you what, let's go to the store now and when we get back you can show me just how happy that is."

The next two weeks were as relaxed as she made them sound that afternoon. She spent time with Elena and began experimenting on her own over the weekends now that she felt she could call the kitchen her own. The hardest thing they did was move her into the house. They came and went together as naturally as they'd been doing it forever. Harry still smiled when he found her there every morning and startled now and then to find her just sitting in a chair reading in the middle of the day or in the courtyard late at night with no need to discuss when she would leave. They were both forever changed and yet comfortable and the same.

He had a pile of documents from his lawyer, accountant, insurance people, and broker and he had a dozen other papers she needed to sign as well. Her business courses and intuitive brilliance made everything including how his book royalties worked easy for her to understand. She occasionally shook her head, never having guessed about all this. One evening in the middle of the second week, she was finally going to sign all of them and Harry was asking her once more about being sure she didn't want to hyphenate her last name when she'd finally had enough of the debate and said in exasperation,

"Haven't we talked about that enough? I just want to be Katherine Logan."

"That's fine Kate and that's who you'll be if you use it on these documents. I know you want to use Beckett in some way though to remember your father."

She smiled, "We still haven't figured out how we do that have we?"

"No, and perhaps it's more important that we do it rather than know how."

"Perhaps, but I'm really finished talking about this hyphenated name business now. I'll use Beckett at school until I'm done and then it'll be on my Degree. I'll decide how to use it later. I really want it to be just Kate Logan. Maybe I'll put Beckett in the company name when I have one. How does that sound?"

"Whatever you want to do with it is fine. Do you have any more questions about all these things?"

"No, I understand it all. I just never knew of it. You never talk about it. For as long as I've known you I thought what you had came from your two books. You seem, I don't know, so unaffected by all this."

Harry shrugged, "You're the first person that ever needed to know of my worth. I suppose Bill suspects because he's my Executor, but he and I never discuss it. I didn't need very much of this while I wandered around on my own, so while it continued to grow I never saw it as a necessity. Accumulating it wasn't what I set out to do in life and perhaps it's why I don't give it as much importance as others might."

She gave him that deadpan look,

"Then no one can accuse me of marrying you for your money if I'm the only one that knows."

"I have that." Harry replied dryly.

She laughed,

"I'm sorry. I'm making too much of this, but I need to get used to all this too."

"I know Kate, and you will and no doubt use it wisely. Now, you have your name, I believe, so will you please sign all these things tonight so we can be rid of them? Let our broker and banker and the others worry over it. It's what I've always done and why we pay them. Start wherever you like."

EPILOGUE

Harry and Kate remained in Tucson until early December. She remained part-time at the nursery until she graduated while Harry wrote reviews and was a visiting lecturer for the semester in the English Department at the University of Arizona.

They spent two weeks in The Cayman Islands in early December and three weeks at Christmas in Hamilton at the insistence of Bill and Martha Powers. Kate spent much of the time being useful and asking questions of the Caruso's while she and Harry looked for a business opportunity and a place to live. Kate found a job south of San Francisco with a couple who were anxious to sell their nursery in the next few years.

Kate learned the fine distinctions of good landscaping and how to manage the business from the remarkably able and friendly Jim Sproll until she fulfilled her state requirements for certification two years later. Jim and Nancy Sproll retired later that year and Harry bought the forty acre nursery and Christmas tree farm. The Sprolls moved to southern California to be near their grandchildren and run a small nursery there in semi-retirement.

"Beckett's Nursery and Landscaping Service" opened for business with a smaller nursery and a landscaping business that grew exponentially. Kate hired a manager for the nursery while she ran the office, drew the designs, and supervised the three landscaping jobs she would accept at once. She quickly became known not only for the flexibility and functionality of her designs but her charismatic personality that Harry watched blossom now as she gained confidence in her work and did what she came to truly love.

The town of 27,000 with its diverse neighborhoods appealed to them and reminded Harry a bit of Hamilton. They found a small, well restored Victorian house in town only five blocks from Harry's favorite coffee shop and within walking distance of nearly anything else that interested them.

Harry involved himself in various town activities where he was known to many of the locals only as the husband of the woman who owned Beckett's and worked at the nursery for the exercise at least one day a week. He also worked as a literary critic and occasional commentator for Public Radio International, BBC America, and lectured for two weeks every semester at the University nearby.

Bill and Martha were frequent visitors now that one of their sons was a sophomore at Stanford and a summer employee of Beckett's. Their other son remained in the East and enrolled at Columbia last fall. Bill was now the Western Region Manager and Martha became ever more active in her work in the city and was being urged to run for the City Council.

Harry remained healthy, had MRIs done once a year nearby and there were no recurrence of symptoms. Bethany Stark now practiced in Palo Alto and he saw her to monitor his aneurysm. Harry continued to insist Bethany's sensual voice had curative powers.

Elspeth asked Christine Morgan to join her agency soon after Harry's wedding with the possibility of buying it from her in several years. Four years on with capitalization from Harry, and the sale of the house in Tucson, the transition was complete. Elspeth was the Chairman of the Board of the city's opera and devoted much of her time there. Chris was now Harry's agent and still booked his airline flights.

Harry's life was settled enough now that another book was forthcoming. Despite his part time endeavors, his passion to write was no less now than his love for Kate. He'd learned on his three book journey that they were all different, conceived and born different, and he was secure enough now to know he could write a good book. He and Chris hadn't agreed yet on the story but he was delighted to have her help him decide.

Drew was finished reorganizing, downsizing, and streamlining the publishing house now and Harry would likely contract with him again primarily because Charlie Winchester was still an editor there and he and Chris thought the VP was doing an excellent job of keeping the small publishing concern competitive in the ever changing publishing business.

A year after they owned the business, Kate surprised him by building a small, two room building with a front porch as an office for Harry on the tree farm a short distance up the hill from the main buildings. She claimed it was reparation for the horror he withstood during her semesters in architecture school, to prove to him she actually learned something about building, and more importantly have him nearer during their workdays. It also provided the room he needed for the remote audio and video equipment quite common now among commentators and reporters. He did his media work and remote lectures from the largest room now and furnished the other as the place he would write. Kate insisted, to Harry's delight, on including a small kitchen that replicated some of the features of the one in the Tucson house. She still brought lunch and they ate at the counter as often as they could to share their news, laugh, and keep score. That time together was important to them and while Kate was still winning, Harry accepted her wit as superior so long ago now that it didn't matter.

Their lives were full and busy as Kate had predicted. She still took on as much as she could handle with the boundless energy that Harry admired in her from the beginning but tempered her competitiveness as she understood now that she was very good at what she did.

Kate was still very glad she'd found him while Harry still wondered everyday what he ever did in his life to deserve her.